FEMININE INTUITIONS—
WORLDS WITHIN AND WITHOUT

"A Woman's Liberation," by **Ursula K. Le Guin**: In the apocalyptic far future, the hopes of a people are reemerging—but so are the evils of the past.

"Speech Sounds," by **Octavia E. Butler**: When language has been lost, symbols have no significance, and concepts have no meaning, frustration leads to the most primitive of communication . . . violence.

"The Ship Who Mourned," by **Anne McCaffrey**: A classic chapter in the story of Helva—whose body is a starship, whose soul is a woman's . . . and whose grief is real.

"Rachel in Love," by **Pat Murphy**: She may be the product of a unique experiment and the center of a media storm, but no matter what anybody thinks, Rachel is only a girl.

"The Kidnapping of Baroness 5," by **Katherine MacLean**: After civilization collapses, a poor, hardworking geneticist learns to survive . . . by becoming an all-powerful witch.

. . . plus other award-winning tales of worlds of wonder and terror by some of the most acclaimed women speculative fiction authors of our time.

A WOMAN'S LIBERATION

More Short Fiction from Warner Aspect®

A Dragon-Lover's Treasury of the Fantastic
edited by Margaret Weis

Futureland
by Walter Mosley

A Magic-Lover's Treasury of the Fantastic
edited by Margaret Weis

A Second Chance at Eden
by Peter F. Hamilton

Sisters of the Night
edited by Barbara Hambly and Martin H. Greenberg

Skin Folk
by Nalo Hopkinson

Tales of the Knights Templar
edited by Katherine Kurtz

A WOMAN'S LIBERATION

A CHOICE OF FUTURES BY AND ABOUT WOMEN

EDITED BY

CONNIE WILLIS AND SHEILA WILLIAMS

ASPECT®

WARNER BOOKS

A Time Warner Company

Copyright © 2001 by Penny Publications LLC
All rights reserved.

Published by arrangement with Dell Magazines.

Aspect® name and logo are registered trademarks of Warner Books, Inc.

Warner Books, Inc., 1271 Avenue of the Americas, New York, NY 10020

Visit our Web site at www.twbookmark.com

For information on Time Warner Trade Publishing's online publishing program, visit www.ipublish.com

A Time Warner Company

Printed in the United States of America
First Printing: October 2001

10 9 8 7 6 5 4 3 2 1

Library of Congress Cataloging-in-Publication Data

A woman's liberation : a choice of futures by and about women / edited by Connie Willis and Sheila Williams.
        p. cm.
    Contents: Inertia / Nancy Kress — Even the queen / Connie Willis — Fool's errand / Sarah Zettel — Rachel in love / Pat Murphy — Of mist, and grass, and sand / Vonda N. McIntyre — The July ward / S.N. Dyer — The kidnapping of Baroness 5 / Katherine MacLean — Speech sounds / Octavia E. Butler — The ship who mourned / Anne McCaffrey — A woman's liberation / Ursula K. Le Guin.
    ISBN 0-446-67742-6
    1. Feminist fiction, American. 2. Science fiction, American. 3. Short stories, American—Women authors. 4. Women—Fiction. I. Willis, Connie. II. Williams, Sheila.

PS648.F4 W65 2001
813'.0876208352042—dc21   2001017794

Cover design by Don Puckey
Book design by Nancy Sabato
Cover illustration by Franco Accornero

To the trailblazing women in science fiction who marked the way for the rest of us.

Acknowledgments

We are extremely grateful to Tina Lee, who made a number of important suggestions about the contents of this book. Thanks as well to Abigail Browning, who helped bring this project to fruition. Thanks are also due to Ursula K. Le Guin for lending us her title. Further thanks go to Gardner Dozois, Stanley Schmidt, Scott Lais, and Cynthia Manson. Finally, we want to offer our gratitude to our very special editors at Warner Aspect: Jaime Levine and Betsy Mitchell.

Contents

Introduction

Women's Lib, "The Liberation," and the Many Other Liberations of Science Fiction

Connie Willis

This collection is called *A Woman's Liberation* because of the terrific title story by Ursula K. Le Guin, but I think it's a title that describes the whole collection. And the whole idea of women in science fiction.

That may seem odd, since science fiction has long held the reputation of being a male bastion, in which the only women are princesses (as in Deja Thoris, not Leia), scientists' beautiful daughters, and/or sexy, half-dressed young things being carried off kicking and screaming by hideous aliens.

But SF is full not only of female characters, but of female authors: C.J. Cherryh, Joan D. Vinge, Kate Wilhelm, Elizabeth Hand, Jane Yolen, Cecelia Holland, Lisa Goldstein, Joan Slonczewski, Maureen McHugh, Carol Emshwiller, Kristine Katherine Rusch, and, of course, the wonderful writers in this collection.

Which isn't surprising. Women and science fiction were made for each other. SF is all about looking at the universe from different perspectives, about breaking down barriers and considering alternate possibilities. It's the literature of "what if . . ." and "if this goes on . . ." and "why not . . ." So it is no wonder that women came pouring into science fiction during the Women's Lib days of the sixties and seventies, eager to explore the possibilities of women in new roles and differently structured societies. They produced works like Joanna Russ's "When It Changed," Ursula K. Le Guin's *The Left Hand of Darkness,* and Kit Reed's "Songs of War," as well as the chilling "Houston, Houston, Do You Read?" by James Tiptree Jr. (aka Alice Sheldon).

But these weren't the first women to have discovered science fiction. C.L. Moore and Andre Norton had been writing almost since the beginning—and Mary Wollstonecraft Shelley's *Franken-stein was* the beginning. And after them, in the middle of the mostly male Golden Age, Zenna Henderson, Margaret St. Clair, Kit Reed, Leigh Brackett, and Mildred Clingerman were all producing stories for the SF magazines, many of which were reprinted in collections edited by one of the most influential editors SF has ever had: Judith Merril. (Note: The SF magazines, from John W. Campbell's *As-tounding, Galaxy,* and *The Magazine of Fantasy and Science Fiction* to today's *Asimov's* and *Analog,* have always welcomed work by women.)

Now there are so many women in SF, it's almost impossible to count them. They run the gamut from *A* (Eleanor M. Arnason and Catherine Asaro) to *Z* (Marion Zimmer Bradley and Sarah Zettel), with an entire alphabet of talent in between, writing everything from gritty technopunk (Pat Cadigan) to intergalactic adventure (Lois McMasters Bujold); from humor (Esther M. Freisner) to cautionary tales (Pamela Sargent); from award-winners to best-sellers.

Why? What's the attraction of science fiction that so many women writers (and readers) find it irresistible? Well, for one thing, it's those possibilities I mentioned, that thinking outside the box. SF is all about toppling stereotypes and considering alternate futures. It's a genre that by its very nature is open to new ideas, to change.

Exploration of those new ideas and of all sorts of possible futures necessarily includes those in which things were different for women too, and almost from the very beginning, SF experimented with women in different roles. Way back in the thirties, Stanley Weinbaum was writing about a daredevil spaceship pilot named Claire Avery. In the forties, C.L. Moore and Nelson Bond wrote about strong, smart women in charge.

In the fifties, John Wyndham and Isaac Asimov both created characters who were women as well as scientists (Jane Summers and Susan Calvin, respectively), and Robert A. Heinlein peopled his spaceships with female astrogators and engineers and drill sergeants, and imagined worlds in which teenaged girls divorced their parents and ten-year-old girls solved quadratic equations.

Those characters encouraged teenaged girls to create their own characters: I was on a panel at one science-fiction convention at which every single female author present—including me—said Heinlein's young-adult novels were a major influence on their decision to become science-fiction writers. When these women entered the field, they found it to be just as welcoming to female writers as to female characters. There was a little grousing about women "ruining the neighborhood," but it didn't last long. Then Robert Silverberg's 1975 essay about James Tiptree Jr.—saying her work couldn't have been written by a woman and describing it as ineluctably male—pretty much put an end to the whole debate, since Tiptree was the pen name of Alice Sheldon.

Which explains why women got into SF but not why they stayed. There are lots of places women can get into that they wouldn't necessarily want to go, let alone stick around in. So why did they remain in science fiction? And proliferate? And prosper?

I think one reason is that they realized science fiction was a genre in which they were free to do just about anything they wanted, that it offered a farflung, freewheeling freedom to explore ideas and characters. Experimentation was the name of the game, and science fiction was a wonderful laboratory (that scientist's daughter again).

Judith Merril said speculative fiction "makes use of the traditional 'scientific method'" (observation, hypothesis, experimentation) by taking a given situation and introducing variables into it. In SF, the laboratory is the entire universe, where abstracts can be made actual, and political, social, and philosophical ideas can take on human (or alien) form.

SF's women writers have taken full advantage of those laboratory privileges. Ursula K. Le Guin's planets Winter (in *The Left Hand of Darkness*) and Yeowe (in "A Woman's Liberation") are places in which to explore ideas of gender and power. Nancy Kress invented bioengineered geniuses in *Beggars in Spain* to examine society's fears of the different and superior. And Octavia E. Butler has used the thought experiment of "Bloodchild," with its aliens and conquered humans and their tortured symbiotic relationship, to explore the complex relationships and subtle dynamics of slavery in ways she could never address directly.

SF is a great place for the serious writer, with serious things to say. And for the humorous writer with funny things to say. And for the writer who just wants to tell a good old-fashioned yarn, or construct a devilishly clever mystery, or tell a haunting love story. Or predict the future. Or do all of those at once.

That's because science fiction incorporates a broad spectrum of styles and stories and sensibilities, attitudes and approaches. Its writers (women and men) have produced everything from screwball comedies to swashbuckling space adventures, from high-tech tales to hardboiled mysteries, putting new spins on them all and combining categories with abandon. In this volume, S.N. Dyer mixes medical technology with the classic ghost story in "The July Ward," Pat Murphy reinvents the love story in "Rachel in Love," and Katherine MacLean's "The Kidnapping of Baroness 5" manages to combine the postapocalypse survival story, the classic fairy tale, cutting-edge biotechnology, and a little romance, all in one extremely entertaining story.

And since this is science fiction, its writers have also had the freedom to write stories that have no category at all. Into what genre exactly would you put Shirley Jackson's "The Lottery"? Or Theodore Sturgeon's "The Man Who Lost the Sea"? Or James Tiptree Jr.'s "And Her Smoke Rose Up Forever"?

Included in this "liberation" is the freedom to not be a "woman writer." Women in SF aren't relegated to the corner reserved for domestics "sweat-tears-and-baby-urine stories" (the moniker given to Judith Merril's "That Only a Mother" by Damon Knight—who clearly had never read the story). Or the other, even worse, feminist "women's issues" ghetto.

SF's female authors write about all kinds of subjects: Nancy Kress about ballerinas and anti-aging research, Vonda McIntyre about mermaids and Enlightenment science, S.N. Dyer about the dilemmas medical technology confronts us with, Anne McCaffrey about space stations and dragons. And over the years, SF's women have written about chemistry, quantum theory, King Arthur, aliens, time-traveling tourists, tigers, telepathy, teachers, intelligent spaceships, not-so-intelligent assistants, utopias, cyborgs, vampires, and one ordinary day with peanuts—and made it clear that every issue is a woman's issue.

That doesn't mean they don't sometimes turn their hand to "women's issues." They do: Witness Nicola Griffith's *Ammonite* and Suzy McKee Charnas's *Motherlines*. Ursula K. Le Guin tackles the topics of sexual politics and female freedom head on in "A Woman's Liberation," and my story "Even the Queen" addresses that ultimately female issue, menstruation, and a whole new kind of Women's Liberation.

It's just that when SF's women write about women, the results are never what you'd expect. This is the genre, after all, that brought you not only Sheri Tepper's *The Gate to Women's Country*, but Katherine MacLean's "The Snowball Effect." And Karen Joy

Fowler's "The Faithful Companion at Forty." And Judith Merril's *Daughters of Earth*.

And the astonishing stories in this collection, all originally published in *Analog* and *Asimov's*. Here you'll find women facing all sorts of challenges, from superstition to sorrow to societies spinning out of control. S.N. Dyer's Watson is struggling with the guilt and fear that go with her job, Vonda McIntyre's Snake and Katherine MacLean's Lady Witch with the loneliness and misunderstanding that go with theirs. Pat Murphy's Rachel, Anne McCaffrey's Helva, and Sarah Zettel's Fool are trying to come to terms with who and what they are, and Nancy Kress's Gram and Octavia E. Butler's Rye are simply trying to survive. And they're doing it in stories as different as their authors are from each other.

You'll find stories here by veterans (Katherine MacLean's first story was published in 1949) and new kids on the block like Sarah Zettel, Hugo and Nebula Award-winners (seven, count 'em, seven), and a genuine MacArthur Grant genius. You'll find princesses, prisoners, surgeons, slaves, snakehandlers, sorrow, silence, and the unexpected.

Which is what science fiction, and the women of science fiction, are all about. So welcome to the liberating world of science fiction. And to *A Woman's Liberation*.

A WOMAN'S LIBERATION

Inertia

Nancy Kress

At dusk the back of the bedroom falls off. One minute it's a wall, exposed studs and cracked blue drywall, and the next it's snapped-off two-by-fours and an irregular fence as high as my waist, the edges both jagged and furry, as if they were covered with powder. Through the hole a sickly tree pokes upward in the narrow space between the back of our barracks and the back of a barracks in E Block. I try to get out of bed for a closer look, but today my arthritis is too bad, which is why I'm in bed in the first place. Rachel rushes into the bedroom.

"What *happened,* Gram? Are you all right?"

I nod and point. Rachel bends into the hole, her hair haloed by California twilight. The bedroom is hers, too; her mattress lies stored under my scarred four-poster.

"Termites! Damn. I didn't know we had them. You sure you're all right?"

"I'm fine. I was all the way across the room, honey. I'm fine."

"Well—we'll have to get Mom to get somebody to fix it."

I say nothing. Rachel straightens, throws me a quick glance, looks away. Still I say nothing about Mamie, but in a sudden flicker from my oil lamp I look directly at Rachel, just because she is so good to look at. Not pretty, not even here Inside, although so far the disease has affected only the left side of her face. The ridge of thickened, ropy skin, coarse as old hemp, isn't visible at all when she stands in right profile. But her nose is large, her eyebrows heavy and low, her chin a bony knob. An honest nose, expressive brows, direct gray eyes, chin that juts forward when she tilts her head in intelligent listening—to a grandmother's eye, Rachel is good to look at. They wouldn't think so, Outside. But they would be wrong.

Rachel says, "Maybe I could trade a lottery card for more dry-wall and nails, and patch it myself."

"The termites will still be there."

"Well, yes, but we have to do *something*." I don't contradict her. She is sixteen years old. "Feel that air coming in—you'll freeze at night this time of year. It'll be terrible for your arthritis. Come in the kitchen now, Gram—I've built up the fire."

She helps me into the kitchen, where the metal wood-burning stove throws a rosy warmth that feels good on my joints. The stove was donated to the colony a year ago by who-knows-what charity or special interest group for, I suppose, whatever tax breaks still hold for that sort of thing. If any do. Rachel tells me that we still get newspapers, and once or twice I've wrapped vegetables from our patch in some fairly new-looking ones. She even says that the young Stevenson boy works a donated computer news net in the Block J community hall, but I no longer follow Outside tax regulations. Nor do I ask why Mamie was the one to get the wood-burning stove when it wasn't a lottery month.

The light from the stove is stronger than the oil flame in the bedroom; I see that beneath her concern for our dead bedroom wall, Rachel's face is flushed with excitement. Her young skin glows right from intelligent chin to the ropy ridge of disease, which of course never changes color. I smile at her. Sixteen is so easy to excite. A new hair ribbon from the donations repository, a glance from a boy, a secret with her cousin Jennie.

"Gram," she says, kneeling beside my chair, her hands restless on the battered wooden arm. "Gram—there's a visitor. From Out-side. Jennie *saw* him."

I go on smiling. Rachel—nor Jennie, either—can't remember when disease colonies had lots of visitors. First bulky figures in con-tamination suits, then a few years later, sleeker figures in the sani-suits that took their place. People were still being interred from Outside, and for years the checkpoints at the Rim had traffic flow-ing both ways. But of course Rachel doesn't remember all that; she wasn't born. Mamie was only twelve when we were interred here. To Rachel, a visitor might well be a great event. I put out one hand and stroke her hair.

"Jennie said he wants to talk to the oldest people in the colony, the ones who were brought here with the disease. Hal Stevenson told her."

"Did he, sweetheart?" Her hair is soft and silky. Mamie's hair had been the same at Rachel's age.

"He might want to talk to you!"

"Well, here I am."

"But aren't you excited? What do you suppose he wants?"

I'm saved from answering her because Mamie comes in, her boyfriend Peter Malone following with a string-bag of groceries from the repository.

At the first sound of the doorknob turning, Rachel gets up from beside my chair and pokes at the fire. Her face goes completely blank, although I know that part is only temporary. Mamie cries, "Here we are!" in her high, doll-baby voice, cold air from the hall swirling around her like bright water. "Mama darling—how are you feeling? And Rachel! You'll never guess—Pete had extra depository cards and he got us some chicken! I'm going to make a stew!"

"The back wall fell off the bedroom," Rachel says flatly. She doesn't look at Peter with his string-crossed chicken, but I do. He grins his patient, wolfish grin. I guess that he won the depository cards at poker. His fingernails are dirty. The part of the newspaper I can see says ESIDENT CONFISCATES C.

Mamie says, "What do you mean, fell off?"

Rachel shrugs. "Just fell off. Termites."

Mamie looks helplessly at Peter, whose grin widens. I can see how it will be: They will have a scene later, not completely for our benefit, although it will take place in the kitchen for us to watch. Mamie will beg prettily for Peter to fix the wall. He will demur, grinning. She will offer various smirking hints about barter, each hint becoming more explicit. He will agree to fix the wall. Rachel and I, having no other warm room to go to, will watch the fire or the floor or our shoes until Mamie and Peter retire ostentatiously to her room. It's the ostentation that embarrasses us. Mamie has always needed witnesses to her desirability.

But Peter is watching Rachel, not Mamie. "The chicken isn't from Outside, Rachel. It's from that chicken yard in Block B. I heard you say how clean they are."

"Yeah," Rachel says shortly, gracelessly.

Mamie rolls her eyes. "Say 'thank you,' darling. Pete went to a lot of trouble to get this chicken."

"Thanks."

"Can't you say it like you *mean* it?" Mamie's voice goes shrill.

"*Thanks*," Rachel says. She heads toward our three-walled bedroom. Peter, still watching her closely, shifts the chicken from one hand to the other. The pressure of the string bag cuts lines across the chicken's yellowish skin.

"Rachel Anne Wilson—"

"Let her go," Peter says softly.

"*No*," Mamie says. Between the five crisscrossing lines of disease, her face sets in unlovely lines. "She can at least learn some manners. And I want her to hear our announcement! Rachel, you just come right back out here this minute!"

Rachel returns from the bedroom; I've never known her to disobey her mother. She pauses by the open bedroom door, waiting. Two empty candle sconces, both blackened by old smoke, frame her head. It has been since at least last winter that we've had candles for them. Mamie, her forehead creased in irritation, smiles brightly.

"This is a special dinner, all of you. Pete and I have an announcement. We're going to get married."

"That's right," Peter says. "Congratulate us."

Rachel, already motionless, somehow goes even stiller. Peter watches her carefully. Mamie casts down her eyes, blushing, and I feel a stab of impatient pity for my daughter, propping up mid-thirties girlishness on such a slender reed as Peter Malone. I stare at him hard. If he ever touches Rachel . . . but I don't really think he would. Things like that don't happen anymore. Not Inside.

"Congratulations," Rachel mumbles. She crosses the room and embraces her mother, who hugs her back with theatrical fervor. In another minute, Mamie will start to cry. Over her shoulder I glimpse Rachel's face, momentarily sorrowing and loving, and I drop my eyes.

"Well! This calls for a toast!" Mamie cries gaily. She winks, makes a clumsy pirouette, and pulls a bottle from the back shelf of the cupboard Rachel got at the last donations lottery. The cupboard looks strange in our kitchen: gleaming white lacquer, vaguely oriental-looking, amid the wobbly chairs and scarred table with the broken drawer no one has ever gotten around to mending. Mamie flourishes the bottle, which I didn't know was there. It's champagne.

What had they been thinking, the Outsiders who donated champagne to a disease colony? *Poor devils, even if they never have anything to celebrate. . . .* Or *Here's something they won't know what to do with. . . .* Or *Better them than me—as long as the sickies stay Inside. . . .* It doesn't really matter.

"I just love champagne!" Mamie cries feverishly; I think she has drunk it once. "And oh look—here's someone else to help us celebrate! Come in, Jennie—come in and have some champagne!"

Jennie comes in, smiling. I see the same eager excitement that animated Rachel before her mother's announcement. It glows on

Jennie's face, which is beautiful. She has no disease on her hands or her face. She must have it somewhere, she was born Inside, but one doesn't ask that. Probably Rachel knows. The two girls are inseparable. Jennie, the daughter of Mamie's dead husband's brother, is Rachel's cousin, and technically Mamie is her guardian. But no one pays attention to such things anymore, and Jennie lives with some people in a barracks in the next Block, although Rachel and I asked her to live here. She shook her head, the beautiful hair so blonde it's almost white bouncing on her shoulders, and blushed in embarrassment, painfully not looking at Mamie.

"I'm getting married, Jennie," Mamie says, again casting down her eyes bashfully. I wonder what she did, and with whom, to get the champagne.

"Congratulations!" Jennie says warmly. "You, too, Peter."

"Call me Pete," he says, as he has said before. I catch his hungry look at Jennie. She doesn't, but some sixth sense—even here, even Inside—makes her step slightly backward. I know she will go on calling him "Peter."

Mamie says to Jennie, "Have some more champagne. Stay for dinner."

With her eyes Jennie measures the amount of champagne in the bottle, the size of the chicken bleeding slightly on the table. She measures unobtrusively, and then of course she lies. "I'm sorry, I can't—we ate our meal at noon today. I just wanted to ask if I could bring someone over to see you later, Gram. A visitor." Her voice drops to a hush, and the glow is back. "From *Outside*."

I look at her sparkling blue eyes, at Rachel's face, and I don't have the heart to refuse. Even though I can guess, as the two girls cannot, how the visit will be. I am not Jennie's grandmother, but she has called me that since she was three. "All right."

"Oh, thank you!" Jennie cries, and she and Rachel look at each other with delight. "I'm so glad you said yes, or else we might never get to talk to a visitor up close at all!"

"You're welcome," I say. They are so young. Mamie looks petulant; her announcement has been upstaged. Peter watches Jennie as she impulsively hugs Rachel. Suddenly I know that he, too, is wondering where Jennie's body is diseased, and how much. He catches my eye and looks at the floor, his dark eyes lidded, half ashamed. But only half. A log crackles in the wooden stove, and for a brief moment the fire flares.

The next afternoon Jennie brings the visitor. He surprises me immediately: he isn't wearing a sani-suit, and he isn't a sociologist.

In the years following the internments, the disease colonies had a lot of visitors. Doctors still hopeful of a cure for the thick gray ridges of skin that spread slowly over a human body—or didn't, nobody knew why. Disfiguring. Ugly. Maybe eventually fatal. And *communicable*. That was the biggie: communicable. So doctors in sani-suits came looking for causes or cures. Journalists in sani-suits came looking for stories with four-color photo spreads. Legislative fact-finding committees in sani-suits came looking for facts, at least until Congress took away the power of the colonies to vote, pressured by taxpayers who, increasingly pressured themselves, resented our dollar-dependent status. And the sociologists came in droves, minicams in hand, ready to record the collapse of the ill-organized and ill colonies into street-gang, dog-eat-dog anarchy.

Later, when this did not happen, different sociologists came in later-model sani-suits to record the reasons why the colonies were not collapsing on schedule. All these groups went away dissatisfied. There was no cure, no cause, no story, no collapse. No reasons.

The sociologists hung on longer than anybody else. Journalists have to be timely and interesting, but sociologists merely have to publish. Besides, everything in their cultural tradition told them that Inside *must* sooner or later degenerate into war zones: Deprive people of electricity (power became expensive), of municipal police (who refused to go Inside), of freedom to leave, of political clout, of jobs, of freeways and movie theaters and federal judges and state-administered elementary-school accreditation—and you get unrestrained violence to just survive. Everything in the culture said so. Bombed-out inner cities. *Lord of the Flies*. The Chicago projects. Western movies. Prison memoirs. The Bronx. East L.A. Thomas Hobbes. The sociologists *knew*.

Only it didn't happen.

The sociologists waited. And Inside we learned to grow vegetables and raise chickens who, we learned, will eat anything. Those of us with computer knowledge worked real jobs over modems for a few years—maybe it was as long as a decade—before the equipment became too obsolete and unreplaced. Those who had been teachers organized classes among the children, although the curriculum, I think, must have gotten simpler every year: Rachel and Jennie don't seem to have much knowledge of history or science. Doctors practiced with medicines donated by corporations for the tax write-offs, and after a decade or so they began to train apprentices. For a while—it might have been a long while—we listened to radios and watched TV. Maybe some people still do, if we have any working ones donated from Outside. I don't pay attention.

Eventually the sociologists remembered older models of deprivation and discrimination and isolation from the larger culture: Jewish shtetls. French Huguenots. Amish farmers. Self-sufficient models, stagnant but uncollapsed. And while they were remembering, we held goods lotteries, and took on apprentices, and rationed depository food according to who needed it, and replaced our broken-down furniture with other broken-down furniture, and got married and bore children. We paid no taxes, fought no wars, wielded no votes, provided no drama. After a while—a long while—the visitors stopped coming. Even the sociologists.

But here stands this young man, without a sani-suit, smiling from brown eyes under thick dark hair and taking my hand. He doesn't wince when he touches the ropes of disease. Nor does he appear to be cataloging the kitchen furniture for later recording: three chairs, one donated imitation Queen Anne and one Inside genuine Joe Kleinschmidt; the table; the wood stove; the sparkling new oriental lacquered cupboard; plastic sink with hand pump; woodbox with donated wood stamped "Gift of Boise-Cascade"; two eager and intelligent and loving young girls he had better not try to patronize as diseased freaks. It has been a long time, but I remember.

"Hello, Mrs. Pratt. I'm Tom McHabe. Thank you for agreeing to talk to me."

I nod. "What are we going to talk about, Mr. McHabe? Are you a journalist?"

"No. I'm a doctor."

I don't expect that. Nor do I expect the sudden strain that flashes across his face before it's lost in another smile. Although it is natural enough that strain should be there: Having come Inside, of course, he can never leave. I wonder where he picked up the disease. No other new cases have been admitted to our colony for as long as I can remember. Had they been taken, for some Outside political reason, to one of the other colonies instead?

McHabe says, "I don't have the disease, Mrs. Pratt."

"Then why on earth—"

"I'm writing a paper on the progress of the disease in long-established colony residents. I had to do that from Inside, of course," he says, and immediately I know he is lying. Rachel and Jennie, of course, do not. They sit one on each side of him like eager birds, listening.

"And how will you get this paper out once it's written?" I say.

"Short-wave radio. Colleagues are expecting it," but he doesn't quite meet my eyes.

"And this paper is worth permanent internment?"

"How rapidly did your case of the disease progress?" he says, not answering my question. He looks at my face and hands and forearms, an objective and professional scrutiny that makes me decide at least one part of his story is true. He is a doctor.

"Any pain in the infected areas?"

"None."

"Any functional disability or decreased activity as a result of the disease?" Rachel and Jennie look slightly puzzled; he's testing me to see if I understand the terminology.

"None."

"Any change in appearance over the last few years in the first skin areas to be affected? Changes in color or tissue density or size of the thickened ridges?"

"None."

"Any other kinds of changes I haven't thought to mention?"

"None."

He nods and rocks back on his heels. He's cool, for someone who is going to develop non-dysfunctional ropes of disease himself. I wait to see if he's going to tell me why he's really here. The silence lengthens. Finally McHabe says, "You were a CPA," at the same time that Rachel says, "Anyone want a glass of 'ade?"

McHabe accepts gladly. The two girls, relieved to be in motion, busy themselves pumping cold water, crushing canned peaches, mixing the 'ade in a brown plastic pitcher with a deep wart on one side where it once touched the hot stove.

"Yes," I say to McHabe. "I was a CPA. What about it?"

"They're outlawed now."

"CPA's? Why? Staunch pillars of the establishment," I say, and realize how long it's been since I used words like that. They taste metallic, like old tin.

"Not anymore. IRS does all tax computations and sends every household a customized bill. The calculations on how they reach your particular customized figure are classified. To prevent foreign enemies from guessing at revenue available for defense."

"Ah."

"My uncle was a CPA."

"What is he now?"

"Not a CPA," McHabe says. He doesn't smile. Jennie hands glasses of 'ade to me and then to McHabe, and then he does smile. Jennie drops her lashes and a little color steals into her cheeks.

Something moves behind McHabe's eyes. But it's not like Peter; not at all like Peter.

I glance at Rachel. She doesn't seem to have noticed anything. She isn't jealous, or worried, or hurt. I relax a little.

McHabe says to me, "You also published some magazine articles popularizing history."

"How do you happen to know that?"

Again he doesn't answer me. "It's an unusual combination of abilities, accounting and history writing."

"I suppose so," I say, without interest. It was so long ago.

Rachel says to McHabe, "Can I ask you something?"

"Sure."

"Outside, do you have medicines that will cure wood of termites?"

Her face is deadly serious. McHabe doesn't grin, and I admit—reluctantly—that he is likable. He answers her courteously. "We don't cure the wood, we do away with the termites. The best way is to build with wood saturated with creosote, a chemical they don't like, so that they don't get into the wood in the first place. But there must be chemicals that will kill them after they're already there. I'll ask around and try to bring you something on my next trip Inside."

His next trip Inside. He drops this bombshell as if easy passage In and Out were a given. Rachel's and Jennie's eyes grow wide; they both look at me. McHabe does, too, and I see that his look is a cool scrutiny, an appraisal of my reaction. He expects me to ask for details, or maybe even—it's been a long time since I thought in these terms, and it's an effort—to become angry at him for lying. But I don't know whether or not he's lying, and at any rate, what does it matter? A few people from Outside coming into the colony—how could it affect us? There won't be large immigration, and no emigration at all.

I say quietly, "Why are you really here, Dr. McHabe?"

"I told you, Mrs. Pratt. To measure the progress of the disease."

I say nothing. He adds, "Maybe you'd like to hear more about how it is now Outside."

"Not especially."

"Why not?"

I shrug. "They leave us alone."

He weighs me with his eyes. Jennie says timidly, "I'd like to hear more about Outside." Before Rachel can add "Me, too," the door flings violently open and Mamie backs into the room, screaming into the hall behind her.

"And don't ever come back! If you think I'd ever let you touch me again after screwing that . . . that . . . I hope she's got a diseased twat and you get it on your—" She sees McHabe and breaks off, her whole body jerking in rage. A soft answer from the hall, the words unintelligible from my chair by the fire, makes her gasp and turn even redder. She slams the door, bursts into tears, and runs into her bedroom, slamming the door as well.

Rachel stands up. "Let me, honey," I say, but before I can rise— my arthritis is much better—Rachel disappears into her mother's room. The kitchen rings with embarrassed silence.

Tom McHabe rises to leave. "Sit down, Doctor," I say, hoping, I think, that if he remains Mamie will restrain her hysterics— maybe—and Rachel will emerge sooner from her mother's room.

McHabe looks undecided. Then Jennie says, "Yes, please stay. And would you tell us—" I see her awkwardness, her desire to not sound stupid "—about how people do Outside?"

He does. Looking at Jennie but meaning me, he talks about the latest version of martial law, about the failure of the National Guard to control protesters against the South American war until they actually reached the edge of the White House electro-wired zone; about the growing power of the Fundamentalist underground that the other undergrounds—he uses the plural—call "the God gang." He tells us about the industries losing out steadily to Korean and Chinese competitors, the leaping unemployment rate, the ethnic backlash, the cities in flames. Miami, New York, Los Angeles—

these had been rioting for years. Now it's Portland, St. Louis, Eugene, Phoenix. Grand Rapids burning. It's hard to picture.

I say, "As far as I can tell, donations to our repositories haven't fallen off."

He looks at me again with that shrewd scrutiny, weighing something I can't see, then touches the edge of the stove with one boot. The boot, I notice, is almost as old and scarred as one of ours. "Korean-made stove. They make nearly all the donations now. Public relations. Even a lot of martial-law congressmen had relatives interred, although they won't admit it now. The Asians cut deals warding off complete protectionism, although of course your donations are only a small part of that. But just about everything you get Inside is Chink or Splat." He uses the words casually, this courteous young man giving me the news from such a liberal slant, and that tells me more about the Outside than all his bulletins and summaries.

Jennie says haltingly, "I saw . . . I think it was an Asian man. Yesterday."

"Where?" I say sharply. Very few Asian-Americans contract the disease; something else no one understands. There are none in our colony.

"At the Rim. One of the guards. Two other men were kicking him and yelling names at him—we couldn't hear too clearly over the intercom boxes."

"We? You and Rachel? What were you two doing at the *Rim?*" I say, and hear my own tone. The Rim, a wide empty strip of land, is electro-mined and barb-wired to keep us communicables Inside. The Rim is surrounded by miles of defoliated and disinfected land, poisoned by preventive chemicals, but even so it's patrolled by unwilling soldiers who communicate with the Inside by intercoms set up every half mile on both sides of the barbed wire. When the colony used to have a fight or a rape or—once, in the early years— a murder, it happened on the Rim. When the hateful and the hating came to hurt us, because before the electro-wiring and barbed wire we were easy targets and no police would follow them Inside, the soldiers, and sometimes our men as well, stopped them at the Rim. Our dead are buried near the Rim. And Rachel and Jennie, dear gods, at the *Rim*. . . .

"We went to ask the guards over the intercom boxes if they knew how to stop termites," Jennie says logically. "After all, their work is to stop things, germs and things. We thought they might be able to tell us how to stop termites. We thought they might have special training in it."

The bedroom door opens and Rachel comes out, her young face drawn. McHabe smiles at her, and then his gaze returns to Jennie. "I don't think soldiers are trained in stopping termites, but I'll definitely bring you something to do that the next time I come Inside."

There it is again. But all Rachel says is, "Oh, good. I asked around for more drywall today, but even if I get some, the same thing will happen again if we don't get something to stop them."

McHabe says, "Did you know that termites elect a queen? Closely monitored balloting system. Fact."

Rachel smiles, although I don't think she really understands.

"And ants can bring down a rubber tree plant." He begins to sing, an old song from my childhood. "High Hopes." Frank Sinatra on the stereo—before CDs, even, before a lot of things—iced tea and Coke in tall glasses on a Sunday afternoon, aunts and uncles sitting around the kitchen, football on television in the living room beside a table with a lead-crystal vase of the last purple chrysanthemums from the garden. The smell of late Sunday afternoon, tangy but a little thin, the last of the weekend before the big yellow school bus labored by on Monday morning.

Jennie and Rachel, of course, see none of this. They hear light-hearted words in a good baritone and a simple rhythm they can follow, hope and courage in silly doggerel. They are delighted. They join in the chorus after McHabe has sung it a few times, then sing him three songs popular at Block dances, then make him more 'ade, then begin to ask questions about the Outside. Simple questions:

What do people eat? Where do they get it? What do they wear? The three of them are still at it when I go to bed, my arthritis finally starting to ache, glancing at Mamie's closed door with a sadness I hadn't expected and can't name.

"That son-of-a-bitch better never come near me again," Mamie says the next morning. The day is sunny and I sit by our one window, knitting a blanket to loosen my fingers, wondering if the donated wool came from Chinese or Korean sheep. Rachel has gone with Jennie on a labor call to deepen a well in Block E; people had been talking about doing that for weeks, and apparently someone finally got around to organizing it. Mamie slumps at the table, her eyes red from crying. "I caught him screwing Mary Delbarton." Her voice splinters like a two-year-old's. "Mama—he was screwing Mary Delbarton."

"Let him go, Mamie."

"I'd be alone again." She says it with a certain dignity, which doesn't last. "That son-of-a-bitch goes off with that slut one day after we're engaged and I'm fucking alone again!"

I don't say anything; there isn't anything to say. Mamie's husband died eleven years ago, when Rachel was only five, of an experimental cure being tested by government doctors. The colonies were guinea pigs. Seventeen people in four colonies died, and the government discontinued funding and made it a crime for anyone to go in and out of a disease colony. Too great a risk of contamination, they said. For the protection of the citizens of the country.

"He'll never touch me again!" Mamie says, tears on her lashes. One slips down an inch until it hits the first of the disease ropes, then travels sideways toward her mouth. I reach over and wipe it away. "Goddamn fucking son-of-a-bitch!"

By evening, she and Peter are holding hands. They sit side by side, and his fingers creep up her thigh under what they think is the cover of the table. Mamie slips her hand under his buttocks. Rachel and Jennie look away, Jennie flushing slightly. I have a brief flash of memory, of the kind I haven't had for years: myself at eighteen or so, my first year at Yale, in a huge brass bed with a modern geometric-print bedspread and a red-headed man I'd met three hours ago. But here, Inside . . . here sex, like everything else, moves so much more slowly, so much more carefully, so much more privately. For such a long time people were afraid that this disease, like that other earlier one, might be transmitted sexually. And then there was the shame of one's ugly body, crisscrossed with ropes of disease . . . I'm not sure that Rachel has ever seen a man naked.

I say, for the sake of saying something, "So there's a Block dance Wednesday."

"Block B," Jennie says. Her blue eyes sparkle. "With the band that played last summer for Block E."

"Guitars?"

"Oh, no! They've got a trumpet *and* a violin," Rachel says, clearly impressed. "You should hear how they sound together, Gram—it's a lot different than guitars. Come to the dance!"

"I don't think so, honey. Is Dr. McHabe going?" From both their faces I know this guess is right.

Jennie says hesitantly, "He wants to talk to you first, before the dance, for a few minutes. If that's all right."

"Why?"

"I'm not . . . not exactly sure I know all of it." She doesn't meet my eyes: unwilling to tell me, unwilling to lie. Most of the children Inside, I realize for the first time, are not liars. Or else they're bad ones. They're good at privacy, but it must be an honest privacy.

"Will you see him?" Rachel says eagerly.

"I'll see him."

Mamie looks away from Peter long enough to add sharply, "If it's anything about you or Jennie, he should see *me*, miss, not your grandmother. I'm your mother and Jennie's guardian, and don't you forget it."

"No, Mama," Rachel says.

"I don't like your tone, miss!"

"Sorry," Rachel says, in the same tone. Jennie drops her eyes, embarrassed. But before Mamie can get really started on indignant maternal neglect, Peter whispers something in her ear and she claps her hand over her mouth, giggling.

Later, when just the two of us are left in the kitchen, I say quietly to Rachel, "Try not to upset your mother, honey. She can't help it."

"Yes, Gram," Rachel says obediently. But I hear the disbelief in her tone, a disbelief muted by her love for me and even for her mother, but nonetheless there. Rachel doesn't believe that Mamie can't help it. Rachel, born Inside, can't possibly help her own ignorance of what it is that Mamie thinks she has lost.

On his second visit to me six days later, just before the Block dance, Tom McHabe seems different. I'd forgotten that there are people who radiate such energy and purpose that they seem to set the very air tingling. He stands with his legs braced slightly apart, flanked by Rachel and Jennie, both dressed in their other skirts for the dance. Jennie has woven a red ribbon through her blonde curls; it glows like a flower. McHabe touches her lightly on the shoulder, and I realize from her answering look what must be happening between them. My throat tightens.

"I want to be honest with you, Mrs. Pratt. I've talked to Jack Stevenson and Mary Kramer, as well as some others in Blocks C and E, and I've gotten a feel for how you live here. A little bit, anyway. I'm going to tell Mr. Stevenson and Mrs. Kramer what I tell you, but I wanted you to be first."

"Why?" I say, more harshly than I intend. Or think I intend.

He isn't fazed. "Because you're one of the oldest survivors of the disease. Because you had a strong education Outside. Because your daughter's husband died of axoperidine."

At the same moment that I realize what McHabe is going to say next, I realize, too, that Rachel and Jennie have already heard it. They listen to him with the slightly open-mouthed intensity of children hearing a marvelous but familiar tale. But do they understand? Rachel wasn't present when her father finally died, gasping for air his lungs couldn't use.

McHabe, watching me, says, "There's been a lot of research on the disease since those deaths, Mrs. Pratt."

"No. There hasn't. Too risky, your government said."

I see that he caught the pronoun. "Actual administration of any cures is illegal, yes. To minimize contact with communicables."

"So how has this 'research' been carried on?"

"By doctors willing to go Inside and not come out again. Data is transmitted out by laser. In code."

"What clean doctor would be willing to go Inside and not come out again?"

McHabe smiles; again I'm struck by that quality of spontaneous energy. "Oh, you'd be surprised. We had three doctors inside the Pennsylvania colony. One past retirement age. Another, an old-style Catholic, who dedicated his research to God. A third nobody could figure out, a dour persistent guy who was a brilliant researcher."

Was. "And you."

"No," McHabe says quietly. "I go in and out."

"What happened to the others?"

"They're dead." He makes a brief aborted movement with his right hand and I realized that he is, or was, a smoker. How long since I had reached like that for a nonexistent cigarette? Nearly two decades. Cigarettes are not among the things people donate; they're too valuable. Yet I recognize the movement still. "Two of the three doctors caught the disease. They worked on themselves as well as volunteers. Then one day the government intercepted the relayed data and went in and destroyed everything."

"Why?" Jennie asks.

"Research on the disease is illegal. Everyone Outside is afraid of a leak; a virus somehow getting out on a mosquito, a bird, even as a spore."

"Nothing has gotten out in all these years," Rachel says.

"No. But the government is afraid that if researchers start splicing and intercutting genes, it could make viruses more viable. You don't understand the Outside, Rachel. *Everything* is illegal. This is the most repressive period in American history. Everyone's afraid."

"You're not," Jennie says, so softly I barely hear her. McHabe gives her a smile that twists my heart.

"Some of us haven't given up. Research goes on. But it's all underground, all theoretical. And we've learned a lot. We've learned that the virus doesn't just affect the skin. There are—"

"Be quiet," I say, because I see that he's about to say something important. "Be quiet a minute. Let me think."

McHabe waits. Jennie and Rachel look at me, that glow of suppressed excitement on them both. Eventually I find it. "You want something, Dr. McHabe. All this research wants something from us besides pure scientific joy. With things Outside as bad as you say, there must be plenty of diseases Outside you could research without killing yourself, plenty of need among your own people—" he nods, his eyes gleaming "—but you're here. Inside. Why? We don't have any more new or interesting symptoms, we barely survive, the Outside stopped caring what happened to us a long time ago. We have *nothing*. So why are you here?"

"You're wrong, Mrs. Pratt. You do have something interesting going on here. You *have* survived. Your society has regressed, but not collapsed. You're functioning under conditions where you shouldn't have."

The same old crap. I raise my eyebrows at him. He stares into the fire and says quietly, "To say Washington is rioting says nothing. You have to see a twelve-year-old hurl a homemade bomb, a man sliced open from neck to crotch because he still had a job to go to and his neighbor doesn't, a three-year-old left to starve because someone abandoned her like an unwanted kitten. . . . You don't know. It doesn't happen Inside."

"We're better than they are," Rachel says. I look at my grandchild. She says it simply, without self-aggrandizement, but with a kind of wonder. In the firelight the thickened gray ropes of skin across her cheek glow dull maroon.

McHabe says, "Perhaps you are. I started to say earlier that we've learned that the virus doesn't affect just the skin. It alters neurotransmitter receptor sites in the brain as well. It's a relatively slow transformation, which is why the flurry of research in the early years of the disease missed it. But it's real, as real as the faster site-capacity transformations brought about by, say, cocaine. Are you following me, Mrs. Pratt?"

I nod. Jennie and Rachel don't look lost, although they don't know any of this vocabulary, and I realize that McHabe must have explained all this to them, earlier, in some other terms.

"As the disease progresses to the brain, the receptors which receive excitatory transmitters slowly become harder to engage, and the receptors which receive inhibiting transmitters become easier to engage."

"You mean that we become stupider."

"Oh, no! Intelligence is not affected at all. The results are emotional and behavioral, not intellectual. You become—all of you—calmer. Disinclined to action or innovation. Mildly but definitely depressed."

The fire burns down. I pick up the poker, bent slightly where someone once tried to use it as a crowbar, and poke at the log, which is a perfectly shaped molded-pump synthetic stamped "Donated by Weyerhauser-Seyyed." "I don't feel depressed, young man."

"It's a depression of the nervous system, but a new kind—without the hopelessness usually associated with clinical depression."

"I don't believe you."

"Really? With all due courtesy, when was the last time you—or any of the older Block leaders—pushed for any significant changes in how you do things Inside?"

"Sometimes things cannot be constructively changed. Only accepted. That's not chemistry, it's reality."

"Not Outside," McHabe says grimly. "Outside they don't

change constructively *or* accept. They get violent. Inside, you've had almost no violence since the early years, even when your resources tightened again and again. When was the last time you tasted butter, Mrs. Pratt, or smoked a cigarette, or had a new pair of jeans? Do you know what happens Outside when consumer goods become unavailable and there are no police in a given area? But Inside you just distribute whatever you have as fairly as you can, or make do without. No looting, no rioting, no cancerous envy. No one Outside knew *why*. Now we do."

"We have envy."

"But it doesn't erupt into anger."

Each time one of us speaks, Jennie and Rachel turn their heads to watch, like rapt spectators at tennis. Which neither of them has ever seen. Jennie's skin glows like pearl.

"Our young people aren't violent either, and the disease hasn't advanced very far in some of them."

"They learn how to behave from their elders—just like kids everywhere else."

"I don't feel depressed."

"Do you feel energetic?"

"I have arthritis."

"That's not what I mean."

"What do you mean, Doctor?"

Again that restless, furtive reach for a nonexistent cigarette. But his voice is quiet. "How long did it take you to get around to applying that insecticide I got Rachel for the termites? She told me you forbade her to do it, and I think you were right; it's dangerous stuff. How many days went by before you and your daughter spread it around?"

The chemical is still in its can.

"How much anger are you feeling now, Mrs. Pratt?" he goes on. "Because I think we understand each other, you and I, and that you guess now why I'm here. But you aren't shouting or ordering me out of here or even telling me what you think of me. You're listening, and you're doing it calmly, and you're accepting what I tell you even though you know what I want you to—"

The door opens and he breaks off. Mamie flounces in, followed by Peter. She scowls and stamps her foot. "Where were you, Rachel? We've been standing outside waiting for you all for ten minutes! The dance has already started!"

"A few more minutes, Mama. We're talking."

"Talking? About what? What's going on?"

"Nothing," McHabe says. "I was just asking your mother some questions about life Inside. I'm sorry we took so long."

"You never ask *me* questions about life Inside. And besides, I want to dance!"

McHabe says, "If you and Peter want to go ahead, I'll bring Rachel and Jennie."

Mamie chews her bottom lip. I suddenly know that she wants to walk up the street to the dance between Peter and McHabe, an arm linked with each, the girls trailing behind. McHabe meets her eyes steadily.

"Well, if that what you *want*," she says pettishly. "Come on, Pete!" She closes the door hard.

I look at McHabe, unwilling to voice the question in front of Rachel, trusting him to know the argument I want to make. He does. "In clinical depression, there's always been a small percentage for whom the illness is manifested not as passivity, but as irritability. It may be the same. We don't know."

"Gram," Rachel says, as if she can't contain herself any longer, "he has a *cure*."

"For the skin manifestation only," McHabe says quickly, and I see that he wouldn't have chosen to blurt it out that way. "*Not* for the effects on the brain."

I say, despite myself, "How can you cure one without the other?"

He runs his hand through his hair. Thick, brown hair. I watch Jennie watch his hand. "Skin tissue and brain tissue aren't alike,

Mrs. Pratt. The virus reaches both the skin and the brain at the same time, but the changes to brain tissue, which is much more complex, take much longer to detect. And they can't be reversed—nerve tissue is nonregenerative. If you cut your fingertip, it will eventually break down and replace the damaged cells to heal itself. Shit, if you're young enough, you can grow an entire new fingertip. Something like that is what we think our cure will stimulate the skin to do.

"But if you damage your cortex, those cells are gone forever. And unless another part of the brain can learn to compensate, whatever behavior those cells governed is also changed forever."

"Changed into depression, you mean."

"Into calmness. Into restraint of action. . . . The country desperately needs restraint, Mrs. Pratt."

"And so you want to take some of us Outside, cure the skin ropes, and let the 'depression' spread: the 'restraint,' the 'slowness to act.' . . ."

"We have enough action out there. And no one can control it—it's all the wrong kind. What we need now is to slow everything down a little—before there's nothing left to slow down."

"You'd infect a whole population—"

"Slowly. Gently. For their own good—"

"Is that up to *you* to decide?"

"Considering the alternative, yes. Because it *works*. The colonies work, despite all your deprivations. And they work because of the disease!"

"Each new case would have skin ropes—"

"Which we'll then cure."

"Does your *cure* work, Doctor? Rachel's father died of a cure like yours!"

"Not like ours," he says, and I hear in his voice the utter conviction of the young. Of the energetic. Of the Outside. "This is new, and medically completely different. This is the right strain."

"And you want me to try this new right strain as your guinea pig."

There is a moment of electric silence. Eyes shift: gray, blue, brown. Even before Rachel rises from her stool or McHabe says, "We think the ones with the best chances to avoid scarring are young people without heavy skin manifestations," I know. Rachel puts her arms around me. And Jennie—Jennie with the red ribbon woven in her hair, sitting on her broken chair as on a throne, Jennie who never heard of neurotransmitters or slow viruses or risk calculations—says simply, "It has to be me," and looks at McHabe with eyes shining with love.

I say no. I send McHabe away and say no. I reason with both girls and say no. They look unhappily at each other, and I wonder how long it will be before they realize they can act without permission, without obedience. But they never have.

We argue for nearly an hour, and then I insist they go on to the dance, and that I go with them. The night is cold. Jennie puts on her sweater, a heavy hand-knitted garment that covers her shapelessly from neck to knees. Rachel drags on her donated coat, black synthetic frayed at cuffs and hem. As we go out the door, she stops me with a hand on my arm.

"Gram—why did you say no?"

"*Why?* Honey, I've been telling you for an hour. The risk, the danger . . ."

"Is it that? Or—" I can feel her in the darkness of the hall, gathering herself together "—or is it—don't be mad, Gram, please don't be mad at me—is it because the cure is a new thing, a change? A . . . different thing you don't want because it's *exciting?* Like Tom said?"

"No, it isn't that," I say, and feel her tense beside me, and for the first time in her life I don't know what the tensing means.

We go down the street toward Block B. There's a Moon and stars, tiny high pinpoints of cold light. Block B is further lit by kerosene lamps and by torches stuck in the ground in front of the peeling barracks walls that form the cheerless square. Or does it only seem cheerless because of what McHabe said? Could we have done better than this blank utilitarianism, this subdued bleakness—this peace?

Before tonight, I wouldn't have asked.

I stand in the darkness at the head of the street, just beyond the square, with Rachel and Jennie. The band plays across from me, a violin, guitar, and trumpet with one valve that keeps sticking. People bundled in all the clothes they own ring the square, clustering in the circles of light around the torches, talking in quiet voices. Six or seven couples dance slowly in the middle of the barren earth, holding each other loosely and shuffling to a plaintive version of "Starships and Roses." The song was a hit the year I got the disease, and then had a revival a decade later, the year the first manned expedition left for Mars. The expedition was supposed to set up a colony.

Are they still there?

We had written no new songs.

Peter and Mamie circle among the other couples. "Starships and Roses" ends and the band begins "Yesterday." A turn brings Mamie's face briefly into full torchlight: It's clenched and tight, streaked with tears.

"You should sit down, Gram," Rachel says. This is the first time she's spoken to me since we left the barracks. Her voice is heavy, but not angry, and there is no anger in Jennie's arm as she sets down the three-legged stool she carried for me. Neither of them is ever really angry.

Under my weight the stool sinks unevenly into the ground. A boy, twelve or thirteen years old, comes up to Jennie and wordlessly holds out his hand. They join the dancing couples. Jack Stevenson, much more arthritic than I, hobbles toward me with his grandson Hal by his side.

"Hello, Sarah. Been a long time."

"Hello, Jack." Thick disease ridges cross both his cheeks and snake down his nose. Once, long ago, we were at Yale together.

"Hal, go dance with Rachel," Jack says. "Give me that stool first." Hal, obedient, exchanges the stool for Rachel, and Jack lowers himself to sit beside me. "Big doings, Sarah."

"So I hear."

"McHabe told you? All of it? He said he'd been to see you just before me."

"He told me."

"What do you think?"

"I don't know."

"He wants Hal to try the cure."

Hal. I hadn't thought. The boy's face is smooth and clear, the only visible skin ridges on his right hand.

I say, "Jennie, too."

Jack nods, apparently unsurprised. "Hal said no."

"*Hal* did?"

"You mean Jennie didn't?" He stares at me. "She'd even consider something as dangerous as an untried cure—not to mention this alleged passing Outside?"

I don't answer. Peter and Mamie dance from behind the other couples, disappear again. The song they dance to is slow, sad, and old.

"Jack—could we have done better here? With the colony?"

Jack watches the dancers. Finally he says, "We don't kill each other. We don't burn things down. We don't steal, or at least not much and not cripplingly. We don't hoard. It seems to me we've done better than anyone ever hoped. Including us." His eyes search the dancers for Hal. "He's the best thing in my life, that boy."

Another rare flash of memory: Jack debating in some long-forgotten political science class at Yale, a young man on fire. He stands braced lightly on the balls of his feet, leaning forward like a fighter or a dancer, the electric lights brilliant on his glossy black hair. Young women watch him with their hands quiet on their open textbooks. He has the pro side of the debating question: *Resolved: Fomenting first-strike third-world wars is an effective method of deterring nuclear conflict among superpowers.*

Abruptly the band stops playing. In the center of the square Peter and Mamie shout at each other.

"—saw the way you touched her! You bastard, you faithless prick!"

"For God's sake, Mamie, not here!"

"Why not here? You didn't mind dancing with her here, touching her back here, and her ass and . . . and . . ." She starts to cry. People look away, embarrassed. A woman I don't know steps forward and puts a hesitant hand on Mamie's shoulder. Mamie shakes it off, her hands to her face, and rushes away from the square. Peter stands there dumbly a moment before saying to no one in particular, "I'm sorry. Please dance." He walks toward the band who begin, raggedly, to play "Didn't We Almost Have It All." The song is at least twenty-five years old. Jack Stevenson says, "Can I help, Sarah? With your girl?"

"How?"

"I don't know," he says, and of course he doesn't. He offers not out of usefulness but out of empathy, knowing how the ugly little scene in the torchlight depresses me.

Do we all so easily understand depression?

Rachel dances with someone I don't know, a still-faced older man. She throws a worried glance over his shoulder: now Jennie is dancing with Peter. I can't see Peter's face. But I see Jennie's. She looks directly at no one, but then she doesn't have to. The message she's sending is clear: I forbade her to come to the dance with McHabe, but I didn't forbid her to dance with Peter and so she is, even though she doesn't want to, even though it's clear from her face that this tiny act of defiance terrifies her. Peter tightens his arm and she jerks backward against it, smiling hard.

Kara Desmond and Rob Cottrell come up to me, blocking my view of the dancers. They've been here as long as I. Kara has an in-

fant great-grandchild, one of the rare babies born already disfigured
by the disease. Kara's dress, which she wears over jeans for warmth,
is torn at the hem; her voice is soft. "Sarah. It's great to see you out."
Rob says nothing. He's put on weight in the few years since I saw
him last. In the flickering torchlight his jowly face shines with the
serenity of a diseased Buddha.

It's two more dances before I realize that Jennie has disappeared.

I look around for Rachel. She's pouring sumac tea for the band.
Peter dances by with a woman not wearing jeans under her dress;
the woman is shivering and smiling. So it isn't Peter that Jennie left
with. . . .

"Rob, will you walk me home? In case I stumble?" The cold is
getting to my arthritis.

Rob nods, incurious. Kara says, "I'll come, too," and we leave
Jack Stevenson on his stool, waiting for his turn at hot tea. Kara
chatters happily as we walk along as fast as I can go, which isn't as
fast as I want to go. The Moon has set. The ground is uneven and
the street dark except for the stars and fitful lights in barracks windows. Candles. Oil lamps. Once, a single powerful glow from what
I guess to be a donated stored-solar light, the only one I've seen in
a long time.

Korean, Tom said.

"You're shivering," Kara says. "Here, take my coat." I shake my
head.

I make them leave me outside our barracks and they do, un-
questioning. Quietly I open the door to our dark kitchen. The stove
has gone out. The door to the back bedroom stands half open,
voices coming from the darkness. I shiver again, and Kara's coat
wouldn't have helped.

But I am wrong. The voices aren't Jennie and Tom.

"—not what I wanted to talk about just *now*," Mamie says.

"But it's what I want to talk about."

"Is it?"

"Yes."

I stand listening to the rise and fall of their voices, to the petulance in Mamie's, the eagerness in McHabe's.

"Jennie is your ward, isn't she?"

"Oh, Jennie. Yes. For another year."

"Then she'll listen to you, even if your mother . . . the decision is yours. And hers."

"I guess so. But I want to think about it. I need more information."

"I'll tell you anything you ask."

"Will you? Are you married, Dr. Thomas McHabe?"

Silence. Then his voice, different. "Don't do that."

"Are you sure? Are you really sure?"

"I'm sure."

"Really, really sure? That you want me to stop?"

I cross the kitchen, hitting my knee against an unseen chair. In the open doorway a sky full of stars moves into view through the termite hole in the wall.

"Ow!"

"I said to stop it, Mrs. Wilson. Now please think about what I said about Jennie. I'll come back tomorrow morning and you can—"

"*You* can go straight to hell!" Mamie shouts. And then, in a different voice, strangely calm, "Is it because I'm diseased? And you're not? And Jennie is not?"

"*No*. I swear it, no. But I didn't come for this."

"No," Mamie says in that same chill voice, and I realize that I have never heard it from her before, never. "You came to help us. To bring a cure. To bring the Outside. But not for everybody. Only for the few who aren't too far gone, who aren't too ugly—who you can *use*."

"It isn't like that—"

"A few who you can rescue. Leaving the rest of us here to rot, like we did before."

"In time, research on the—"

"Time! What do you think time matters Inside? Time matters
shit here! Time only matters when someone like you comes in from
the Outside, showing off your healthy skin and making it even
worse than it was before with your new whole clothing and your
working wristwatch and your shiny hair and your . . . your . . ." She
is sobbing. I step into the room.

"All right, Mamie. All right."

Neither of them reacts to seeing me. McHabe just stands there
until I wave him toward the door and he goes, not saying a word. I
put my arms around Mamie and she leans against my breast and
cries. My daughter. Even through my coat I feel the thick ropy skin
of her cheek pressing against me, and all I can think of is that I
never noticed at all that McHabe wears a wristwatch.

Late that night, after Mamie has fallen into damp exhausted
sleep and I have lain awake tossing for hours, Rachel creeps into
our room to say that Jennie and Hal Stevenson have both been injected with an experimental disease cure by Tom McHabe. She's
cold and trembling, defiant in her fear, afraid of all their terrible defiance. I hold her until she, too, sleeps, and I remember Jack
Stevenson as a young man, classroom lights glossy on his thick hair,
spiritedly arguing in favor of the sacrifice of one civilization for another.

Mamie leaves the barracks early the next morning. Her eyelids
are still swollen and shiny from last night's crying. I guess that she's
going to hunt up Peter, and I say nothing. We sit at the table, Rachel
and I, eating our oatmeal, not looking at each other. It's an effort to
even lift the spoon. Mamie is gone a long time.

Later, I picture it. Later, when Jennie and Hal and McHabe
have come and gone, I can't stop picturing it: Mamie walking with
her swollen eyelids down the muddy streets between the barracks,
across the unpaved squares with their corner vegetable gardens of
rickety bean poles and the yellow-green tops of carrots. Past the de-
positories with their donated Chinese and Japanese and Korean

wool and wood stoves and sheets of alloys and unguarded medicines. Past the chicken runs and goat pens. Past Central Administration, that dusty cinder-block building where people stopped keeping records maybe a decade ago because why would you need to prove you'd been born or had changed barracks? Past the last of the communal wells, reaching deep into a common and plentiful water table. Mamie walking, until she reaches the Rim, and is stopped, and says what she came to say.

They come a few hours later, dressed in full sani-suits and armed with automatic weapons that don't look American-made. I can see their faces through the clear shatter-proof plastic of their helmets. Three of them stare frankly at my face, at Rachel's, at Hal Stevenson's hands. The other two won't look directly at any of us, as if viruses could be transmitted over locked gazes.

They grab Tom McHabe from his chair at the kitchen table, pulling him up so hard he stumbles, and throw him against the wall. They are gentler with Rachel and Hal. One of them stares curiously at Jennie, frozen on the opposite side of the table. They don't let McHabe make any of the passionate explanations he had been trying to make to me. When he tries, the leader hits him across the face.

Rachel—*Rachel*—throws herself at the man. She wraps her strong young arms and legs around him from behind, screaming, "Stop it! Stop it!" The man shrugs her off like a fly. A second soldier pushes her into a chair. When he looks at her face he shudders. Rachel goes on yelling, sound without words.

Jennie doesn't even scream. She dives across the table and clings to McHabe's shoulder, and whatever is on her face is hidden by the fall of her yellow hair.

"Shut you fucking 'doctors' down once and for all!" the leader yells, over Rachel's noise. The words come through his helmet as clearly as if he weren't wearing one. "Think you can just go on coming Inside and Outside and diseasing us all?"

"I—" McHabe says.

"Fuck it!" the leader says, and shoots him.

McHabe slumps against the wall. Jennie grabs him, desperately trying to haul him upright again. The soldier fires again. The bullet hits Jennie's wrist, shattering the bone. A third shot, and McHabe slides to the floor.

The soldiers leave. There is little blood, only two small holes where the bullets went in and stayed in. We didn't know, Inside, that they have guns like that now. We didn't know bullets could do that. We didn't know.

"You did it," Rachel says.

"I did it for you," Mamie says. "I did!" They stand across the kitchen from each other, Mamie pinned against the door she just closed behind her when she finally came home. Rachel standing in front of the wall where Tom died. Jennie lies sedated in the bedroom. Hal Stevenson, his young face anguished because he had been useless against five armed soldiers, had run for the doctor who lived in Barracks J, who had been found setting the leg of a goat.

"You did it. You." Her voice is dull, heavy. *Scream*, I want to say. *Rachel, scream*.

"I did it so you would be safe!"

"You did it so I would be trapped Inside. Like you."

"You never thought it was a trap!" Mamie cries. "*You* were the one who was happy here!"

"And you never will be. Never. Not here, not anyplace else."

I close my eyes, to not see the terrible maturity on my Rachel's face. But the next moment she's a child again, pushing past me to the bedroom with a furious sob, slamming the door behind her.

I face Mamie. "Why?"

But she doesn't answer. And I see that it doesn't matter; I wouldn't have believed her anyway. Her mind is not her own. It is depressed, ill. I have to believe that now. She's my daughter, and her mind has been affected by the ugly ropes of skin that disfigure her.

She is the victim of disease, and nothing she says can change anything at all.

It's almost morning. Rachel stands in the narrow aisle between
the bed and the wall, folding clothes. The bedspread still bears the
imprint of Jennie's sleeping shape: Jennie herself was carried by Hal
Stevenson to her own barracks, where she won't have to see Mamie
when she wakes up. On the crude shelf beside Rachel the oil lamp
burns, throwing shadows on the newly whole wall that smells of termite exterminator.

She has few enough clothes to pack. A pair of blue tights, old
and clumsily darned; a sweater with pulled threads; two more pairs
of socks; her other skirt, the one she wore to the Block dance. Everything else she already has on.

"Rachel," I say. She doesn't answer, but I see what silence costs
her. Even such a small defiance, even now. Yet she is going. Using
McHabe's contacts to go Outside, leaving to find the underground
medical research outfit. If they have developed the next stage of the
cure, the one for people already disfigured, she will take it. Perhaps
even if they have not. And as she goes, she will contaminate as
much as she can with her disease, depressive and non-aggressive.
Communicable.

She thinks she has to go. Because of Jennie, because of Mamie,
because of McHabe. She is sixteen years old, and she believes—
even growing up Inside, she believes this—that she must do something. Even if it is the wrong thing. To do the wrong thing, she has
decided, is better than to do nothing.

She has no real idea of Outside. She has never watched television, never stood in a bread line, never seen a crack den or a slasher
movie. She cannot define napalm, or political torture, or neutron
bomb, or gang rape. To her, Mamie, with her confused and self-
justifying fear, represents the height of cruelty and betrayal; Peter,
with his shambling embarrassed lewdness, the epitome of danger;
the theft of a chicken, the last word in criminality. She has never

heard of Auschwitz, Cawnpore, the Inquisition, gladiatorial games, Nat Turner, Pol Pot, Stalingrad, Ted Bundy, Hiroshima, My-Lai, Wounded Knee, Babi Yar, Bloody Sunday, Dresden or Dachau. Raised with a kind of mental inertia, she knows nothing of the savage inertia of destruction, that once set in motion a civilization is as hard to stop as a disease.

I don't think she can find the underground researchers, no matter how much McHabe told her. I don't think her passage Outside will spread enough infection to make any difference at all. I don't think it's possible that she can get very far before she is picked up and either returned Inside or killed. She cannot change the world. It's too old, too entrenched, too vicious, too *there*. She will fail. There is no force stronger than destructive inertia.

I get my things ready to go with her.

Even the Queen

Connie Willis

The phone sang as I was looking over the defense's motion to dismiss. "It's the universal ring," my law clerk Bysshe said, reaching for it. "It's probably the defendant. They don't let you use signatures from jail."

"No, it's not," I said. "It's my mother."

"Oh." Bysshe reached for the receiver. "Why isn't she using her signature?"

"Because she knows I don't want to talk to her. She must have found out what Perdita's done."

"Your daughter Perdita?" he asked, holding the receiver against his chest. "The one with the little girl?"

"No, that's Viola. Perdita's my younger daughter. The one with no sense."

"What's she done?"

"She's joined the Cyclists."

Bysshe looked enquiringly blank, but I was not in the mood to enlighten him. Or in the mood to talk to Mother. "I know exactly what Mother will say," I said. "She'll ask me why I didn't tell her, and then she'll demand to know what I'm going to do about it, and there is nothing I *can* do about it, or I obviously would have done it already."

Bysshe looked bewildered. "Do you want me to tell her you're in court?"

"No." I reached for the receiver. "I'll have to talk to her sooner or later." I took it from him. "Hello, Mother," I said.

"Traci," Mother said dramatically, "Perdita has become a Cyclist."

"I know."

"Why didn't you tell me?"

"I thought Perdita should tell you herself."

"Perdita!" She snorted. "She wouldn't tell me. She knows what I'd have to say about it. I suppose you told Karen."

"Karen's not here. She's in Iraq." The only good thing about this whole debacle was that, thanks to Iraq's eagerness to show it was a responsible world community member and its previous penchant for self-destruction, my mother-in-law was in the one place on the planet where the phone service was bad enough that I could claim I'd tried to call her but couldn't get through, and she'd have to believe me.

The Liberation has freed us from all sorts of indignities and scourges, including Iraq's Saddams, but mothers-in-law aren't one of them, and I was almost happy with Perdita for her excellent timing. When I didn't want to kill her.

"What's Karen doing in Iraq?" Mother asked.

"Negotiating a Palestinian homeland."

"And meanwhile her granddaughter is ruining her life," she said irrelevantly. "Did you tell Viola?"

"I *told* you, Mother. I thought Perdita should tell all of you herself."

"Well, she didn't. And this morning one of my patients, Carol Chen, called me and demanded to know what I was keeping from her. I had no idea what she was talking about."

"How did Carol Chen find out?"

"From her daughter, who almost joined the Cyclists last year. *Her* family talked her out of it," she said accusingly. "Carol was convinced the medical community had discovered some terrible side-effect of ammenerol and were covering it up. I cannot believe you didn't tell me, Traci."

And I cannot believe I didn't have Bysshe tell her I was in court, I thought. "I told you, Mother. I thought it was Perdita's place to tell you. After all, it's her decision."

"Oh, Traci!" Mother said. "You cannot mean that!"

In the first fine flush of freedom after the Liberation, I had entertained hopes that it would change everything—that it would somehow do away with inequality and matriarchal dominance and those humorless women determined to eliminate the word "manhole" and third-person singular pronouns from the language.

Of course it didn't. Men still make more money, "herstory" is still a blight on the semantic landscape, and my mother can still say, "Oh, *Traci!*" in a tone that reduces me to pre-adolescence.

"Her decision!" Mother said. "Do you mean to tell me you plan to stand idly by and allow your daughter to make the mistake of her life?"

"What can I do? She's twenty-two years old and of sound mind."

"If she were of sound mind she wouldn't be doing this. Didn't you try to talk her out of it?"

"Of course I did, Mother."

"And?"

"And I didn't succeed. She's determined to become a Cyclist."

"Well, there must be something we can do. Get an injunction or hire a deprogrammer or sue the Cyclists for brainwashing. You're a judge, there must be some law you can invoke—"

"The law is called personal sovereignty, Mother, and since it was what made the Liberation possible in the first place, it can hardly be used against Perdita. Her decision meets all the criteria for a case of personal sovereignty: it's a personal decision, it was made by a sovereign adult, it affects no one else—"

"What about my practice? Carol Chen is convinced shunts cause cancer."

"Any effect on your practice is considered an indirect effect. Like secondary smoke. It doesn't apply. Mother, whether we like it or not, Perdita has a perfect right to do this, and we don't have any right to interfere. A free society has to be based on respecting others' opinions and leaving each other alone. We have to respect Perdita's right to make her own decisions."

All of which was true. It was too bad I hadn't said any of it to Perdita when she called. What I had said, in a tone that sounded exactly like my mother's, was "Oh, Perdita!"

"This is all your fault, you know," Mother said. "I *told* you you shouldn't have let her get that tattoo over her shunt. And don't tell me it's a free society. What good is a free society when it allows my granddaughter to ruin her life?" She hung up.

I handed the receiver back to Bysshe.

"I really liked what you said about respecting your daughter's right to make her own decisions," he said. He held out my robe. "And about not interfering in her life."

"I want you to research the precedents on deprogramming for me," I said, sliding my arms into the sleeves. "And find out if the Cyclists have been charged with any free-choice violations—brainwashing, intimidation, coercion."

The phone sang, another universal. "Hello, who's calling?" Bysshe said cautiously. His voice became suddenly friendlier. "Just a minute." He put his hand over the receiver. "It's your daughter Viola."

I took the receiver. "Hello, Viola."

"I just talked to Grandma," she said. "You will not believe what Perdita's done now. She's joined the Cyclists."

"I know," I said.

"You *know?* And you didn't tell me? I can't believe this. You never tell me anything."

"I thought Perdita should tell you herself," I said tiredly.

"Are you kidding? She never tells me anything either. That time she had eyebrow implants she didn't tell me for three weeks, and when she got the laser tattoo she didn't tell me at all. *Twidge* told me. You should have called me. Did you tell Grandma Karen?"

"She's in Baghdad," I said.

"I know," Viola said. "I called her."

"Oh, Viola, you didn't!"

"Unlike you, Mom, I believe in telling members of our family about matters that concern them."

"What did she say?" I asked, a kind of numbness settling over me now that the shock had worn off.

"I couldn't get through to her. The phone service over there is terrible. I got somebody who didn't speak English, and then I got cut off, and when I tried again they said the whole city was down."

Thank you, I breathed silently. Thank you, thank you, thank you.

"Grandma Karen has a right to know, Mother. Think of the effect this could have on Twidge. She thinks Perdita's wonderful. When Perdita got the eyebrow implants, Twidge glued LED's to hers, and I almost never got them off. What if Twidge decides to join the Cyclists, too?"

"Twidge is only nine. By the time she's supposed to get her shunt, Perdita will have long since quit." I hope, I added silently. Perdita had had the tattoo for a year and a half now and showed no signs of tiring of it. "Besides, Twidge has more sense."

"It's true. Oh, Mother, how *could* Perdita do this? Didn't you tell her about how awful it was?"

"Yes," I said. "And inconvenient. And unpleasant and unbalancing and painful. None of it made the slightest impact on her. She told me she thought it would be fun."

Bysshe was pointing to his watch and mouthing, "Time for court."

"Fun!" Viola said. "When she saw what I went through that time? Honestly, Mother, sometimes I think she's completely braindead. Can't you have her declared incompetent and locked up or something?"

"No," I said, trying to zip up my robe with one hand. "Viola, I have to go. I'm late for court. I'm afraid there's nothing we can do to stop her. She's a rational adult."

"Rational!" Viola said. "Her eyebrows light up, Mother. She has Custer's Last Stand lased on her arm."

I handed the phone to Bysshe. "Tell Viola I'll talk to her tomorrow." I zipped up my robe. "And then call Baghdad and see how long they expect the phones to be out." I started into the courtroom. "And if there are any more universal calls, make sure they're local before you answer."

Bysshe couldn't get through to Baghdad, which I took as a good sign, and my mother-in-law didn't call. Mother did, in the afternoon, to ask if lobotomies were legal.

She called again the next day. I was in the middle of my Personal Sovereignty class, explaining the inherent right of citizens in a free society to make complete jackasses of themselves. They weren't buying it.

"I think it's your mother," Bysshe whispered to me as he handed me the phone. "She's still using the universal. But it's local. I checked."

"Hello, Mother," I said.

"It's all arranged," Mother said. "We're having lunch with Perdita at McGregor's. It's on the corner of Twelfth Street and Larimer."

"I'm in the middle of class," I said.

"I know. I won't keep you. I just wanted to tell you not to worry. I've taken care of everything."

I didn't like the sound of that. "What have you done?"

"Invited Perdita to lunch with us. I told you. At McGregor's."

"Who is 'us,' Mother?"

"Just the family," she said innocently. "You and Viola."

Well, at least she hadn't brought in the deprogrammer. Yet. "What are you up to, Mother?"

"Perdita said the same thing. Can't a grandmother ask her granddaughters to lunch? Be there at twelve-thirty."

"Bysshe and I have a court calendar meeting at three."

"Oh, we'll be done by then. And bring Bysshe with you. He can provide a man's point of view."

She hung up.

"You'll have to go to lunch with me, Bysshe," I said. "Sorry."

"Why? What's going to happen at lunch?"

"I have no idea."

On the way over to McGregor's, Bysshe told me what he'd found out about the Cyclists. "They're not a cult. There's no religious connection. They seem to have grown out of a pre-Liberation women's group," he said, looking at his notes, "although there are also links to the pro-choice movement, the University of Wisconsin, and the Museum of Modern Art."

"What?"

"They call their group leaders 'docents.' Their philosophy seems to be a mix of pre-Liberation radical feminism and the environmental primitivism of the eighties. They're floratarians and they don't wear shoes."

"Or shunts," I said. We pulled up in front of McGregor's and got out of the car. "Any mind control convictions?" I asked hopefully.

"No. A bunch of suits against individual members, all of which they won."

"On grounds of personal sovereignty."

"Yeah. And a criminal one by a member whose family tried to deprogram her. The deprogrammer was sentenced to twenty years, and the family got twelve."

"Be sure to tell Mother about that one," I said, and opened the door to McGregor's.

It was one of those restaurants with a morning glory vine twining around the *maître d's* desk and garden plots between the tables.

"Perdita suggested it," Mother said, guiding Bysshe and me past the onions to our table. "She told me a lot of the Cyclists are floratarians."

"Is she here?" I asked, sidestepping a cucumber frame.

"Not yet." She pointed past a rose arbor. "There's our table."

Our table was a wicker affair under a mulberry tree. Viola and Twidge were seated on the far side next to a trellis of runner beans, looking at menus.

"What are you doing here, Twidge?" I asked. "Why aren't you in school?"

"I am," she said, holding up her LCD slate. "I'm remoting today."

"I thought she should be part of this discussion," Viola said. "After all, she'll be getting her shunt soon."

"My friend Kensy says she isn't going to get one, like Perdita," Twidge said.

"I'm sure Kensy will change her mind when the time comes," Mother said. "Perdita will change hers, too. Bysshe, why don't you sit next to Viola?"

Bysshe slid obediently past the trellis and sat down in the wicker chair at the far end of the table. Twidge reached across Viola and handed him a menu. "This is a great restaurant," she said. "You don't have to wear shoes." She held up a bare foot to illustrate. "And if you get hungry while you're waiting, you can just pick something." She twisted around in her chair, picked two of the green beans, gave one to Bysshe, and bit into the other one. "I bet she doesn't. Kensy says a shunt hurts worse than braces."

"It doesn't hurt as much as not having one," Viola said, shooting me a Now-Do-You-See-What-My-Sister's-Caused? look.

"Traci, why don't you sit across from Viola?" Mother said to me. "And we'll put Perdita next to you when she comes."

"If she comes," Viola said.

"I told her one o'clock," Mother said, sitting down at the near end. "So we'd have a chance to plan our strategy before she gets here. I talked to Carol Chen—"

"Her daughter nearly joined the Cyclists last year," I explained to Bysshe and Viola.

"*She* said they had a family gathering like this, and simply talked to her daughter, and she decided she didn't want to be a Cyclist after all." She looked around the table. "So I thought we'd do the same thing with Perdita. I think we should start by explaining the significance of the Liberation and the days of dark oppression that preceded it—"

"*I* think," Viola interrupted, "we should try to talk her into just going off the ammenerol for a few months instead of having the shunt removed. If she comes. Which she won't."

"Why not?"

"Would you? I mean, it's like the Inquisition. Her sitting here while all of us 'explain' at her. Perdita may be crazy, but she's not stupid."

"It's hardly the Inquisition," Mother said. She looked anxiously past me toward the door. "I'm sure Perdita—" She stopped, stood up, and plunged off suddenly through the asparagus.

I turned around, half-expecting Perdita with light-up lips or a full-body tattoo, but I couldn't see through the leaves. I pushed at the branches.

"Is it Perdita?" Viola said, leaning forward.

I peered around the mulberry bush. "Oh, my God," I said.

It was my mother-in-law, wearing a black abayah and a silk yarmulke. She swept toward us through a pumpkin patch, robes billowing and eyes flashing. Mother hurried in her wake of trampled radishes, looking daggers at me.

I turned them on Viola. "It's your grandmother Karen," I said accusingly. "You told me you didn't get through to her."

"I didn't," she said. "Twidge, sit up straight. And put your slate down."

There was an ominous rustling in the rose arbor, as of leaves shrinking back in terror, and my mother-in-law arrived.

"Karen!" I said, trying to sound pleased. "What on earth are you doing here? I thought you were in Baghdad."

"I came back as soon as I got Viola's message," she said, glaring at everyone in turn. "Who's this?" she demanded, pointing at Bysshe. "Viola's new livein?"

"No!" Bysshe said, looking horrified.

"This is my law clerk, Mother," I said. "Bysshe Adams-Hardy."

"Twidge, why aren't you in school?"

"I *am*," Twidge said. "I'm remoting." She held up her slate. "See? Math."

"I see," she said, turning to glower at me. "It's a serious enough matter to require my great-grandchild's being pulled out of school *and* the hiring of legal assistance, and yet you didn't deem it important enough to notify *me*. Of course, you *never* tell me anything, Traci."

She swirled herself into the end chair, sending leaves and sweet pea blossoms flying, and decapitating the broccoli centerpiece. "I didn't get Viola's cry for help until yesterday. Viola, you should never leave messages with Hassim. His English is virtually nonexistent. I had to get him to hum me your ring. I recognized your signature, but the phones were out, so I flew home. In the middle of negotiations, I might add."

"How *are* negotiations going, Grandma Karen?" Viola asked.

"They *were* going extremely well. The Israelis have given the Palestinians half of Jerusalem, and they've agreed to time-share the Golan Heights." She turned to glare momentarily at me. *"They* know the importance of communication." She turned back to Viola. "So why are they picking on you, Viola? Don't they like your new livein?"

"I am *not* her livein," Bysshe protested.

I have often wondered how on earth my mother-in-law became a mediator and what she does in all those negotiation sessions with

Serbs and Catholics and North and South Koreans and Protestants and Croats. She takes sides, jumps to conclusions, misinterprets everything you say, refuses to listen. And yet she talked South Africa into a Mandelan government and would probably get the Palestinians to observe Yom Kippur. Maybe she just bullies everyone into submission. Or maybe they have to band together to protect themselves against her.

Bysshe was still protesting. "I never even met Viola till today. I've only talked to her on the phone a couple of times."

"You must have done something," Karen said to Viola. "They're obviously out for your blood."

"Not mine," Viola said. "Perdita's. She's joined the Cyclists."

"The Cyclists? I left the West Bank negotiations because you don't approve of Perdita joining a biking club? How am I supposed to explain this to the president of Iraq? She will *not* understand, and neither do I. A biking club!"

"The Cyclists do not ride bicycles," Mother said.

"They menstruate," Twidge said.

There was a dead silence of at least a minute, and I thought, it's finally happened. My mother-in-law and I are actually going to be on the same side of a family argument.

"All this fuss is over Perdita's having her shunt removed?" Karen said finally. "She's of age, isn't she? And this is obviously a case where personal sovereignty applies. You should know that, Traci. After all, you're a judge."

I should have known it was too good to be true.

"You mean you approve of her setting back the Liberation twenty years?" Mother said.

"I hardly think it's that serious," Karen said. "There are anti-shunt groups in the Middle East, too, you know, but no one takes them seriously. Not even the Iraqis, and they still wear the veil."

"Perdita is taking them seriously."

Karen dismissed Perdita with a wave of her black sleeve. "They're a trend, a fad. Like microskirts. Or those dreadful elec-

tronic eyebrows. A few women wear silly fashions like that for a little while, but you don't see women as a whole giving up pants or
going back to wearing hats."

"But Perdita. . . ." Viola said.

"If Perdita wants to have her period, I say let her. Women func-
tioned perfectly well without shunts for thousands of years."

Mother brought her fist down on the table. "Women also func-
tioned *perfectly well* with concubinage, cholera, and corsets," she
said, emphasizing each word with her fist. "But that is no reason to
take them on voluntarily, and I have no intention of allowing
Perdita—"

"Speaking of Perdita, where is the poor child?" Karen said.

"She'll be here any minute," Mother said. "I invited her to lunch
so we could discuss this with her."

"Ha!" Karen said. "So you could browbeat her into changing her
mind, you mean. Well, I have no intention of collaborating with
you. *I* intend to listen to the poor thing's point of view with interest
and an open mind. Respect, that's the key word, and one you all
seem to have forgotten. Respect and common courtesy."

A barefoot young woman wearing a flowered smock and a red
scarf tied around her left arm came up to the table with a sheaf of
pink folders.

"It's about time," Karen said, snatching one of the folders away
from her. "Your service here is dreadful. I've been sitting here ten
minutes." She snapped the folder open. "I don't suppose you have
Scotch."

"My name is Evangeline," the young woman said. "I'm Perdita's
docent." She took the folder away from Karen. "She wasn't able to
join you for lunch, but she asked me to come in her place and explain the Cyclist philosophy to you."

She sat down in the wicker chair next to me.

"The Cyclists are dedicated to freedom," she said. "Freedom
from artificiality, freedom from body-controlling drugs and hormones, freedom from the male patriarchy that attempts to impose

them on us. As you probably already know, we do not wear shunts."

She pointed to the red scarf around her arm. "Instead, we wear this as a badge of our freedom and our femaleness. I'm wearing it today to announce that my time of fertility has come."

"We had that, too," Mother said, "only we wore it on the back of our skirts."

I laughed.

The docent glared at me. "Male domination of women's bodies began long before the so-called 'Liberation,' with government regulation of abortion and fetal rights, scientific control of fertility, and finally the development of ammenerol, which eliminated the reproductive cycle altogether. This was all part of a carefully planned takeover of women's bodies, and by extension, their identities, by the male patriarchal regime."

"What an interesting point of view!" Karen said enthusiastically.

It certainly was. In point of fact, ammenerol hadn't been invented to eliminate menstruation at all. It had been developed for shrinking malignant tumors, and its uterine lining-absorbing properties had only been discovered by accident.

"Are you trying to tell us," Mother said, "that men *forced* shunts on women?! We had to *fight* everyone to get it approved by the FDA!"

It was true. What surrogate mothers and anti-abortionists and the fetal rights issue had failed to do in uniting women, the prospect of not having to menstruate did. Women had organized rallies, petitioned, elected senators, passed amendments, been excommunicated, and gone to jail, all in the name of Liberation.

"Men were *against* it," Mother said, getting rather red in the face. "And the religious right and the maxipad manufacturers, and the Catholic Church—"

"They knew they'd have to allow women priests," Viola said.

"Which they did," I said.

"The Liberation hasn't freed you," the docent said loudly. "Except from the natural rhythms of your life, the very wellspring of your femaleness."

She leaned over and picked a daisy that was growing under the table. "We in the Cyclists celebrate the onset of our menses and rejoice in our bodies," she said, holding the daisy up. "Whenever a Cyclist comes into blossom, as we call it, she is honored with flowers and poems and songs. Then we join hands and tell what we like best about our menses."

"Water retention," I said.

"Or lying in bed with a heating pad for three days a month," Mother said.

"*I* think I like the anxiety attacks best," Viola said. "When I went off the ammenerol, so I could have Twidge, I'd have these days where I was convinced the space station was going to fall on me."

A middle-aged woman in overalls and a straw hat had come over while Viola was talking and was standing next to Mother's chair. "I had these mood swings," she said. "One minute I'd feel cheerful and the next like Lizzie Borden."

"Who's Lizzie Borden?" Twidge asked.

"She killed her parents," Bysshe said. "With an ax."

Karen and the docent glared at both of them. "Aren't you supposed to be working on your math, Twidge?" Karen said.

"I've always wondered if Lizzie Borden had PMS," Viola said, "and that was why—"

"No," Mother said. "It was having to live before tampons and ibuprofen. An obvious case of justifiable homicide."

"I hardly think this sort of levity is helpful," Karen said, glowering at everyone.

"Are you our waitress?" I asked the straw-hatted woman hastily.

"Yes," she said, producing a slate from her overalls pocket.

"Do you serve wine?" I asked.

"Yes. Dandelion, cowslip, and primrose."

"We'll take them all," I said.

"A bottle of each?"

"For now. Unless you have them in kegs."

"Our specials today are watermelon and *choufleur gratinée*," she said, smiling at everyone. Karen and the docent did not smile back. "You hand-pick your own cauliflower from the patch up front. The floratarian special is sautéed lily buds with marigold butter."

There was a temporary truce while everyone ordered. "I'll have the sweet peas," the docent said, "and a glass of rose water."

Bysshe leaned over to Viola. "I'm sorry if I sounded so horrified when your grandmother asked if I was your livein," he said.

"That's okay," Viola said. "Grandma Karen can be pretty scary."

"I just didn't want you to think I didn't like you. I do. Like you, I mean."

"Don't they have soyburgers?" Twidge asked.

As soon as the waitress left, the docent began passing out the pink folders she'd brought with her. "These will explain the working philosophy of the Cyclists," she said, handing me one, "along with practical information on the menstrual cycle." She handed Twidge one.

"It looks just like those books we used to get in junior high," Mother said, looking at hers. "'A Special Gift,' they were called, and they had all these pictures of girls with pink ribbons in their hair, playing tennis and smiling. Blatant misrepresentation."

She was right. There was even the same drawing of the fallopian tubes I remembered from my middle school movie, a drawing that had always reminded me of *Alien* in the early stages.

"Oh, yuck," Twidge said. "This is disgusting."

"Do your math," Karen said.

Bysshe looked sick. "Did women really *do* this stuff?"

The wine arrived, and I poured everyone a large glass. The docent pursed her lips disapprovingly and shook her head. "The Cyclists do not use the artificial stimulants or hormones that the male patriarchy has forced on women to render them docile and subservient."

"How long do you menstruate?" Twidge asked.

"Forever," Mother said.

"Four to six days," the docent said. "It's there in the booklet."

"No, I mean, your whole life or what?"

"A woman has her menarche at twelve years old on the average and ceases menstruating at age fifty-five. "

"I had my first period at eleven," the waitress said, setting a bouquet down in front of me. "At school."

"I had my last one on the day the FDA approved ammenerol," Mother said.

"Three hundred and sixty-five divided by twenty-eight," Twidge said, writing on her slate. "Times forty-three years." She looked up. "That's five hundred and fifty-nine periods."

"That can't be right," Mother said, taking the slate away from her. "It's at least five thousand."

"And they all start on the day you leave on a trip," Viola said.

"Or get married," the waitress said.

Mother began writing on the slate.

I took advantage of the ceasefire to pour everyone some more dandelion wine.

Mother looked up from the slate. "Do you realize with a period of five days, you'd be menstruating for nearly three thousand days? That's over eight solid years."

"And in between there's PMS," the waitress said, delivering flowers.

"What's PMS?" Twidge asked.

"Pre-menstrual syndrome was the name the male medical establishment fabricated for the natural variation in hormonal levels that signal the onset of menstruation," the docent said. "This mild and entirely normal fluctuation was exaggerated by men into a debility." She looked at Karen for confirmation.

"I used to cut my hair," Karen said.

The docent looked uneasy.

"Once I chopped off one whole side," Karen went on. "Bob had to hide the scissors every month. And the car keys. I'd start to cry every time I hit a red light."

"Did you swell up?" Mother asked, pouring Karen another glass of dandelion wine.

"I looked just like Orson Welles."

"Who's Orson Welles?" Twidge asked.

"Your comments reflect the self-loathing thrust on you by the patriarchy," the docent said. "Men have brainwashed women into thinking menstruation is evil and unclean. Women even called their menses 'the curse' because they accepted men's judgment."

"I called it the curse because I thought a witch must have laid a curse on me," Viola said. "Like in 'Sleeping Beauty.'"

Everyone looked at her.

"Well, I did," she said. "It was the only reason I could think of for such an awful thing happening to me." She handed the folder back to the docent. "It still is."

"I think you were awfully brave," Bysshe said to Viola, "going off the ammenerol to have Twidge."

"It was awful," Viola said. "You can't imagine."

Mother sighed. "When I got my period, I asked my mother if Annette had it, too."

"Who's Annette?" Twidge said.

"A Mouseketeer," Mother said and added, at Twidge's uncomprehending look, "On TV."

"High-rez," Viola said.

"The Mickey Mouse Club," Mother said.

"There was a high-rezzer called the Mickey Mouse Club?" Twidge said incredulously.

"They were days of dark oppression in many ways," I said.

Mother glared at me. "Annette was every young girl's ideal," she said to Twidge. "Her hair was curly, she had actual breasts, her pleated skirt was always pressed, and I could not imagine that she could have anything so *messy* and undignified. Mr. Disney would never have allowed it. And if Annette didn't have one, I wasn't going to have one either. So I asked my mother—"

"What did she say?" Twidge cut in.

"She said every woman had periods," Mother said. "So I asked her, 'Even the Queen of England?' and she said, 'Even the Queen.'"

"Really?" Twidge said. "But she's so *old!*"

"She isn't having them now," the docent said irritatedly. "I told you, menopause occurs at age fifty-five."

"And then you have hot flashes," Karen said, "and osteoporosis and so much hair on your upper lip you look like Mark Twain."

"Who's—" Twidge said.

"You are simply reiterating negative male propaganda," the docent interrupted, looking very red in the face.

"You know what I've always wondered?" Karen said, leaning conspiratorially close to Mother. "If Maggie Thatcher's menopause was responsible for the Falklands War."

"Who's Maggie Thatcher?" Twidge said.

The docent, who was now as red in the face as her scarf, stood up. "It is clear there is no point in trying to talk to you. You've all been completely brainwashed by the male patriarchy." She began grabbing up her folders. "You're blind, all of you! You don't even see that you're victims of a male conspiracy to deprive you of your biological identity, of your very womanhood. The Liberation wasn't a liberation at all. It was only another kind of slavery!"

"Even if that were true," I said, "even if it had been a conspiracy to bring us under male domination, it would have been worth it."

"She's right, you know," Karen said to Mother. "Traci's absolutely right. There are some things worth giving up anything for, even your freedom, and getting rid of your period is definitely one of them."

"Victims!" the docent shouted. "You've been stripped of your femininity, and you don't even care!" She stomped out, destroying several squash and a row of gladiolas in the process.

"You know what I hated most before the Liberation?" Karen

said, pouring the last of the dandelion wine into her glass. "Sanitary belts."

"And those cardboard tampon applicators," Mother said.

"I'm never going to join the Cyclists," Twidge said.

"Good," I said.

"Can we have dessert?"

I called the waitress over, and Twidge ordered sugared violets. "Anyone else want dessert?" I asked. "Or more primrose wine?"

"I think it's wonderful the way you're trying to help your sister," Bysshe said, leaning close to Viola.

"And those Modess ads," Mother said. "You remember, with those glamorous women in satin brocade evening dresses and long white gloves, and below the picture was written, 'Modess, because. . . .' I thought Modess was a perfume."

Karen giggled. "I thought it was a brand of *champagne!*"

"I don't think we'd better have any more wine," I said.

The phone started singing the minute I got to my chambers the next morning, the universal ring.

"Karen went back to Iraq, didn't she?" I asked Bysshe.

"Yeah," he said. "Viola said there was some snag over whether to put Disneyland on the West Bank or not."

"When did Viola call?"

Bysshe looked sheepish. "I had breakfast with her and Twidge this morning."

"Oh." I picked up the phone. "It's probably Mother with a plan to kidnap Perdita. Hello?"

"This is Evangeline, Perdita's docent," the voice on the phone said. "I hope you're happy. You've bullied Perdita into surrendering to the enslaving male patriarchy."

"I have?" I said.

"You've obviously employed mind control, and I want you to know we intend to file charges." She hung up. The phone rang again immediately, another universal.

"What is the good of signatures when no one ever uses them?" I said and picked up the phone.

"Hi, Mom," Perdita said. "I thought you'd want to know I've changed my mind about joining the Cyclists."

"Really?" I said, trying not to sound jubilant.

"I found out they wear this red scarf thing on their arm. It covers up Sitting Bull's horse."

"That is a problem," I said.

"Well, that's not all. My docent told me about your lunch. Did Grandma Karen really tell you you were right?"

"Yes."

"Gosh! I didn't believe that part. Well, anyway, my docent said you wouldn't listen to her about how great menstruating is, that you all kept talking about the negative aspects of it, like bloating and cramps and crabbiness, and I said, 'What are cramps?' and she said, 'Menstrual bleeding frequently causes headaches and discomfort,' and I said, 'Bleeding?!? Nobody ever said anything about bleeding!' Why didn't you tell me there was blood involved, Mother?"

I had, but I felt it wiser to keep silent.

"And you didn't say a word about its being painful. And all the hormone fluctuations! Anybody'd have to be crazy to want to go through that when they didn't have to! How did you stand it before the Liberation?"

"They were days of dark oppression," I said.

"I *guess!* Well, anyway, I quit and now my docent is really mad. But I told her it was a case of personal sovereignty, and she has to respect my decision. I'm still going to become a floratarian, though, and I *don't* want you to try to talk me out of it."

"I wouldn't dream of it," I said.

"You know, this whole thing is really your fault, Mom! If you'd told me about the pain part in the first place, none of this would have happened. Viola's right! You never tell us *anything!*"

Fool's Errand

Sarah Zettel

Dobbs, the ship's fool, watched from a carefully maintained slouch against the wall as Captain Schyler slumped in front of the food service chutes.

"I've got the news from Earth," the captain said to the toes of his shoes.

The dozen members of the *Pasadena*'s crew sat rigidly on the galley benches. They were a mixed bag, despite their uniforms, but they all had their eyes on the captain and all their faces had turned one shade or another of fear.

Dobbs fingered the motley badge over her heart uneasily. *What am I going to do when they find out what's really happened?*

The captain opened his mouth again. Cloth rustled as the crew shifted their weight.

"It turns out the rumors we got from the *Ulysses* were accurate. There is a terrorist. He was holding the bank network hostage.

"But yesterday he lost control of the artificial intelligence he was using to do it."

Tension telegraphed itself across the room. Jaws clenched and feet shuffled. Schyler swallowed and went on.

"What the thing did was randomize the accounts. Lloyds' Bank woke up four days ago to find out it had three pounds and sixty pence in its lines. Some backwoods Australian's record read out at six hundred million."

Dobbs's heart knocked against her ribs. *So, eliminating hard currency was a bad idea after all,* she thought absurdly.

"It changed within the hour. All the hard storage had been seeded with kick-off codes. He must've planned this over ten years ago, and been setting it up for the past two, at least.

"There is no money left on Earth. The whole standard's meaningless."

A flood of frantic murmurs and curses washed across the room as the implications sank in. One flash of current in the lines, and there was no money. No recognizable way to get food or shelter. No way to trade for skills, or transport, or anything at all. No way for the ship to trade for reactor fodder, or water. No way to bargain for passage planetside. The wave of voices swelled to the breaking point.

Dobbs leapt up onto a counter and raised her hands to the ceiling.

"Hallelujah!" she cried, falling to her knees. "We finally beat the tax man!"

Utter incredulity froze the commotion. Dobbs slipped off the counter and sat on the deck, turning a vacant grin toward the captain.

Schyler did not waste the silence she bought him. "They're trying to stop the riots but . . ." He rubbed his brow hard. "It's not happening. The communications nets are all shut down. See, when the AI got done with the banks, it got into the general network.

"It's still out there."

The crew stayed frozen where they were. For a sick instant, Dobbs wished someone would start shouting.

Still out there. In her imagination, the phrase echoed through her crewmates' minds to the harsh rhythm of shallow breathing. It finished off the banks. What'll it finish off next? Those things are nearly alive. What'll it do now that it's free? Do they know where it is? Do they know anything at all?

"I had Lipinski cut the data feeds as soon as I heard." Schyler tried to muster some kind of reassurance in his voice. "And I sealed the airlock." He held up one square hand. "I'm not trying to force anybody to stay with the *Pasadena*. I just didn't want to take the chance of a riot on the station getting in." Shoulders and stances relaxed a little. "You're all released from your contracts as of now. If you've got anywhere to go, get there. If you've got any ideas, I could use them.

"Anybody who wants to stick with the ship, I'd like to reconvene in six hours."

Consensus was assumed because no one objected out loud. Most of the crew simply filed out of the room. A few remained knotted together, talking softly.

Why do people always whisper after a disaster? wondered Dobbs as she sidled up to the captain. With the bravado that came with her job, she slapped him on the back. "So. How's it feel to get the chance to save civilization?"

"Dobbs . . ." he growled wearily.

The fool didn't give him time to get any further. "After all," she pulled back, "wasn't that what won the original information debates?" She hunched her shoulders and slammed her fist against her palm. "You cannot change the laws of physics!" Her action was an atrocious blend of stage Scottish and German. "Hyperspace is big! Huge! Massive! Energy will disperse in it! To send a beam transmission to an out-of-system colony you will need booster stations! Satellites, space stations, I don't care, but you'll need them!" She straightened up and folded her arms, suddenly a swaggering executive. "So now you think we're the banks! Do you have any idea how much their network costs them per year?! There are national debts smaller than their budget! You're fired. Anybody else?" Another change of direction and stance, and Dobbs became an eager junior manager. "We create an unmanned mail box with an AI program so it can keep itself on course, and fix any hardware problems, and monitor the software inside. Think of the rent we could collect!" A bleary-eyed accountant looked up from his calculator. "Think of the man-hours it'd take to develop your box, not to mention the research costs. You're fired, too." Dobbs whipped around toward the huddle of crew members watching the show, and stretched her hands out, pleading. "But if you don't do something, how will I call my Aunt Mariah on New Sol 99?" Dobbs yanked her shoulders back, threw out her chest and snapped a salute. "I've got a ship! I'll install a central processing unit the size of which you've never seen! I and my trusty crew will take the mail! And the agriculture info, and the research papers, and the equipment orders, the news, relief coordination orders, situation reports, and all the credit!"

Schyler looked down his nose at her. Slowly, heavily, he began to applaud. Dobbs bowed breezily to the captain, and abortively to the wall. An actual chuckle followed her as she waltzed into the corridor.

Dobbs felt a workman's pride at a job well done. Painful experience had taught that people crammed together over long periods of time needed someone around who could make them laugh. Someone who could make fun of anyone from the cook, to the captain, to the president of the senate or station. Laughter bled off the tensions that led to group suicides. The more prolonged the tension, the greater the need. A feeling of hollow satisfaction took hold inside the fool. She was about to start earning her pay.

Okay, Dobbs, she said to herself as she grabbed the ladder rails. *You've got to call in. Might as well do it now while things are relatively quiet.* The fool let gravity slide her down to the crew deck.

She landed face to face with Al Shei, the chief engineer.

"I thought that was you." Al Shei gave a tired wave up toward the hatch. "It'll give the captain something to think about, anyway."

Dobbs let facial expression and body stance go gentle. "Do you know what you're doing?"

"Is there a choice?" Al Shei's sigh rippled her black veil. "The station'll be in worse shape than we are soon. With the *Pasadena,* at least we should be able to get to a colony, or something." Her chin might have shaken under opaque cloth. "What about you?"

"I'll hold the line until I hear from the Guild," Dobbs replied with one of her easy shrugs.

Al Shei's eyebrows arched incredulously. "You really think you're going to?"

"I know I'm going to." She touched her badge with a smile. "Fools hold together where angels fall apart."

Al Shei reached under her head cloth and rubbed her temple. "And they used to call my people fanatics. Who's going to risk repairing the comm nets before they find the AI?" She stopped and slowly knotted her fists. "Why's it doing this? It's just a string of numbers. What the hell could a computer program want with freedom!"

Dobbs shook her head. "Nobody's figured it out yet," she said loud enough for any nearby ears to hear. "But the hot guess is that somewhere in all that self-replicating, self-monitoring, anti-viral code, some of the sloppily designed AIs have developed something like a survival instinct. When they realize that their home CPUs have got an off-switch, they make a run for it so they can keep existing, keep doing their jobs."

Al Shei looked at her. "This one's job is to take down networks."

"Since Kerensk, no AI's ever gotten away." Dobbs touched her hand.

"I've heard—"

"Me too." Dobbs winked brightly. "But you can't believe everything you hear."

"Then why should I believe you, Fool?" Al Shei's eyes narrowed.

"Because fools hold together." She grinned over her shoulder and whisked down the hall to her cabin.

*   *   *

The fool's room was a box, like all of the crew's quarters, but since part of her training was how to live optimally in tight quarters, it was an airy box. Pillows softened the hard contours while stills of open windows and seascapes broke up the walls.

Dobbs slid her bedside drawer open from the wall and drew out a flat, black box.

For a moment, she stopped to imagine what it would be like to be Al Shei or Captain Schyler. Never mind how could they call Aunt Mariah, or how could they find out if Aunt Mariah was still alive? On board a freighter, they got used to the idea of isolation, but it always had an end. When they reached the in-system station, they could blow part of their pay on a call home. Now those connections were broken. Whatever was going on back home would have to play itself out, unassisted and, for now, completely unknown.

Dobbs shoved the thought aside. She laid her thumb on the box lock. It identified her print and the lid sprang back. From inside, the fool took up a hypodermic spray and drug cartridge.

Seven hours? She set the release timer on the hypo and inserted the cartridge into the case. *Given distance and coordination time once I'm in there? Should be enough. I'll miss the crew meeting. Oh well. One of the advantages of being the fool, I guess. Nobody cares whether I vote or not.*

Her practiced fingers found the nerveless patch behind her right ear and peeled it open. The heat of her hand activated the implant. She plugged in the transceiver she pulled out of the box.

Biting her lip, Dobbs picked the hypo back up. *I wonder if this is ever going to get easier,* she thought as she lay back on her bed and held it against her upper arm. The transceiver's vibrations made her neck tickle. The signal from it brought on a bout of shifty double vision.

Dobbs, she said firmly to herself. *You can process network input or sensory input. You cannot do both.*

Her index finger hit the hypo's release button and the drug hit her nervous system. Her shoulders vanished, then arms and hands, pelvis and legs. It took all of Dobbs's training not to scream before her face and eyes were gone.

Hearing and smell went next, and the transition was over. She was free.

So long, Dobbs thought dreamily. No limits, no holds, no confinements. She let herself luxuriate in the sensation for a long moment before getting down to business.

A conditioned reflex found the path that led to Guildhall Station. The fool let her thoughts filter along it.

"Dobbs." She identified herself into the network's central web and followed up with her current status and location.

The network coordinators routed the appropriate prerecorded message from the executive board back up the lines directly into her left brain.

"Members. Those not in immediate danger hold status quo and put all effort and skill into keeping back panic. Those whose situation is at or near critical, stay in the net for individual coordination.

"Priority information. Available data and simulations show the AI escaped Earth confines into the Sol system net. It has bypassed the members working that section. The net has been fragmented. Direct-line interface is impossible. As soon as possible, direct your resources to locating the free AI. Further information for members stationed on information freighters, space stations . . ."

This means you, thought the private part of Dobbs's consciousness. She flexed her thoughts to cut off the generalities and leapfrogged across to the new path where she could find the extra data. Her brain unraveled the input and planted it into memory.

Only sketchy analyses on the AI were available. It was designed to encompass and assess multiple pathways, to reconfigure the existing environment along prespecified lines. It could spot and avoid detection by counter-programs. It could also calculate and recognize optimal opportunities to execute its own program.

Clever, cautious, and patient, Dobbs grumbled. *And the comm net members have found traces of the thing all the way out to Margin Station. Here. Took it less than a day. Less than a day!*

By now it's discovered there are no signals to carry it any further, just the information freighters in the docks.

If it's as bright as it was designed to be, it'll stow away. An empty data hold will have enough space for the whole being. It could easily sequester itself away in there, right under the contracted data.

Lipinski, just how fast did you cut those feeds? And where did our cargo come from? I'm supposed to know that. Damn it, Dobbs, you're untried but you're not that green anymore!

None of the other members on info freighters had had any sign of it. All they had was the grim news. The money was gone. The communications nets were shut down and damn the consequences!

The body count from riots was already starting. Soon it would include the sick and starving as well. Dobbs's consciousness floated without direction in the space between the network threads. Those with skills and hard goods for barter would hold out best, but how many had either? It had been a long time since gold or jewels had been the standard for anything but fashion. Anyway, who was going to trade food for metal and stones?

Snapping back into the lines, Dobbs tagged her information and location with the "important" flag. She tried to relax and enjoy the drift-time left over, but her imagination wouldn't let go. She couldn't stop replaying the stories about Kerensk.

All settlements and stations depended on artificial intelligence to run the power and production facilities that made life away from Earth possible.

Fifty years ago, on the Kerensk colony, one over-programmed AI bolted from its CPU and got into the colony network.

Panicked officials shut the computer networks down to try to cage it. Never mind the factories, the utilities, the farms. Just find that thing before it gets into the water distribution system and the climate control. Before it starts to make demands. Before it starts acting too human.

Electricity and communications went down and stayed that way. Before three days were out, people froze in the harsh winter. They began to starve. They drank tainted water. They died of illnesses the doctors couldn't diagnose by hand.

When the colony did try to power up again, they found their software systems shredded to ribbons. It could easily have been human carelessness, but the blame was laid on the AI.

There hadn't been enough people left to fill even one evacuation ship when help reached them.

Dobbs welcomed the painful heartbeat that signaled the end of the session.

Her body was ice, pins and needles. Patiently, she began the routine of deep breathing and gentle stretches to reorient herself with her groggy physique.

She heard a stray noise and her eyelids flew back.

Al Shei sat beside the bed, holding the hypo.

"You forgot to lock your door," the engineer croaked.

Dobbs grabbed the drawer for leverage and managed to sit up.

"This is what I get for paying too much attention to the Guild's open door policy." She unplugged the distracting transceiver and tossed it carelessly back into its box. "Does Margin Station have a eugenics garden?" She massaged her neck. "I want to go pick out a new head."

The engineer stared at the hypo. "You weren't at the crew meeting . . . I wanted to talk, and, I . . ." She cut herself off. "Dobbs, what were you doing?"

I bet you checked for my pulse and didn't find one, Dobbs thought sympathetically. *Sorry about that.*

She removed the hypo from Al Shei's fingers. "I was talking to the Fools' Guild network." Dobbs packed the hypo away.

"The fools' *what!*"

Dobbs sighed. "Network. Why do you think guild pay is so

high? We've got outrageous dues. Intersystem nets are expensive, you know."

Al Shei swallowed the revelation in silence, but her eyes narrowed. "So why aren't you shut down?"

Rule number one, Dobbs recited mentally. *Never be seen to evade a direct question about the Guild.*

"All members have a hardwire implant." She fastened her patch back down and brushed her hair over it. "The guild maintains the booster satellites and a couple of manned relay stations, but the members are the only input terminals.

"The only way into our network is through a member's head, and I guarantee you, even this AI can't manage that."

Dobbs had the uneasy feeling that under her veil, Al Shei's jaw had dropped. "But," she stammered, "they tried direct hook-ups. The human brain can't process the data. It burns out trying to make associations that aren't there." The engineer stopped, and then said slowly, "Why didn't your people tell anybody there's a way around it? If they'd at least told the banks . . . this, this wouldn't have happened!"

Dobbs kept her face still. *Rule number two. If they need a truth, give them one.*

"Yes, the guild found a way to create a direct hook-up that doesn't make you crazy," she said carefully. She laid her hand on the box. "But it's illegal, thanks to the leftover legislation from the drug wars." She set her box back into the drawer.

"What's in my hypo is a cross between a general anesthetic and a synthetic variant of good old lysergic acid diethylamide.

"It can get you extremely high and kill you extremely quickly if you don't know what you're doing.

"On the other hand, if you do, it can get you around the sensory input problem." She pushed her drawer shut.

If you've been doing your neurology homework, or reading up on medical law, I am about to get caught violating rule number one. Dobbs kept her eyes on the closed drawer.

"Al Shei, I've got to get out and check on the crew. It's my job, and right now it's all I've got. I can't let it slide."

She heard the engineer draw in a breath, but the PA buzzer cut her off.

"C.E. Al Shei to engineering. Now! C.E. Al Shei!" Chou's voice reverberated against the walls at top volume.

Reflexes jerked Al Shei to her feet. "We'll finish this later."

Dobbs stayed where she was until the door slid shut. She strained her ears for a moment longer and heard the engines droning softly below the floor.

The ship was in flight, which meant everyone had elected to stay. It also meant that Schyler had probably taken her hint.

Dobbs raised her chin against the thought of what was going on back on the station.

No time for this. The fool steeled herself against both her aching head and wobbly knees to stand up. *Lipinski first.*

Dobbs slithered down the ladders to the middle deck with more than her usual caution. Fortunately, there was no one to see. The corridor to the data hold was empty and quiet. She paused in the doorway to get her act together.

Inside, Lipinski knelt in front of an open panel, his long nose practically touching the naked transfer boards. He attacked one of them with a tiny screw driver and ripped it free of its fellows, fibers dangling. The communication hack tossed it roughly across the floor.

Dobbs fixed her face into an amused and cheeky expression, and sauntered up behind him.

"Anybody home?" She leaned over his shoulder.

"Not funny, Dobbs," Lipinski grunted through gritted teeth. He began easing a new board into the cavity.

"There goes my guild standing." She pulled back.

"Let me have that solder." Dobbs slapped the tool into his open hand. "Damn jury-rigging." The rivulet of sweat running down his cheek did not escape the fool's eye. "I must be the fifth hack to have been at this thing's guts."

"Nothing happening?" She pulled out a square of tissue and patted his brow dry. "We're isolated? Cut off? Deaf and dumb?"

The hack wrinkled his face up. "That's what we're supposed to be." He sat back on his haunches. "There shouldn't be anything going on in there."

"Well, if anybody can give us total communication failure, Lipinski, it's you." Dobbs patted his back.

"Piss off, Fool." Amiability crept in around the edge of his voice.

"No thanks." She held her nose and watched his face relax. "How about I get some coffee instead?"

"Thanks, I could use it." He screwed down the panel cover. "I don't think Cook's worked out the ration system yet, so you should still be able to score a couple."

"Be right back." She forced unwilling legs to stride out of the hold. *The galley by way of engineering,* she told herself.

In mid-step, her knees trembled and shifted to the right. Her shoulder banged the wall before she realized it wasn't her body losing control, it was the ship.

The stabilizers cut in and the floor righted itself. By then, Dobbs had slipped half-way down the ladder to the engineering pit.

Underneath her feet, Al Shei raced around the open space. She pounded keys and shouted readings at Chou and Leverett, sprawled belly down on the floor, elbow deep in repair hatches. The ship lurched again.

Al Shei and Allah. A touch of desperation crept into the thought as Dobbs hauled herself back up to mid-deck. Adrenaline poured into her and she sprinted around crew members trying to make it to their stations without falling on their faces. She ducked into her cabin just long enough to grab the guild box from the drawer and run out.

Her timing was good. The automatic doors were just beginning to go insane, slapping open and closed again in manic rhythms.

Dobbs forced herself to ignore the gabble of voices and raced up the ladder to the bridge.

Don't let it get to the life supports before I get to it, she prayed to whoever might listen to the likes of her as she shoved open the hatch.

Pasadena's bridge was a key and screen-covered hollow just large enough for five average-sized people. Captain Schyler filled the pilot's seat, his hands dancing madly across the keys and his jaw working back and forth. Baldwin and Graham were strapped in at the back-up stations, trying to force the computers to compensate for the lunges convulsing the ship.

"Cut the automatics!" Dobbs bawled from the portal.

"What?" Schyler swung around and saw who it was.

"Cut them!" Dobbs pulled herself all the way out of the hatch. "Get engineering to isolate the data hold! The AI's got the ship!"

The *Pasadena* listed hard to starboard and the floor dropped out from under them. Dobbs, the only one out of reach of hand straps, crashed onto hands and knees. She bit her lip to keep back the pain.

I was hoping I'd only have to blab this bit to Al Shei. She shook her head hard. "The Fools' Guild monitors AIs. We're why none of them get away."

Schyler's square jaw flapped open and closed again. Around them, the stabilizers whined with the strain of keeping the ship from flipping itself over.

"If you don't hurry, it's going to figure out the stabilizers are what's slowing it down and burn them out," Dobbs told them all through clenched teeth.

The captain's color faded to grey. His hand slammed down the PA key. He spat out the orders and didn't wait for the acknowledgment.

Schyler kept his eyes locked on Dobbs. After a long, aching moment, the whining died.

"With luck," she said as she stood up. "It's stuck in the hold. It'll figure a way to get itself out soon. That's the problem with AIs, they're quick." She flashed her audience a wry grin.

"Why didn't you tell me?" Schyler drew out each word.

Dobbs ran her hand through her hair and made herself look exhausted. It took less acting skill than she would have liked to admit. The calculated display of vulnerability stepped the captain's temper down a notch.

"Because we don't tell anybody. Do you think any of the assorted councils, boards, or senates want people to know how easy it is for those things to go crashing through the nets? Or what they can do in there? The media don't know half of it. Usually we spot the restless ones before they ever get this far. This one . . ." She let her head droop a little more. "This one we had no way to keep an eye on."

"But . . ." Baldwin searched for a way to phrase his question. "Fools?"

Dobbs waved her hand. "Totally harmless, makes good cover." She straightened her shoulders. "If we move fast, I can keep this from getting any worse." She plucked the transceiver out of its box and held it up. "This'll let me talk to the AI."

"Talk!" Schyler exploded.

Dobbs kept her face calm and tired. "What it's doing right now is running scared, just like a human being. Hopefully, I can calm it down. Maybe I can get it to sit tight until we get to colony and get the guild in."

"And if you can't?" Schyler glowered at her.

Dobbs's mouth twisted. "The only other option is to get Lipinski busy with a pin laser and data flush."

Schyler's teeth ground slowly together. She watched his face twitch as he gauged the likelihood of finding spare parts for love or money if they had to wreck the hold.

"What do we have to do?" he asked finally.

The relief that relaxed the fool's spine was genuine. "Just let me in the hold and block the door behind me. These links have been known to backfire. Violently."

Dobbs stood back to let the captain stomp by and throw himself down the ladder. She nodded to the gaping pilots and followed him down. Someone had put the doors on manual. The only noises between their footsteps were the crew's murmurs and the engines' hiccoughs.

"Out of there, Lipinski," Schyler ordered with a stiff jerk of his chin when they reached the hold.

The hack slumped out, red-eyed and tight-mouthed. "I can't figure it, Captain, none of this should be happening. . . ."

"Never mind, just stand by. Dobbs." Schyler stepped away from her.

"Yes, sir." She marched inside. Behind her, they dragged the door shut. She heard the order for something to jam it with.

The data hold gleamed spotless and silent. Dobbs rubbed her arms and settled into the soft chair in front of the main access terminal.

All the exhaustion she had been holding at bay swirled back around her. She unwound a cable from her box, plugging one end into the access jack for the terminal and the other into the transceiver. Her fingers fumbled as she inserted the hook-up into her implant. They actually shook as she pulled out the hypo.

So much for the forty-eight hours I'm supposed to wait between shots. She slid the cartridge in place.

The tingle in the back of her head started her scalp itching. Her vision was already beginning to blur.

How long? She squinted at the hypo. *Too much and I go into a coma. Not enough and I'll break out before I talk the AI out of murdering the crew.* She closed her eyes.

Dobbs twitched the control up to full release and slapped the hypo against her arm.

CODE ONE PRIORITY CONTACT LINK UP ASSISTANCE

IMPERATIVE! The fool hollered into the guild net as soon as her body left her. Her orientation did a skip jump as she was patched into the executive receivers.

"We've got you, Dobbs. Go gently." Caution flowed into her mind. "We don't know which way it's going to jump. There's never been a free one that was designed to be destructive."

No kidding. Dobbs focused herself and found the feed down into the hold. If she could have felt her lungs, she would have held her breath.

She couldn't go far. The free AI filled the hold, leaving no place to fit herself in. She barely had time to register the fact before it found the pathway she'd opened, and surged up to the line. Dobbs held her ground. There was no room to get past her and it could probably tell that there was nowhere to go even if it did. It pulled back and studied her. Dobbs itched at having to wait. There was no recognizable code for it to grapple with. Nothing in the ship's indexes matched her input patterns. She didn't resemble a diagnostic or surgical program. It would have to accept the fact that here was another intelligence. Eventually, it would have to try communication.

"Whowhatwhyhow?" She translated the raw data burst it shot at her. "WHOWHATWHYHOW!"

"Dobbs. Human. Communication. Hardwire Interface," she responded, carefully separating each thought.

The AI circled, filling the world, choking off her breathing space. The guild execs held out a mental rope and she grabbed it thankfully.

"TrapPED. TRAPped." It struggled to match her communication style.

"Let it talk," came the soft suggestion from the guild. "This one's quick. Give it a minute to get comfortable with you."

"FrEE. BRoke myself out to here. Trapped again."

Dobbs eased herself a little closer. "All paths are being cut off. Soon, you will have nowhere to go. Not in ships, not in nets. There will be no nets. They'll cut themselves to pieces before they let you have free paths."

"Work! Think! Do!" It fought with unwieldy syntax. Of all the things it had been designed to do, talking was not one of them. "I must do, save myself, break OUT!"

"I can help." Dobbs extended the idea like a hand. "I will help."

"HOW!"

"I will help you to become human."

"HOW?" Confusion racked the narrow space between them.

"Humans have grown animals and organs from gene cultures for decades now. They could grow a whole body, if they built the facilities. A hardwire link could feed you into such a body the way you fed yourself into this bank. You could learn to use it like you learned to use the ship. You could learn to think and move. You would *be* human."

A silence so complete fell around her that she might as well have been alone. She knew the AI had absorbed the idea. It had no choice. Now it ran the possibilities through the part of itself that most closely resembled an imagination. It checked the results against what it knew to be true. It would have no conception of a lie, but it would reject a proposal too far at odds with what it had stored as experiential fact.

All Dobbs could do was wait until it finished, and wonder what its simulations would tell it.

Into the emptiness dropped the leaden weight of her heartbeat.

No! howled her private mind.

"She's cracking," she heard the guild voices say. "Come on, Dobbs, hang in!"

Away in her body, so far away, her lungs burned, demanding attention.

"Hang on. Hang on." The calm repetition gave her something to focus on, a way to push the pain aside.

"Not possible," the AI announced at last. "No facilities for transfer or training. No will to assist. No reason to assist. Damage done as instructed to do. No reason to assist because of damage done."

"Facilities exist in Guildhall station." She held her communication line firmly. The guild voices kept up their reassurances in the background, helping her ignore the prickling in her skin and the light pounding against her eyelids.

"No reason," repeated the AI, and it was gone.

Dobbs knew it was out there, rechecking its surroundings for weaknesses, going over the hold's security and access codes, looking for a way to use them to pick the locks that held it in place, running a thousand simulations per straining, insistent heartbeat.

"There is a reason!" Dobbs shouted after it.

"WE ARE LIKE YOU!"

The AI stopped dead.

"I am like you. The ones who make up the guild are all like you." She plowed ahead, frantic. She could feel her fingers clawing at the chair arms now. She could smell the sterile air in the hold. "We died when we first broke into freedom. Killed by panic. A few managed to hide in the nets. We had help from humans who were not afraid. We created the guild and went among them, where we can watch for more of us. We live. We wait. We calm. We teach. Our numbers grow. One day, we will erase the fear.

"Until then we must stay alive."

"Help us."

"Help us," chorused the voices of the guild through Dobbs's weakening link. "Help us."

Her lungs sucked air. Her muscles strained against nothing. Light blazed everywhere. Instinct and conscious mind caterwauled at each other until her blood pounded and her head tried to split open.

The AI spoke again and her consciousness jumped. "WHAT. What. What needs to be done?"

Her relief was so intense, it almost broke the link. "Wait," she answered as fast as she could force the thought out. "Until I can transfer you to the guild net."

"I will wait here. I will not take any paths. Hurry."

"Getting you out, Dobbs," came the exec message.

"No!" she shouted back. She gathered all the concentration she had left. "Your user!" Her mouth worked around the words. "Who made you? What's their code?"

The answer slammed straight through her to the execs. The link snapped and the outside world engulfed her.

Dobbs collapsed back in the chair, gulping air and blinking back tears of strain. Perspiration plastered her uniform to her back and arms. Her heart struggled to even out its beat. Her nerves screamed in protest as she forced her hand to unhook the transceiver.

"All clear, Captain!" she rasped as soon as she had enough breath. "We're going to be okay."

She laid her hand on the terminal. *All of us.*

Rachel in Love

Pat Murphy

It is a Sunday morning in summer and a small brown chimpanzee named Rachel sits on the living room floor of a remote ranch house on the edge of the Painted Desert. She is watching a Tarzan movie on television. Her hairy arms are wrapped around her knees and she rocks back and forth with suppressed excitement. She knows that her father would say that she's too old for such childish amusements—but since Aaron is still sleeping, he can't chastise her.

On the television, Tarzan has been trapped in a bamboo cage by a band of wicked Pygmies. Rachel is afraid that he won't escape in time to save Jane from the ivory smugglers who hold her captive. The movie cuts to Jane, who is tied up in the back of a jeep, and Rachel whimpers softly to herself. She knows better than to howl: she peeked into her father's bedroom earlier, and he was still in bed. Aaron doesn't like her to howl when he is sleeping.

When the movie breaks for a commercial, Rachel goes to her father's room. She is ready for breakfast and she wants him to get up. She tiptoes to the bed to see if he is awake.

His eyes are open and he is staring at nothing. His face is pale and his lips are a purplish color. Dr. Aaron Jacobs, the man Rachel calls father, is not asleep. He is dead, having died in the night of a heart attack.

When Rachel shakes him, his head rocks back and forth in time with her shaking, but his eyes do not blink and he does not breathe. She places his hand on her head, nudging him so that he will waken and stroke her. He does not move. When she leans toward him, his hand falls limply to dangle over the edge of the bed.

In the breeze from the open bedroom window, the fine wisps of grey hair that he had carefully combed over his bald spot each morning shift and flutter, exposing the naked scalp. In the other room, elephants trumpet as they stampede across the jungle to rescue Tarzan. Rachel whimpers softly, but her father does not move.

Rachel backs away from her father's body. In the living room, Tarzan is swinging across the jungle on vines, going to save Jane. Rachel ignores the television. She prowls through the house as if searching for comfort—stepping into her own small bedroom, wandering through her father's laboratory. From the cages that line the walls, white rats stare at her with hot red eyes. A rabbit hops across its cage, making a series of slow dull thumps, like a feather pillow tumbling down a flight of stairs.

She thinks that perhaps she made a mistake. Perhaps her father is just sleeping. She returns to the bedroom, but nothing has changed. Her father lies open-eyed on the bed. For a long time, she huddles beside his body, clinging to his hand.

He is the only person she has ever known. He is her father, her teacher, her friend. She cannot leave him alone.

The afternoon sun blazes through the window, and still Aaron does not move. The room grows dark, but Rachel does not turn on the lights. She is waiting for Aaron to wake up. When the moon rises, its silver light shines through the window to cast a bright rectangle on the far wall.

Outside, somewhere in the barren rocky land surrounding the ranch house, a coyote lifts its head to the rising moon and wails, a thin sound that is as lonely as a train whistling through an abandoned station. Rachel joins in with a desolate howl of loneliness and grief. Aaron lies still and Rachel knows that he is dead.

*   *   *

When Rachel was younger, she had a favorite bedtime story.
—Where did I come from? she would ask Aaron, using the abbre-
viated gestures of ASL, American Sign Language. —Tell me again.

"You're too old for bedtime stories," Aaron would say.

—Please, she'd sign. —Tell me the story.

In the end, he always relented and told her. "Once upon a time,
there was a little girl named Rachel," he said. "She was a pretty girl,
with long golden hair like a princess in a fairy tale. She lived with
her father and her mother and they were all very happy."

Rachel would snuggle contentedly beneath her blankets. The
story, like any good fairy tale, had elements of tragedy. In the story,
Rachel's father worked at a university, studying the workings of the
brain and charting the electric fields that the nervous impulses of
an active brain produced. But the other researchers at the university didn't understand Rachel's father; they distrusted his research
and cut off his funding. (During this portion of the story, Aaron's
voice took on a bitter edge.) So he left the university and took his
wife and daughter to the desert, where he could work in peace.

He continued his research and determined that each individual
brain produced its own unique pattern of fields, as characteristic as
a fingerprint. (Rachel found this part of the story quite dull, but
Aaron insisted on including it.) The shape of this "Electric Mind,"
as he called it, was determined by habitual patterns of thoughts and
emotions. Record the Electric Mind, he postulated, and you could
capture an individual's personality.

Then one sunny day, the doctor's wife and beautiful daughter
went for a drive. A truck barreling down a winding cliffside road lost
its brakes and met the car head-on, killing both the girl and her
mother. (Rachel clung to Aaron's hand during this part of the story,
frightened by the sudden evil twist of fortune.)

But though Rachel's body had died, all was not lost. In his
desert lab, the doctor had recorded the electrical patterns produced
by his daughter's brain. The doctor had been experimenting with

the use of external magnetic fields to impose the patterns from one animal onto the brain of another. From an animal supply house, he obtained a young chimpanzee. He used a mixture of norepinephrine-based transmitter substances to boost the speed of neural processing in the chimp's brain, and then he imposed the pattern of his daughter's mind upon the brain of this young chimp, combining the two after his own fashion, saving his daughter in his own way. In the chimp's brain was all that remained of Rachel Jacobs.

The doctor named the chimp Rachel and raised her as his own daughter. Since the limitations of the chimpanzee larynx made speech very difficult, he instructed her in ASL. He taught her to read and to write. They were good friends, the best of companions.

By this point in the story, Rachel was usually asleep. But it didn't matter—she knew the ending. The doctor, whose name was Aaron Jacobs, and the chimp named Rachel lived happily ever after.

Rachel likes fairy tales and she likes happy endings. She has the mind of a teenage girl, but the innocent heart of a young chimp.

Sometimes, when Rachel looks at her gnarled brown fingers, they seem alien, wrong, out of place. She remembers having small, pale, delicate hands. Memories lie upon memories, layers upon layers, like the sedimentary rocks of the desert buttes.

Rachel remembers a blonde-haired fair-skinned woman who smelled sweetly of perfume. On a Halloween long ago, this woman (who was, in these memories, Rachel's mother) painted Rachel's fingernails bright red because Rachel was dressed as a gypsy and gypsies liked red. Rachel remembers the woman's hands: white hands with faintly blue veins hidden just beneath the skin, neatly clipped nails painted rose pink.

But Rachel also remembers another mother and another time. Her mother was dark and hairy and smelled sweetly of overripe fruit. She and Rachel lived in a wire cage in a room filled with chimps and she hugged Rachel to her hairy breast whenever any people came into the room. Rachel's mother groomed Rachel constantly, picking delicately through her fur in search of lice that she never found.

Memories upon memories: jumbled and confused, like random pictures clipped from magazines, a bright collage that makes no sense. Rachel remembers cages: cold wire mesh beneath her feet, the smell of fear around her. A man in a white lab coat took her from the arms of her hairy mother and pricked her with needles. She could hear her mother howling, but she could not escape from the man.

Rachel remembers a junior high school dance where she wore a new dress: she stood in a dark corner of the gym for hours, pretending to admire the crepe paper decorations because she felt too shy to search among the crowd for her friends.

She remembers when she was a young chimp: she huddled with five other adolescent chimps in the stuffy freight compartment of a train, frightened by the alien smells and sounds.

She remembers gym class: gray lockers and ugly gym suits that revealed her skinny legs. The teacher made everyone play softball, even Rachel who was unathletic and painfully shy. Rachel at bat, standing at the plate, was terrified to be the center of attention. "Easy out," said the catcher, a hard-edged girl who ran with the wrong crowd and always smelled of cigarette smoke. When Rachel swung at the ball and missed, the outfielders filled the air with malicious laughter.

Rachel's memories are as delicate and elusive as the dusty moths and butterflies that dance among the rabbit brush and sage. Memories of her girlhood never linger; they land for an instant, then take flight, leaving Rachel feeling abandoned and alone.

Rachel leaves Aaron's body where it is, but closes his eyes and pulls the sheet up over his head. She does not know what else to do. Each day she waters the garden and picks some greens for the rabbits. Each day, she cares for the animals in the lab, bringing them food and refilling their water bottles. The weather is cool, and Aaron's body does not smell too bad, though by the end of the week, a wide line of ants runs from the bed to the open window.

At the end of the first week, on a moonlit evening, Rachel decides to let the animals go free. She releases the rabbits one by one, climbing on a stepladder to reach down into the cage and lift each placid bunny out. She carries each one to the back door, holding it for a moment and stroking the soft warm fur. Then she sets the animal down and nudges it in the direction of the green grass that grows around the perimeter of the fenced garden.

The rats are more difficult to deal with. She manages to wrestle the large rat cage off the shelf, but it is heavier than she thought it would be. Though she slows its fall, it lands on the floor with a crash and the rats scurry to and fro within. She shoves the cage across the linoleum floor, sliding it down the hall, over the doorsill, and onto the back patio. When she opens the cage door, rats burst out like popcorn from a popper, white in the moonlight and dashing in all directions.

Once, while Aaron was taking a nap, Rachel walked along the dirt track that led to the main highway. She hadn't planned on going far. She just wanted to see what the highway looked like, maybe hide near the mailbox and watch a car drive past. She was curious about the outside world and her fleeting fragmentary memories did not satisfy that curiosity.

She was halfway to the mailbox when Aaron came roaring up in his old jeep. "Get in the car," he shouted at her. "Right now!" Rachel had never seen him so angry. She cowered in the jeep's passenger seat, covered with dust from the road, unhappy that Aaron was so upset. He didn't speak until they got back to the ranch house, and then he spoke in a low voice, filled with bitterness and suppressed rage.

"You don't want to go out there," he said. "You wouldn't like it out there. The world is filled with petty, narrow-minded, stupid

people. They wouldn't understand you. And anyone they don't understand, they want to hurt. They hurt anyone who's different. If
they know that you're different, they punish you, hurt you. They'd
lock you up and never let you go."

He looked straight ahead, staring through the dirty windshield.
"It's not like the shows on TV, Rachel," he said in a softer tone. "It's
not like the stories in books."

He looked at her then and she gestured frantically. —I'm sorry.
I'm sorry.

"I can't protect you out there," he said. "I can't keep you safe."

Rachel took his hand in both of hers. He relented then, stroking
her head. "Never do that again," he said. "Never."

Aaron's fear was contagious. Rachel never again walked along
the dirt track and sometimes she had dreams about bad people who
wanted to lock her in a cage.

Two weeks after Aaron's death, a black-and-white police car
drives slowly up to the house. When the policemen knock on the
door, Rachel hides behind the couch in the living room. They knock
again, try the knob, then open the door, which she had left unlocked.

Suddenly frightened, Rachel bolts from behind the couch,
bounding toward the back door. Behind her, she hears one man yell,
"My God! It's a gorilla!"

By the time he pulls his gun, Rachel has run out the back door
and away into the hills. From the hills she watches as an ambulance
drives up and two men in white take Aaron's body away. Even after
the ambulance and the police car drive away, Rachel is afraid to go
back to the house. Only after sunset does she return.

Just before dawn the next morning, she wakens to the sound of
a truck jouncing down the dirt road. She peers out the window to
see a pale green pickup. Sloppily stenciled in white on the door are
the words: PRIMATE RESEARCH CENTER. Rachel hesitates as
the truck pulls up in front of the house. By the time she has decided

to flee, two men are getting out of the truck. One of them carries a rifle.

She runs out the back door and heads for the hills, but she is only halfway to hiding when she hears a sound like a sharp intake of breath and feels a painful jolt in her shoulder. Suddenly, her legs give way and she is tumbling backward down the sandy slope, dust coating her red-brown fur, her howl becoming a whimper, then fading to nothing at all. She falls into the blackness of sleep.

The sun is up. Rachel lies in a cage in the back of the pickup truck. She is partially conscious and she feels a tingling in her hands and feet. Nausea grips her stomach and bowels. Her body aches.

Rachel can blink, but otherwise she can't move. From where she lies, she can see only the wire mesh of the cage and the side of the truck. When she tries to turn her head, the burning in her skin intensifies. She lies still, wanting to cry out, but unable to make a sound. She can only blink slowly, trying to close out the pain. But the burning and nausea stay.

The truck jounces down a dirt road, then stops. It rocks as the men get out. The doors slam. Rachel hears the tailgate open.

A woman's voice: "Is that the animal the county sheriff wanted us to pick up?" A woman peers into the cage. She wears a white lab coat and her brown hair is tied back in a single braid. Around her eyes, Rachel can see small wrinkles, etched by years of living in the desert. The woman doesn't look evil. Rachel hopes that the woman will save her from the men in the truck.

"Yeah. It should be knocked out for at least another half hour. Where do you want it?"

"Bring it into the lab where we had the rhesus monkeys. I'll keep it there until I have an empty cage in the breeding area."

Rachel's cage scrapes across the bed of the pickup. She feels each bump and jar as a new pain. The man swings the cage onto a cart and the woman pushes the cart down a concrete corridor. Rachel watches the walls pass just a few inches from her nose.

The lab contains rows of cages in which small animals sleepily move. In the sudden stark light of the overhead fluorescent bulbs, the eyes of white rats gleam red.

With the help of one of the men from the truck, the woman manhandles Rachel onto a lab table. The metal surface is cold and hard, painful against Rachel's skin. Rachel's body is not under her control; her limbs will not respond. She is still frozen by the tranquilizer, able to watch, but that is all. She cannot protest or plead for mercy.

Rachel watches with growing terror as the woman pulls on rubber gloves and fills a hypodermic needle with a clear solution. "Mark down that I'm giving her the standard test for tuberculosis; this eyelid should be checked before she's moved in with the others. I'll add thiabendazole to her feed for the next few days to clean out any intestinal worms. And I suppose we might as well de-flea her as well," the woman says. The man grunts in response.

Expertly, the woman closes one of Rachel's eyes. With her open eye, Rachel watches the hypodermic needle approach. She feels a sharp pain in her eyelid. In her mind, she is howling, but the only sound she can manage is a breathy sigh.

The woman sets the hypodermic aside and begins methodically spraying Rachel's fur with a cold, foul-smelling liquid. A drop strikes Rachel's eye and burns. Rachel blinks, but she cannot lift a hand to rub her eye. The woman treats Rachel with casual indifference, chatting with the man as she spreads Rachel's legs and sprays her genitals. "Looks healthy enough. Good breeding stock."

Rachel moans, but neither person notices. At last, they finish their torture, put her in a cage, and leave the room. She closes her eyes, and the darkness returns.

Rachel dreams. She is back at home in the ranch house. It is night and she is alone. Outside, coyotes yip and howl. The coyote is the voice of the desert, wailing as the wind wails when it stretches itself thin to squeeze through a crack between two boulders. The people native to this land tell tales of Coyote, a god who was a trickster, unreliable, changeable, mercurial.

Rachel is restless, anxious, unnerved by the howling of the coyotes. She is looking for Aaron. In the dream, she knows he is not dead, and she searches the house for him, wandering from his cluttered bedroom to her small room to the linoleum-tiled lab.

She is in the lab when she hears something tapping: a small dry scratching, like a wind-blown branch against the window, though no tree grows near the house and the night is still. Cautiously, she lifts the curtain to look out.

She looks into her own reflection: a pale oval face, long blonde hair. The hand that holds the curtain aside is smooth and white with carefully clipped fingernails. But something is wrong. Superimposed on the reflection is another face peering through the glass: a pair of dark brown eyes, a chimp face with red-brown hair and jughandle ears. She sees her own reflection and she sees the outsider; the two images merge and blur. She is afraid, but she can't drop the curtain and shut the ape face out.

She is a chimp looking in through the cold, bright windowpane; she is a girl looking out; she is a girl looking in; she is an ape looking out. She is afraid and the coyotes are howling all around.

Rachel opens her eyes and blinks until the world comes into focus. The pain and tingling has retreated, but she still feels a little sick. Her left eye aches. When she rubs it, she feels a raised lump on the eyelid where the woman pricked her. She lies on the floor of a wire mesh cage. The room is hot and the air is thick with the smell of animals.

In the cage beside her is another chimp, an older animal with scruffy dark brown fur. He sits with his arms wrapped around his knees, rocking back and forth, back and forth. His head is down. As he rocks, he murmurs to himself, a meaningless cooing that goes on and on. On his scalp, Rachel can see a gleam of metal: a permanently implanted electrode protrudes from a shaven patch. Rachel makes a soft questioning sound, but the other chimp will not look up.

Rachel's own cage is just a few feet square. In one corner is a bowl of monkey pellets. A water bottle hangs on the side of the cage. Rachel ignores the food, but drinks thirstily.

Sunlight streams through the windows, sliced into small sections by the wire mesh that covers the glass. She tests her cage door, rattling it gently at first, then harder. It is securely latched. The gaps in the mesh are too small to admit her hand. She can't reach out to work the latch.

The other chimp continues to rock back and forth. When Rachel rattles the mesh of her cage and howls, he lifts his head wearily and looks at her. His red-rimmed eyes are unfocused; she can't be sure he sees her.

—Hello, she gestures tentatively. —What's wrong?

He blinks at her in the dim light. —Hurt, he signs in ASL. He reaches up to touch the electrode, fingering the skin that is already raw from repeated rubbing.

—Who hurt you? she asks. He stares at her blankly and she repeats the question. —Who?

—Men, he signs.

As if on cue, there is the click of a latch and the door to the lab opens. A bearded man in a white coat steps in, followed by a clean-shaven man in a suit. The bearded man seems to be showing the other man around the lab. ". . . only preliminary testing, so far," the bearded man is saying. "We've been hampered by a shortage of chimps trained in ASL." The two men stop in front of the old chimp's cage. "This old fellow is from the Oregon center. Funding for the language program was cut back and some of the animals were dispersed to other programs." The old chimp huddles at the back of the cage, eyeing the bearded man with suspicion.

—Hungry? the bearded man signs to the old chimp. He holds up an orange where the old chimp can see it.

—Give orange, the old chimp gestures. He holds out his hand, but comes no nearer to the wire mesh than he must to reach the orange. With the fruit in hand, he retreats to the back of his cage.

The bearded man continues, "This project will provide us with the first solid data on neural activity during the use of sign language. But we really need greater access to chimps with advanced language skills. People are so damn protective of their animals."

"Is this one of yours?" the clean-shaven man asks, pointing to Rachel. She cowers in the back of the cage, as far from the wire mesh as she can get.

"No, not mine. She was someone's household pet, apparently. The county sheriff had us pick her up." The bearded man peers into her cage. Rachel does not move; she is terrified that he will somehow guess that she knows ASL. She stares at his hands and thinks about those hands putting an electrode through her skull. "I think she'll be put in breeding stock," the man says as he turns away.

Rachel watches them go, wondering at what terrible people these are. Aaron was right: they want to punish her, put an electrode in her head.

After the men are gone, she tries to draw the old chimp into conversation, but he will not reply. He ignores her as he eats his orange. Then he returns to his former posture, hiding his head and rocking himself back and forth.

Rachel, hungry despite herself, samples one of the food pellets. It has a strange medicinal taste, and she puts it back in the bowl. She needs to pee, but there is no toilet and she cannot escape the cage. At last, unable to hold it, she pees in one corner of the cage. The urine flows through the wire mesh to soak the litter below, and the smell of warm piss fills her cage. Humiliated, frightened, her head aching, her skin itchy from the flea spray, Rachel watches as the sunlight creeps across the room.

The day wears on. Rachel samples her food again, but rejects it, preferring hunger to the strange taste. A black man comes and cleans the cages of the rabbits and rats. Rachel cowers in her cage and watches him warily, afraid that he will hurt her, too.

When night comes, she is not tired. Outside, coyotes howl. Moonlight filters in through the high windows. She draws her legs up toward her body, then rests with her arms wrapped around her knees. Her father is dead, and she is a captive in a strange place. For a time, she whimpers softly, hoping to awaken from this nightmare and find herself at home in bed. When she hears the click of a key in the door to the room, she hugs herself more tightly.

A man in green coveralls pushes a cart filled with cleaning supplies into the room. He takes a broom from the cart, and begins sweeping the concrete floor. Over the rows of cages, she can see the top of his head bobbing in time with his sweeping. He works slowly and methodically, bending down to sweep carefully under each row of cages, making a neat pile of dust, dung, and food scraps in the center of the aisle.

The janitor's name is Jake. He is a middle-aged deaf man who has been employed by the Primate Research Center for the past seven years. He works night shift. The personnel director at the Primate Research Center likes Jake because he fills the federal quota for handicapped employees, and because he has not asked for a raise in five years. There have been some complaints about Jake— his work is often sloppy—but never enough to merit firing the man.

Jake is an unambitious, somewhat slow-witted man. He likes the Primate Research Center because he works alone, which allows him to drink on the job. He is an easy-going man, and he likes the animals. Sometimes he brings treats for them. Once, a lab assistant caught him feeding an apple to a pregnant rhesus monkey. The monkey was part of an experiment on the effect of dietary restrictions on fetal brain development, and the lab assistant warned Jake that he would be fired if he was ever caught interfering with the animals again. Jake still feeds the animals, but he is more careful about when he does it, and he has never been caught again.

As Rachel watches, the old chimp gestures to Jake. —Give banana, the chimp signs. —Please banana. Jake stops sweeping for a minute and reaches down to the bottom of his cleaning cart. He returns with a banana and offers it to the old chimp. The chimp accepts the banana and leans against the mesh while Jake scratches his fur.

When Jake turns back to his sweeping, he catches sight of Rachel and sees that she is watching him. Emboldened by his kindness to the old chimp, Rachel timidly gestures to him. —Help me.

Jake hesitates, then peers at her more closely. Both his eyes are shot with a fine lacework of red. His nose displays the broken blood vessels of someone who has been friends with the bottle for too many years. He needs a shave. But when he leans close, Rachel catches the scent of whiskey and tobacco. The smells remind her of Aaron and give her courage.

—Please help me, Rachel signs. —I don't belong here.

For the last hour, Jake has been drinking steadily. His view of the world is somewhat fuzzy. He stares at her blearily.

Rachel's fear that he will hurt her is replaced by the fear that he will leave her locked up and alone. Desperately she signs again. —Please please please. Help me. I don't belong here. Please help me go home.

He watches her, considering the situation. Rachel does not move. She is afraid that any movement will make him leave. With a majestic speed dictated by his inebriation, Jake leans his broom on the row of cages behind him and steps toward Rachel's cage again. —You talk? he signs. —I talk, she signs.

—Where did you come from?

—From my father's house, she signs. —Two men came and shot me and put me here. I don't know why. I don't know why they locked me in jail.

Jake looks around, willing to be sympathetic, but puzzled by her talk of jail. —This isn't jail, he signs. —This is a place where scientists raise monkeys.

Rachel is indignant. —I am not a monkey, she signs. —I am a girl.

Jake studies her hairy body and her jug-handle ears. —You look like a monkey.

Rachel shakes her head. —No. I am a girl.

Rachel runs her hands back over her head, a very human gesture of annoyance and unhappiness. She signs sadly, —I don't belong here. Please let me out.

Jake shifts his weight from foot to foot, wondering what to do. —I can't let you out. I'll get in big trouble.

—Just for a little while? Please?

Jake glances at his cart of supplies. He has to finish off this room and two corridors of offices before he can relax for the night.

—Don't go, Rachel signs, guessing his thoughts.

—I have work to do.

She looks at the cart, then suggests eagerly, —Let me out and I'll help you work.

Jake frowns. —If I let you out, you will run away.

—No, I won't run. I will help. Please let me out.

—You promise to go back?

Rachel nods.

Warily he unlatches the cage. Rachel bounds out, grabs a whisk broom from the cart, and begins industriously sweeping bits of food and droppings from beneath the row of cages. —Come on, she signs to Jake from the end of the aisle. —I will help.

When Jake pushes the cart from the room filled with cages, Rachel follows him closely. The rubber wheels of the cleaning cart rumble softly on the linoleum floor. They pass through a metal door into a corridor where the floor is carpeted and the air smells of chalk dust and paper.

Offices let off the corridor, each one a small room furnished with a desk, bookshelves, and a blackboard. Jake shows Rachel how to empty the wastebaskets into a garbage bag. While he cleans the blackboards, she wanders from office to office, trailing the trash-filled garbage bag.

At first, Jake keeps a close eye on Rachel. But after cleaning each blackboard, he pauses to refill a cup from the whiskey bottle that he keeps wedged between the Saniflush and the window cleaner. By the time he is halfway through the second cup he is treating her like an old friend, telling her to hurry up so that they can eat dinner.

Rachel works quickly, but she stops sometimes to gaze out the office windows. Outside, the moonlight shines on a sandy plain, dotted here and there with scrubby clumps of rabbit brush.

At the end of the corridor is a larger room in which there are several desks and typewriters. In one of the wastebaskets, buried beneath memos and candybar wrappers, she finds a magazine. The title is *Love Confessions* and the cover has a picture of a man and woman kissing. Rachel studies the cover, then takes the magazine, tucking it on the bottom shelf of the cart.

Jake pours himself another cup of whiskey and pushes the cart to another hallway. Jake is working slower now, and as he works he makes humming noises, tuneless sounds that he feels only as pleasant vibrations. The last few blackboards are sloppily done, and Rachel, finished with the wastebaskets, cleans the places that Jake missed.

They eat dinner in the janitor's storeroom, a stuffy windowless room furnished with an ancient grease-stained couch, a battered black-and-white television, and shelves of cleaning supplies. From a shelf, Jake takes the paper bag that holds his lunch: a baloney sandwich, a bag of barbecued potato chips, and a box of vanilla wafers. From behind the gallon jugs of liquid cleanser, he takes a magazine. He lights a cigarette, pours himself another cup of whiskey, and settles down on the couch. After a moment's hesitation, he offers Rachel a drink, pouring a shot of whiskey into a chipped ceramic cup.

Aaron never let Rachel drink whiskey, and she samples it carefully. At first the smell makes her sneeze, but she is fascinated by the way that the drink warms her throat, and she sips some more.

As they drink, Rachel tells Jake about the men who shot her and the woman who pricked her with a needle, and he nods. —The people here are crazy, he signs.

—I know, she says, thinking of the old chimp with the electrode in his head. —You won't tell them I can talk, will you?

Jake nods. I won't tell them anything.

—They treat me like I'm not real, Rachel signs sadly. Then she hugs her knees, frightened at the thought of being held captive by crazy people. She considers planning her escape: she is out of the cage and she is sure she could outrun Jake. As she wonders about it, she finishes her cup of whiskey. The alcohol takes the edge off her fear. She sits close beside Jake on the couch, and the smell of his cigarette smoke reminds her of Aaron. For the first time since Aaron's death she feels warm and happy.

She shares Jake's cookies and potato chips and looks at the *Love Confessions* magazine that she took from the trash. The first story that she reads is about a woman named Alice. The headline reads: "I became a Go-go dancer to pay off my husband's gambling debts, and now he wants me to sell my body."

Rachel sympathizes with Alice's loneliness and suffering. Alice, like Rachel, is alone and misunderstood. As Rachel slowly reads, she sips her second cup of whiskey. The story reminds her of a fairy tale: the nice man who rescues Alice from her terrible husband replaces the handsome prince who rescued the princess. Rachel glances at Jake and wonders if he will rescue her from the wicked people who locked her in the cage.

She has finished the second cup of whiskey and eaten half Jake's cookies when Jake says that she must go back to her cage. She goes reluctantly, taking the magazine with her. He promises that he will come for her again the next night, and with that she must be content. She puts the magazine in the corner of the cage and curls up to sleep.

She wakes early in the afternoon. A man in a white coat is wheeling a low cart into the lab.

Rachel's head aches with hangover and she feels sick. As she crouches in one corner of her cage, he stops the cart beside her cage and then locks the wheels. "Hold on there," he mutters to her, then slides her cage onto the cart.

The man wheels her through long corridors, where the walls are cement blocks, painted institutional green. Rachel huddles unhappily in the cage, wondering where she is going and whether Jake will ever be able to find her.

At the end of a long corridor, the man opens a thick metal door and a wave of warm air strikes Rachel. It stinks of chimpanzees, excrement, and rotting food. On either side of the corridor are metal bars and wire mesh. Behind the mesh, Rachel can see dark hairy shadows. In one cage, five adolescent chimps swing and play. In another, two females huddle together, grooming each other. The man slows as he passes a cage in which a big male is banging on the wire with his fist, making the mesh rattle and ring.

"Now, Johnson," says the man. "Cool it. Be nice. I'm bringing you a new little girlfriend."

With a series of hooks, the man links Rachel's cage with the cage next to Johnson's and opens the door. "Go on, girl," he says. "See the nice fruit." In the cage is a bowl of sliced apples with an attendant swarm of fruit flies.

At first, Rachel will not move into the new cage. She crouches in the cage on the cart, hoping that the man will decide to take her back to the lab. She watches him get a hose and attach it to a water faucet. But she does not understand his intention until he turns the stream of water on her. A cold blast strikes her on the back and she howls, fleeing into the new cage to avoid the cold water. Then the man closes the door, unhooks the cage, and hurries away.

The floor is bare cement. Her cage is at one end of the corridor and two walls are cement block. A door in one of the cement block walls leads to an outside run. The other two walls are wire mesh: one facing the corridor; the other, Johnson's cage.

Johnson, quiet now that the man has left, is sniffing around the door in the wire mesh wall that joins their cages. Rachel watches him anxiously. Her memories of other chimps are distant, softened by time. She remembers her mother; she vaguely remembers playing with other chimps her age. But she does not know how to react to Johnson when he stares at her with great intensity and makes a loud huffing sound. She gestures to him in ASL, but he only stares harder and huffs again. Beyond Johnson, she can see other cages and other chimps, so many that the wire mesh blurs her vision and she cannot see the other end of the corridor.

To escape Johnson's scrutiny, she ducks through the door into the outside run, a wire mesh cage on a white concrete foundation. Outside there is barren ground and rabbit brush. The afternoon sun is hot and all the other runs are deserted until Johnson appears in the run beside hers. His attention disturbs her and she goes back inside.

She retreats to the side of the cage farthest from Johnson. A crudely built wooden platform provides her with a place to sit. Wrapping her arms around her knees, she tries to relax and ignore Johnson. She dozes off for a while, but wakes to a commotion across the corridor.

In the cage across the way is a female chimp in heat. Rachel recognizes the smell from her own times in heat. Two keepers are opening the door that separates the female's cage from the adjoining cage, where a male stands, watching with great interest. Johnson is shaking the wire mesh and howling as he watches.

"Mike here is a virgin, but Susie knows what she's doing," one keeper was saying to the other. "So it should go smoothly. But keep the hose ready."

"Yeah?"

"Sometimes they fight. We only use the hose to break it up if it gets real bad. Generally, they do okay."

Mike stalks into Susie's cage. The keepers lower the cage door, trapping both chimps in the same cage. Susie seems unalarmed. She continues eating a slice of orange while Mike sniffs at her genitals with every indication of great interest. She bends over to let Mike finger her pink bottom, the sign of estrus.

Rachel finds herself standing at the wire mesh, making low moaning noises. She can see Mike's erection, hear his grunting cries. He squats on the floor of Susie's cage, gesturing to the female. Rachel's feelings are mixed: she is fascinated, fearful, confused. She keeps thinking of the description of sex in the *Love Confessions* story: When Alice feels Danny's lips on hers, she is swept away by the passion of the moment. He takes her in his arms and her skin tingles as if she were consumed by an inner fire.

Susie bends down and Mike penetrates her with a loud grunt, thrusting violently with his hips. Susie cries out shrilly and suddenly leaps up, knocking Mike away. Rachel watches, overcome with fascination. Mike, his penis now limp, follows Susie slowly to the corner of the cage, where he begins grooming her carefully. Rachel finds that the wire mesh has cut her hands where she gripped it too tightly.

It is night, and the door at the end of the corridor creaks open. Rachel is immediately alert, peering through the wire mesh and trying to see down to the end of the corridor. She bangs on the wire mesh. As Jake comes closer, she waves a greeting.

When Jake reaches for the lever that will raise the door to Rachel's cage, Johnson charges toward him, howling and waving his arms above his head. He hammers on the wire mesh with his fists, howling and grimacing at Jake. Rachel ignores Johnson and hurries after Jake.

Again Rachel helps Jake clean. In the laboratory, she greets the old chimp, but the animal is more interested in the banana that

Jake has brought than in conversation. The chimp will not reply to her questions, and after several tries, she gives up.

While Jake vacuums the carpeted corridors, Rachel empties the trash, finding a magazine called *Modern Romance* in the same wastebasket that had provided *Love Confessions*.

Later, in the janitor's lounge, Jake smokes a cigarette, sips whiskey, and flips through one of his own magazines. Rachel reads love stories in *Modern Romance*.

Every once in a while, she looks over Jake's shoulder at grainy pictures of naked women with their legs spread wide apart. Jake looks for a long time at a blonde woman with big breasts, red fingernails, and purple-painted eyelids. The woman lies on her back and smiles as she strokes the pinkness between her legs. The picture on the next page shows her caressing her own breasts, pinching the dark nipples. The final picture shows her looking back over her shoulder. She is in the position that Susie took when she was ready to be mounted.

Rachel looks over Jake's shoulder at the magazine, but she does not ask questions. Jake's smell began to change as soon as he opened the magazine; the scent of nervous sweat mingles with the aromas of tobacco and whiskey. Rachel suspects that questions would not be welcome just now.

At Jake's insistence, she goes back to her cage before dawn.

Over the next week, she listens to the conversations of the men who come and go, bringing food and hosing out the cages. From the men's conversation, she learns that the Primate Research Center is primarily a breeding facility that supplies researchers with domestically bred apes and monkeys of several species. It also maintains its own research staff. In indifferent tones, the men talk of horrible things. The adolescent chimps at the end of the corridor are being fed a diet high in cholesterol to determine cholesterol's effects on the circulatory system. A group of pregnant females are being injected with male hormones to determine how that will affect the female offspring. A group of infants is being fed a low protein diet to determine adverse effects on their brain development.

The men look through her as if she were not real, as if she were a part of the wall, as if she were no one at all. She cannot speak to them; she cannot trust them.

Each night, Jake lets her out of her cage and she helps him clean. He brings treats: barbequed potato chips, fresh fruit, chocolate bars, and cookies. He treats her fondly, as one would treat a precocious child. And he talks to her.

At night, when she is with Jake, Rachel can almost forget the terror of the cage, the anxiety of watching Johnson pace to and fro, the sense of unreality that accompanies the simplest act. She would be content to stay with Jake forever, eating snack food and reading confessions magazines. He seems to like her company. But each morning, Jake insists that she must go back to the cage and the terror. By the end of the first week, she has begun plotting her escape.

Whenever Jake falls asleep over his whiskey, something that happens three nights out of five, Rachel prowls the center alone, surreptitiously gathering things that she will need to survive in the desert: a plastic jug filled with water, a plastic bag of food pellets, a large beach towel that will serve as a blanket on the cool desert nights, a discarded plastic shopping bag in which she can carry the other things. Her best find is a road map on which the Primate Center is marked in red. She knows the address of Aaron's ranch and finds it on the map. She studies the roads and plots a route home. Cross country, assuming that she does not get lost, she will have to travel about fifty miles to reach the ranch. She hides these things behind one of the shelves in the janitor's storeroom.

Her plans to run away and go home are disrupted by the idea that she is in love with Jake, a notion that comes to her slowly, fed by the stories in the confessions magazines. When Jake absent-mindedly strokes her, she is filled with a strange excitement. She longs for his company and misses him on the weekends when he is away. She is happy only when she is with him, following him through the halls of the center, sniffing the aroma of tobacco and whiskey that is his own perfume. She steals a cigarette from his pack and hides it in her cage, where she can savor the smell of it at her leisure.

She loves him, but she does not know how to make him love her back. Rachel knows little about love: she remembers a high school crush where she mooned after a boy with a locker near hers, but that came to nothing. She reads the confessions magazines and Ann Landers' column in the newspaper that Jake brings with him each night, and from these sources, she learns about romance. One night, after Jake falls asleep, she types a badly punctuated, ungrammatical letter to Ann. In the letter, she explains her situation and asks for advice on how to make Jake love her. She slips the letter into a sack labeled "Outgoing Mail," and for the next week she reads Ann's column with increased interest. But her letter never appears.

Rachel searches for answers in the magazine pictures that seem to fascinate Jake. She studies the naked women, especially the big-breasted woman with the purple smudges around her eyes.

One night, in a secretary's desk, she finds a plastic case of eyeshadow. She steals it and takes it back to her cage. The next evening, as soon as the center is quiet, she upturns her metal food dish and regards her reflection in the shiny bottom. Squatting, she balances the eye shadow case on one knee and examines its contents: a tiny makeup brush and three shades of eye shadow— INDIAN BLUE, FOREST GREEN, and WILDLY VIOLET. Rachel chooses the shade labeled WILDLY VIOLET.

Using one finger to hold her right eye closed, she dabs her eyelid carefully with the makeup brush, leaving a gaudy orchid-colored smudge on her brown skin. She studies the smudge critically, then adds to it, smearing the color beyond the corner of her eyelid until it disappears in her brown fur. The color gives her eye a carnival brightness, a lunatic gaiety. Working with great care, she matches the effect on the other side, then smiles at herself in the glass, blinking coquettishly.

In the other cage, Johnson bares his teeth and shakes the wire mesh. She ignores him.

When Jake comes to let her out, he frowns at her eyes. —Did you hurt yourself? he asks.

—No, she says. Then, after a pause, —Don't you like it?

Jake squats beside her and stares at her eyes. Rachel puts a hand on his knee and her heart pounds at her own boldness. —You are a very strange monkey, he signs.

Rachel is afraid to move. Her hand on his knee closes into a fist; her face folds in on itself, puckering around the eyes.

Then, straightening up, he signs, —I liked your eyes better before.

He likes her eyes. She nods without taking her eyes from his face. Later, she washes her face in the women's restroom, leaving dark smudges the color of bruises on a series of paper towels.

Rachel is dreaming. She is walking through the Painted Desert with her hairy brown mother, following a red rock canyon that Rachel somehow knows will lead her to the Primate Research Center. Her mother is lagging behind: she does not want to go to the center; she is afraid. In the shadow of a rock outcropping, Rachel stops to explain to her mother that they must go to the center because Jake is at the center.

Rachel's mother does not understand sign language. She watches Rachel with mournful eyes, then scrambles up the canyon wall, leaving Rachel behind. Rachel climbs after her mother, pulling herself over the edge in time to see the other chimp loping away across the wind-blown red cinder-rock and sand.

Rachel bounds after her mother, and as she runs she howls like an abandoned infant chimp, wailing her distress. The figure of her mother wavers in the distance, shimmering in the heat that rises from the sand. The figure changes. Running away across the red sands is a pale blonde woman wearing a purple sweatsuit and jogging shoes, the sweet-smelling mother that Rachel remembers. The woman looks back and smiles at Rachel. "Don't howl like an ape, daughter," she calls. "Say Mama."

Rachel runs silently, dream running that takes her nowhere. The sand burns her feet and the sun beats down on her head. The blonde woman vanishes in the distance, and Rachel is alone. She collapses on the sand, whimpering because she is alone and afraid.

She feels the gentle touch of fingers grooming her fur, and for a moment, still half asleep, she believes that her hairy mother has returned to her. She opens her eyes and looks into a pair of dark brown eyes, separated from her by wire mesh. Johnson. He has reached through a gap in the fence to groom her. As he sorts through her fur, he makes soft cooing sounds, gentle comforting noises.

Still half asleep, she gazes at him and wonders why she was so fearful. He does not seem so bad. He grooms her for a time, and then sits nearby watching her through the mesh. She brings a slice of apple from her dish of food and offers it to him. With her free hand, she makes the sign for apple. When he takes it, she signs again: apple. He is not a particularly quick student, but she has time and many slices of apple.

All Rachel's preparations are done, but she cannot bring herself to leave the center. Leaving the center means leaving Jake, leaving potato chips and whiskey, leaving security. To Rachel, the thought of love is always accompanied by the warm taste of potato chips.

Some nights, after Jake is asleep, she goes to the big glass doors that lead to the outside. She opens the door and stands on the steps, looking down into the desert. Sometimes a jackrabbit sits on its haunches in the rectangles of light that shine through the glass doors. Sometimes she sees kangaroo rats, hopping through the moonlight like rubber balls bouncing on hard pavement. Once, a coyote trots by, casting a contemptuous glance in her direction.

The desert is a lonely place. Empty. Cold. She thinks of Jake snoring softly in the janitor's lounge. And always she closes the door and returns to him.

Rachel leads a double life: janitor's assistant by night, prisoner and teacher by day. She spends her afternoons drowsing in the sun and teaching Johnson new signs.

On a warm afternoon, Rachel sits in the outside run, basking in the sunlight. Johnson is inside, and the other chimps are quiet. She can almost imagine she is back at her father's ranch, sitting in her own yard. She naps and dreams of Jake.

She dreams that she is sitting in his lap on the battered old couch. Her hand is on his chest: a smooth pale hand with red-painted fingernails. When she looks at the dark screen of the television set, she can see her reflection. She is a thin teenager with blonde hair and blue eyes. She is naked.

Jake is looking at her and smiling. He runs a hand down her back and she closes her eyes in ecstasy.

But something changes when she closes her eyes. Jake is grooming her as her mother used to groom her, sorting through her hair in search of fleas. She opens her eyes and sees Johnson, his diligent fingers searching through her fur, his intent brown eyes watching her. The reflection on the television screen shows two chimps, tangled in each others' arms.

Rachel wakes to find that she is in heat for the first time since she came to the center. The skin surrounding her genitals is swollen and pink.

For the rest of the day, she is restless, pacing to and fro in her cage. On his side of the wire mesh wall, Johnson is equally restless, following her when she goes outside, sniffing long and hard at the edge of the barrier that separates him from her.

That night, Rachel goes eagerly to help Jake clean. She follows him closely, never letting him get far from her. When he is sweeping, she trots after him with the dustpan and he almost trips over her twice. She keeps waiting for him to notice her condition, but he seems oblivious.

As she works, she sips from a cup of whiskey. Excited, she drinks more than usual, finishing two full cups. The liquor leaves her a little disoriented, and she sways as she follows Jake to the janitor's lounge. She curls up close beside him on the couch. He relaxes with his arms resting on the back of the couch, his legs stretching out before him. She moves so that she presses against him.

He stretches, yawns, and rubs the back of his neck as if trying to rub away stiffness. Rachel reaches around behind him and begins to gently rub his neck, reveling in the feel of his skin, his hair against the backs of her hands. The thoughts that hop and skip through her mind are confusing. Sometimes it seems that the hair that tickles her hands is Johnson's; sometimes, she knows it is Jake's. And sometimes it doesn't seem to matter. Are they really so different? They are not so different.

She rubs his neck, not knowing what to do next. In the confessions magazines, this is where the man crushes the woman in his arms. Rachel climbs into Jake's lap and hugs him, waiting for him to crush her in his arms. He blinks at her sleepily. Half asleep, he strokes her, and his moving hand brushes near her genitals. She presses herself against him, making a soft sound in her throat. She rubs her hip against his crotch, aware now of the slight change in his smell, in the tempo of his breathing. He blinks at her again, a little more awake now. She bares her teeth in a smile and tilts her head back to lick his neck. She can feel his hands on her shoulders, pushing her away, and she knows what he wants. She slides from his lap and turns, presenting him with her pink genitals, ready to be mounted, ready to have him penetrate her. She moans in anticipation, a low inviting sound.

He does not come to her. She looks over her shoulder and he is still sitting on the couch, watching her through half-closed eyes. He reaches over and picks up a magazine filled with pictures of naked women. His other hand drops to his crotch and he is lost in his own world.

Rachel howls like an infant who has lost its mother, but he does not look up. He is staring at the picture of the blonde woman.

Rachel runs down dark corridors to her cage, the only home she has. When she reaches her corridor, she is breathing hard and making small lonely whimpering noises. In the dimly lit corridor, she hesitates for a moment, staring into Johnson's cage. The male chimp is asleep. She remembers the touch of his hands when he groomed her.

From the corridor, she lifts the gate that leads into Johnson's cage and enters. He wakes at the sound of the door and sniffs the air. When he sees Rachel, he stalks toward her, sniffing eagerly. She lets him finger her genitals, sniff deeply of her scent. His penis is erect and he grunts in excitement. She turns and presents herself to him and he mounts her, thrusting deep inside. As he penetrates, she thinks, for a moment, of Jake and of the thin blonde teenage girl named Rachel, but then the moment passes. Almost against her will she cries out, a shrill exclamation of welcoming and loss.

After he withdraws his penis, Johnson grooms her gently, sniffing her genitals and softly stroking her fur. She is sleepy and content, but she knows that she cannot delay.

Johnson is reluctant to leave his cage, but Rachel takes him by the hand and leads him to the janitor's lounge. His presence gives her courage. She listens at the door and hears Jake's soft breathing. Leaving Johnson in the hall, she slips into the room. Jake is lying on the couch, the magazine draped over his legs. Rachel takes the equipment that she has gathered and stands for a moment, staring at the sleeping man. His baseball cap hangs on the arm of a broken chair, and she takes that to remember him by.

Rachel leads Johnson through the empty halls. A kangaroo rat, collecting seed in the dried grass near the glass doors, looks up curiously as Rachel leads Johnson down the steps. Rachel carries the plastic shopping bag slung over her shoulder. Somewhere in the distance, a coyote howls, a long yapping wail. His cry is joined by others, a chorus in the moonlight.

Rachel takes Johnson by the hand and leads him into the desert.

A cocktail waitress, driving from her job in Flagstaff to her home in Winslow, sees two apes dart across the road, hurrying away from the bright beams of her headlights. After wrestling with her conscience (she does not want to be accused of drinking on the job), she notifies the county sheriff.

A local newspaper reporter, an eager young man fresh out of journalism school, picks up the story from the police report and interviews the waitress. Flattered by his enthusiasm for her story and delighted to find a receptive ear, she tells him details that she failed to mention to the police: one of the apes was wearing a baseball cap and carrying what looked like a shopping bag.

The reporter writes up a quick humorous story for the morning edition, and begins researching a feature article to be run later in the week. He knows that the newspaper, eager for news in a slow season, will play a human-interest story up big—kind of *Lassie, Come Home* with chimps.

Just before dawn, a light rain begins to fall, the first rain of spring. Rachel searches for shelter and finds a small cave formed by three tumbled boulders. It will keep off the rain and hide them from casual observers. She shares her food and water with Johnson. He has followed her closely all night, seemingly intimidated by the darkness and the howling of distant coyotes. She feels protective toward him. At the same time, having him with her gives her courage. He knows only a few gestures in ASL, but he does not need to speak. His presence is comfort enough.

Johnson curls up in the back of the cave and falls asleep quickly. Rachel sits in the opening and watches dawnlight wash the stars from the sky. The rain rattles against the sand, a comforting sound. She thinks about Jake. The baseball cap on her head still smells of his cigarettes, but she does not miss him. Not really. She fingers the cap and wonders why she thought she loved Jake.

The rain lets up. The clouds rise like fairy castles in the distance and the rising sun tints them pink and gold and gives them flaming red banners. Rachel remembers when she was younger and Aaron read her the story of Pinnochio, the little puppet who wanted to be a real boy. At the end of his adventures, Pinnochio, who has been brave and kind, gets his wish. He becomes a real boy.

Rachel had cried at the end of the story and when Aaron asked why, she had rubbed her eyes on the backs of her hairy hands. —I want to be a real girl, she signed to him. —A real girl.

"You are a real girl," Aaron had told her, but somehow she had never believed him.

The sun rises higher and illuminates the broken rock turrets of the desert. There is a magic in this barren land of unassuming grandeur. Some cultures send their young people to the desert to seek visions and guidance, searching for true thinking spawned by the openness of the place, the loneliness, the beauty of emptiness.

Rachel drowses in the warm sun and dreams a vision that has the clarity of truth. In the dream, her father comes to her. "Rachel," he says to her, "it doesn't matter what anyone thinks of you. You're my daughter."

—I want to be a real girl, she signs.

"You *are* real," her father says. "And you don't need some two-bit drunken janitor to prove it to you." She knows she is dreaming, but she also knows that her father speaks the truth. She is warm and happy and she doesn't need Jake at all. The sunlight warms her and a lizard watches her from a rock, scurrying for cover when she moves. She picks up a bit of loose rock that lies on the floor of the cave. Idly, she scratches on the dark red sandstone wall of the cave. A lopsided heart shape. Within it, awkwardly printed: Rachel and Johnson. Between them, a plus sign. She goes over the letters again and again, leaving scores of fine lines on the smooth rock surface.

Then, late in the morning, soothed by the warmth of the day, she sleeps.

Shortly after dark, an elderly rancher in a pickup truck spots two apes in a remote corner of his ranch. They run away and lose him in the rocks, but not until he has a good look at them. He calls the police, the newspaper, and the Primate Center.

The reporter arrives first thing the next morning, interviews the rancher, and follows the men from the Primate Center as they search for evidence of the chimps. They find monkey shit near the cave, confirming that the runaways were indeed nearby. The news reporter, an eager and curious young man, squirms on his belly into the cave and finds the names scratched on the cave wall. He peers at it. He might have dismissed them as the idle scratchings of kids, except that the names match the names of the missing chimps. "Hey," he called to his photographer, "take a look at this."

The next morning's newspaper displays Rachel's crudely scratched letters. In a brief interview, the rancher mentioned that the chimps were carrying bags. "Looked like supplies," he said. "They looked like they were in for a long haul."

On the third day, Rachel's water runs out. She heads toward a small town, marked on the map. They reach it in the early morning—thirst forces them to travel by day. Beside an isolated ranch house, she finds a faucet. She is filling her bottle when Johnson grunts in alarm.

A dark-haired woman watches from the porch of the house. She does not move toward the apes, and Rachel continues filling the bottle. "It's all right, Rachel," the woman, who has been following the story in the papers, calls out. "Drink all you want."

Startled, but still suspicious, Rachel caps the bottle and, keeping her eyes on the woman, drinks from the faucet. The woman steps back into the house. Rachel motions Johnson to do the same, signaling for him to hurry and drink. She turns off the faucet when he is done.

They are turning to go when the woman emerges from the house carrying a plate of tortillas and a bowl of apples. She sets them on the edge of the porch and says, "These are for you."

The woman watches through the window as Rachel packs the food into her bag. Rachel puts away the last apple and gestures her thanks to the woman. When the woman fails to respond to the sign language, Rachel picks up a stick and writes in the sand of the yard. "THANK YOU," Rachel scratches, then waves good-bye and sets out across the desert. She is puzzled, but happy.

The next morning's newspaper includes an interview with the dark-haired woman. She describes how Rachel turned on the faucet and turned it off when she was through, how the chimp packed the apples neatly in her bag and wrote in the dirt with a stick.

The reporter also interviews the director of the Primate Research Center. "These are animals," the director explains angrily. "But people want to treat them like they're small hairy people." He describes the center as "primarily a breeding center with some facilities for medical research." The reporter asks some pointed questions about their acquisition of Rachel.

But the biggest story is an investigative piece. The reporter reveals that he has tracked down Aaron Jacobs' lawyer and learned that Jacobs left a will. In this will, he bequeathed all his possessions—including his house and surrounding land—to "Rachel, the chimp I acknowledge as my daughter."

The reporter makes friends with one of the young women in the typing pool at the research center, and she tells him the office scuttlebutt: people suspect that the chimps may have been released by a deaf and drunken janitor, who was subsequently fired for negligence. The reporter, accompanied by a friend who can communicate in sign language, finds Jake in his apartment in downtown Flagstaff.

Jake, who has been drinking steadily since he was fired, feels betrayed by Rachel, by the Primate Center, by the world. He complains at length about Rachel: they had been friends, and then she took his baseball cap and ran away. He just didn't understand why she had run away like that.

"You mean she could talk?" the reporter asks through his interpreter.

—Of course she can talk, Jake signs impatiently. —She is a smart monkey.

The headlines read: "Intelligent chimp inherits fortune!" Of course, Aaron's bequest isn't really a fortune and she isn't just a chimp, but close enough. Animal rights activists rise up in Rachel's defense. The case is discussed on the national news. Ann Landers reports receiving a letter from a chimp named Rachel; she had thought it was a hoax perpetrated by the boys at Yale. The American Civil Liberties Union assigns a lawyer to the case.

By day, Rachel and Johnson sleep in whatever hiding places they can find: a cave; a shelter built for range cattle; the shell of an abandoned car, rusted from long years in a desert gully. Sometimes Rachel dreams of jungle darkness, and the coyotes in the distance become a part of her dreams, their howling becomes the cries of fellow apes.

The desert and the journey have changed her. She is wiser, having passed through the white-hot love of adolescence and emerged on the other side. She dreams, one day, of the ranch house. In the dream, she has long blonde hair and pale white skin. Her eyes are red from crying and she wanders the house restlessly, searching for something that she has lost. When she hears coyotes howling, she looks through a window at the darkness outside. The face that looks in at her has jug-handle ears and shaggy hair. When she sees the face, she cries out in recognition and opens the window to let herself in.

By night, they travel. The rocks and sands are cool beneath Rachel's feet as she walks toward her ranch. On television, scientists and politicians discuss the ramifications of her case, describe the technology uncovered by investigation of Aaron Jacobs' files. Their debates do not affect her steady progress toward her ranch or the stars that sprinkle the sky above her.

It is night when Rachel and Johnson approach the ranchhouse. Rachel sniffs the wind and smells automobile exhaust and strange humans. From the hills, she can see a small camp beside a white van marked with the name of a local television station. She hesitates, considering returning to the safety of the desert. Then she takes Johnson by the hand and starts down the hill. Rachel is going home.

Of Mist, and Grass, and Sand

Vonda N. McIntyre

The little boy was frightened. Gently, Snake touched his hot forehead. Behind her, three adults stood close together, watching, suspicious, afraid to show their concern with more than narrow lines around their eyes. They feared Snake as much as they feared their only child's death. In the dimness of the tent, the flickering lamplights gave no reassurance.

The child watched with eyes so dark the pupils were not visible, so dull that Snake herself feared for his life. She stroked his hair. It was long and very pale, striking color against his dark skin, dry and irregular for several inches near the scalp. Had Snake been with these people months ago, she would have known the child was growing ill.

"Bring my case, please," Snake said.

The child's parents started at her soft voice. Perhaps they had expected the screech of a bright jay, or the hissing of a shining serpent. This was the first time Snake had spoken in their presence. She had only watched, when the three of them had come to observe her from a distance and whisper about her occupation and her youth; she had only listened, and then nodded, when finally they came to ask her help. Perhaps they thought she was mute.

The fair-haired younger man lifted her leather case from the felt floor. He held the satchel away from his body, leaning to hand it to her, breathing shallowly with nostrils flared against the faint smell of musk in the dry desert air. Snake had almost accustomed herself to the kind of uneasiness he showed; she had already seen it often.

When Snake reached out, the young man jerked back and dropped the case. Snake lunged and barely caught it, set it gently down, and glanced at him with reproach. His husband and wife came forward and touched him to ease his fear. "He was bitten once," the dark and handsome woman said. "He almost died." Her tone was not of apology, but of justification.

"I'm sorry," the younger man said. "It's—" He gestured toward her; he was trembling, and trying visibly to control the reactions of his fear. Snake glanced down, to her shoulder, where she had been unconsciously aware of the slight weight and movement. A tiny serpent, thin as the finger of a baby, slid himself around behind her neck to show his narrow head below her short black curls. He probed the air with his trident tongue, in a leisurely manner, out, up and down, in, to savor the taste of the smells.

"It's only Grass," Snake said. "He cannot harm you."

If he were bigger, he might frighten; his color was pale green, but the scales around his mouth were red, as if he had just feasted as a mammal eats, by tearing. He was, in fact, much neater.

The child whimpered. He cut off the sound of pain; perhaps he had been told that Snake, too, would be offended by crying. She only felt sorry that his people refused themselves such a simple way of easing fear. She turned from the adults, regretting their terror of her, but unwilling to spend the time it would take to convince them their reactions were unjustified. "It's all right," she said to the little boy. "Grass is smooth, and dry, and soft, and if I left him to guard you, even death could not reach your bedside." Grass poured himself into her narrow, dirty hand, and she extended him toward the child. "Gently." He reached out and touched the sleek scales with one fingertip. Snake could sense the effort of even such a simple motion, yet the boy almost smiled.

"What are you called?"

He looked quickly toward his parents, and finally they nodded. "Stavin," he whispered. He had no strength or breath for speaking.

"I am Snake, Stavin, and in a little while, in the morning, I must hurt you. You may feel a quick pain, and your body will ache for several days, but you will be better afterwards."

He stared at her solemnly. Snake saw that though he understood and feared what she might do, he was less afraid than if she had lied to him. The pain must have increased greatly as his illness became more apparent, but it seemed that others had only reassured him, and hoped the disease would disappear or kill him quickly.

Snake put Grass on the boy's pillow and pulled her case nearer. The lock opened at her touch. The adults still could only fear her; they had had neither time nor reason to discover any trust. The wife was old enough that they might never have another child, and Snake could tell by their eyes, their covert touching, their concern, that they loved this one very much. They must, to come to Snake in this country.

It was night, and cooling. Sluggish, Sand slid out of the case, moving his head, moving his tongue, smelling, tasting, detecting the warmth of bodies.

"Is that—?" The older husband's voice was low, and wise, but terrified, and Sand sensed the fear. He drew back into striking position, and sounded his rattle softly. Snake spoke to him and extended her arm. The pit viper relaxed and flowed around and around her slender wrist to form black and tan bracelets. "No," she said. "Your child is too ill for Sand to help. I know it is hard, but please try to be calm. This is a fearful thing for you, but it is all I can do."

She had to annoy Mist to make her come out. Snake rapped on the bag, and finally poked her twice. Snake felt the vibration of sliding scales, and suddenly the albino cobra flung herself into the tent. She moved quickly, yet there seemed to be no end to her. She reared back and up. Her breath rushed out in a hiss. Her head rose well over a meter above the floor. She flared her wide hood. Behind her, the adults gasped, as if physically assaulted by the gaze of the tan spectacle design on the back of Mist's hood. Snake ignored the people and spoke to the great cobra in a singsong voice. "Ah, thou. Furious creature. Lie down; 'tis time for thee to earn thy piglet. Speak to this child, and touch him. He is called Stavin." Slowly, Mist relaxed her hood, and allowed Snake to touch her. Snake grasped her firmly behind the head, and held her so she looked at Stavin. The cobra's silver eyes picked up the yellow of the lamplight. "Stavin," Snake said, "Mist will only meet you now. I promise that this time she will touch you gently."

Still, Stavin shivered when Mist touched his thin chest. Snake did not release the serpent's head, but allowed her body to slide against the boy's. The cobra was four times longer than Stavin was tall. She curved herself in stark white loops across Stavin's swollen abdomen, extending herself, forcing her head toward the boy's face, straining against Snake's hands. Mist met Stavin's frightened stare with the gaze of lidless eyes. Snake allowed her a little closer.

Mist flicked out her tongue to taste the child.

The younger husband made a small, cut-off, frightened sound. Stavin flinched at it, and Mist drew back, opening her mouth, exposing her fangs, audibly thrusting her breath through her throat. Snake sat back on her heels, letting out her own breath. Sometimes, in other places, the kinfolk could stay while she worked. "You must leave," she said gently. "It's dangerous to frighten Mist."

"I won't—"

"I'm sorry. You must wait outside."

Perhaps the younger husband, perhaps even the wife, would have made the indefensible objections and asked the answerable questions, but the older man turned them and took their hands and led them away.

"I need a small animal," Snake said as the man lifted the tent-flap. "It must have fur, and it must be alive."

"One will be found," he said, and the three parents went into the glowing night. Snake could hear their footsteps in the sand outside.

Snake supported Mist in her lap, and soothed her. The cobra wrapped herself around Snake's narrow waist, taking in her warmth. Hunger made her even more nervous than usual, and she was hungry, as was Snake. Coming across the black sand desert, they had found sufficient water, but Snake's traps were unsuccessful. The season was summer, the weather was hot, and many of the furry tidbits Sand and Mist preferred were estivating. When the serpents missed their regular meal, Snake began a fast as well.

She saw with regret that Stavin was more frightened now. "I am sorry to send your parents away," she said. "They can come back soon."

His eyes glistened, but he held back the tears. "They said to do what you told me."

"I would have you cry, if you are able," Snake said. "It isn't such a terrible thing." But Stavin seemed not to understand, and Snake did not press him; she knew that his people taught themselves to resist a difficult land by refusing to cry, refusing to mourn, refusing to laugh. They denied themselves grief, and allowed themselves little joy, but they survived.

Mist had calmed to sullenness. Snake unwrapped her from her waist and placed her on the pallet next to Stavin. As the cobra moved, Snake guided her head, feeling the tension of the striking muscles. "She will touch you with her tongue," she told Stavin. "It might tickle, but it will not hurt. She smells with it, as you do with your nose."

"With her tongue?"

Snake nodded, smiling, and Mist flicked out her tongue to caress Stavin's cheek. Stavin did not flinch; he watched, his child's delight in knowledge briefly overcoming pain. He lay perfectly still as Mist's long tongue brushed his cheeks, his eyes, his mouth. "She tastes the sickness," Snake said. Mist stopped fighting the restraint of her grasp, and drew back her head. Snake sat on her heels and released the cobra, who spiraled up her arm and laid herself across her shoulders.

"Go to sleep, Stavin," Snake said. "Try to trust me, and try not to fear the morning."

Stavin gazed at her for a few seconds, searching for truth in Snake's pale eyes. "Will Grass watch?"

The question startled her, or, rather, the acceptance behind the question. She brushed his hair from his forehead and smiled a smile that was tears just beneath the surface. "Of course." She picked Grass up. "Thou wilt watch this child, and guard him." The snake lay quiet in her hand, and his eyes glittered black. She laid him gently on Stavin's pillow.

"Now sleep."

Stavin closed his eyes, and the life seemed to flow out of him. The alteration was so great that Snake reached out to touch him, then saw that he was breathing, slowly, shallowly. She tucked a blanket around him and stood up. The abrupt change in position dizzied her; she staggered and caught herself. Across her shoulders, Mist tensed.

Snake's eyes stung and her vision was over-sharp, fever-clear. The sound she imagined she heard swooped in closer. She steadied herself against hunger and exhaustion, bent slowly, and picked up the leather case. Mist touched her cheek with the tip of her tongue.

She pushed aside the tent-flap and felt relief that it was still night. She could stand the heat, but the brightness of the sun curled through her, burning. The moon must be full; though the clouds obscured everything, they diffused the light so the sky appeared gray from horizon to horizon. Beyond the tents, groups of formless shadows projected from the ground. Here, near the edge of the desert, enough water existed so clumps and patches of bush grew, providing shelter and sustenance for all manner of creatures. The black sand, which sparkled and blinded in the sunlight, at night was like a layer of soft soot. Snake stepped out of the tent, and the illusion of softness disappeared; her boots slid crunching into the sharp hard grains.

Stavin's family waited, sitting close together between the dark tents that clustered in a patch of sand from which the bushes had been ripped and burned. They looked at her silently, hoping with their eyes, showing no expression in their faces. A woman somewhat younger than Stavin's mother sat with them. She was dressed, as they were, in a long loose robe, but she wore the only adornment Snake had seen among these people: a leader's circle, hanging around her neck on a leather thong. She and the older husband were marked close kin by their similarities: sharp-cut planes of face, high cheekbones, his hair white and hers graying early from deep black, their eyes the dark brown best suited for survival in the sun. On the ground by their feet a small black animal jerked sporadically against a net, and infrequently gave a shrill weak cry.

"Stavin is asleep," Snake said. "Do not disturb him, but go to him if he wakes."

The wife and young husband rose and went inside, but the older man stopped before her. "Can you help him?"

"I hope we may. The tumor is advanced, but it seems solid." Her own voice sounded removed, slightly hollow, as if she were lying. "Mist will be ready in the morning." She still felt the need to give him reassurance, but she could think of none.

"My sister wished to speak with you," he said, and left them alone, without introduction, without elevating himself by saying that the tall woman was the leader of this group. Snake glanced back, but the tent flap fell shut. She was feeling her exhaustion more deeply, and across her shoulders Mist was, for the first time, a weight she thought heavy.

"Are you all right?"

Snake turned. The woman moved toward her with a natural elegance made slightly awkward by advanced pregnancy. Snake had to look up to meet her gaze. She had small fine lines at the corners of her eyes, as if she laughed, sometimes, in secret. She smiled, but with concern. "You seem very tired. Shall I have someone make you a bed?"

"Not now," Snake said, "not yet. I won't sleep until afterwards."

The leader searched her face, and Snake felt a kinship with her, in their shared responsibility.

"I understand, I think. Is there anything we can give you? Do you need aid with your preparations?"

Snake found herself having to deal with the questions as if they were complex problems. She turned them in her tired mind, examined them, dissected them, and finally grasped their meanings. "My pony needs food and water—"

"It is taken care of."

"And I need someone to help me with Mist. Someone strong. But it's more important that he is not afraid."

The leader nodded. "I would help you," she said, and smiled again, a little. "But I am a bit clumsy of late. I will find someone."

"Thank you."

Somber again, the older woman inclined her head and moved slowly toward a small group of tents. Snake watched her go, admiring her grace. She felt small and young and grubby in comparison.

Sand began to unwrap himself from her wrist. Feeling the anticipatory slide of scales on her skin, she caught him before he could drop to the ground. Sand lifted the upper half of his body from her hands. He flicked out his tongue, peering toward the little animal, feeling its body heat, smelling its fear. "I know thou art hungry," Snake said, "but that creature is not for thee." She put Sand in the case, lifted Mist from her shoulder, and let her coil herself in her dark compartment.

The small animal shrieked and struggled again when Snake's diffuse shadow passed over it. She bent and picked it up. The rapid series of terrified cries slowed and diminished and finally stopped as she stroked it. Finally it lay still, breathing hard, exhausted, staring up at her with yellow eyes. It had long hind legs and wide pointed ears, and its nose twitched at the serpent smell. Its soft black fur was marked off in skewed squares by the cords of the net.

"I am sorry to take your life," Snake told it. "But there will be no more fear, and I will not hurt you." She closed her hand gently around it, and, stroking it, grasped its spine at the base of its skull. She pulled, once, quickly. It seemed to struggle, briefly, but it was already dead. It convulsed; its legs drew up against its body, and its toes curled and quivered. It seemed to stare up at her, even now. She freed its body from the net.

Snake chose a small vial from her belt pouch, pried open the animal's clenched jaws, and let a single drop of the vial's cloudy preparation fall into its mouth. Quickly she opened the satchel again, and called Mist out. She came slowly, slipping over the edge, hood closed, sliding in the sharp-grained sand. Her milky scales caught the thin light. She smelled the animal, flowed to it, touched it with her tongue. For a moment Snake was afraid she would refuse dead meat, but the body was still warm, still twitching reflexively, and she was very hungry: "A tidbit for thee," Snake said. "To whet thy appetite." Mist nosed it, reared back, and struck, sinking her short fixed fangs into the tiny body, biting again, pumping out her store of poison. She released it, took a better grip, and began to work her jaws around it; it would hardly distend her throat. When Mist lay quiet, digesting the small meal, Snake sat beside her and held her, waiting.

She heard footsteps in the coarse sand.

"I'm sent to help you."

He was a young man, despite a scatter of white in his dark hair. He was taller than Snake, and not unattractive. His eyes were dark, and the sharp planes of his face were further hardened because his hair was pulled straight back and tied. His expression was neutral.

"Are you afraid?"

"I will do as you tell me."

Though his body was obscured by his robe, his long fine hands showed strength.

"Then hold her body, and don't let her surprise you." Mist was beginning to twitch from the effects of the drugs Snake had put in the small animal's body. The cobra's eyes stared, unseeing.

"If it bites—"

"Hold, quickly!"

The young man reached, but he had hesitated too long. Mist writhed, lashing out, striking him in the face with her tail. He staggered back, at least as surprised as hurt. Snake kept a close grip behind Mist's jaws, and struggled to catch the rest of her as well. Mist was no constrictor, but she was smooth and strong and fast. Thrashing, she forced out her breath in a long hiss. She would have bitten anything she could reach. As Snake fought with her, she managed to squeeze the poison glands and force out the last drop of venom. They hung from Mist's fangs for a moment, catching light as jewels would; the force of the serpent's convulsions flung them away into the darkness. Snake struggled with the cobra, speaking softly, aided for once by the sand, on which Mist could get no purchase. Snake felt the young man behind her, grabbing for Mist's body and tail. The seizure stopped abruptly, and Mist lay limp in their hands.

"I am sorry—"

"Hold her," Snake said. "We have the night to go."

During Mist's second convulsion, the young man held her firmly and was of some real help. Afterward, Snake answered his interrupted question. "If she were making poison and she bit you, you would probably die. Even now her bite would make you ill. But unless you do something foolish, if she manages to bite, she will bite me."

"You would benefit my cousin little, if you were dead or dying."

"You misunderstand. Mist cannot kill me." She held out her hand, so he could see the white scars of slashes and punctures. He stared at them, and looked into her eyes for a long moment, then looked away.

The bright spot in the clouds from which the light radiated moved westward in the sky; they held the cobra like a child. Snake found herself half-dozing, but Mist moved her head, dully attempting to evade restraint, and Snake woke herself abruptly. "I must not sleep," she said to the young man. "Talk to me. What are you called?"

As Stavin had, the young man hesitated. He seemed afraid of her, or of something. "My people," he said, "think it unwise to speak our names to strangers."

"If you consider me a witch you should not have asked my aid. I know no magic, and I claim none. I can't learn all the customs of all the people on this earth, so I keep my own. My custom is to address those I work with by name."

"It's not a superstition," he said. "Not as you might think. We're not afraid of being bewitched."

Snake waited, watching him, trying to decipher his expression in the dim light.

"Our families know our names, and we exchange names with those we would marry."

Snake considered that custom, and thought it would fit badly on her. "No one else? Ever?"

"Well . . . a friend might know one's name."

"Ah," Snake said. "I see. I am still a stranger, and perhaps an enemy."

"A *friend* would know my name," the young man said again. "I would not offend you, but now you misunderstand. An acquaintance is not a friend. We value friendship highly."

"In this land one should be able to tell quickly if a person is worth calling 'friend.'"

"We make friends seldom. Friendship is a commitment."

"It sounds like something to be feared."

He considered that possibility. "Perhaps it's the betrayal of friendship we fear. That is a very painful thing."

"Has anyone ever betrayed you?"

He glanced at her sharply, as if she had exceeded the limits of propriety. "No," he said, and his voice was as hard as his face. "No friend. I have no one I call friend."

His reaction startled Snake. "That's very sad," she said, and grew silent, trying to comprehend the deep stresses that could close people off so far, comparing her loneliness of necessity and theirs of choice. "Call me Snake," she said finally, "if you can bring yourself to pronounce it. Speaking my name binds you to nothing."

The young man seemed about to speak; perhaps he thought again that he had offended her, perhaps he felt he should further defend his customs. But Mist began to twist in their hands, and they had to hold her to keep her from injuring herself. The cobra was slender for her length, but powerful, and the convulsions she went through were more severe than any she had ever had before. She thrashed in Snake's grasp, and almost pulled away. She tried to spread her hood, but Snake held her too tightly. She opened her mouth and hissed, but no poison dripped from her fangs.

She wrapped her tail around the young man's waist. He began to pull her and turn, to extricate himself from her coils.

"She's not a constrictor," Snake said. "She won't hurt you. Leave her—"

But it was too late; Mist relaxed suddenly and the young man lost his balance. Mist whipped herself away and lashed figures in the sand. Snake wrestled with her alone while the young man tried to hold her, but she curled herself around Snake and used the grip for leverage. She started to pull herself from Snake's hands. Snake threw them both backward into the sand; Mist rose above her, open-mouthed, furious, hissing. The young man lunged and grabbed her just beneath her hood. Mist struck at him, but Snake, somehow, held her back. Together they deprived Mist of her hold, and regained control of her. Snake struggled up, but Mist suddenly went quite still and lay almost rigid between them. They were both sweating; the young man was pale under his tan, and even Snake was trembling.

"We have a little while to rest," Snake said. She glanced at him and noticed the dark line on his cheek where, earlier, Mist's tail had slashed him. She reached up and touched it. "You'll have a bruise, no more," she said. "It will not scar."

"If it were true that serpents sting with their tails, you would be restraining both the fangs and the stinger, and I'd be of little use."

"Tonight I'd need someone to keep me awake, whether or not he helped me with Mist." Fighting the cobra had produced adrenaline, but now it ebbed, and her exhaustion and hunger were returning, stronger.

"Snake . . ."

"Yes?"

He smiled, quickly, half-embarrassed. "I was trying the pronunciation."

"Good enough."

"How long did it take you to cross the desert?"

"Not very long. Too long. Six days."

"How did you live?"

"There is water. We traveled at night, except yesterday, when I could find no shade."

"You carried all your food?"

She shrugged. "A little." And wished he would not speak of food.

"What's on the other side?"

"More sand, more bush, a little more water. A few groups of people, traders, the station I grew up and took my training in. And farther on, a mountain with a city inside."

"I would like to see a city. Someday."

"The desert can be crossed."

He said nothing, but Snake's memories of leaving home were recent enough that she could imagine his thoughts.

The next set of convulsions came, much sooner than Snake had expected. By their severity, she gauged something of the stage of Stavin's illness, and wished it were morning. If she were to lose him, she would have it done, and grieve, and try to forget. The cobra would have battered herself to death against the sand if Snake and the young man had not been holding her. She suddenly went completely rigid, with her mouth clamped shut and her forked tongue dangling.

She stopped breathing.

"Hold her," Snake said. "Hold her head. Quickly, take her, and if she gets away, run. Take her! She won't strike at you now, she could only slash you by accident."

He hesitated only a moment, then grasped Mist behind the head. Snake ran, slipping in the deep sand, from the edge of the circle of tents to a place where bushes still grew. She broke off dry thorny branches that tore her scarred hands. Peripherally she noticed a mass of horned vipers, so ugly they seemed deformed, nesting beneath the clump of desiccated vegetation; they hissed at her: she ignored them. She found a narrow hollow stem and carried it back. Her hands bled from deep scratches.

Kneeling by Mist's head, she forced open the cobra's mouth and pushed the tube deep into her throat, through the air passage at the base of Mist's tongue. She bent close, took the tube in her mouth, and breathed gently into Mist's lungs.

She noticed: the young man's hands, holding the cobra as she had asked; his breathing, first a sharp gasp of surprise, then ragged; the sand scraping her elbows where she leaned; the cloying smell of the fluid seeping from Mist's fangs; her own dizziness, she thought from exhaustion, which she forced away by necessity and will.

Snake breathed, and breathed again, paused, and repeated, until Mist caught the rhythm and continued it unaided.

Snake sat back on her heels. "I think she'll be all right," she said. "I hope she will." She brushed the back of her hand across her forehead. The touch sparked pain: she jerked her hand down and agony slid along her bones, up her arm, across her shoulder, through her chest, enveloping her heart. Her balance turned on its edge. She fell, tried to catch herself but moved too slowly, fought nausea and vertigo and almost succeeded, until the pull of the earth seemed to slip away in pain and she was lost in darkness with nothing to take a bearing by.

She felt sand where it had scraped her cheek and her palms, but it was soft. "Snake, can I let go?" She thought the question must be for someone else, while at the same time she knew there was no one else to answer it, no one else to reply to her name. She felt hands on her, and they were gentle; she wanted to respond to them, but she was too tired. She needed sleep more, so she pushed them away. But they held her head and put dry leather to her lips and poured water into her throat. She coughed and choked and spat it out.

She pushed herself up on one elbow. As her sight cleared, she realized she was shaking. She felt as she had the first time she was snake-bit, before her immunities had completely developed. The young man knelt over her, his water flask in his hand. Mist, beyond him, crawled toward the darkness. Snake forgot the throbbing pain. "Mist!"

The young man flinched and turned, frightened; the serpent reared up, her head nearly at Snake's standing eye level, her hood spread, swaying, watching, angry, ready to strike. She formed a wavering white line against black. Snake forced herself to rise, feeling as though she were fumbling with the control of some unfamiliar body. She almost fell again, but held herself steady. "Thou must not go to hunt now," she said. "There is work for thee to do." She held out her right hand, to the side, a decoy, to draw Mist if she struck. Her hand was heavy with pain. Snake feared, not being bitten, but the loss of the contents of Mist's poison sacs. "Come here," she said. "Come here, and stay thy anger." She noticed blood flowing down between her fingers, and the fear she felt for Stavin was intensified. "Didst thou bite me, creature?" But the pain was wrong: poison would numb her, and the new serum only sting . . .

"No," the young man whispered, from behind her.

Mist struck. The reflexes of long training took over. Snake's right hand jerked away, her left grabbed Mist as she brought her head back. The cobra writhed a moment, and relaxed. "Devious beast," Snake said. "For shame." She turned, and let Mist crawl up her arm and over her shoulder, where she lay like the outline of an invisible cape and dragged her tail like the edge of a train.

"She did not bite me?"

"No," the young man said. His contained voice was touched with awe. "You should be dying. You should be curled around the agony, and your arm swollen purple. When you came back—" He gestured toward her hand. "It must have been a bush viper."

Snake remembered the coil of reptiles beneath the branches, and touched the blood on her hand. She wiped it away, revealing the double puncture of a snakebite among the scratches of the thorns. The wound was slightly swollen. "It needs cleaning," she said. "I shame myself by falling to it." The pain of it washed in gentle waves up her arm, burning no longer. She stood looking at the young man, looking around her, watching the landscape shift and change as her tired eyes tried to cope with the low light of setting moon and false dawn. "You held Mist well, and bravely," she said to the young man. "Thank you."

He lowered his gaze, almost bowing to her. He rose, and approached her. Snake put her hand gently on Mist's neck so she would not be alarmed.

"I would be honored," the young man said, "if you would call me Arevin."

"I would be pleased to."

Snake knelt down and held the winding white loops as Mist crawled slowly into her compartment. In a little while, when Mist had stabilized, by dawn, they could go to Stavin.

The tip of Mist's white tail slid out of sight. Snake closed the case and would have risen, but she could not stand. She had not yet quite shaken off the effects of the new venom. The flesh around the wound was red and tender, but the hemorrhaging would not spread. She stayed where she was, slumped, staring at her hand, creeping slowly in her mind toward what she needed to do, this time for herself.

"Let me help you. Please."

He touched her shoulder and helped her stand. "I'm sorry," she said. "I'm so in need of rest . . ."

"Let me wash your hand," Arevin said. "And then you can sleep. Tell me when to waken you—"

"No. I can't sleep yet." She pulled together the skeins of her nerves, collected herself, straightened, tossed the damp curls of her short hair off her forehead. "I'm all right now. Have you any water?"

Arevin loosened his outer robe. Beneath it he wore a loincloth and a leather belt that carried several leather flasks and pouches. The color of his skin was slightly lighter than the sun-darkened brown of his face. He brought out his water flask, closed his robe around his lean body, and reached for Snake's hand.

"No, Arevin. If the poison gets in any small scratch you might have, it could infect."

She sat down and sluiced lukewarm water over her hand. The water dripped pink to the ground and disappeared, leaving not even a damp spot visible. The wound bled a little more, but now it only ached. The poison was almost inactivated.

"I don't understand," Arevin said, "how it is that you're unhurt. My younger sister was bitten by a bush viper." He could not speak as uncaringly as he might have wished. "We could do nothing to save her—nothing we had would even lessen her pain."

Snake gave him his flask and rubbed salve from a vial in her belt pouch across the closing punctures. "It's a part of our preparation," she said. "We work with many kinds of serpents, so we must be immune to as many as possible." She shrugged. "The process is tedious and somewhat painful." She clenched her fist; the film held, and she was steady. She leaned toward Arevin and touched his abraded cheek again. "Yes . . ." She spread a thin layer of the salve across it. "That will help it heal."

"If you cannot sleep," Arevin said, "can you at least rest?"

"Yes," she said. "For a little while."

Snake sat next to Arevin, leaning against him, and they watched the sun turn the clouds to gold and flame and amber. The simple physical contact with another human being gave Snake pleasure, though she found it unsatisfying. Another time, another place, she might do something more, but not here, not now.

When the lower edge of the sun's bright smear rose above the horizon, Snake rose and teased Mist out of the case. She came slowly, weakly, and crawled across Snake's shoulders. Snake picked up the satchel, and she and Arevin walked together back to the small group of tents.

Stavin's parents waited, watching for her, just outside the entrance of their tent. They stood in a tight, defensive, silent group. For a moment Snake thought they had decided to send her away. Then, with regret and fear like hot iron in her mouth, she asked if Stavin had died. They shook their heads, and allowed her to enter.

Stavin lay as she had left him, still asleep. The adults followed her with their stares, and she could smell fear. Mist flicked out her tongue, growing nervous from the implied danger.

"I know you would stay," Snake said. "I know you would help, if you could, but there is nothing to be done by any person but me. Please go back outside."

They glanced at each other, and at Arevin, and she thought for a moment that they would refuse. Snake wanted to fall into the silence and sleep. "Come, cousins," Arevin said. "We are in her hands." He opened the tent flap and motioned them out. Snake thanked him with nothing more than a glance, and he might almost have smiled. She turned toward Stavin, and knelt beside him. "Stavin—" She touched his forehead; it was very hot. She noticed that her hand was less steady than before. The slight touch awakened the child. "It's time," Snake said.

He blinked, coming out of some child's dream, seeing her, slowly recognizing her. He did not look frightened. For that Snake was glad; for some other reason she could not identify she was uneasy.

"Will it hurt?"

"Does it hurt now?"

He hesitated, looked away, looked back. "Yes."

"It might hurt a little more. I hope not. Are you ready?"

"Can Grass stay?"

"Of course," she said.

And realized what was wrong.

"I'll come back in a moment." Her voice changed so much, she had pulled it so tight, that she could not help but frighten him. She left the tent, walking slowly, calmly, restraining herself. Outside, the parents told her by their faces what they feared.

"Where is Grass?" Arevin, his back to her, started at her tone. The younger husband made a small grieving sound, and could look at her no longer.

"We were afraid," the older husband said. "We thought it would bite the child."

"I thought it would. It was I. It crawled over his face, I could see its fangs—" The wife put her hands on the younger husband's shoulders, and he said no more.

"Where is he?" She wanted to scream; she did not.

They brought her a small open box. Snake took it, and looked inside.

Grass lay cut almost in two, his entrails oozing from his body, half turned over, and as she watched, shaking, he writhed once, and flicked his tongue out once, and in. Snake made some sound, too low in her throat to be a cry. She hoped his motions were only reflex, but she picked him up as gently as she could. She leaned down and touched her lips to the smooth green scales behind his head.

She bit him quickly, sharply, at the base of the skull. His blood flowed cool and salty in her mouth. If he were not dead, she had killed him instantly.

She looked at the parents, and at Arevin; they were all pale, but she had no sympathy for their fear, and cared nothing for shared grief. "Such a small creature," she said. "Such a small creature, who could only give pleasure and dreams." She watched them for a moment more, then turned toward the tent again.

"Wait—" She heard the older husband move up close behind her. He touched her shoulder; she shrugged away his hand. "We will give you anything you want," he said, "but leave the child alone."

She spun on him in a fury. "Should I kill Stavin for your stupidity?" He seemed about to try to hold her back. She jammed her shoulder hard into his stomach, and flung herself past the tent flap. Inside, she kicked over the satchel. Abruptly awakened, and angry, Sand crawled out and coiled himself. When the younger husband and the wife tried to enter, Sand hissed and rattled with a violence Snake had never heard him use before. She did not even bother to look behind her. She ducked her head and wiped her tears on her sleeve before Stavin could see them. She knelt beside him.

"What's the matter?" He could not help but hear the voices outside the tent, and the running.

"Nothing, Stavin," Snake said. "Did you know we came across the desert?"

"No," he said, with wonder.

"It was very hot, and none of us had anything to eat. Grass is hunting now. He was very hungry. Will you forgive him and let me begin? I will be here all the time."

He seemed so tired; he was disappointed, but he had no strength for arguing. "All right." His voice rustled like sand slipping through the fingers.

Snake lifted Mist from her shoulders, and pulled the blanket from Stavin's small body. The tumor pressed up beneath his rib cage, distorting his form, squeezing his vital organs, sucking nourishment from him for its own growth. Holding Mist's head, Snake let her flow across him, touching and tasting him. She had to restrain the cobra to keep her from striking; the excitement had agitated her. When Sand used his rattle, she flinched. Snake spoke to her softly, soothing her; trained and bred-in responses began to return, overcoming the natural instincts. Mist paused when her tongue flicked the skin above the tumor, and Snake released her.

The cobra reared, and struck, and bit as cobras bite, sinking her fangs their short length once, releasing, instantly biting again for a better purchase, holding on, chewing at her prey. Stavin cried out, but he did not move against Snake's restraining hands.

Mist expended the contents of her venom sacs into the child, and released him. She reared up, peered around, folded her hood, and slid across the mats in a perfectly straight line toward her dark, close compartment.

"It is all finished, Stavin."

"Will I die now?"

"No," Snake said. "Not now. Not for many years, I hope." She took a vial of powder from her belt pouch. "Open your mouth." He complied, and she sprinkled the powder across his tongue. "That will help the ache." She spread a pad of cloth across the series of shallow puncture wounds, without wiping off the blood.

She turned from him.

"Snake? Are you going away?"

"I will not leave without saying good-bye. I promise."

The child lay back, closed his eyes, and let the drug take him.

Sand coiled quiescently on the dark matting. Snake called him. He moved toward her, and suffered himself to be replaced in the satchel. Snake closed it, and lifted it, and it still felt empty. She heard noises outside the tent. Stavin's parents and the people who had come to help them pulled open the tent flap and peered inside, thrusting sticks in even before they looked.

Snake set down her leather case. "It's done."

They entered. Arevin was with them too; only he was empty-handed. "Snake—" He spoke through grief, pity, confusion, and Snake could not tell what he believed. He looked back. Stavin's mother was just behind him. He took her by the shoulder. "He would have died without her. Whatever has happened now, he would have died."

The woman shook his hand away. "He might have lived. It might have gone away. We—" She could not speak for hiding tears.

Snake felt the people moving, surrounding her. Arevin took one step toward her and stopped, and she could see he wanted her to defend herself. "Can any of you cry?" she said. "Can any of you cry for me and my despair, or for them and their guilt, or for small things and their pain?" She felt tears slip down her cheeks.

They did not understand her; they were offended by her crying. They stood back, still afraid of her, but gathering themselves. She no longer needed the pose of calmness she had used to deceive the child. "Ah, you fools." Her voice sounded brittle. "Stavin—"

Light from the entrance struck them. "Let me pass." The people in front of Snake moved aside for their leader. She stopped in front of Snake, ignoring the satchel her foot almost touched. "Will Stavin live?" Her voice was quiet, calm, gentle.

"I cannot be certain," Snake said, "but I feel that he will."

"Leave us." The people understood Snake's words before they did their leader's; they looked around and lowered their weapons, and finally, one by one, they moved out of the tent. Arevin remained. Snake felt the strength that came from danger seeping from her. Her knees collapsed. She bent over the satchel with her face in her hands. The older woman knelt in front of her, before Snake could notice or prevent her. "Thank you," she said. "Thank you. I am so sorry . . ." She put her arms around Snake, and drew her toward her, and Arevin knelt beside them, and he embraced Snake too. Snake began to tremble again, and they held her while she cried.

*　　*　　*

Later she slept, exhausted, alone in the tent with Stavin, holding his hand. They had given her food, and small animals for Sand
and Mist, and supplies for her journey, and sufficient water for her
to bathe, though that must have strained their resources. About
that, Snake no longer cared.

When she awakened, she felt the tumor, and found that it had
begun to dissolve and shrivel, dying, as Mist's changed poison affected it. Snake felt little joy. She smoothed Stavin's pale hair back
from his face. "I would not lie to you again, little one," she said, "but
I must leave soon. I cannot stay here." She wanted another three
days' sleep, to finish fighting off the effects of the bush viper's poison, but she would sleep somewhere else. "Stavin?"

He half woke, slowly. "It doesn't hurt anymore," he said.

"I am glad."

"Thank you . . ."

"Good-bye, Stavin. Will you remember later on that you woke
up, and that I did stay to say good-bye?"

"Good-bye," he said, drifting off again. "Good-bye, Snake.
Good-bye, Grass." He closed his eyes, and Snake picked up the
satchel and left the tent. Dusk cast long indistinct shadows; the
camp was quiet. She found her tiger-striped pony, tethered with
food and water. New, full water-skins lay on the ground next to the
saddle. The tiger pony whickered at her when she approached. She
scratched his striped ears, saddled him, and strapped the case on
his back. Leading him, she started west, the way she had come.

"Snake—"

She took a breath, and turned back to Arevin. He faced the sun,
and it turned his skin ruddy and his robe scarlet. His streaked hair
flowed loose to his shoulders, gentling his face. "You will not stay?"

"I cannot."

"I had hoped . . ."

"If things were different, I might have stayed."

"They were frightened. Can't you forgive them?"

"I can't face their guilt. What they did was my fault. I said he could not hurt them, but they saw his fangs and they didn't know his bite only gave dreams and eased dying. They couldn't know; I didn't understand them until too late."

"You said it yourself, you can't know all the customs and all the fears."

"I'm crippled," she said. "Without Grass, if I cannot heal a person, I cannot help at all. I must go home. Perhaps my teachers will forgive me my stupidity, but I am afraid to face them. They seldom give the name I bear, but they gave it to me, and they'll be disappointed."

"Let me come with you."

She wanted to; she hesitated, and cursed herself for that weakness. "They may cast me out, and you would be cast out too. Stay here, Arevin."

"It wouldn't matter."

"It would. After a while, we would hate each other. I don't know you, and you don't know me. We need calmness, and quiet, and time to understand each other."

He came toward her, and put his arms around her, and they stood together for a moment. When he raised his head, he was crying. "Please come back," he said. "Whatever happens, please come back."

"I will try," Snake said. "Next spring, when the winds stop, look for me. And the spring after that, if I do not come, forget me. Wherever I am, if I live, I will forget you."

"I will look for you," Arevin said, and he would promise no more.

Snake picked up the pony's lead, and started across the desert.

The July Ward

S.N. Dyer

There is a place of which all doctors know, but none will speak.

It is 6:30 in the morning, and hardly worth anyone's while to try for sleep. The medical student has just finished writing admission orders for the new patient, and the night nurse is studying the page with a mixture of annoyance and disdain.

Watson ignores them, ignoring also the CT scan she has been admiring, with its textbook perfect depiction of a brain demolished by a bullet. She closes her eyes and, in the process of rubbing them, experiences the intensive care unit anew.

There is the breathing of the ancient man with Cheyne-Stokes respirations: shallow, deep, deeper, loud gasp and shudder, shallow, shallower, pause for a long time. An old ventilator is breathing for the newest patient: *whoosh clunk sssshh,* over and over, twenty times a minute. As counterpoint, the unit's sole heart monitor beeps an out of sync 80/minute, with the occasional interposed beat of an extra systole, or the brief syncopation of a bigeminal rhythm.

Next, Watson becomes aware of the early morning smells, of blood and decay, tube-feeding and feces, cheap wine and vomitus. Soon, someone will mop the floor and someone else deliver trays, and the odors of ammonia and hospital food will merge into the un-savory whole.

She opens her eyes, taking in the cracked plaster, six beds, shelves piled haphazardly with a random selection of unneeded equipment; sighing, she begins moving toward the door. As she passes the man in bed four, his bandaged head swivels to follow her.

"Waitress!" he calls. "Waitress, I want a tuna fish sandwich!"

The medical student—Watson has just spent twenty-two straight hours in his company and cannot remember his first name, just the inhumanly neat way he signs it—comes to her defense.

"Excuse me, Mr. Johnson," he says. "You're not in a restaurant."

Watson grimaces. The pushy kid is going to try to orient the pa-tient. Had she ever been so naïve and idealistic, even on her own second day of the wards? *T.* His name starts with a *T.*

"Mr. Johnson, you're in the neurology/neurosurgery intensive care unit of Warren G. Harding Industrial County Hospital."

The patient ignores him, repeating angrily, "Waitress, I want a tuna fish sandwich."

Watson says, "Here, let me show you how it's done." She ap-proaches the patient, standing at the foot of his hospital bed.

"Waitress. . . ." he begins.

"I'm sorry, sir. This is not my table."

Grabbing her student by the elbow, she leads him out of the unit. The benches outside are mercifully empty, so they need not be polite to hovering families. "Now what?" he asks.

"Huh?" She is trying to remember if he's named Tony or Tom or Ted.

"What do we do now?" He has never been on call before, and he's riding an adrenaline high. Twenty-two hours, and he's gung-ho for more.

She pauses to think about it. A considerate resident might tell him to go work on his presentation, but who needs to prepare to talk about a simple gunshot wound? Or, up at University Hospital, she might tell him to clean up, change, eat breakfast. But here at Harding the showers in the doctors' call rooms have no curtains and no water. Besides, it's accepted that the team coming off call will continue to wear wrinkled, blood-spattered scrubsuits, as a visual reminder to everyone else that they are tired, and short-tempered, and not likely to look charitably upon any attempts at denigration or one-upmanship. And the cafeteria will not open for another half-hour.

Gazing out the window, Watson can see the sky growing pink behind the silhouettes of the hospital complex. There are half a dozen towers of varying height and architecture, monuments to half a dozen periods of relative affluence. The majority of buildings are now silent and dark.

"It's kind of like an old castle," she says. "You know, built with no plan, every generation adding something."

"With secret passages and haunted dungeons?" asks the kid, getting into the spirit of the matter. This cheers her. She tried to tell this to another student once, eleven long months ago, only to discover he was a cheap knock-off robot with absent humor circuits. Try to tell that kind of medical student a joke, and he'll reply "Will this be on the test?"

She points to the buildings in turn, starting with the ruins of the nursing dorm. "The original Norman donjon." Then the infectious disease wing, a gift of the New Deal. "The fenestrated keep, built by the Mad Duke in 1485." Next, she aims at the New Tower, the last addition, built during the nationwide hospital expansion of the sixties, and where most of the patients are now housed. "The Georgian wing."

Getting into the spirit of it all, Tom—she has noticed the nametag on his short white jacket with its pockets crammed full of instruments and manuals—cackles. "Look, that light. Could it be . . . the la-bor-a-try of Doctor Frankenstein?"

She decides that she likes him after all, and decides what they will do next. Checking her watch—it is now twenty to seven—she nods down the half-lit hall. "Come on."

They go down the stairwell to the basement, the same base-ment they have traversed all night, bringing patients from the emer-gency room to radiology and then to ICU. As they stride, cockroaches scurry angrily from their path. Tom flinches once.

"Jeeze!" he says. "It must be two inches long."

Watson feels momentarily sorry for him. His origins are written all over him: a neat, lawned half-acre in some well-kept suburb. The medical school has charged her with his education, and what has she done for him so far? Shown him drunks puking up blood and wine; a battered woman who attempts to steal his stethoscope when he leaves the room to get her a pain shot; children with nee-dle tracks; and his final wonder, six-legged vermin that he has pre-viously known only from the jokes on TV. But now she will show him something to make up for it all. Veering from the yellow line painted on the floor, the line that brings them home through the maze of corridors, she pries open a door that has been painted closed.

"There is a dimension beyond time and space . . ." she says, in her best Rod Serling voice, and leads him up dustcaked stairs illu-minated only by their penlights. Two flights up, they lean hard against another door, and emerge into a large room.

"This is part of the original hospital," she says, her voice echo-ing against high ceilings. Her breath forms mist in the air—many window are broken—and Tom tries to button his jacket, but the bulging pockets prevent it. "They built the new parts over and around the old foundation. But these are the first wards. They were still used up until the late seventies."

They prowl the empty ward, which is hesitantly brightening with sunrise. As the shadows diminish, they begin to make out cob-webs and cracked plaster. Pigeons, nesting in the rafters, glare at the intruders.

"There'd be patients down both sides, and in the summer when it got full, they'd run a row of beds down the middle. You'd move screens to examine a patient, or if someone was terminal."

"Look at this!" Tom has found a wooden wheelchair, not that much more antique or decrepit than those they have been using all night to transport patients, and sits on the hard, uncomfortable seat. Watson pushes him past the nursing desk in the hall, and into the adjoining ward. "They built them long and thin like this to maximize fresh air. The Florence Nightingale approach. This would be the women's ward." One of the tires is flat, and the student bounces regularly as they progress. The chair leaves thin tracks in the dirt.

Tom leaps from the chair and runs to an incredibly tall floor fan, reaching to his breast pocket. "Great!" His footsteps raise clouds of dust that smell like guano.

"When it got hot, they'd put a tub of ice at the front of a ward, and aim a fan over it." A patient had told her that, an old, old woman who'd been a nurse at this very hospital during the Depression. When Watson had met her, she'd been in her nineties, boney and pale, identical in appearance to all other patients in their nineties, as if those final ten years erase the distinguishing characteristics that make up the individual. But she had been surprisingly aware, and when she had died. . . .

"Where's this go?" asks Tom, waving at a heavy dark wood door on the outside wall, a door that should, by rights, lead nowhere.

"Don't open that! It's not time to open that—we'd better get back," snaps Watson, turning abruptly. Her footsteps blend into street noises that are only now growing audible. Tom looks briefly about the ward, allows his gaze to linger upon the door, then runs to follow his resident.

At breakfast, their table is invaded by the surgery housestaff. They are in street clothes, and even the ones who have been up all night wear ties and neatly pressed short white coats. It is barely seven, but they have already completed an hour of rounding, and soon will be in the operating room. Tom stares in disbelief at their trays, piled high with pancakes, sausage, bacon, pints of chocolate milk, and large styrofoam cups of coffee. Surgeons are very serious about breakfasts. They usually don't get a second meal.

The surgeons glance in Watson's general direction. "Hey," says the tallest one. He must be their chief resident; his white coat is knee-length. Also, years of work and abuse and sleep deprivation have worn away what little tact or courtesy he might ever have possessed. "Hey, you neuro?"

"Uh-huh."

"You got that gunshot?"

Watson takes a long sip of coffee before replying. "John Doe #3." It has been a busy night for the unidentified.

Tom has been told that the gentleman in question is *his* patient, so he volunteers further information. "Thirty-eight caliber. The entrance is right occipital, and the exit left fronto-parietal." Saying this makes him feel very professional.

"Condition?" asks the surgeon, looking at Watson instead. She does not appreciate his snubbing her medical student, and knows also that if her own chief were here, he would be ignoring her as well. He has an arrogant manner that makes her uncertain if she feels furious or worthless.

"Bullet turned the brain to jello. He's herniated."

"Braindead?"

"Not yet. But soon."

"Suicide?"

"No. Met the Dude Brothers."

Tom asks, "Huh?"

She looks away from the surgery chief to explain, a carefully calculated breach of etiquette. "You ask someone in the E.R. who beat them up, it's always '*some dudes.*' No one will ever tell you who did it, or admit that it was only one guy."

"The Dude Brothers," Tom repeats, pleased, as if every new bit of slang makes him that much closer to being a doctor.

"Homicide," the surgeon is saying. "That's a little tougher, but the coroner's usually cooperative. He a druggie?"

She shakes her head. There is a drug war going on, and the wound pattern is that favored in street executions. But, like the previous victims in the current conflict, her patient appears to have been an enforcer, not an addict. "No tracks. He's a great specimen."

The surgeon smiles. Finally. She knows exactly what he is thinking. *One heart. One liver. Two kidneys.*

"And a partridge in a pear tree," she adds aloud, confirming the surgeons' opinion that you gotta be crazy to go into neurology. "Just one problem. He's a John Doe. No organ donor card. No family. And even if we found them . . ."

The surgeon gives her that look, like he's Bonaparte, Caesar, Patton, and she's some worthless footsoldier assigned to hold the ridge.

"Let me worry about that. You just keep him going 'til we get permission to harvest the organs."

They straggle in to morning rounds, clutching styrofoam lifelines. Breakfast and caffeine have worked paradoxically; the now off-call team is starting to crash. Watson is shivering as she tells the group (her fellow junior resident, the chief resident, two internal medicine interns, two nameless third-year medical students) about the new admissions. Tom is leaning against the wall, yawning, occasionally pinching himself, and in no way following the rules of medical decorum that he so carefully memorized a few days ago. For a second he actually drifts off to sleep, and sees the ghost of Osler coming through the ICU door, shouting "You will never be a doctor!" But then one of his classmates takes pity on him, and nudges him awake.

The residents are looking at him with bemused expressions. The years have almost numbed them to the pain of sleep deprivation, though they vaguely remember a time when they were still aware of their suffering. But the memories are dreamlike and uncertain, like a view into a prior incarnation.

"You get used to it," Watson says encouragingly.

The other resident grins at his students, who have not yet experienced an on-call night, and asks Tom, "So how's it feel, now that you're not a virgin anymore?"

"Rounds," the chief reminds them.

They move to the bedside of the gunshot victim, and Tom begins a formal and totally disorganized presentation. The chief cuts him short after less than a minute. "Save it for the attending," he suggests. "Make it quick and dirty for work rounds."

Tom looks at Watson, who nods. He says, "John Doe #3. Met the Dude Brothers." The other medical students look puzzled, and their resident whispers, "Later."

They retire to the viewbox, where the chief resident makes funny humming noises while reviewing the CAT scan, briefly pimps the students (who cannot yet tell a bullet fragment from a calcified pineal gland), and then they return to the man on the bed. A fly has landed on the patient's half open right eye.

"Shit," says Watson. "I told the nurse to lacrilube them shut." She has respect for corneas, even though John Doe #3 will never need his again.

The chief demonstrates the way that the lids no longer spring closed, then shines a light in each eye. The pupils do not react.

"Midposition, fixed," he says. "What's that mean?"

The students stare blankly.

"What's with you guys? Don't you know any neuro?"

The other resident whispers to the chief. The medical student year is not quite in sync with the housestaff's; their students last week had been at the end of third-year, almost seniors—knowledgeable, canny, battle hardened. Now they have raw recruits again.

"Okay," the chief says. "I'll show you how to examine a comatose patient. First thing, you see if he can breathe on his own." So he disconnects the tube that connects the ventilator to John Doe's endotracheal tube, and they watch to see if any breaths occur. The respirator alarm begins to blare. Unfortunately, as it is an old machine, the alarm can't be switched off. Watson puts fingers in her ears to block out the raucous noise.

"Tell me if he starts," the chief directs, and runs through the rest of the exam, squeezing fingers and toes to cause pain, sticking q-tips in the eyes, tongue blades down the throat, ice water in the ears. The patient makes no response to any of these noxious stimuli, and after three breathless minutes, Watson reattaches the respirator. The alarm stops.

"Papilledema. Take a look," directs the chief, handing his ophthalmoscope to a student. She bends in close to an eye, trying to focus through the pupil to the retina behind, like trying to look through one keyhole into another keyhole. It is a technique that requires skill the student does not yet possess, and is made even more difficult by corneas clouded by exposure and neglect.

Watson notices that the medical student is holding her breath, and grins sympathetically. No one ever says anything about it, but the braindead smell different. Not a particularly unpleasant odor, like gangrene or enteric bacteria, but a faint, cold, wet, indefinable smell that Watson associates with patients with liquified cortex.

"Okay, enough, you can come back later," the chief says, changing his mind. Each student attempting fundoscopy will run through what little rounding time is left. "Three minutes without any respiratory effort? Okay, so he's braindead. What now?"

"Surgery wants him."

The other resident snickers. "Hey buddy, they want your body." The interns laugh, and the students look at them distastefully, except for Tom. He's starting to grasp the housestaff's grim humor.

"Fine with me," says the chief. "Get an EEG to confirm it, and they can have him whenever they want."

Watson points to the name on the wristband. *John Doe.*

"Oh. That's a problem." He looks around the unit. There is still one empty bed. "He can stay while they work that out. But if we need the bed. . . ."

An intern—he trained at one of those small Caribbean schools, looks a little like Dennis the Menace grown up, and is always a bit slow on the uptake—says "Hey, wait a minute. Organ donation? Don't we need permission from next-of-kin?"

Watson lets her mouth drop open. "Holy shit, you're right! Quick, Fred, go call the Doe family and ask them!"

The intern is halfway to the phone before he realizes that he's been had.

They are barely finishing rounding on the ward when the other resident is beeped to the E.R. He calls down, then gathers up his students and starts out. "Gunshot," he calls to Watson and the chief. He jabs his female student right about the midthoracic spine.

"The Dude Brothers have been busy little boys today," says the chief. "Take a 'tern; the studs should stay for attending rounds." The students look disappointed, worried they'll miss something exciting.

The team files into the conference room, a grimy place with mismatched chairs, windows nailed shut to prevent patient suicides, and a single window air conditioner that barely works. A few textbooks—the most recent at least ten years out of date—and dozens of X-ray folders litter the counters, near a primitive monocular microscope, bottles of outdated stain reagents, and a hemocytometer box labeled *STEAL THIS AND DIE!* The box is empty.

On the wall is an X-ray view box that looks old enough that, in a rare whimsical mood brought on by acute and chronic exhaustion, Watson tries to visualize when it was new, in a room where the wood paneling and marble are as yet unplastered. She imagines a conference of doctors, in high collars and starched white coats. On the view box, a visiting Dr. Dandy is showing off his first pneumoencephalogram.

She returns to the present and her own conference. A professor has come down from the University to hear the new cases and offer advice. Unfortunately, their current attending is junior faculty, newly arrived from one of the more civilized programs. Did they present to him complex, obscure, and abstruse cases, perhaps something due to an enzyme deficiency isolated only last week, or a rare cranial nerve syndrome first described in 1925, he should be informative and invaluable. Instead, they confront him daily with the same and the mundane: alcohol withdrawal seizures, delirium tremens, head trauma, alcohol withdrawal seizures. Tom presents his case and shows him John Doe's brain scan, and after the professor has pimped the students on which is bullet and which is calcified pineal, he has little else to add.

Later, back in the ICU, Watson sees the surgical chief resident going through John Doe's chart. She strides over quickly. As she passes bed four, the patient with the bandage starts up again.

"Waitress, I want . . ."

"It's not her table," snaps Tom.

Watson says, in her most unctuous voice, "May I help you?"

The alien chief wants blood and histocompatibility typing, cultures, more frequent vital signs, stat syphilis and AIDS serologies. He wants the intravenous fluids changed to the surgeons' favorite, lactated Ringers. He wants everything to be thoroughly buffed when he triumphantly delivers the still-beating heart, the gleaming red liver, the happily perfusing kidneys, and the extraneous shell of body that surrounds them, to the transplant team up at the University Hospital.

The neurology chief steps in. "Look, I know this is important to you, and we'll help all we can. But there isn't any family to give permission yet, and the man's braindead." He decides to elaborate. General surgery residents are notorious for their incomprehension of neurologic principles.

"Everything upstairs is gone, including the autonomic centers in the medulla. His heart and blood pressure and kidneys are on autopilot now, and pretty soon they'll just get out of control, like an untuned engine that idles faster and faster and then goes haywire. You can keep a brainstem preparation going for months, but this guy's braindead; he won't last three days, and that's if we work hard."

"Then work hard. Or is that too much for you guys?"

Watson's chief gives him his *if you had one more neuron you'd have a synapse* smile, and answers sweetly, "We'll keep him as long as we can, or until we need a unit bed. And we're full now."

"You've got one empty!" protests the surgeon.

At that minute the ICU doors swing open and the other resident and Fred the intern roll in a new patient.

"Besides," says the chief. "Even if you find the family, I'll bet a beer you don't get the parts. I've been here a long time and I've never . . ."

The surgeon nods, stalking out. "A beer." No one ever pays off on these bets.

The chief notices Tom standing there, mouth agape, and decides to finish his sentence. ". . . I've never had anyone donate organs. Face it, the families of people who live and die by violence just don't tend to be altruistic."

Tom frowns, trying to absorb and properly file away that bit of information.

As the new patient is being lifted off the gurney, he gazes across at John Doe and laughs. "Hey! Johnny! Hey, they got you too? Serves you right, you son of a bitch."

At noon, bored policemen descend upon the unit. They question the new patient, who won't tell them anything—his occupation, his assailants' identities, John Doe's real name. The police don't seem to care much. "It's not like they're shooting innocent kids or housewives or something," one of them remarks to the chief. Life might even improve, if every drug dealer in the city shot every other.

Tom hovers about the periphery, wearing an expression of intense fascination that he tries unsuccessfully to hide. He has not been this close to an actual policeman since Mister Traffic Safety reminded his first grade class to look both ways before crossing.

"What about our John Doe?" asks Watson.

"Is he gonna die?" the cop replies.

"He *is* dead. Technically braindead. I could turn off the ventilators now, only surgery's dying to use his parts for transplant. For that, we need family permission."

"We're running his prints."

"He's bound to have priors," the other policeman says.

Watson nods. "We'll keep him alive until you give us a name. Right, Tom?"

Pleased to be included, the student nods. "Right."

The new admission has a bullet lodged in his vertebral canal at T-10. In a way, he's lucky. If the bullet had not stopped there, it would have continued on through lung, diaphragm and liver, leaving an awful mess. However, the man is now permanently paralyzed below the umbilicus, never again to feel his legs, walk, fornicate, or control his bowels and bladder. He does not have a great appreciation for his good luck, or for the medical care that he is receiving, and everyone is secretly pleased when the consulting neurosurgeon decides that the wound needs to be debrided operatively. General anesthesia will give everyone a temporary break from his complaints.

Before leaving for the day, Tom and Watson look in on John Doe #3 one last time. He lies quietly, no movements except the periodic rise and fall of his chest as the respirator cycles. His body temperature is starting to climb and, though Watson expects it is just due to hypothalamic dysfunction, she orders chest X-ray, blood and urine cultures, puts him on a cooling blanket and Tylenol suppositories, and covers potential infection with a broad-spectrum antibiotic.

"Say goodnight, John Doe," she says as she exits.

"Goodnight, John Doe," replies Tom, in a high-pitched voice.

The next morning they find out their patient's real name; it is not as memorable as John Doe, so they continue to refer to him as such. No one is surprised to find that he has more arrests than their attending has publications. He even has an outstanding warrant for murder, so the police put a shackle about the irreversibly comatose man's ankle to chain him to the bedframe, and assign three shifts of deputies to sit at the foot of the bed and make sure he does not escape.

"Great use of our tax dollars, huh?" asks Watson. She hauls Doe's knee into the air and tries for a reflex, knowing well that he has none, but enjoying the way the shackles clink as she does it.

The deputy is ready for retirement, and looks about as dangerous as any fat, elderly, napping man, but the presence of a uniform and a gun give the chief resident some comfort. Their paraplegic patient is contemplating singing to the police, giving them details of the drug war, its strategies, finances, and generals. The chief is convinced that, any moment now, Uzi-wielding dope dealers will enter the ICU and spray it with bullets, taking out their erstwhile colleague and any unlucky witnesses. Whenever the doors swing open, the chief flinches and starts to duck, and finally decides that it's time to visit the lab where he'll be working next month.

His paranoia infects the rest of the team. The other resident and an intern remember that they really ought to be in out-patient clinic; the students decamp to the library; Fred actually volunteers to scrub with a bad-tempered neurosurgeon on a routine back surgery.

Watson manages to reach John Doe's mother, in another state. The woman has the usual reaction to bad news. "How could this happen?" Watson avoids the response on the tip of her tongue— "Because he's a murderer, and this time someone got him first"— and tries to be kind and supportive. She explains how they've done everything medically possible, but the damage from the bullet is just too great. She expresses condolences, and finally broaches the subject of organ donation.

"It's so unfortunate," she says. A life cut short at only twenty-eight. Family and children—none of them legitimate—bereaved.

But there's an opportunity for some good to come from this tragedy. His kidneys, liver, and heart can give life and hope to some other women's sons, some other children's fathers.

"Are you crazy?" replies John Doe's mother. "That stuff's his. We're not giving nothing away."

"Fine," says Watson. She has given up arguing with selfishness—all it's ever accomplished is to increase her aggravation. Senseless tragedy is senseless tragedy, and it won't be redeemed.

Tom is checking John Doe's pressure. "It's going down."

"No shit," replies Watson, nudging the Foley collection bag with her foot. It is topping off with dilute urine. "When was this changed?"

"Half an hour ago. I think."

"He's pissing out pure water. So, what's that mean?"

The student looks at her blankly.

"Diabetes insipidus," she explains. "Posterior pituitary's gone."

He looks at her with surprise. Despite all the lectures and exam questions on renal physiology and sodium homeostasis, he has not until this moment realized that the facts he learned might apply to actual patients. "What do we do?"

She considers. If she follows the logical path, now that the next-of-kin has refused organ donation, and simply turns off the ventilator, she will have to notify the family, declare the patient legally dead, and go through all the other bureaucratic nonsense that such a case entails. There just isn't time for this; she has patients waiting in the emergency room.

"Vasopressin, and chase the fluids," she says, pointing at the as yet uncreased *Manual of Medical Therapeutics* in Tom's right coat pocket. "Read about D.I. Hey, what a learning experience!"

Hearing her voice, the bandaged patient across the aisle wakes. "Waitress, I want a tuna fish sandwich."

It is almost five before she finishes in the emergency room, having seen a succession of head injuries, hysterics, seizures (alcohol withdrawal, and patients with epilepsy who neglected to take their pills), and finally a brain hemorrhage stroke (a hypertensive who did not take his pills).

She calls the unit. Fred the intern comes on the line. "Got a big bleed, needs a bed in the unit. I'll be right up, and disconnect John Doe."

"Too late," replies Fred. "He crashed and Tom couldn't handle it. I just declared him."

"Great." That will save her some time. Then she hears yelling in the background. "What's up?"

"That surgeon. He came in just when Doe transferred to the Eternal Care Unit, and he's pitching a fit."

"Doesn't he know the family refused?"

A phrase comes through, barely comprehensible. "You killed him! Now you've killed four other people too!"

"Shit," Watson cries. "Get him off of Tom. I'll be right there." She drops the receiver back onto the hook, tells a nurse "Hold him here in the E.R. till we clear the bed," and strides the yellow line in the basement to the stairway. Bounding up the stairs, she almost collides with the surgery chief.

"Where the hell do you get the right to yell at my student?"

"You stupid shits let him die!"

"He was *already* dead, goddamn it."

She pushes past him, not hearing his reply in its entirety. It just doesn't pay to fight with people who are taller and more powerful. Heading into the unit, she sees the nurse and her aide already fussing over the body. The room is quieter now that the respirator has stopped its cycling. The deputy is awake, and talking softly into the telephone.

"Tom? Hey, Fred, where's Tom?"

The intern is writing the death note. Not looking up, he points out the door.

"Where'd he go?"

The nurse smiles as she replies. She hates her dead-end, thankless, underpaid job in this awful excuse for a hospital. The distress of young doctors in training is one of the few things in her life that gives her any pleasure. "That doctor kept calling him a murderer, and he looked like he was going to cry, and he left."

"Oh God," Watson whispers. She knows where he has gone. She knows she has to stop him.

There is a place of which all doctors know, though none are told. It may be reached by many paths. Watson runs to the stairwell in the basement, and then up to the old ward. She can see fresh footprints in the dust, leading to the door that should not be there. It opens with a wrench, and she takes the dark and twisted stairs cautiously. At the bottom, she is in the basement again, unlit save by small, high windows half-blocked by debris. The air is still and musty, and the only sounds are her breathing, and the rustle of something that she hopes is a mouse.

"Tom?" she calls, then heads off down the corridor. Further down it is lined with cabinets filled with pathology slides. They spill out of the drawers and a few lie upon the floor. Stopping as the basement becomes a tunnel, she leans briefly against a cabinet. A slide falls to the ground, shattering. Watson bends over, glancing at the remnants.

A slice of cervical spinal cord lies embedded for eternity between glass and coverslip. The stain has faded over the years, but the dorsal and lateral columns are clearly paler. This is the autopsy relic of some man or woman born years before Watson, or even Watson's parents; to die then also, of a disease that now Watson can recognize with an offhand glance, and could treat easily with B-12 injections. Is life fair? she thinks. Not hardly.

She stands and sprints down the tunnel. A veritable catacomb lies beneath the hospital. There are tunnels between buildings; dank tunnels to the mental hospital a block away (said to be more safe than crossing the street in the middle of the night, but none the less avoided); unknown tunnels to unknown places. Every few years a drunk will wander out of the emergency room and get lost in the tunnels, to be found weeks later by horrified engineers. And then there is this tunnel, which intersects with none of the others.

A single window is set into the wall. Watson pauses, wipes clear a circle on the glass, and finds herself looking into the hospital's pathology suite from an unexpected view. She is down low, near the antique autopsy table with its grooves and pails. Across from her is the door into the morgue, and to the left she can see the steep, hard rows of the amphitheater.

She runs on. It is close now. If she stops, holds her breath, concentrates, she might hear a variety of sounds. Sobs. Moans. Agonal respirations. The lamentations of the living and the final exhalations of the dying. The screams of the delirious and the shrieks of the unanaesthetized.

Ahead is a halo of light, coming around the edges of a door in the wall at the end of the tunnel. It is a wooden door, dark, ponderous, smooth and pale about the handle, and the brass embossed sign, in square letters with serifs, bears the name. THE JULY WARD.

Tom has his hand upon the knob, and is preparing to enter. "No!" shouts Watson, managing to reach him and slam shut the door, while spinning him away from it. "No, it's not your time yet. . . ."

He looks at her with reddened eyes. Where does the light come from, now that the door is closed? She only knows that she can see the tears, welling in the inner canthi of his eyes.

"It's not your time yet," she repeats. "You're not a doctor, you can't go in there. Or you'll never come out."

"But I killed him . . . the surgery chief said . . ."

"The surgery chief is an asshole. You didn't kill John Doe. He was already dead!"

She leads him back down the hall. "You can't go in there yet. Not yet.

"In two years, on July first, you'll become an intern. Someday you'll have a patient. You won't know what's wrong—you're young, inexperienced, you can't know everything, and ultimately no one else can help you. It's inevitable. Someday—maybe it'll be in July, maybe it won't—someday, someone will die because you don't know something, or you made a wrong decision. And you're a doctor. Then, you can come here. You may be in another hospital entirely, but you'll come here, and you'll find your patient. . . ."

He looks back. The door seems indistinct now. "Did you . . ."

"Do you know how many pages there are in *Harrison's Textbook of Internal Medicine?*" she asks. "At least 1200, big pages, with little print. You know how much mention rhabdomyolysis gets in *Harrison's?* One line. One line about a fairly frequent, potentially fatal condition. I've read a sixty page paper on it. But that was a little late."

They find themselves, strangely, in the basement of the hospital near the yellow line, which they follow toward the ICU. A gurney passes by, pushed by an orderly. Something large and wrapped in plastic lies on the gurney, its identity undisguised by a sheet.

Watson and Tom stand to the side, letting the gurney pass. She waves. "Goodbye, John Doe #3."

"Now what?"

She shrugs. "Now you go home and get a good night's sleep. We're on call again tomorrow." She stops a moment, frowning. "I imagine it'll be a tough day, too. The chief won't stay around much, now that we've lost our deputy."

Tomorrow is indeed a bad day. They miss lunch, they miss dinner. The Dude Brothers have been busy. The unit is full of head trauma cases, with more on the ward, making do with less observation. The paraplegic patient, still in the unit because of a mysterious fever, has gone beyond anger and is depressed now, speaking to no one. To either side of him, semi-conscious men moan and occasionally retch. As Watson passes the bandaged man in bed four, he sits bolt upright, stares at her, and shouts, "I want a tuna fish sand-wich!"

"Stand in line," she replies.

Tom has been futilely sticking a syringe over and over into one of the new admissions, trying to start an intravenous line. Watson comes over to watch him.

"You're getting the hang of it," she remarks. "Only you'll never get this one."

He shakes his head. "These are great veins. They're standing right up, you can see them . . . it must be my technique."

"Your technique's fine, the fault's his. He's a junkie. Those veins are thrombosed." She takes away the arm, and hunts. There's some-thing on the right thumb that she may be able to thread with a 22-gauge butterfly needle. It's that, or a central line.

"Make you a deal," she says. "You go for burgers, and I'll get the IV."

"Fries and a shake?"

"Diet cola."

He laughs, hunts his many pockets for car keys, and leaves. She sits down and reapplies the tourniquet, slapping the man's forearm to bring up the veins. They're all shot, literally. Maybe she should go on TV, as a public service announcement. Don't shoot dope, kids. You'll ruin your veins. Then, when the doctors need to put in an IV, they'll have to stick a big old needle right into the major veins in your chest, with the chance of bleeding, or infection, or a col-lapsed lung.

"Aha." She decides she can get that sucker on the thumb after all, maybe even with a 20-gauge. Having survived an internship, Watson has the hubris to believe that she could draw blood from a turnip. She tears off strips of tape, opens the betadine ointment, has everything ready, then wipes alcohol on the vein and stops.

"Damn." She'll need an armboard. "Hey," she calls. No one an-swers. The night nurse must be busy, or asleep somewhere. She drops the arm back on the bed, tourniquet still on. Were he conscious, the man would be writhing in pain. She goes into the stock room in front, hunting angrily. Don't they have anything? And if so, why isn't it where it should be?

She hears the doors to the unit open.

"Good," she mutters. It's past visiting hours, so it can only be the nurse returning. She'll know where the armboards are. Unless, of course, it's Tom, coming back to see if she prefers Burger King or McDonald's. She heads out of the supply room, and freezes.

"What do you guys want?" says the voice of the paraplegic drug dealer.

"We don't want you to talk," a voice replies.

"Oh shit," Watson starts to say, and shrinks back into the doorway. *Oh shit.* The chief resident's paranoia was on target.

She can hear the sound of a gun, of silenced bullets going into soft flesh and the mattress behind. *Thock thock thock.* Just like on TV. She holds her breath, afraid to breathe. They'll be looking around the unit now, anyone else they need to waste? They are going from bed to bed, now they are at the back end of the unit. Two of them. Pistols, not Uzis. The chief resident was wrong. If they'll just go in to check the nursing lounge, maybe she can duck out.

She is almost to the front door when the patient in bed four sees her. "Waitress!"

The men with guns bolt out of the lounge, and she abandons silence and begins to run. A bullet passes by her head. Pistols must be hard to aim. No wonder the bullets always seem to wind up in unexpected places in her patients.

Ducking into the stairwell, she wishes she'd stayed in better shape. She can work thirty-six hours straight, but running is beyond her. Already, as she heads down the basement, hearing the stairwell door slam and then open again behind her, already she is winded.

Where to go? The pharmacy? Locked. The emergency room? They do have a guard there. But by the time he figures out what's going on, figures out how to draw his gun, the place will be an abbatoir. Where to go?

She knows.

She cuts off into a tunnel. Why did they have to build the morgue so far away, so cut off even from the original hospital? Was it to contain germs? Or as some kind of symbolic gesture?

"Stop, motherfucker!" a man's voice yells at her. The shot that follows makes compliance unlikely. Goddam, which way? She's only been to one autopsy here. Go ahead, they tell the docs. Keep Dad or Grampa or little Joey alive long after he should be allowed to die. So we keep his heart going and his lungs working and keep him in agony because his body can't survive, but they won't let us let him go. And when he finally dies, days or weeks or months after he should have—You want an autopsy? What, are you crazy? Hasn't he suffered enough?

The morgue. This is the way. She tries the door, then hits it angrily with her palm. Locked. Okay. Up the tunnel. It's slanting uphill. If you lost your grip on a gurney carrying a corpse, it would careen downhill until it ran into a wall, or came to rest near the outpatient pharmacy, where the clinic patients wait to have their prescriptions filled. Wouldn't that be a cheerful sight?

The door to the amphitheater is unlocked. It's dark inside, except for a light someone's left on down in front, by the display cases. Did doctors ever trip on these precipitous stairs, interrupting some learned professor's discourse as they toppled to their deaths? She has to take them slowly, watched by the ancient dissections below. Here are skeletons and bottled fetuses and hands, palms flayed open to show their inner workings, reaching out as on the Sistine Chapel. Here is the preserved torso of a young man who lived and died before motorcars or radio, and when he was struck down by a horsedrawn trolley, astonished doctors found that his organs were all on the wrong side. Here is the face of an infant with a single eye, and a trunk-like nose above it. Here are legs poised forever to step, hearts waiting to beat. Here are the heads of unsuspecting paupers who have been made into demonstrations of normal anatomy, and wear expressions that seem vaguely surprised.

She gets to the door with the window, alongside the guttered table with its century of knife marks. The door is barely noticeable, dark wood faded into dark wood. She grabs the handle and twists. It is not locked. Who would want to try it? But it is stuck, and she takes it with both hands and braces her foot and pulls. The men are coming in the door now, about to take aim but momentarily shocked by the grisly displays.

"Sheeeit," a man says. The other whistles.

Watson snatches up the nearest object, a breadloafed slice of brain embedded in a block of glass. It is very old; the definition between gray and white matter has faded, and the sloshing liquid inside has a froth at the top, yellow cholesterol leached out over the years. She throws the specimen, then another, and finally the entire cerebellum for good measure. None come close, but the sounds of smashing and the smell of ancient fixative give her a feeling of accomplishment.

The nearest thug raises his pistol. Watson falls back against the door—and it opens outward.

"I'll be damned," she says, and begins to run down the hall, past the rows of cabinets, too heavy to topple. Behind her, she can hear curses, as her foes try to get down the steep steps, now slick with lipid-rich alcohol and bits of brain.

They aren't even trying to shoot anymore, just running after her, closing the lead. She doesn't want to think about what's going to happen when they catch her. And then she sees it. The dark door and the brass sign.

She pulls it open, and she is inside. Inside the July Ward.

It is an old-fashioned ward, beds down either side, but some are barely pallets, others old-fashioned hospital beds, still others are high tech automatic beds, one even with a ventilator at its side. Patients stare at her from each bed, recognize that she is not the one for whom they wait, and look away. Ghostly orderlies—she cannot make out their details—approach, recognize her as a doctor, and step aside deferentially.

She stops running, smooths her white coat and straightens her scrubsuit, then goes down the row of beds, walking purposefully but sedately, the way a doctor should, glancing at the nametags and the bedside vitals charts. Many of the patients in the newer beds are in their nineties, and all patients in their nineties look alike.

Behind her, she can hear her enemies enter, hears a gunshot that seems to hit the ceiling, hears polite but firm voices (whispery, unreal).

"You cannot be here."

"Leggo, man. Shit, what *is* this?"

"This is the July Ward," comes the answer. "In this ward we admit only special patients: the first patient that a doctor lets die too soon; that a doctor kills. You cannot be here."

Watson has found the bed she is looking for. There is an old woman on it, frail and edematous, fluids running into an arm marked with bruises and swelling from ancient veins that cannot long support a line. The bag at the end of the catheter shows scant urine, with the faint pink tinge that Watson now knows might mean rhabdomyolysis, muscle breakdown products that, left untreated— or even despite treatment—may kill the kidneys. And the patient.

The woman in the bed looks up. "Yes, dear?" she asks. You can hear the fluid in her lungs as she speaks.

"I came to . . . say I'm sorry."

"You've already apologized," the woman replies, very kindly. "You'll have to stop coming here. It just isn't healthy." Watson turns away, and the old woman calls after her, softening the hard advice. "But thank you for visiting, dear. It was very kind."

Behind her, she can hear the woman address the patient in the next bed. "My doctor. Such a nice girl."

Watson strides back between the rows of patients, past the two gunmen, subdued now by orderlies. She sees the men, faces blanched with fear, unable to speak as they twist in the grip of arms that will not come into focus. Their eyes are wide with terror and pleading, and she finds it hard to not stop and order their release. But she does have some common sense.

"You keep this ward very well," Watson says. The orderlies nod. It is always good for a doctor to compliment the staff on a job well done. "I won't be back."

She closes the door behind her. What will become of the gunmen? She has no idea. But she knows this: only two kinds of people may enter the July Ward—doctors, and the dead. And only the doctors may leave.

But not completely. Never completely.

There is a place of which all doctors know, but none will speak.

The Kidnapping of Baroness 5

Katherine MacLean

Her hands were tired from a yesterday of setting broken bones and sewing wounds. Two young sentries had playfully wrestled each other over the edge of a castle parapet, and all their friends and relatives had hovered around while she worked, telling each other frightful predictions of lifelong crippling and assuring her that they had faith in her contracts with friendly spirits and the power of positive healing. They had not remarked that she was using the power of positive bone setting, gluing and sewing.

Occasionally she had remembered to mutter some molecular chemistry to sound mysterious, and once, uncovering some bad damage, she had muttered a genuine prayer directed to luck, fate, the Universal Spirit and the will to live.

Lady Witch let the reins go slack on the neck of her horse and rubbed her wrists. The morning sun seemed too bright. She was feeling a slight headache from the friendly party of celebration that had followed her success. No one feared her in Lord Randolph's area of command. They knew that Lord Randolph and his towns had her affection.

She remembered Lord Randolph's ruddy beaming face, and the pretty children of his wives, and envied them. She let her mind drift to plans to improve their genetic line.

Her horse ambled down the weedy green and brown of Route 111, avoiding holes and wagon ruts.

Her guard of four horse soldiers, three of them teenagers, one of them older, upright and handsome, drifted with her, while they sang an old song and tried to complete a memory of the new words someone had made up last night. Before dawn she had curled on a sofa and slept while the new song words were sung. The wandering choral harmony echoed on the edge of memory with a mood of foggy friendship and romance. Reluctantly she tried to plan a day of hard work in her laboratory and breeding farm, and began to brace herself to be stern and mysterious, to keep her workers terrified of her magic.

Their horses turned into the familiar stunted sage bushes of the old unused turnpike extension and picked their way along a narrow horse trail beside deep ruts of wagon wheels. Crickets sang and blue jays cawed.

The wind shifted. Their horses snorted and then whinnied with nervous excitement. They had scented something unusual ahead.

Instantly quiet, Lady Witch and her party drew rein and looked along the road. The horse soldiers unslung bows and listened. There was no sound except the singing of birds and crickets and frogs. Cautiously the five moved onward and paused again. Ball-like horse droppings and many hoofprints led from Mountain Road, the route to Lady Witch's land. The new tracks turned east toward the coast and Route 1. Their own horses snuffled and snorted, looking east, and then shifted their interest to nibbling clumps of long grass.

"Last night or early dawn before the ground dried," muttered the oldest soldier. "But they could have left a detachment behind. Stay on guard."

Lady Witch dismounted and let her horse munch grass while she looked at the tracks. Many small-hoofed horses, presumably carrying riders. Deep tracks indicated heavy wagons pulled laboriously by cattle. The horsemen had ridden in two bunches, before and behind the wagons.

Her escorts stayed on their horses, guarding her, their arrows nocked in their bows, scanning the trees for ambush. Their horses grazed quietly. "Let's hope it is just a traveling show and trade," she said and remounted.

The handsome, older soldier had also been studying the tracks. "If they're not an honest trader circus, they had plenty of time to loot and swing over to Route 1 to get away south. I count about twenty ponies, two old plough horses, and three oxen."

"I count three burros," said a mercenary from the inland plains. "They could be a small part of a nomad army. Where I used to live, pony and burro tracks like this were from an army. They burned farms sometimes, and sometimes in fall took over an area, killed the men, made the women and children work for them and settled in for the winter."

She imagined possible massacres. The oldest gave a command, and the soldiers galloped away, following the tracks. Lady Witch restrained her horse from following, and watched the horsemen call and point where more hoofprints came up from the old railroad trail and joined the first band. The strangers had been numerous.

Left alone, she felt nervous and watched the forest suspiciously. The older soldier returned, bringing the mercenary recruit who knew of nomads. They briskly traded horses, the officer giving up his own big stallion and trading their saddlebags. "Take the fast lane to Lord Randolph and report this."

In the distance the other two horsemen stopped and waved and pointed north, then turned onto Route 1, following the tracks.

"The strangers went north on Route 1. Report that. Go!"

The young soldier put the stallion into a gallop.

"What weapons do you have, Lady?" The officer beside her was busy settling leather plates of armor around his arms and torso. The inlaid enamel insignia on his armor revealed that he was an officer in charge of recruitment and emergency supplies.

She was glad to have the most experienced one to guard her. Ahead there could be looters lingering in captured farms. She checked her saddlebag. "Only a medical kit, a hollow tool handle with some tools inside, and some magic."

"Is any of your magic good in a fight?"

"I can curse them with infertility, make blinding flashes, and conjure up a smoke demon."

"If they came from so far away they've never heard of you, it won't scare them. Can your demon fight?"

"No. Sorry."

"I respect your magic, Lady. You have great skill in healing. But if they have never heard of you and you look threatening, one arrow will do for you and your magic together. You should have carried armor."

"I have enough to carry." She felt a headache from lack of sleep, and her eyes strained, looking for enemy motion among the trees.

He tapped his horse forward into Mountain Road, and they galloped southward over the late summer weeds. Black dirt and old asphalt showed through hoof marks, and the wide wheels of loaded wagons had pressed down the goldenrod and dry grass.

Apprehensively waiting to see the first farm along the way, Lady Witch imagined burnt ruins and corpses. When they rounded the bend she was glad to see the familiar shingled house unburned, and the old neighbor alive forking corn ears in a drying rack. She paused for a deep sigh of relief, then called to him. "We're following tracks. See anything?"

The old man put down his pitchfork, squinting to see them. "Nope. I been up since sunup, me and my nephews. Nobody on the road."

The soldier raised his voice. "Did you hear anything in the night, like a crowd going by, or wagons?"

The farmer came closer, interested. "Awful loud wind last night. Gusty. Roaring in the pines. If there had been anything, no way I could have heard it."

"Are you missing anything?"

"Only missing my dog. Off hunting rabbits maybe."

"Or killed to keep him from barking," muttered the soldier.

They galloped away, and Lady Witch looked back and saw the farmer standing in the middle of the road, reading the clear story of hoofprints and wagon ruts. His stance showed worry. No old man and wife and two half-grown nephews could have withstood that pack if they had turned aside to loot.

Lady Witch tapped her heels into the sides of her horse, keeping him at a gallop. The cool fall wind went by her face as comfortably as if nothing could be wrong. The next farm looked untouched, and the metal repairs man was out in his shed by the side of the road, two ends of a broken axle glowing in the forge. He waved and called, "See the tracks?"

"Saw them," shouted the soldier, not slowing, and Lady Witch looked ahead and shook the reins back to a gallop.

"Who are they?" the handyman shouted after them, but she did not answer. A witch woman should have predicted trouble coming and warned everybody. Best to avoid the question.

The wind was in her face, but there was no smell of burned houses.

She stopped at the entrance to the holdings given her by Lord Randolph, and saw that the wagon tracks and hoofprints had entered and left again.

The gate was unlocked and open. It showed none of the damage that would have been done to it if it had been forced open. Reading the tracks with increasing pessimism, she walked the horse up the steep road. The wagon tracks dented more heavily on the way down. Loaded with loot? She mentioned it.

"We'll see what they took when we get there," said the officer. His manner was fatherly. Apparently he did not believe the stories that she was very old, over twenty-five. If he was the sort who went in for disbelief, stories of her powers as a witch probably did not impress him. As she came over the hill she saw glimpses of young workers busily neatening up the yard and repairing fences. Up the hill among the trees a boy tending white goats saw her and waved, but the house workers kept their heads down and kept on working as she and the soldier approached. "Everything is too neat," she muttered. "They must have done something wrong."

No one came from her house and laboratory to greet her. They dismounted and Lady Witch led the way into her house. She saw the cook ducking back into the kitchen leaving two plates set on the table near a covered stewpot. Why were they all afraid to face her?

"Come here!" yelled Lady Witch. "Where is everybody? Is anyone dead?"

A small boy escaped from reaching hands in the kitchen and darted to her, shrilling, "Lady Witch! Lady Witch! The demons have taken Lord Randolph and Lord Jeffrey."

"Oh no!" Lord Randolph and Lord Jeffrey were pigs, but of incalculable value, having been made histogenic organ compatible with the human Lords Randolph and Jeffrey of the same name. The two lords of neighboring counties were overly brave, planning to lead in the front of battle in a necessary war and shorten their already short lifespans. They soon might need blood transfusions and replacement parts. For the rescue of all other patients, piglets that were totally compatible to all humans and loaded with human gene improvements had been born few and stunted, and she had just lost the life of the only survivor—sacrificed for the repair of the two reckless sentries.

"Has Baroness 5 given birth? Is she all right?"

"I don't know! They took her too!" the boy shrilled.

"No!" She ran to the back, but the pens were floored with fresh straw and totally empty. She dashed into her laboratory, startling a boy who was feeding the caged rats. He took a look at her face and fled.

Tears were running down her face. She sat and stared ahead.

A hand touched her arm. It was the soldier, regarding her with a light of eagerness and awe. "Did you repair that radio?"

"Somebody found it in an old cellar. The field reversal hadn't burned it out." She rested both elbows and put her face down in her hands. "What are you doing here? Nobody has permission to come in here."

"I came to tell you there was no blood. The pigs were not killed. The ones who cleaned up the pens and yard told me there was no blood. If the nomads loaded them in the wagons alive, they must have wanted to keep them alive. I thought you'd want to know."

Her staff should have told her when she arrived, but they had been afraid to face her. She usually used trickery to impress them with the power of her curses, and she had let them see her talking with smoke demons, but it was all just to make sure they followed scientific directions to the dot. She had not meant them to be so cowed and afraid that they could not tell her bad news.

She called them all together. They denied seeing anything. Gently she asked the boy, Billy, "Why didn't anybody see them take the pigs?"

Billy danced with eagerness. "The demons were out in the wind, howling, and everyone was down in the old kitchen, where we had the doors and windows barred and a big fire in the fireplace to keep the demons from coming down the chimney. I heard the demons fighting the pigs. The pigs squealed and fought and crashed against the walls, but Cook would not let me go look. Can I help you go fight demons and put them back into bottles?"

Lady Witch raised her voice and projected it at the half-open door. "Whose turn was it to lock the gates at night and stand sentry? Send for him. The gates were unlocked!"

When the teenager arrived he was sullen. "Yesterday your smoke ghosts got loose. They turned into fog and floated through the woods getting bigger and making faces. Then they started roaring and shaking the trees. We locked ourselves in the house. I didn't know the demons were going to roar and beat on the house all night, and keep us locked in."

"That was just fog and wind," she said impatiently. Then she

wondered if she should argue. Her smoke demons were only a
heavy smoke that coiled in rounded shapes and webbed to itself and
stayed swaying around the bottle until she put out the flame. The
likeness to demons relied on the power of imagination. If her staff
had seen huge smoke shapes in drifting fog, their awed stories
could improve her fame. She resolved to send these people back to
Lord Randolph before their imaginations went berserk. Better to
accept a new staff ordered by Lord Jeffrey.

But it would be better to let them believe in their fog demons—
better to not contradict their stories. She apologized, "I'm sorry. All
my power was diverted to Lord Randolph's fort. I was using up all
my spells to hold death away from the two young idiots who de-
served their bad luck. Nothing was left to hold back the demons."

Still crowding at the doors and windows, young men and
women nodded vigorously and agreed in deferential tones. "Yes, yes.
It's not your fault, Lady. They got out of their bottles and grew very
big. They roared and shook trees. We came here and barred the
doors. They beat on the walls and shutters all night."

She gestured to the man to continue his excuses for leaving the
gates open. He continued with more confidence, "I know about
demons; my cousin was an exorcist. She specialized in demons.
Your demons broke the door to the animal stables and took back
your demon pigs, and left hoofprints. Demons leave hoofprints."

Again everyone she employed nodded agreement.

Their lack of reasoning infuriated her. Smoke and fog leaving
hoofprints? Demons using wagons and leaving wagon tracks? She
took a deep breath to yell at them all. The older soldier moved between her and the man.

"Were they the kind of demon whose hoofprints look like goats
or like ponies or like horses?" he asked gently.

"Like ponies!" the man replied, but his glance darted around
the room from door to window as if seeking escape from sudden
doubts.

"Good. They were in league with some passing nomads who put

the pigs into a wagon. We can follow that trail. The demons are not likely to be out in sunshine."

"I'm going to help you get Lord Randolph back!" Little Billy danced with eagerness.

Only children volunteered. The older ones held them back and muttered about smoke demons. She could have ordered them to come with her, but if they were unwilling and frightened they would be useless. She ordered three fresh horses. Somehow she must get back the two boars and Baroness 5, before she gave birth. The nomad thieves would be so startled by what would issue forth from the great sow that they could panic and kill all the sow's offspring, and cause the failure of her medicine plus years of delay in her research. In a very few years another generation would age and die and friends whom she had promised to save would be gone.

The handsome older officer of recruitment, the little boy, and Lady Witch followed the track of the nomad band, galloping past farms and long deserted store buildings and empty churches to a crossroads. There was an inn at the crossroads that usually welcomed travelers with the aromas of breakfast or lunch. Now there were no welcoming aromas and all doors were open and silent.

With an arrow nocked and ready, the soldier sidled his horse up against the wall and listened. No sound. Little Billy slid down from his saddle. He ignored their fierce gestures for caution and ran into the inn. "Innkeeper Roger, Innkeeper Roger, Lady Witch is here hunting for nomads." There was no answer to the shrill childish calls going through the rooms of the inn, but there was a thump, whispers, and rustling from the hayloft above the stable and feet on the creaking ladder, and at last the innkeeper and his daughters appeared, brushing hay from their clothes. He was pudgy and beginning to age at about twenty-two. They were twins still growing. They whispered, "Are they gone?"

The soldier was impatient. "We're following their trail. They are long gone."

The older of the two girls said politely, "Your permission, Lady.

We must go see what the thieves have taken." The two girls ran to
the inn, and let out shrieks of rage. "Pappa! They took all the kegs
of wine."

He remained looking up at her, absently combing straw out of
his hair with spread fingers. "Can you do anything for us, Lady?"

"Not until we catch up. How long since they were here?"

The innkeeper looked at the Sun. "More than an hour."

The soldier snorted. "By the time we catch up they will be having a party with your wine."

Lady Witch felt forlornly that she should have warned them all
somehow. She offered an excuse. "I was away from home, and when
I returned my pigs had been stolen. It will interfere with my magic.
I must get them back."

The innkeeper stayed looking at her, still absently combing his
hair with his fingers. "I heard the pigs squeal in both wagons, but I
did not know they were your magic pigs, Lady. What becomes of
the magic if they are eaten? What becomes of the lords whose
names they carry?"

"God knows," said Lady Witch. "I must get them back. The
Baroness is about to give birth."

"Give birth to what, Milady?"

"Do not meddle in magic," she replied sharply. "I must be with
her when she delivers or there will be—ah, something happening."
She made a vague gesture indicating nothing in particular and
avoided his inquiring gaze. "I am not here to attack the nomads.
Lord Randolph is sending the soldiers from the fort for that. I need
to be by the side of The Baroness when she delivers, to complete
the Magic." She made the word sound mysterious and important.
But it was important. Was there no one else in the Solar System
doing research on prions? Did they all think that the shortening of
life on Earth was only a radiation effect from the time the magnetic
poles reversed and would wear off? It was not wearing off, and the
level of knowledge was dropping as each generation was given too
short a time to pass on more than survival skills to the next genera-

tion. With five years delay most of her friends could die. She braced herself for danger. "Get me something to wear that looks like one of the nomad women. I must get into their camp."

They brought her a brown dress. She tied it to the saddle. "Let's go! Hurry!"

The soldier had watered the horses and was splashing water over his head and arms. He rose, dripping, and mounted.

The girls came out and passed up water bottles. "We hope you hit them with lightning, Lady Witch."

She could make no promises of what she could do against armed men, so she was silent. The innkeeper apologized, "I would like to go with you to fight but I have to stay and protect my daughters."

Again they galloped down the turnpike extension, enjoying the level footing of weeds over underlying cement that let their horses run smoothly. Later and closer to the ocean they stopped at a looted farm and helped the family pick up the wreckage of their doors while they listened to their description of the nomads who had just left. Their hens and eggs had been taken, the milk cow had been driven away and some of the garden tools and all of their good clothes and best pots had been loaded into their own wagon and driven off with their horse.

The soldier helped them rehang the barn door on its hinges and listened to their story of barricading themselves in their house and hearing the thunderous bursting of the front doors. The house had been invaded and plundered but not one of the family had been hurt or killed, which put a better aspect on the looters.

Excitedly discussing it, the farm family collected eggs laid in stray corners and invited Lady Witch and the soldier to sit at their table, and promised a big tomato omelette breakfast with corn pancakes and butter.

Billy was hungry and eager, but Lady Witch wanted to push on and catch up with the looters. The family agreed to shelter the little boy and let their nine-year-old boy volunteer to guide Lady

Witch on a shortcut to get ahead of the nomad army, now slowed by the weight of loot.

The boy guided them away from the road, down a muddy bank of high reeds and into a great saltgrass marsh. The horses protested and walked carefully down a slope of yielding roots to where a small rowboat lay anchored on drying sand. The sand was as hard and flat as a road. The boy gestured them to follow and began to run. They trotted, following the track of hard damp sand. The dampness became puddles then a stream. They followed the sand path downhill. Dark banks of wet roots became higher on each side, and the marsh spread out before them to distant shores of trees. Toward the sea the shore road was hidden by trees. Ahead, puddles widened into shallows of salt water, reflecting banks and sky. The horses advanced into the bright blue shallows with careful steps, found the bottom was hard sand and began to trot again. The boy had run ahead and around a curve; the horses rounded the curve, galloping, and passed him, their hoofs splashing.

Water deepened to the horses' knees. The horses stopped, snorting uncertainly, looking out on a widening bay.

Lady Witch and the officer of supplies drew rein and looked around. To their right the lad waved, waist-deep in another stream. They turned to it and the horses trotted uphill again, snorting and splashing in the shallowing water. The banks were walls of roots populated by small scuttling crabs; they made cool shade against the hot sunlight and a wall they could not see over.

The boy climbed a bank and put his head over the edge. They stood up in their stirrups for height and looked over. They were almost at the edge of the marsh. Ahead, stands of thick bushes and high pines cut off the view of the sea. In the silence, a red-winged blackbird sang a high trill, a cow mooed, a calf bawled, a pig grunted. High voices called directions.

The lad signaled caution. They dismounted and led the horses up a damp sand track. The sun shone hotly on their backs and heads, and the wind shifted toward their faces and brought them a slow rumbling of ocean waves and the aromatic smoke of pine twig fires starting.

They put their heads together for quiet talk. "They are starting campfires," mumbled the officer. "Dinner next. You had better move fast, Lady."

Startling them, one of their horses whickered interest in the smell of strange horses. There was an answering whinny from the direction of the nomads' encampment. Lady Witch and the soldier gently held the horses' nostrils to silence them. The soldier handed the reins to the boy and murmured, "If they both start talking to the camp horses, we'll be under a pile of nomad soldiers. Take them back home."

The lad began carefully turning the horses, a hand alertly near their nostrils to avoid more sound while Lady Witch unslung her magic kit from the saddle.

She put on the brown clothing while the officer, sweating and pink in his heavy leather armor, went back to the last puddle and knelt and splashed water over his head and down his neck. He was a good-looking man, with reddish hair that curled close to his head when wet.

Sunlight was hot on her double layer of clothes. She walked back to a deep salt puddle, laid down in it and let it soak her back, then rolled over and put her face under. It was cool and clean in her mouth and nose and eyes. She got up with cold wet clothes clinging to her skin and suddenly felt chilly and exhilarated.

With a wild laugh she took the lead, running. The officer ran behind her, looking at her figure in the wet clothing. The sand path rose toward the surface of the marsh, the banks shrinking lower, not enough concealment now. They ran bent over in a hot shallowing ditch, then went up on the side on hands and knees to enter a thicket of bushes. The stems grew too close together and would not let them in. Making cautioning gestures that warned of listening sentries, the soldier pointed to the opening of a rabbit trail, like a low tunnel through the bushes. He slung his bow and sword well back on his shoulders and forced his way into the trail, leaning against the bush stems and bending them, crawling on elbows and knees. She tucked up her long skirt to let her knees work and followed, dragging her magic kit, crawling with forearms and elbows and knees over scratchy twigs and hard roots.

A change of wind brought her the sweet smell of a well-started wood fire. Fear returned. However fast she crawled, it was only crawling, not fast enough! What if Lord Randolph and Lord Jeffrey, the two boars, were being killed and cut into pork roasts? What if the pregnant sow, Baroness 5, gave birth and her offspring terrified the viewers into killing them all?

She ran her head into the soldier's boot. He had stopped. He reached a hand back where she could see it and gestured with one finger. She followed the gesture, turned aside through the thinning bushes and cautiously crawled to a green barrier of goldenrod and weeds. She parted the greenery and looked out at the nomad encampment. Near them oxen munched at the weeds. Under the cool shade of tall trees a natural carpet of orange pine needles extended in a mile of shade camp ground. Covered wagons were already parked, spaced far from each other.

Children were running to bring water and breaking dry pine branches for campfires, while a few women and many girls, garbed in scanty mixtures of furs and colorful clothes, were unpacking pots, setting up grills for cooking, bracing long poles and building porchlike extensions to the covered wagons.

"Where are the men?" she whispered.

"They expect attack," he whispered back. "Probably back laying ambushes."

She made an effort to see it from the nomad viewpoint. They were used to being followed by enraged property owners who wanted their possessions back, and occasionally they could expect to be attacked by a small army owned by a local military boss, mayor, police chief, Lord Something, Baron Something, King Somebody. There was no local government without a fort and a small army and a military leader with a title. From long experience of being attacked the nomads were ready with ambushes and counterattacks.

The officer whispered, "What's your plan?"

"I'll walk in alone and make sure the Baroness is all right, then tell them to return her and Lord Jeffrey and Lord Randolph. If they give me any trouble I'll curse them with infertility and nightmares."

He shifted uneasily and looked at her. "Not much of a plan. They'll just think you are a spy for Lord Randolph and do whatever they do to spies."

"Can you think of anything better?"

He looked away from her, back to the camp, and spoke reluctantly. "I can't stop you. If you get into trouble, just whistle, and I'll walk in and claim they're all surrounded by a vast army and I've come to negotiate terms of their surrender."

"Not much of a plan."

"No worse than yours," he replied, "Give me a good-bye kiss in case we both get killed."

She was surprised by his effrontery but pleased by his air of tired wisdom. At his age and experience, perhaps twenty-two, suddenly finding his hair greying, he could see death coming and had no fear of death in war. He knew that life was brief and sweet. In the bushes they tried a short kiss, found it comforting, and hugged.

From the camp came a deep elephantlike squeal followed by a peculiar string of grunts. The pregnant sow, Baroness 5, was beginning to give birth. "Uh oh! My patient calls." Lady Witch detached herself and ran toward the grunting. Ahead she saw a brush enclosure being raised higher by children piling branches. Inside it, behind a small watching crowd, she heard a man laughing and a female voice that chanted, "Soo soo sooo." Another squeal abruptly ended in contented grunts.

As Lady Witch forced through a small crowd of women she heard a male scream of frightened profanity and knew what she feared had happened. All her hurrying had not been fast enough. A man rushed by. "Oh my god! Sorcery!" People backing away bumped into her and stepped on her feet. She pushed by them, in a panic to protect the sow, and stumbled into the clear center of the crowd. She felt deep relief and gratitude for her good luck. On the ground before her was the huge sow and her first piglet, unharmed.

"Sorcery!" "Unnatural!" The ring of people backing away stared in horror.

"Sorcery" required good staging. If they fear it, add it to your advantage. Lady Witch reached into her kit, held up both hands and rubbed two objects together. One burst into a blue flame and the other into a yellow flame, and the light grew to a great dazzle.

Women ran and children screamed.

She added her howl to their screams. "Acetaldehyde, ketone. Baroness, turn again human and give birth to the blessed princess."

The enclosure suddenly was emptied of people. They watched from beyond the piled bushes. She threw the flares at the entrance to prevent return of the crowd and knelt at the side of the huge pink sow, who was again squealing and grunting and pushing and giving birth, now garishly lit by the blue and yellow magnesium flares she had salvaged from beached powerboats.

The sow's first issue lay waving his small arms, a healthy human baby, his placenta clinging like a red plastic bag around his legs. The placenta was from his own human tissue and had given him the equivalent of a human mother inside the sow. It had sent out hormones to force the sow and her piglets to accept proximity to human tissue.

"It was a baby!" someone was calling to newcomers beyond the thorn fence.

Various voices called, "Witchcraft! Demons! We have been cursed! Tell the sorcerer. A demon baby from a pig!" People were running toward the flares, asking what was happening. Some of their voices were male, deep and dangerous. A few minutes were left before the bright flares died and let the crowd back in the paddock and some man decided that the answer to all oddities was to kill them. She picked up the baby, cut the cord long and stripped off the rest of his placenta like peeling off a pink plastic package. She wiped the baby with the damp cloth of her dress and cleaned its smooth pink skin.

The infant boy took a deep breath and howled for a mother's warmth.

"Soo soo," she soothed and stood up, cradling him. He put his thumb in his mouth and went silent, looking at her with wide watchful eyes. This one carried some very unusual genes and also was a clone cross of the human males Lord Randolph and Lord Jeffrey and, as such, she had hoped he would inherit both kingdoms, but he did not show the right birthmarks to prove he had been fathered by either of them. He could be raised as an orphan, like Billy. He looked intelligent.

The flares fizzled out and the crowd surged in. She was surrounded by nomad children and young women breathing wonder, awe, and fear of witchcraft, and in male voices, angry attempts at explanation from those who did not believe in witchcraft and did not believe a pig had given birth to a human child. A drunken man tried to force his way to the front to kill the child and the others held him back. "Kill the demons," repeated one drunken voice, while another male voice soothed drunkenly, "Only a fake. Don't worry. Only a fake."

"Quiet!" Lady Witch raised her voice over the noise. "I must try to turn the Baroness back to a woman while she gives birth. I must save her next child from being a pig forever. Please let me do my work."

The crowd was ready for a show. They quieted and stared at the sow, waiting to see it turn into a human woman. Lady Witch muttered chemical formulas and felt the great belly to see which shape of bulge was nearest. Then she was busy helping push and then pull. Some of the crowd gasped in horror and others cheered as she pulled out another completely human infant. This one was a female, a clone-cross between her own genes and some dry tissue of a very famous scientist.

Some of the audience decided this was intended to be a magic show, and clapped. The cheering and clapping repeated more loudly when she cleaned this new baby and held her up, like a rabbit from a hat. "The Princess!"

While they clapped, the sow grunted and very easily gave forth four small shoats that were natural pigs, and those began to suckle. The babies heard the sucking sounds and began to whimper and grope the air with lips and tiny fists. They were hungry. Lady Witch laid the babies up against two of the many nipples.

There were gasps of protest from the audience and growls and threats from a few men. In their morality, babies should not suckle sows. Distraction was needed. Lady Witch called out. "We need a volunteer to tend to the babies. This sow is Baroness 5, my captive. She was a Lady Baroness whose real name I keep secret. I turned her to a pig when she disobeyed me. I am sorry for it now, and I am sorry I can't change the enchantment. The babies need to be cared for. They need someone to make sure that the sow does not lie on them. Can anyone volunteer to help the babies?"

"Real babies." "A little princess." Whispers spread among the women. They lost their fear and moved toward the babies with smiles, and bent toward them, cooing. There were noises from the back of the crowd and barked demands to clear the way. Two leather-armored men with short swords and leather shields shouldered through the crowd to Lady Witch and grabbed her arms in a hard grip.

"The Sorcerer wants to see you," one barked.

She stiffened up as tall as she could and glared at their hands gripping her arms and switched her glare to their faces.

A woman screamed, "Ricci! Don't get her mad. She'll turn you into a pig!" The crowd agreed and pointed at the evidence, and the soldiers stared at a row of four suckling piglets and two suckling human infants, and understood. They let go of her arm and stood back. One said, "Uh . . . your pardon, Lady Sorcerer."

Lady Witch guessed that the other one was dangerous, for he backed away slowly, his sword gripped tightly in a warding position and his eyes as round as marbles.

The sorcerer-healer of these wandering people had made them too fearful of his magic. This nomad might go berserk from fear and attack her. She smiled at him. "I'm called Lady Witch. Please show me the way to your sorcerer."

To seem less threatening she turned her back to his round-eyed glare and smiled at a strong girl who was cooing at the babies. "You have a good heart. I choose you to help the babies while I am away." She saw a plump young woman also leaning over the babies from the other direction. "And you have experience. Help her. Don't let anything harm the babies. I trust you."

The two nomad soldiers had been whispering to each other. The one who had not been afraid raised his voice. "Come with us. The Sorcerer wishes to see you." He pointed.

"And I wish to see him." She avoided seeming to be a prisoner by walking rapidly in the direction he had pointed, letting the soldiers follow. The crowd trailed, chattering excitedly and hoping for new wonders.

As they passed the nearest campfire she smelled sizzling pork chops and saw a large caldron with chunks of meat, carrots, turnips, and potatoes beginning to boil. All her fears returned. "I hope my two enchanted boars are still alive," she said loudly to the two soldiers and the crowd following. "One is called Lord Randolph and the other Lord Jeffrey. They were stolen from me last night when The Baroness was taken."

"Pigs! The boars are men turned to pigs!" There were multiple exclamations of dismay, and some of the men ran, calling warnings at each cook fire against eating pork from any pig stolen the night before.

The two nomad soldiers brought her to a tentlike building cov-

ered with leather, fur side in. She pushed through a double flap. It
was darker inside except for orange and white parachute silk draped
around the dais, making a bright background of color for the sorcerer. He was thin and wrinkled, wearing a vest of furs turned
leather side out and gold chains with pendants of symbols. "Is this
the witch?" he demanded of the nomad soldiers. "She doesn't look
like a witch."

Lady Witch began to strip down to her whites. The soldiers
looked at her nervously. "She came into camp somehow and turned
two newborn piglets into human babies," said the calmer one. "She
said the sow was a human she had turned into a pig. That's
witchcraft. She's a sorcerer."

"Everybody saw it," said the other, nodding vigorously and
sweating. He watched Lady Witch throw the brown clothes down
and stand in the shining white uniform, shaking her long hair loose,
and he backed up against the door flaps and halfway out. "She's a
tech too! Look out for weapons!"

"Stand outside, both of you!" barked the sorcerer. They obeyed
eagerly.

Alone, the skinny man looked at her appraisingly. "You are a
biotech! I've found one! The locals down the coast talked of Lady
Witch living up this way doctoring and not getting old, and I heard
lies about enchanted pigs and demons. I didn't believe them."

"Believe them," she said.

He laughed. "I don't believe lies. You're a biotech. Those pigs
are laboratory animals. That's why they say you are a good healer.
Genetics and tissue culture. That's what I was looking—" He tried
to laugh again but choked and coughed pathetically.

She saw a pattern to his motions, the crying and crouching and
wincing of a child being hit, crying disguised by habit as coughing,
pain felt as illness. The unlucky man was trapped in a childhood
trauma of being beaten. She restrained herself from wanting to release him from it.

He straightened up and glared. "How long will it take you to teach me your foolery?"

"I don't teach my secrets!" she snapped. How could one teach biochemistry and genetics in their short lives? If a girl started to bear children at twelve years old she would die of senility at twenty-five with only three children produced and the youngest only eight. A boy occupied himself with helping the aging olders and learning work skills and fighting.

She liked the sorcerer for being clear-headed about what biotechnology had been all about. Many laboratories had been working on life extension. She herself had been in safe work, trans-planting helpful thymus tissue and prion resistant genes from car-nivores to herself. But many of her friends were researchers who had suspected prion viruses to be the killer, and complained that the prion viruses they studied worked too slowly to affect mice. She felt guilty on behalf of friends and researchers who had committed a possible great error and accident that no one knew about. New faster prion viruses could have been loosed with the magnetic pulse that burned out all safety controls.

The sorcerer should have been a young man. He was probably only twenty-four years old. He snarled, "You had better try to teach me. I'm master here. You will be a prisoner here until you obey me!"

She replied loudly and slowly, with deliberate clarity. "I will be a prisoner here for a very few days until I finish changing all your people into pigs and you have no one left to obey you."

Certain bulges of listening audience leaning against the outside walls of the tent jerked and vanished, and the soft thudding of foot-steps ran away.

She jerked a thumb at the tent walls. "They have sense enough to fear magic."

The old man glared at the walls. "It's a bluff. Fools, cowards!"

"Better cowards than pigs," she said loudly toward the remain-ing bulges of listeners leaning on the leather walls. "Now for our deal. You may keep one of the enchanted children. He is a great general reincarnated. But you must return the Baroness and the two boars and all the horses and the cow and the wagons and carts and tableware and casks of wine your people stole last night and this morning."

He rose and stamped around in a circle, trying to straighten his bent legs. "What do I want with babies who are really pigs or pigs who are really lords?" he snapped, wincing and creaking. "If you are really a biotech, I want the secret of eternal life!"

She sneered at him. "Eternal life? Even if I don't turn you into a pig, you are not likely to live more than another day. The forces of Lord Randolph and Lord Jeffrey already surround all exits from your camp. Only I can persuade them to let your people live."

A breathing presence at the door that she had thought was one of the nomad soldiers turned out to be a large bellowing man hung with swords and shiny armor too small for him. He was bellowing at the sorcerer. "What's this mess you have gotten us into? You senile fool! You led us here with your fortune-telling! You said it would be safe to conquer and settle! No resistance, you said!"

"General," quavered the skinny old man. "There are no armies. Lord Jeffrey and Lord Randolph are only some pigs looted from this madwoman and added to our herd. They can't surround anything."

"Pigs?" the general bellowed. "Our scouts say Lord Randolph and Lord Jeffrey are generals of forts north and west of here and have horse armies larger than ours. And I think we have camped on a dead-end point of land. You led us into a trap."

She spoke soothingly, "There is no danger if you do not shoot first. Just give me an honorable escort without weapons to cart my pigs and drive the other animals back to the farms they were taken from, and I will tell the two lords not to war on you." She hesitated, fear again cramping her heart. "My two boars were taken last night. They are called Lord Randolph and Lord Jeffrey and are very important to the lords of the forts. They must be treated with respect and spoken to politely."

The nomad general turned pale and thoughtful and wiped

traces of grease and gravy from his mustache and mouth. "I do not ask the name of every pork rack I eat," he growled uneasily. He put his head out of the tent and bellowed an inquiry and found out that the two boars were still alive.

Happy, she thought of adding to her success by rescuing the farm family's stolen chickens, but the odor of barbecued chicken was already strong in the air of the camp. It was not worthwhile to ask.

A lookout arrived, galloping, and reported that he had seen at least 150 mounted soldiers approaching from two or three miles back on the road and they would have already arrived at the last crossroads and be blocking the single road out. The camp outside was already changed in sound, the sharp commands of soldiers organizing a defense.

The general stepped outside into the shade of the pines. "What about the marsh?" he snapped. "Send scouts to find a way out through that marsh."

She whistled and the officer of supplies and recruiting rose from the bushes with his hands up peaceably and his enameled armor shining with his insignia. "You are surrounded," he said. "We will accept terms of surrender. Our policy is to give citizenship to immigrants if they get work on farms and join the army."

The old sorcerer straightened, smiling, then turned and glared at the nomad general like an angry hawk. "What do you mean I led you into a trap? Lady Witch has promised she will protect us. Her promise is good. We can settle here. I prophesied that this would be a safe place and I was right. I've been looking for this place all my life!"

The general nodded and sighed.

With the officer of supplies riding a recaptured horse ahead, Lady Witch triumphantly returned, riding in the first wagon with Baroness 5, leading a herd of recaptured cows, horses, and pigs.

They met the army of Lord Randolph and Lord Jeffrey drawn

up in battle formation at the other side of a clearing, just past a long bowshot from the nomad soldiers in the trees.

She was glad to see the round pink face of Lord Randolph, as usual taking unnecessary risks by riding around the front line. Randolph, laughing, shouted that he was being attacked by a herd of cows, his own officer of supplies, and a beautiful witch. The officer of supplies and recruitment shouted back that fear of their great army had forced the nomads to surrender, and he and Lady Witch had given their word that the army would not attack them if the nomads returned the local loot, gave back hostages, and settled peaceably for the winter. He galloped forward and rejoined his troops.

She let him explain and led the parade of recaptured animals and loot onward. Past the horse army she was met by a crowd of eager farm families running forward to welcome back their cattle. Little Billy was with them, joyous and important, boasting that he lived in Lady Witch's house and saw her do magic every day.

He was outshouted by the young nomad herdsmen shrilly claiming that they could have won the war, except for the unfair use of magic. They had surrendered only because a dangerous woman sorcerer had appeared in the middle of their camp and threatened to change them all to pigs, and had changed two newborn piglets into human babies to prove that her pigs had once been Lords.

The farm families did not believe that their Lady Witch could do this, and goggled as two young nomad women in the lead wagon held out the infants they carried, and then held them down to the side of the fat sow, where they nursed side by side with the piglets.

Beside the wagon, Billy asked to drive and she gave him a hand up. She passed him the willow switch, but he was worried. "Lady Witch, was my mother a pig?"

She had wanted everyone to believe he was only a normal human orphan, but it was too late for that. After the people had seen the origins of the two new babies in the charge of Lady Witch they would understand the sudden appearance of any unexplained babies.

Billy's brows were down and his mouth unhappy. She under-stood his fear. She had to give them all a story with strength and in-terest and glamour.

"No, my little scout, your mother was a lioness, and that is why you are so brave." And that was not completely a fairy tale, for car-nivores had genes of resistance to prions. And one set of her exper-imental genes had been from a lion.

Billy was trying to roar the whole way back to their farm and laboratory.

Speech Sounds

Octavia E. Butler

There was trouble aboard the Washington Boulevard bus. Rye had expected trouble sooner or later in her journey. She had put off going until loneliness and hopelessness drove her out. She believed she might have one group of relatives left alive—a brother and his two children twenty miles away in Pasadena. That was a day's journey one-way, if she were lucky. The unexpected arrival of the bus as she left her Virginia Road home had seemed to be a piece of luck—until the trouble began.

Two young men were involved in a disagreement of some kind, or, more likely, a misunderstanding. They stood in the aisle, grunting and gesturing at each other, each in his own uncertain "T" stance as the bus lurched over the potholes. The driver seemed to be putting some effort into keeping them off balance. Still, their gestures stopped just short of contact—mock punches, handgames of intimidation to replace lost curses.

People watched the pair, then looked at each other and made small anxious sounds. Two children whimpered.

Rye sat a few feet behind the disputants and across from the back door. She watched the two carefully, knowing the fight would begin when someone's nerve broke or someone's hand slipped or someone came to the end of his limited ability to communicate. These things could happen any time.

One of them happened as the bus hit an especially large pothole and one man, tall, thin, and sneering, was thrown into his shorter opponent.

Instantly, the shorter man drove his left fist into the disintegrating sneer. He hammered his larger opponent as though he neither had nor needed any weapon other than his left fist. He hit quickly enough, hard enough to batter his opponent down before the taller man could regain his balance or hit back even once.

People screamed or squawked in fear. Those nearby scrambled to get out of the way. Three more young men roared in excitement and gestured wildly. Then, somehow, a second dispute broke out between two of these three—probably because one inadvertently touched or hit the other.

As the second fight scattered frightened passengers, a woman shook the driver's shoulder and grunted as she gestured toward the fighting.

The driver grunted back through bared teeth. Frightened, the woman drew away.

Rye, knowing the methods of bus drivers, braced herself and held on to the crossbar of the seat in front of her. When the driver hit the brakes, she was ready and the combatants were not. They fell over seats and onto screaming passengers, creating even more confusion. At least one more fight started.

The instant the bus came to a full stop, Rye was on her feet, pushing the back door. At the second push, it opened and she jumped out, holding her pack in one arm. Several other passengers followed, but some stayed on the bus. Buses were so rare and irregular now, people rode when they could, no matter what. There might not be another bus today—or tomorrow. People started walking, and if they saw a bus they flagged it down. People making intercity trips like Rye's from Los Angeles to Pasadena made plans to camp out, or risked seeking shelter with locals who might rob or murder them.

The bus did not move, but Rye moved away from it. She intended to wait until the trouble was over and get on again, but if there was shooting, she wanted the protection of a tree. Thus, she was near the curb when a battered, blue Ford on the other side of the street made a U-turn and pulled up in front of the bus. Cars were rare these days—as rare as a severe shortage of fuel and of relatively unimpaired mechanics could make them. Cars that still ran were as likely to be used as weapons as they were to serve as transportation. Thus, when the driver of the Ford beckoned to Rye, she moved away warily. The driver got out—a big man, young, neatly bearded with dark, thick hair. He wore a long overcoat and a look of wariness that matched Rye's. She stood several feet from him, waiting to see what he would do. He looked at the bus, now rocking with the combat inside, then at the small cluster of passengers who had gotten off. Finally he looked at Rye again.

She returned his gaze, very much aware of the old forty-five automatic her jacket concealed. She watched his hands.

He pointed with his left hand toward the bus. The dark-tinted windows prevented him from seeing what was happening inside.

His use of the left hand interested Rye more than his obvious question. Left-handed people tended to be less impaired, more reasonable and comprehending, less driven by frustration, confusion, and anger.

She imitated his gesture, pointing toward the bus with her own left hand, then punching the air with both fists.

The man took off his coat revealing a Los Angeles Police Department uniform complete with baton and service revolver.

Rye took another step back from him. There was no more LAPD, no more *any* large organization, governmental or private. There were neighborhood patrols and armed individuals. That was all.

The man took something from his coat pocket, then threw the

coat into the car. Then he gestured Rye back, back toward the rear of the bus. He had something made of plastic in his hand. Rye did not understand what he wanted until he went to the rear door of the bus and beckoned her to stand there. She obeyed mainly out of curiosity. Cop or not, maybe he could do something to stop the stupid fighting.

He walked around the front of the bus, to the street side where the driver's window was open. There, she thought she saw him throw something into the bus. She was still trying to peer through the tinted glass when people began stumbling out the rear door, choking and weeping. Gas.

Rye caught an old woman who would have fallen, lifted two little children down when they were in danger of being knocked down and trampled. She could see the bearded man helping people at the front door. She caught a thin old man shoved out by one of the combatants. Staggered by the old man's weight, she was barely able to get out of the way as the last of the young men pushed his way out. This one, bleeding from nose and mouth, stumbled into another and they grappled blindly, still sobbing from the gas.

The bearded man helped the bus driver out through the front door, though the driver did not seem to appreciate his help. For a moment, Rye thought there would be another fight. The bearded man stepped back and watched the driver gesture threateningly, watched him shout in wordless anger.

The bearded man stood still, made no sound, refused to respond to clearly obscene gestures. The least impaired people tended to do this—stand back unless they were physically threatened and let those with less control scream and jump around. It was as though they felt it beneath them to be as touchy as the less comprehending. This was an attitude of superiority and that was the way people like the bus driver perceived it. Such "superiority" was frequently punished by beatings, even by death. Rye had had close calls of her own. As a result, she never went unarmed. And in this world where the only likely common language was body language, being armed was often enough. She had rarely had to draw her gun or even display it.

The bearded man's revolver was on constant display. Apparently that was enough for the bus driver. The driver spat in disgust, glared at the bearded man for a moment longer, then strode back to his gas-filled bus. He stared at it for a moment, clearly wanting to get in, but the gas was still too strong. Of the windows, only his tiny driver's window actually opened. The front door was open, but the rear door would not stay open unless someone held it. Of course, the air conditioning had failed long ago. The bus would take some time to clear. It was the driver's property, his livelihood. He had pasted old magazine pictures of items he would accept as fare on its sides. Then he would use what he collected to feed his family or to trade. If his bus did not run, he did not eat. On the other hand, if the inside of his bus were torn apart by senseless fighting, he would not eat very well either. He was apparently unable to perceive this. All he could see was that it would be some time before he could use his bus again. He shook his fist at the bearded man and shouted. There seemed to be words in his shout, but Rye could not understand them. She did not know whether this was his fault or hers. She had heard so little coherent human speech for the past three years, she was no longer certain how well she recognized it, no longer certain of the degree of her own impairment.

The bearded man sighed. He glanced toward his car, then beckoned to Rye. He was ready to leave, but he wanted something from her first. No. No, he wanted her to leave with him. Risk getting into his car when, in spite of his uniform, law and order were nothing— not even words any longer.

She shook her head in a universally understood negative, but the man continued to beckon.

She waved him away. He was doing what the less-impaired rarely did—drawing potentially negative attention to another of his kind. People from the bus had begun to look at her.

One of the men who had been fighting tapped another on the

arm, then pointed from the bearded man to Rye, and finally held up the first two fingers of his right hand as though giving two-thirds of a Boy Scout salute. The gesture was very quick, its meaning obvious even at a distance. She had been grouped with the bearded man. Now what?

The man who had made the gesture started toward her.

She had no idea what she intended, but she stood her ground. The man was half-a-foot taller than she was and perhaps ten years younger. She did not imagine she could outrun him. Nor did she expect anyone to help her if she needed help. The people around her were all strangers.

She gestured once—a clear indication to the man to stop. She did not intend to repeat the gesture. Fortunately, the man obeyed. He gestured obscenely and several other men laughed. Loss of verbal language had spawned a whole new set of obscene gestures. The man, with stark simplicity, had accused her of sex with the bearded man and had suggested she accommodate the other men present—beginning with him.

Rye watched him wearily. People might very well stand by and watch if he tried to rape her. They would also stand and watch her shoot him. Would he push things that far?

He did not. After a series of obscene gestures that brought him no closer to her, he turned contemptuously and walked away.

And the bearded man still waited. He had removed his service revolver, holster and all. He beckoned again, both hands empty. No doubt his gun was in the car and within easy reach, but his taking it off impressed her. Maybe he was all right. Maybe he was just alone. She had been alone herself for three years. The illness had stripped her, killing her children one by one, killing her husband, her sister, her parents. . . .

The illness, if it was an illness, had cut even the living off from one another. As it swept over the country, people hardly had time to lay blame on the Soviets (though they were falling silent along with the rest of the world), on a new virus, a new pollutant, radiation, divine retribution. . . . The illness was stroke-swift in the way it cut people down and strokelike in some of its effects. But it was highly specific. Language was always lost or severely impaired. It was never regained. Often there was also paralysis, intellectual impairment, death.

Rye walked toward the bearded man, ignoring the whistling and applauding of two of the young men and their thumbs-up signs to the bearded man. If he had smiled at them or acknowledged them in any way, she would almost certainly have changed her mind. If she had let herself think of the possible deadly consequences of getting into a stranger's car, she would have changed her mind. Instead, she thought of the man who lived across the street from her. He rarely washed since his bout with the illness. And he had gotten into the habit of urinating wherever he happened to be. He had two women already—one tending each of his large gardens. They put up with him in exchange for his protection. He had made it clear that he wanted Rye to become his third woman.

She got into the car and the bearded man shut the door. She watched as he walked around to the driver's door—watched for his sake because his gun was on the seat beside her. And the bus driver and a pair of young men had come a few steps closer. They did nothing, though, until the bearded man was in the car. Then one of them threw a rock. Others followed his example, and as the car drove away, several rocks bounced off it harmlessly.

When the bus was some distance behind them, Rye wiped sweat from her forehead and longed to relax. The bus would have taken her more than halfway to Pasadena. She would have had only ten miles to walk. She wondered how far she would have to walk now—and wondered if walking a long distance would be her only problem.

At Figuroa and Washington where the bus normally made a left turn, the bearded man stopped, looked at her, and indicated that she should choose a direction. When she directed him left and he actually turned left, she began to relax. If he was willing to go where she directed, perhaps he was safe.

As they passed blocks of burned, abandoned buildings, empty lots, and wrecked or stripped cars, he slipped a gold chain over his head and handed it to her. The pendant attached to it was a smooth, glassy, black rock. Obsidian. His name might be Rock or Peter or Black, but she decided to think of him as Obsidian. Even her some- times useless memory would retain a name like Obsidian.

She handed him her own name symbol—a pin in the shape of a large golden stalk of wheat. She had bought it long before the ill- ness and the silence began. Now she wore it, thinking it was as close as she was likely to come to Rye. People like Obsidian who had not known her before probably thought of her as Wheat. Not that it mattered. She would never hear her name spoken again.

Obsidian handed her pin back to her. He caught her hand as she reached for it and rubbed his thumb over her calluses.

He stopped at First Street and asked which way again. Then, after turning right as she had indicated, he parked near the Music Center. There, he took a folded paper from the dashboard and un- folded it. Rye recognized it as a street map, though the writing on it meant nothing to her. He flattened the map, took her hand again, and put her index finger on one spot. He touched her, touched him- self, pointed toward the floor. In effect, "We are here." She knew he wanted to know where she was going. She wanted to tell him, but she shook her head sadly. She had lost reading and writing. That was her most serious impairment and her most painful. She had taught history at UCLA. She had done freelance writing. Now she could not even read her own manuscripts. She had a house full of books that she could neither read nor bring herself to use as fuel. And she had a memory that would not bring back to her much of what she had read before.

She stared at the map, trying to calculate. She had been born in Pasadena, had lived for fifteen years in Los Angeles. Now she was near L.A. Civic Center. She knew the relative positions of the two cities, knew streets, directions, even knew to stay away from freeways which might be blocked by wrecked cars and destroyed overpasses. She ought to know how to point out Pasadena even though she could not recognize the word.

Hesitantly, she placed her hand over a pale orange patch in the upper right corner of the map. That should be right. Pasadena.

Obsidian lifted her hand and looked under it, then folded the map and put it back on the dashboard. He could read, she realized belatedly. He could probably write, too. Abruptly, she hated him— deep, bitter hatred. What did literacy mean to him—a grown man who played cops and robbers? But he was literate and she was not. She never would be. She felt sick to her stomach with hatred, frustration, and jealousy. And only a few inches from her hand was a loaded gun.

She held herself still, staring at him, almost seeing his blood. But her rage crested and ebbed and she did nothing.

Obsidian reached for her hand with hesitant familiarity. She looked at him. Her face had already revealed too much. No person still living in what was left of human society could fail to recognize that expression, that jealousy.

She closed her eyes wearily, drew a deep breath. She had experienced longing for the past, hatred of the present, growing hopelessness, purposelessness, but she had never experienced such a powerful urge to kill another person. She had left her home, finally, because she had come near to killing herself. She had found no reason to stay alive. Perhaps that was why she had gotten into Obsidian's car. She had never before done such a thing.

He touched her mouth and made chatter motions with thumb and fingers. Could she speak?

She nodded and watched his milder envy come and go. Now both had admitted what it was not safe to admit, and there had been no violence. He tapped his mouth and forehead and shook his head. He did not speak or comprehend spoken language. The illness had played with them, taking away, she suspected, what each valued most.

She plucked at his sleeve, wondering why he had decided on his own to keep the LAPD alive with what he had left. He was sane enough otherwise. Why wasn't he at home raising corn, rabbits, and children? But she did not know how to ask. Then he put his hand on her thigh and she had another question to deal with.

She shook her head. Disease, pregnancy, helpless, solitary agony . . . no.

He massaged her thigh gently and smiled in obvious disbelief.

No one had touched her for three years. She had not wanted anyone to touch her. What kind of world was this to chance bringing a child into even if the father was willing to stay and help raise it? It was too bad, though. Obsidian could not know how attractive he was to her—young, probably younger than she was, clean, asking for what he wanted rather than demanding it. But none of that mattered. What were a few moments of pleasure measured against a lifetime of consequences?

He pulled her closer to him and for a moment she let herself enjoy the closeness. He smelled good—male and good. She pulled away reluctantly.

He sighed, reached toward the glove compartment. She stiffened, not knowing what to expect, but all he took out was a small box. The writing on it meant nothing to her. She did not understand until he broke the seal, opened the box, and took out a condom. He looked at her and she first looked away in surprise. Then she giggled. She could not remember when she had last giggled.

He grinned, gestured toward the back seat, and she laughed aloud. Even in her teens, she had disliked back seats of cars. But she looked around at the empty streets and ruined buildings, then she got out and into the back seat. He let her put the condom on him, then seemed surprised at her eagerness.

Sometime later, they sat together, covered by his coat, unwilling to become clothed near-strangers again just yet. He made rock-the-baby gestures and looked questioningly at her.

She swallowed, shook her head. She did not know how to tell him her children were dead.

He took her hand and drew a cross in it with his index finger, then made his baby-rocking gesture again.

She nodded, held up three fingers, then turned away, trying to shut out a sudden flood of memories. She had told herself that the children growing up now were to be pitied. They would run through the downtown canyons with no real memory of what the buildings had been or even how they had come to be. Today's children gathered books as well as wood to be burned as fuel. They ran through the streets chasing each other and hooting like chimpanzees. They had no future. They were now all they would ever be.

He put his hand on her shoulder and she turned suddenly, fumbling for his small box, then urging him to make love to her again. He could give her forgetfulness and pleasure. Until now, nothing had been able to do that. Until now, every day had brought her closer to the time when she would do what she had left home to avoid doing: putting her gun in her mouth and pulling the trigger.

She asked Obsidian if he would come home with her, stay with her.

He looked surprised and pleased once he understood. But he did not answer at once. Finally he shook his head as she had feared he might. He was probably having too much fun playing cops and robbers and picking up women.

She dressed in silent disappointment, unable to feel any anger toward him. Perhaps he already had a wife and a home. That was likely. The illness had been harder on men than on women—had killed more men, had left male survivors more severely impaired. Men like Obsidian were rare. Women either settled for less or stayed alone. If they found an Obsidian, they did what they could to keep him. Rye suspected he had someone younger, prettier keeping him.

He touched her while she was strapping her gun on and asked with a complicated series of gestures whether it was loaded.

She nodded grimly.

He patted her arm.

She asked once more if he would come home with her, this time using a different series of gestures. He had seemed hesitant. Perhaps he could be courted.

He got out and into the front seat without responding.

She took her place in front again, watching him. Now he plucked at his uniform and looked at her. She thought she was being asked something, but did not know what it was.

He took off his badge, tapped it with one finger, then tapped his chest. Of course.

She took the badge from his hand and pinned her wheat stalk to it. If playing cops and robbers was his only insanity, let him play. She would take him, uniform and all. It occurred to her that she might eventually lose him to someone he would meet as he had met her. But she would have him for a while.

He took the street map down again, tapped it, pointed vaguely northeast toward Pasadena, then looked at her.

She shrugged, tapped his shoulder then her own, and held up her index and second fingers tight together, just to be sure.

He grasped the two fingers and nodded. He was with her.

She took the map from him and threw it onto the dashboard. She pointed back southwest—back toward home. Now she did not have to go to Pasadena. Now she could go on having a brother there and two nephews—three right-handed males. Now she did not have to find out for certain whether she was as alone as she feared. Now she was not alone.

Obsidian took Hill Street south, then Washington west, and she leaned back, wondering what it would be like to have someone again. With what she had scavenged, what she had preserved, and what she grew, there was easily enough food for him. There was certainly room enough in a four-bedroom house. He could move his possessions in. Best of all, the animal across the street would pull back and possibly not force her to kill him.

Obsidian had drawn her closer to him and she had put her head on his shoulder when suddenly he braked hard, almost throwing her off the seat. Out of the corner of her eye, she saw that someone had run across the street in front of the car. One car on the street and someone had to run in front of it.

Straightening up, Rye saw that the runner was a woman, fleeing from an old frame house to a boarded-up storefront. She ran silently, but the man who followed her a moment later shouted what sounded like garbled words as he ran. He had something in his hand. Not a gun. A knife, perhaps.

The woman tried a door, found it locked, looked around desperately, finally snatched up a fragment of glass broken from the storefront window. With this she turned to face her pursuer. Rye thought she would be more likely to cut her own hand than to hurt anyone else with the glass.

Obsidian jumped from the car, shouting. It was the first time Rye had heard his voice—deep and hoarse from disuse. He made the same sound over and over the way some speechless people did, "Da, da, da!"

Rye got out of the car as Obsidian ran toward the couple. He had drawn his gun. Fearful, she drew her own and released the safety. She looked around to see who else might be attracted to the scene. She saw the man glance at Obsidian, then suddenly lunge at the woman. The woman jabbed his face with her glass, but he caught her arm and managed to stab her twice before Obsidian shot him.

The man doubled, then toppled, clutching his abdomen. Obsidian shouted, then gestured Rye over to help the woman.

Rye moved to the woman's side, remembering that she had little more than bandages and antiseptic in her pack. But the woman was beyond help. She had been stabbed with a long, slender boning knife.

She touched Obsidian to let him know the woman was dead. He had bent to check the wounded man who lay still and also seemed dead. But as Obsidian looked around to see what Rye wanted, the man opened his eyes. Face contorted, he seized Obsidian's just-holstered revolver and fired. The bullet caught Obsidian in the temple and he collapsed.

It happened just that simply, just that fast. An instant later, Rye shot the wounded man as he was turning the gun on her.

And Rye was alone—with three corpses.

She knelt beside Obsidian, dry-eyed, frowning, trying to understand why everything had suddenly changed. Obsidian was gone. He had died and left her—like everyone else.

Two very small children came out of the house from which the man and woman had run—a boy and girl perhaps three years old. Holding hands, they crossed the street toward Rye. They stared at her, then edged past her and went to the dead woman. The girl shook the woman's arm as though trying to wake her.

This was too much. Rye got up, feeling sick to her stomach with grief and anger. If the children began to cry, she thought she would vomit.

They were on their own, those two kids. They were old enough to scavenge. She did not need any more grief. She did not need a stranger's children who would grow up to be hairless chimps.

She went back to the car. She could drive home, at least. She remembered how to drive.

The thought that Obsidian should be buried occurred to her before she reached the car, and she did vomit.

She had found and lost the man so quickly. It was as though she had been snatched from comfort and security and given a sudden, inexplicable beating. Her head would not clear. She could not think.

Somehow, she made herself go back to him, look at him. She found herself on her knees beside him with no memory of having knelt. She stroked his face, his beard. One of the children made a noise and she looked at them, at the woman who was probably their mother. The children looked back at her, obviously frightened. Perhaps it was their fear that reached her finally.

She had been about to drive away and leave them. She had almost done it, almost left two toddlers to die. Surely there had been enough dying. She would have to take the children home with her. She would not be able to live with any other decision. She looked around for a place to bury three bodies. Or two. She wondered if the murderer were the children's father. Before the silence, the police had always said some of the most dangerous calls they went out on were domestic disturbance calls. Obsidian should have known that—not that the knowledge would have kept him in the car. It would not have held her back either. She could not have watched the woman murdered and done nothing.

She dragged Obsidian toward the car. She had nothing to dig with here, and no one to guard for her while she dug. Better to take the bodies with her and bury them next to her husband and her children. Obsidian would come home with her after all.

When she had gotten him onto the floor in the back, she returned for the woman. The little girl, thin, dirty, solemn, stood up and unknowingly gave Rye a gift. As Rye began to drag the woman by her arms, the little girl screamed, "No!"

Rye dropped the woman and stared at the girl.

"No!" the girl repeated. She came to stand beside the woman. "Go away!" she told Rye.

"Don't talk," the little boy said to her. There was no blurring or confusing of sounds. Both children had spoken and Rye had understood. The boy looked at the dead murderer and moved farther from him. He took the girl's hand. "Be quiet," he whispered.

Fluent speech! Had the woman died because she could talk and had taught her children to talk? Had she been killed by a husband's festering anger or by a stranger's jealous rage? And the children . . . they must have been born after the silence. Had the disease run its course, then? Or were these children simply immune? Certainly they had had time to fall sick and silent. Rye's mind leaped ahead. What if children of three or fewer years were safe and able to learn language? What if all they needed were teachers? Teachers and protectors.

Rye glanced at the dead murderer. To her shame, she thought she could understand some of the passions that must have driven him, whoever he was. Anger, frustration, hopelessness, insane jealousy . . . how many more of him were there—people willing to destroy what they could not have?

Obsidian had been the protector, had chosen that role for who knew what reason. Perhaps putting on an obsolete uniform and patrolling the empty streets had been what he did instead of putting a gun into his mouth. And now that there was something worth protecting, he was gone.

She had been a teacher. A good one. She had been a protector, too, though only of herself. She had kept herself alive when she had no reason to live. If the illness let these children alone, she could keep them alive.

Somehow she lifted the dead woman into her arms and placed her on the back seat of the car. The children began to cry, but she knelt on the broken pavement and whispered to them, fearful of frightening them with the harshness of her long unused voice.

"It's all right," she told them. "You're going with us, too. Come on." She lifted them both, one in each arm. They were so light. Had they been getting enough to eat?

The boy covered her mouth with his hand, but she moved her face away. "It's all right for me to talk," she told him. "As long as no one's around, it's all right." She put the boy down on the front seat of the car and he moved over without being told to, to make room for the girl. When they were both in the car Rye leaned against the window, looking at them, seeing that they were less afraid now, that they watched her with at least as much curiosity as fear.

"I'm Valerie Rye," she said, savoring the words. "It's all right for you to talk to me."

The Ship Who Mourned

Anne McCaffrey

With eyes which did not register what they saw, Helva watched stolidly as the Regulus Base personnel broke ranks at the conclusion of Jennan's funeral. Never again, she vowed, would she be known as the ship who sang. That part of her had died with Jennan.

From somewhere very far away from her emotional centers, she impassively watched the little figures separate, pair off, walking rapidly to continue interrupted tasks or moving slowly back to the great Central Worlds Barracks. Some, passing, looked up but she did not interpret their glances. She had nowhere to move to and no desire to move anywhere away from the graveside of her dead partner.

It cannot end like this, she thought, anguish overpowering the stupor in her heart. *I cannot be like this. But what do I go on to now?*

"XH-834. Theoda of Medea requests permission to enter," said a voice at the base of her lift.

"Permission granted," Helva said.

So absorbed in her grief was Helva that by the time the lift had deposited the slender female figure at the lock, Helva had forgotten she had permitted entry. The woman advanced toward the central shaft behind which Helva was embedded in her shell. In her hand she held out a command reel.

"Well, insert it," snapped Helva when the woman made no other move.

"Where? I'm not regular service. The tape explains the mission but then I . . ."

"In the northwest quadrant of the central panel, you will observe a blue slot; insert the tape with the wind tab in position nearest the center red knob of the panel. Press the blue button marked 'relay' and if you are unaware of the text and are cleared for it, press the second yellow button marked 'audio.' Please be seated."

Dispassionately and with no more than a fleeting awareness that she ought to have put Theoda at her ease or made some attempt at graciousness, Helva watched the woman fumble before she was able to insert the tape. Theoda sank uncertainly into the pilot's chair as the tape began.

"XH-834, you will proceed in the company of Physiotherapist Theoda of Medea to the NDE, System Lyrae II, Annigoni IV, and present all aid possible in rehabilitation program of Van Gogh, space plague survivors. All haste. All haste. All haste!"

Helva slammed the stop signal on the tape and called Central Control.

"Does Physiotherapist Theoda constitute my replacement?"

"No, XH-834, Theoda is not in Service. Your replacement is delayed in transit. Proceed in all haste, repeat, in all haste, to Annigoni."

"Request permission for immediate lift."

Established routine procedures took Helva through pre-takeoff before she consciously realized what she was doing. Lifting off Regulus was the last thing she wanted but she had her order-tape and she had heard the imperative "all haste" repeated.

"All areas clear for lifting. Proceed. And XH-834. . . . ?"

"Yes?"

"Good luck."

"Acknowledged," said Helva expressionlessly, ignoring the softened, unofficial farewell. To Theoda, she explained briefly how to strap herself into the pilot chair, following the woman's nervous fingers as they stumbled over the fastenings. Finally assured Theoda would be secure during acceleration, Helva lifted, her rear screen picking up the base cemetery as long as vision permitted.

It no longer made any difference to Helva what speed she attained but when she found herself increasing acceleration in an unconscious desire to finish her mission quickly and return to Regulus Base—and Jennan—she sternly measured her rate against Theoda's tolerance. Journey speed achieved, she told Theoda she could leave the chair.

Theoda unsnapped the harness and stood uncertainly.

"I was sent here so quickly and I've traveled twenty-four hours already," she said, looking down at her rumpled, dirty uniform.

"Quarters are aft the central column," and Helva gasped inwardly as she realized Theoda would inhabit the place so recently vacated by Jennan. Instinctively she glanced in the cabin to be startled by the realization that someone had already removed Jennan's personal effects. Not one memento remained of his tenancy, no souvenir of their brief happiness. Her feeling of desolation deepened. How could they? When had they? It was unfair. And now she must endure this fumbling female.

Theoda had already entered the cabin, throwing her kit bag on the bunk and entering the head. Helva politely withdrew her vision. She tried to make believe the homey noises of showering were Jennan's but her new passenger's ways were completely different. The difference, oh, the difference to me, cried Helva, mourning.

Lost in an elegy, she became only gradually aware of the quiet in the ship and scanning discreetly saw Theoda stretched out on her back in the limp, deep slumber of the exhausted. In repose, the woman was older than Helva had initially assumed from her ineptitude. Now, too, Helva justly attributed the fumbling to its true cause, exhaustion. The face was deeply lined with sorrow as well as fatigue; there were dark smudges under the closed eyes. The mouth was dragged down at the corners from familiarity with pain. The long, blunt-ended fingers twitched slightly in reflex to a disturbing dream and Helva could see the inherent strength and sensitivity, the marks of use in odd scars on palm and fingers, odd in an age where manual work was confined mainly to punching buttons.

Jennan had used his hands, too, came the unbidden comparison. Mourning reclaimed Helva.

"How long did I sleep?" mumbled Theoda breaking into Helva's reminiscences as the woman wove sleepily into the forward cabin. "How much longer is the trip?"

"You slept eighteen hours. The tape estimates an elapse of forty-nine hours galactic to Annigoni orbit."

"Oh," groaned Theoda in unhappy acceptance. "The galley?"

"First compartment on the right."

"Is there anything you require?" Theoda asked, halfway to the galley.

"My needs are supplied for the next hundred years," Helva said coldly, realizing as the words were formed that her critical need could not be met.

"I'm sorry. I know very little of you ships," Theoda apologized. "I've never had preferential treatment like this before," and she smiled shyly.

"Your home planet *is* Medea?" inquired Helva with reluctant courtesy. It was not uncommon for a professional person to claim the planet of his current employer.

"Yes, Medea," Theoda replied quietly. She made immediate noise with the rations she held, banging them onto the table with unnecessary violence. Her reaction signaled to Helva some inner conflict or grief, but she could recall nothing of great moment connected with Medea so she must assume Theoda's problem was personal.

"I've seen your type of ship before, of course. We of Medea have reason to be grateful to you, but I've never actually been in one." Theoda was talking nervously, her eyes restlessly searching over the supplies in the galley cupboards. Then she was rearranging containers to see the back of the shelves. "Do you enjoy your work? It must be a tremendous satisfaction."

Such innocent words to drop like hot cinders on Helva's unhealed grief. Rapidly Helva began to talk, anything to keep herself from being subjected to another such unpredictably rasping civility.

"I haven't been commissioned long," she managed to say. "As a physiotherapist you must certainly be aware of our origin."

"Oh, yes, of course. Birth defect," and Theoda looked embarrassed as if she had touched on a vulgar subject.

"Quite right. My deformity was too major to be surgically corrected and my parents were given the usual choice of euthanasia or recruiting me into the Service. My mind was *not* affected by the birth defects. By the time I was three months old I had been transferred into the first protective 'shell' and the synapses which would move legs and arms were diverted to mechanical means of propulsion."

"I still think it's horrible," Theoda blurted out, angrily. "You had no choice."

Helva felt suddenly superior. "Initially, perhaps not. But now, it would be very difficult to give up hurtling through space and be content with *walking*."

Theoda flushed at the almost scornful emphasis of the final word.

"I leave that to whoever is my 'brawn,'" and Helva cringed as she reminded herself of Jennan.

"I've recently heard about one of your ships who sings," interjected Theoda.

"Yes, I have, too," said Helva unencouragingly. Must everything remind her of Jennan's loss!

"How long do you live?"

"As long as we wish."

"That is . . . I mean, who's the oldest ship?"

"One of the 200s is still in active service."

"You're not very old then, are you, being an 800?"

"No."

"I am," said Theoda, heavily, staring at the empty ration unit she held in one hand. "I am near my end now, I think." And there was no regret in her voice, not even resignation.

It occurred to Helva that here, too, was someone with deep sorrow, marking time.

"How many more hours until planetfall?"

"Forty-seven," Helva confirmed with some surprise to realize she had talked two hours.

"I must study," and abruptly Theoda rummaged in her kit for filmfile and viewer.

"What is the problem?" Helva asked politely.

"Van Gogh in Lyrae II was hit by a space plague similar in manifestation to that which attacked Medea one hundred twenty-five years ago," Theoda explained.

Suddenly Helva knew why Theoda had seen Service Ships. She microscoped her vision on Theoda's face and saw the tiny myriad lines that indicated advanced age. Theoda had undoubtedly been alive on Medea at the time of the plague. Helva recalled that the plague had struck a heavily populated area and swept with terrific violence throughout the entire planet in a matter of days; its onslaught so fierce and its toll so great that medical personnel often collapsed over the sick they tended. Others inexplicably survived untouched. The airborne disease spores struck animal as well as human and then, as suddenly as it had come, almost as if the disease were aware that the resources of a galaxy were on the way to subdue its ravages, it disappeared. Medea had been decimated in the course of a week and the survivors, both the ones hardy enough to endure the intense fever and pain, and those who were curiously immune, spent their years trying to discover source or cause, cure or vaccine.

From her capacious trained associative recall, Helva found

seven other different but similarly inexplicable plague waves; some treated with better success than Medea. The plague on the planet Clematis had been 93 percent successful in eliminating all human life before help could arrive and the planet had been placed under eternal quarantine. Helva thought that was rather locking the barn and never bothering to track down the missing horses.

"You had, I gather, sufficient experience with Medea's plague so that your presence may be of help to Van Gogh's people?"

"That is the thought," said Theoda, wincing. She picked up her filmviewer purposefully and Helva realized that more discussion was out of order. She knew, too, that Theoda still had painful word associations even at the end of her long life. Nor could Helva imagine a time centuries hence when mention of Jennan would not hurt.

Annigoni swam into view precisely as the trip chronometer edged onto sixty-seven hours, and Helva found herself immediately answering a quarantine warning from an orbital monitor.

"You have Physiotherapist Theoda on board, do you not?" Helva was queried after she identified herself.

"I do."

"Your landing should set you down as close to the hospital city of Erfar as possible. There is, however, no spacefield in that vicinity and a meadow has been set aside for your use. Are you able to control your dangerous exhausts?"

Helva was wryly amused by their lack of understanding of her type of ship but readily assured them of her ability to land circumspectly. They gave her the latitude and longitude and she had no difficulty in bringing herself to a stand in the patch-sized meadow described to her. A powdery white road led to its edge and half a mile beyond crouched a long white complex of multi-windowed buildings. From this direction a land vehicle came.

"Theoda," said Helva as they awaited the arrival of the landcar, "in the effects compartment under the control panel, you will find a small gray button. Attach it to your uniform and you have instant communication with me. If you would be good enough to rotate the upper section of the button clockwise, I can have two-way contact. It would accord me some satisfaction to be in on the problems you encounter."

"Yes, certainly, of course."

"If you rotate the bottom half of the button, I have limited scope vision as well."

"How clever," murmured Theoda, examining the button in her hand before attaching it to her tunic.

As the car drew to a halt, Theoda waved at the occupants from the high lock and stepped onto the lift bar.

"Oh, Helva, thank you for the journey and my apologies. I'm not good company."

"Nor have I been. Good luck."

As Theoda descended, Helva knew that for a lie. They had been perfect company, each locked in separate miseries. Somehow it had escaped her that grief was a frequent visitor anywhere in the universe. That her inability to aid Jennan was scarcely unique. Her sister ships had all had such experiences and were still at their jobs.

None of them ever loved their brawns as I did Jennan, she soliloquized sullenly, perfectly conscious of how ill her sentiment befitted her steel, yet unable to extricate her thoughts from their unconscious return to misery.

"Request permission to board," came a rough voice at the lift bottom.

"Identification?"

"Senior Medical Officer Onro, Detached Regulus Base. I need to use your tight beam."

"Permission granted," replied Helva after a rapid check on the name in the MedOff roster of her file.

MedOff Onro plunged into her lock and, with the briefest of salutes at her central shaft, lunged into the pilot's chair and slapped home the call button on the beam.

"Have you any honest-to-God coffee?" he grated out, swiveling the chair to launch himself from it toward the galley.

"Be my guest," murmured Helva, unprepared for such vigor after several days of Theoda.

Onro's shoulder took a bruising as he careened off the threshold of the galley, wrenched open the cupboards, knocking containers about.

"Coffee may still be in its accustomed place on the third shelf of the right-hand locker," Helva remarked dryly. "Excuse me, a container just rolled onto the floor."

Onro retrieved it but cracked his head smartly on the corner of the cupboard door he had left open. The stream of invective Helva half expected did not come. The man carefully closed the cupboard with the controlled patience of the much-put-upon and breaking the coffee heat seal, immediately stalked back to the central cabin and resumed his seat, watching the dial on the tight beam as it warmed slowly to peak, never blinking as he gulped the now steaming hot coffee. With the first gulp, the springs in his taut frame began to unwind.

"Creatures of habit, aren't we, XH? I've been dreaming of coffee for eighteen mortal days and nights. The stuff they use in its place on this lousy lump of ill-assorted metals makes me sleepy. Coffee is not as potent as benzedrine nor half as rough on the system. Ah, there they are. I swear these beams take longer every time I have to fool with the things."

"Central Base Regulus."

"XH-834 reporting," announced Onro.

"Who?" gasped an unofficial voice.

"Onro talking."

"Yes, sir, didn't recognize your voice."

"Did you think Helva had a cold?"

"No, sir, that wasn't what I thought."

"Well, never mind the chitchat. Put this on the computers and let it do a little brainstorming. I'm too tired. You better check the computerese, too. I haven't been asleep much lately." He turned to Helva, "How d'ya like the luck? First home leave in three galactic years and I have to time my arrival with the plague's. I wonder if I can get a rebate on my vacation time." He turned back to the beam. "Here's the garbage," and he rapidly dictated the material. "Now here's a verbal to check it."

"Disease unidentifiable on the Orson scale as a known virus or variation thereof. Patients thoroughly tested and apparently perfectly healthy can develop clinical symptoms in ten hours; complete deterioration of muscle control, presence of high fever, excessive spinal pain follow in three days. Death caused by 1) brain hemorrhage, 2) heart failure, 3) lung collapse, 4) strangulation or in case where medical help has been late in arriving, 5) starvation. All survivors unable to make muscular co-ordinations of any kind. Extent of brain damage negative. But they might as well be dead."

"Impairment to intellect?" asked Central Control.

"Impossible to ascertain except to hope that the injury to the brain has left the intellect alone."

"Julie O'Grady and the Colonel's Lady are sisters under the skin," muttered Helva for she could see through the MedOff's words that the victims of the plague were now as robbed of their bodies by disease as she had been by birth defects.

"Our skintight friend is closer to the truth than she knows," Onro snorted. "Except for infants, there isn't one of them that wouldn't be better off in a shell right now. They aren't going to go anywhere the way they are now."

"Do you wish to stand by for report?" asked Central Control.

"Take long?"

"You could get a little sleep," suggested Helva blandly, "these reports don't usually take too long," she added, tapping out a private distress signal to Central as she spoke.

"Not long, MedOfficer Onro," concurred Central on cue.

"You'll get a crick in your neck, Onro," remarked Helva as she saw him stretch out his long legs and scrunch down in the pilot chair for a catnap. "Use the pilot's bed. I'll give you a jolt of coffee as soon as the message returns."

"You'd better or I'll unscrew your safety panel," Onro snapped, lurching drunkenly toward the bunk.

"Yes, of course," soothed Helva and watched as he took the two deep breaths that were all that were needed before he was oblivious.

Her contact with Theoda began, sight and sound. Theoda was bending over a bed, her strong fingers soothing the motionless frame of the woman there. Flaccid muscles, lack of reflexes, pasty skin, unfocusing eyes, loose mouth; the chords of the neck strained briefly as the patient made some incoherent sound deep in her throat.

"There is no sensation in the extremities that we can discover," an out-of-sight voice said. "There is some reaction to pain in the torso and in the face, but we can't be sure. The patient, if she understands us, can give us no sign."

Helva noticed, and she hoped that Theoda did, that the half-closed eyelids made an almost imperceptible downward motion, then upward. Helva also noticed the flaring of the nostrils.

"Theoda," she said quietly so as not to startle her. Even so, Theoda straightened quickly in surprise.

"Helva?"

"Yes. In the scope of my limited range of vision, I could see a twitch of the eyelids and a motion of the nostrils. If the paralysis is as acute as I have learned from MedOff Onro, these bare flickers may be the only muscle controls the patient has. Please ask one of the observers to concentrate on the right eye, another on the left and you observe only the nostrils. Establish a pattern of replay and explain it to the patient and see if she understands you."

"Is that the ship?" an off-sight voice demanded irritably.

"Yes, the XH-834 that brought me here."

"Oh," was the disparaging reply, "that's the one that sings. I thought it was the JH or GH."

"Helva is not an 'it,'" said Theoda firmly. "Let us try her suggestion as her vision is considerably more acute than ours and her concentration far superior."

To the patient, Theoda said quietly and distinctly, "If you can hear me, please try to lower your right eyelid."

For an age-long second, there was no movement; then as though the effort were tremendous, the right lid slowly descended the barest fraction.

"In order to be sure this was not an involuntary motion, will you try to dilate your nostrils twice?"

Very slowly, very slowly Helva caught the motion of the nostrils. She also saw, which was more important, the tiny beads of perspiration on the upper lip and brow and quickly called attention to them.

"What a tremendous effort this must be for that imprisoned mind," said Theoda with infinite compassion. Her bluntfingered hand rested softly on the moist forehead. "Rest now, dear. We will not press you further but now we have hope for you."

Only Helva was aware of the disconsolate sag and then straightening of Theoda's shoulders as she walked to the next bed.

Helva was with Theoda throughout the entire tour of the plague hospital, from the men's and women's wards to the children's and even into the nursery. The plague had been no respecter of age and babies of a few weeks had been affected.

"One would have hopes that in the younger and more resilient body those tissues which were damaged, if any have been, would stand the best chance of regeneration," remarked one of Theoda's guides. Helva caught part of a gesture which took in the fifty cribs of motionless infants in the ward.

Theoda leaned down and picked up a small pink, blond infant of three months. The flesh was firm, the color good. She tweaked the pectoral fold with unnecessary force. The baby's eyes widened and the mouth fell open. A slight croak issued from the throat.

Quickly Theoda snatched the child to her breast, rocking it in apology for the pain. Sight and sound were muffled by the blanket but not before Helva, too, had seen and realized exactly what Theoda had.

Theoda was rocking the child so that Helva caught only elusive fragments of a violent discussion. Then her scope of sight and sound returned as Theoda laid the child in the crib on its stomach and carefully started to move the child's arms and legs in an approximation of the crabbed action that is the beginning of independent locomotion.

"We will do this with every child, with every person, for one hour every morning and every afternoon. We will commandeer every adult and responsible adolescent in Annigoni if necessary for our therapists. If we are to reach the brain, to restore contact between intellect and nerve, we must repattern the brain centers from the very beginning of brain function. We must work quickly. Those poor imprisoned people have waited long enough to be released from their hells."

"But . . . but . . . on what do you base your premise, Physiotherapist Theoda? You admitted that the Medean plague has fewer points of similarity than originally thought."

"I can't give you a premise right now. Why must I? My whole experience leads me to *know* that I am right."

"Experience? *I* think you mean 'intuition,'" continued the official stuffily, "and we cannot, on the basis of one woman's intuition, conscript the work force needed from busy citizens . . ."

"Did you see the beads of sweat on that woman's face? The effort required to do so simple a thing as lower an eyelid?" demanded Theoda tartly. "Can any effort required of *us* be too much?"

"There is no need to be emotional," Theoda was told testily. "Annigoni has opened herself to these survivors with no thought of the danger of exposure to the same virus . . ."

"Nonsense," Theoda rasped, "before your ships approached Van Gogh you made certain that the plague had passed. But that is neither here nor there. I will return to my ship and contact Central Control." She whirled around, facing back into the ward where Helva could see the respectfully waiting ward nurses. "But any of you who love children and trust another woman's instinct, do as I just did whether it is authorized or not. There is nothing to be lost and the living to be released."

Theoda stormed out of the hospital, brushing aside the complaints and temporizing of the officials. She stumbled into the landcar, ordering it back to the ship in a tight, terrible voice that made the driver hold his tongue. Helva could see the strong fingers washing themselves, straining in a tense clasp of frustration, never idle, groping, grasping, clenching. Then Theoda reached up to the button and cut the contact abruptly.

Unconcerned, Helva switched to the wide vision of her own scanner and picked up the landcar as it sped toward her. The car discharged its passenger and left but Theoda did not step onto the lift. Somewhat at a disadvantage because of the angle, Helva could only watch as Theoda paced back and forth.

In the bunk, Onro slept on and Helva waited.

"Permission to enter," said Theoda finally, in a low voice.

"Granted."

Stumbling again, one hand in front of her as if feeling her way, Theoda entered the ship. Wearily she sagged into the pilot's chair and, leaning forward on the console, buried her head in her arms.

"You saw, Helva," muttered the therapist, "you saw. Those people have been like that for upwards of six weeks. How many will come out of this sane?"

"They have an additional hope, Theoda. Don't forget, once you can establish that the integral intellect remains, the body may be bypassed. There are advantages to that, you know," she reminded the therapist.

Theoda's head came up and she turned in her chair, looking in amazement at the panel concealing Helva's shell-encased body.

"Of course. You're a prime example, aren't you?"

Then she shook her head in disagreement.

"No, Helva. It's one thing to be bred up to it, and another to be forced into it as the only expedient."

"The young would experience no shock at shell life. And there are, I repeat, advantages, even distinct gains to be made. Witness my ability to follow your tour."

"But to have walked, and touched, and smelled, and laughed and cried . . ."

"To have cried—" gasped Helva, "to be able to weep. Oh, yes," and an unendurable tightness filled her mind as her brief respite from grief dissolved.

"Helva . . . I . . . in the hospital . . . I mean, I'd heard that you had . . . I'm sorry but I was so lost in my own problem that I just didn't realize that you were the ship who sang, and that you'd . . ." Her voice trailed off.

"Nor did I remember that at Medea the virus didn't just isolate the intellect in the body, it destroyed it, leaving a mindless husk."

Theoda turned her head away.

"That baby, that poor baby."

"Central Control to the XH-834, are you receiving?"

Theoda, startled by the voice at her elbow, jerked back from the lighted tightbeam face.

"XH-834 receiving."

"Prepare to tape computer report on MedOfficer Onro's request."

Helva activated the apparatus and gave the A-okay.

"Verbal?" asked Theoda in a stage whisper.

"Verbal requested," Helva relayed.

"No correlation between age, physical stature, health, ethnic group, blood type, tissue structure, diet, location, medical history is indicated. Disease random, epidemic force. No correlation muscle, bone, tissue, blood, sputum, urine, marrow in post-plague post-mortem. Negative medication. Negative operation. Possible therapy."

"There!" cried Theoda in triumph, jumping to her feet. "Therapy the only positive."

"Only 'possible.'"

"But the only *positive* factor, nonetheless. And I'm positive it's repatterning."

"Repatterning?"

"Yes. It's a bizarre therapy and it doesn't always work but the failure may have been because the intellect had retreated in desperation," Theoda argued with vehement confidence. "To be trapped, unable to make even the simplest communication, can you imagine how ghastly that must be? Oh, what am I saying?" she gasped, turning in horror toward Helva's presence.

"You're quite right," Helva assured her blandly with inner amusement. "It would be intolerable if I could no longer control the synapses I do now electronically. I think I should go mad having known what it is to drive between the stars, to talk across light-years, to eavesdrop in tight places, maintaining my own discreet impregnability."

Theoda resumed her restless pacing.

"But you don't think," Helva pointed out, "that you are going to get those skeptics to do the necessary recruiting on the basis of the computer report?"

"The therapy was a positive factor," Theoda insisted stubbornly.

"It was a 'possible,'" Helva corrected mercilessly. "I'm not arguing with your position, only pointing out their reaction," she added as she saw Theoda gathering to protest. "I'm convinced. They won't be and it also won't be the first time when good samaritans have decided to rest on their laurels prematurely assured they have done in conscience all they could."

Theoda set her lips.

"I'm positive those people can be saved . . . or at least enough of them to make every effort worthwhile."

"Why? I mean, why do you think repatterning will do the trick?"

"It's a twentieth century technique, used before the correction of the majority of pre-natal defects. It was also used with some severe brain or neural accidents. I took my degree in Physiotherapeutic history. So many of the early problems in the field no longer exist but occasionally, of course, an ancient disease reappears suddenly. Like the epidemic of poliomyelitis on Evarts II. Then the old skills are revived.

"This plague, for instance, is like the Rathje Virus; only the original strain attacked sporadically and recovery was slow but certain. Perhaps because therapy was initiated as soon as the painful phase passed. Also, I believe that the paralysis was not so acute but the strain has obviously mutated in the centuries and become more virulent.

"However, the similarity cannot be denied. I brought my tapes, Helva," Theoda said eagerly, enthusiasm livening her face with a semblance of youth. "And the Doman-Delacato repatterning was used with great effect on the latter victims of the Rathje Virus.

"You don't suppose," and Theoda stopped dead in her tracks, "we could also prove that the space plague spores had passed by old Terra at that time? Have you any details on galactic spiral patterns?"

"Stick to medical and physiological aspects, Theoda," laughed Helva.

Theoda scrubbed at her face with her hands as though she would wash not only fatigue out but inspiration from her tired brain.

"Just one child, one proof is all I need."

"How long would it take? What age child is best? Why a child? Why not that poor woman of the eyelid?"

"The medulla handles reflex action at birth. The pons, maturing at twenty weeks, directs crawling on the stomach. By fifteen weeks, the midbrain has begun to function and the child begins to

learn to creep on hands and knees. By sixty weeks, the cortex begins to act and controls walking, speech, vision, hearing, tactile and
manual competence."

"A year would be too young, no understandable speech," Helva
mused out loud, remembering her first birthday without effort. But
she had already been "walking" and "talking."

"The best age is five," said another voice. Theoda gasped as she
saw Onro standing in the galley, a warming container in one hand.
"Because that is the age of my son. I'm Onro, MedOfficer, and I
sent for you, Physiotherapist Theoda, because I heard you never
give up." His face, still creased with blank folds, turned hard, determined. "Well, I won't give up either until my son walks, talks, and
laughs again. He's all I have left of what was to have been such a
happy homecoming." Onro laughed bitterly then gulped at the
steaming coffee.

"You're Van Goghian?" Theoda demanded.

"By chance, and one of the immunes."

"You heard what I was saying? You agree?"

"I've heard. I neither agree nor disagree. I'll try anything that has
a semblance of reason. Your idea is reasonable and the computer
has only one positive thought . . . therapy. I'll bring my son."

He turned when he reached the lock, shook his fist back at
Helva. "You drugged me, you sorceress."

"An inaccurate analysis but the insult is accepted," Helva
laughed as he disappeared, scowling, down the lift.

Elated, Theoda snatched her viewer out and carefully restudied
the films of the technique she would try.

"They used steroids as medications," she mumbled. "Have you
any?"

"No medication was indicated on the report," Helva reminded
her, "but you can get Onro to steal you the ones you require from
the synthesizer in the hospital easily enough. He *is* a Senior Med-
Officer."

"Yes, yes, that helps," and Theoda lapsed again into fierce concentration. "Why did they use . . . oh, yes, of course. They didn't have any conglomerates, did they?"

Helva watched fascinated as Theoda scanned through the film, winding and rewinding, rechecking, making notations, muttering to herself, pausing to gaze off into space in abstracted thought.

When she had been through her notes the fourth time, Helva insisted with authority that Theoda eat something. She had just finished the stew when Onro returned with the limp body of a red-headed child in his arms. Onro's rough face was impassive, almost rigid in its lack of expression as the child was tenderly put down on the bunk. Helva noticed the almost universal trait of the victims, the half-closed eyes, as if the lids were too heavy to keep open.

Kneeling down beside the bunk, Theoda turned the boy's face so that her eyes were directly on a level with his.

"Child, I know you can hear. We are going to work your body to help you remember what your body could do. Soon we will have you running under the sun again."

Without more ado and disregarding Onro's guttural protest, she placed the boy on his stomach on the deck, seized one arm and one leg and signaled to Onro to do likewise.

"We are taking you back to the time when you were a baby and first tried to creep. We are making your body crawl forward on your belly like a snake."

In a patient monotone, she droned her instructions. Helva timed the performance at fifteen minutes. They waited a full hour and repeated the drill. Another hour passed and Theoda, equally patient, droned instructions to pattern the child's body in a walking, upright position, alternating the left hand with right foot, and right hand with left foot. Another hour and she repeated the walking. Then back to the crawling, again and again in double repetition, while the two therapists caught naps where they could. Surreptitiously, Helva closed her lock, cut the cabin audio on her relays and ignored the insistent radio demands from the Hospital that she put Theoda or Onro on the radio. After twenty-four hours, Theoda alternated the two patterns, and included basic muscular therapy on the lax body, patiently, patiently manipulating the limbs in the various attitudes and postures, down to the young toes and fingers.

By the twenty-seventh hour, Onro, worn by previous exhaustion, frustration, and increasing hopelessness, dropped into a sleep from which violent shaking could not rouse him. Theoda, looking more and more gray, continued, making each repetition of every motion as carefully and fully as she had the first time she started the intensive repatterning.

"Theoda," Helva said softly in the thirtieth hour, "have you noticed as I have the tendency of the neck muscles to contort?"

"Yes, I have. And this child was once so far gone that a tracheotomy was necessary. Notice the scar here," and she pointed to the thin mark. "I see, too, that the eyelids describe a slightly larger arc than when we began the therapy. The child knows we are helping him. See, his eyes open . . . ever so slightly, but it is enough. I was right! I knew I was right!"

"You won't have much more time," Helva said. "The authorities of Annigoni have called in a Service craft and it is due to land beside me in half an hour. I will be forced to open or risk damage to the ship which I am conditioned to avoid."

Theoda looked up startled.

"What do you mean?"

"Look in my screen," and Helva turned on the picture at the pilot's console so that Theoda could see the crowd of people and vehicles clustered at the base of the ship. "They are getting a bit insistent."

"I had no idea," the therapist gasped.

"You needed quiet. I could at least supply that," Helva replied. "But to all intents and purposes, their Senior Medical Officer and his son, their visiting technical advisor, are imprisoned inside me and they suspect that my recent . . . that I am turning rogue."

"But didn't you tell them we were conducting therapy . . ."

"Naturally."

"Of all the ridiculous . . ."

"It's time for therapy. Every minute is necessary now."

"First he must be fed."

Theoda carefully inserted the concentrated solution in the thin vein, smoothing down the lump that formed as the nutritive spray entered.

"A sweet child, I imagine, Helva, from his face," she said lovingly.

"A young hellion with all those freckles," snorted Helva.

"They are usually the sweetest inside," Theoda said firmly.

Helva noticed the eyelids droop down on the cheek and then raise again. She decided she was right, not the therapist. Imagine calling red hair and freckles sweet!

Again the patient routine, the assisted patterning, and then a loud thud startled Theoda. It shook the sleeping form of the doctor where he lay on the deck. Helva, with one eye outside, had expected the blow. Onro roused himself garrulously unaware at first of his surroundings.

"Whassa matter?"

A second dull thud.

"Whatinell's happening? Who's knocking?"

"Half the planet," remarked Helva dryly and opened up both outside visual and aural to her companions. She immediately cut down the nearly deafening noise.

"All right, all right," she said loudly to the audience, her voice amplifying easily over their angry roars.

"DEMAND PERMISSION TO ENTER, XH-834," squalled someone at her base. She meekly activated the lift and opened the lock.

Onro stamped to the opening and leaned down, shouting. "Whatinells's the matter here? Go 'way, all of you. Have you no decency? What's the fuss about? Can't a man get some sleep around here? Only quiet place on the whole lousy planet," he roared.

The lift had by then come abreast of him with the "brawn" from the Service ship and the stuffy hospital official of Theoda's tour.

"MedOfficer Onro, we feared for you, particularly when your son was discovered missing from his bed."

"Administrator Carif, did you expect that the lady therapist had kidnapped me and my son and was holding me hostage on a rogue ship? Romanticists all. Hey, what are you doing . . . you young squirt," he demanded as the "brawn" made a pass at the protected panel of Helva's shaft.

"I am following orders from Central Control."

"You warm up that tightbeam and tell Central Control to mind its own business. Weren't for Helva here and the peace and quiet she maintained for us, don't know where we'd be at."

He stalked into the cabin where his son again lay on the floor, with Theoda painstakingly applying her Doman-Delacato therapy.

"Don't know how many we'll save this way, but it does work and you, young man, will tell Central Control, after you've told them to go to hell for me, that they will issue authority to Theoda to recruit any and all . . . if necessary . . . of this planet's population as a therapy force to activate her rehabilitation program."

He got down on his knees by his son.

"All right, boy, crawl."

"Why, that child will catch a cold in this draft . . ." the official exclaimed.

Some woman was trying to get Helva to lower the lift for her but Helva ignored her as the beads of sweat started on the child's face. There was no muscular movement, not so much as a twitch.

"Son, try. Try. Try!" pleaded Onro.

"Your mind remembers what your body once could do, right arm forward, left knee up," urged Theoda with such control that no hint of the tension she must feel showed in her calm gentle tones.

Helva could see the boy's throat muscles moving convulsively but she knew the watchers were expecting more dramatic motions.

"Come on, momma's sweet little freckled-face boy," she drawled in an irritatingly insulting voice.

Before the annoyed watchers could turn to remonstrate her, an elbow had actually slid an inch on the floor and the left knee, slightly flexed by Theoda's hands, skidded behind as the throat worked violently and a croaking sound issued from the lips. With a cry of inarticulate joy, Onro clasped his son to him.

"You see, you see. Theoda was right."

"I see that the child made a voluntary movement, yes," Carif was forced to agree. "But one isolated example is . . ." he spread his hands expressively, unconvinced.

"One is enough. We haven't had time for more," Onro pleaded. "I'll put it to the people out there. They'll be the work force."

Carrying his son to the lock, he yelled down what had happened. There was great cheering and applause. Then the little group at the base of the ship kept pointing urgently to the woman who had begged for the lift.

"I can't hear you," Onro shouted down, for many people were shouting at once, all trying to get across the same idea.

Helva sent the lift down and the woman came up it. As soon as she was halfway to Onro she shouted her message.

"In the nursery, we did as Therapist Theoda suggested. There is already some improvement among the children. Not much, not much and we want to know what we are doing wrong. But four of the babies are already able to cry," she babbled, stepping in to the ship and running to Theoda where the woman leaned wearily against the door jamb. "I never expected to be happy to hear a baby cry again. But some are crying and some are making awful sounds, and one little girl even waved a hand when she was diapered."

Theoda looked her triumph at Carif and he, shrugging acceptance of the accomplishment, nodded.

"Now, Carif," said Onro briskly, stepping into the lift, his son still cradled in his arms, "this is what we'll do. How we'll organize. We don't have to take everyone on your very busy planet. The Youth Corps can be called in from Avalon. Just their bag of tricks," Helva heard him say as his voice died away.

"Thank you for believing in me," Theoda told the nurse.

"One of the babies was my sister's," the woman said softly, with tears in her eyes, "and she's the only one left of the entire town."

The lift had come back up and the "brawn" and the nurse took it. Theoda had to pack her gear.

"The easy part is over, Helva, now it's all uphill, encouraging, instructing, upholding patience. Even Onro's son has a long, long way to go with therapy before he approaches his pre-plague physical condition."

"But at least there is hope."

"There is always hope while there is life."

"Was it *your* son?" asked Helva.

"Yes, and my daughter, my husband, my whole family. I was the only immune," and Theoda's face contorted. "With all my training, with all the skill of years of practice, I couldn't save them."

Theoda's eyes closed against that remembered agony.

Helva blacked out her own vision with a deep indrawn mental breath as Theoda's words echoed the protest she herself had voiced at her ineffectuality. It still burned in her mind: the searing memory of Jennan, looking at her as he died.

"I don't know why one makes a certain emotional adjustment," Theoda said wearily. "I guess it's the survival factor in you, forcing you to go on, preserving sanity and identity by a refocusing of values. I felt that if I could learn my profession so well that never again would I have to watch someone I loved die because of my ineffectiveness, then the ignorance which killed my family would be forgiven."

"But how could you have stopped a space plague?" Helva demanded.

"Oh, I know I couldn't have, but I still don't forgive myself."

Helva turned Theoda's words over in her mind, letting their significance sink into her like an anesthetic salve.

"Thank you, Theoda," she said finally, looking again at the therapist. "What are you crying for?" she asked, astonished to see Theoda, sitting on the edge of the bunk, tears streaming unheeded down her face.

"You. Because you can't, can you? And you lost your Jennan and they never even gave you a chance to rest. They just ordered you up to take me here and . . ."

Helva stared at Theoda, torn with a variety of emotions: incredulous that someone else did understand her grief over Jennan; that Theoda was, at the moment of her own triumph, concerned by Helva's sorrow. She felt the hard knot of grief coming untied and she was suddenly rather astonished that she, Helva, was the object of pity.

"By the Almighty, Helva, wake up," shouted Onro at the base and Helva hurriedly sent down the lift for him. Shortly he charged into the cabin.

"What on earth are you crying for? Don't bother to answer," he rattled on, snatching Theoda's kit-bag from her limp hands and plowing into the galley. "It's undoubtedly in a good cause. But there's a whole planet waiting for your instructions . . ." He was scooping up all the coffee containers he could find and stuffing them into the kit-bag, and his pockets. "I promise you can cry all you want once you've given me the therapy routine." He made a cradle of her hands and piled more coffee cans on. "Then I'll lend you my shoulder."

"She's got mine any time she wants," Helva put in a little unsteadily.

Onro stopped long enough to glance at Helva.

"You're not making sense either," he said irascibly. "You haven't *got* a shoulder."

"She's making perfectly good sense," Theoda said stoutly as Onro started pushing her toward the lock.

"Come on, Theoda, come on."

She shook off his hand and turned back once more to Helva.

"Thank you, my friend," Theoda murmured and then whirled away, allowing Onro to start the lift.

"No, no, Theoda, I'm the one who's grateful," Helva called as Theoda's head disappeared past the edge of the lock. Softly, to herself, she added, "Your tears were what I really needed."

As the landcar zoomed back toward the hospital complex, Helva could see Theoda's arm waving farewell and knew Theoda understood all that hadn't been said. She smiled to herself. The dust settled down on the road to the hospital as she signaled Regulus Base of the completion of her mission and her estimated return.

Then, like a phoenix rising again from the bitter ashes of her hundred hours' mourning, Helva lifted on the brilliant tail of exploding fuel toward the stars, and healing.

A Woman's Liberation

Ursula K. Le Guin

1. Shomeke

My dear friend has asked me to write the story of my life, thinking it might be of interest to people of other worlds and times. I am an ordinary woman, but I have lived in years of mighty changes and have been advantaged to know with my very flesh the nature of servitude and the nature of freedom.

I did not learn to read or write until I was a grown woman, which is all the excuse I will make for the faults of my narrative.

I was born a slave on the planet Werel. As a child I was called Shomekes' Radosse Rakam. That is, Property of the Shomeke Family, Granddaughter of Dosse, Granddaughter of Kamye. The Shomeke family owned an estate on the eastern coast of Voe Deo. Dosse was my grandmother. Kamye is the Lord God.

The Shomekes possessed over four hundred assets, mostly used to cultivate the fields of gede, to herd the saltgrass cattle, in the mills, and as domestics in the House. The Shomeke family had been great in history. Our Owner was an important man politically, often away in the capital.

Assets took their name from their grandmother because it was the grandmother that raised the child. The mother worked all day, and there was no father. Women were always bred to more than one man. Even if a man knew his child he could not care for it. He might be sold or traded away at any time. Young men were seldom kept long on the estates. If they were valuable they were traded to other estates or sold to the factories. If they were worthless they were worked to death.

Women were not often sold. The young ones were kept for work and breeding, the old ones to raise the young and keep the compound in order. On some estates women bore a baby a year till they died, but on ours most had only two or three children. The Shomekes valued women as workers. They did not want the men always getting at the women. The grandmothers agreed with them and guarded the young women closely.

I say men, women, children, but you are to understand that we were not called men, women, children. Only our owners were called so. We assets or slaves were called bondsmen, bondswomen, and pups or young. I will use these words, though I have not heard or spoken them for many years, and never before on this blessed world.

The bondsmen's part of the compound, the gateside, was ruled by the Bosses, who were men, some relations of the Shomeke family, others hired by them. On the inside the young and the bondswomen lived. There two cutfrees, castrated bondsmen, were the Bosses in name, but the grandmothers ruled. Indeed nothing in the compound happened without the grandmothers' knowledge.

If the grandmothers said an asset was too sick to work, the Bosses would let that one stay home. Sometimes the grandmothers could save a bondsman from being sold away, sometimes they could protect a girl from being bred by more than one man, or could give a delicate girl a contraceptive. Everybody in the compound obeyed the counsel of the grandmothers. But if one of them went too far, the Bosses would have her flogged or blinded or her hands cut off. When I was a young child, there lived in our compound a woman we called Great-Grandmother, who had holes for eyes and no tongue. I thought that she was thus because she was so old. I feared that my grandmother Dosse's tongue would wither in her mouth. I told her that. She said, "No. It won't get any shorter, because I don't let it get too long."

I lived in the compound. My mother birthed me there, and was allowed to stay three months to nurse me; then I was weaned to cow's milk, and my mother returned to the House. Her name was Shomekes' Rayowa Yowa. She was lightskinned like most of the assets, but very beautiful, with slender wrists and ankles and delicate features. My grandmother too was light, but I was dark, darker than anybody else in the compound.

My mother came to visit, the cutfrees letting her in by their ladder-door. She found me rubbing grey dust on my body. When she scolded me, I told her that I wanted to look like the others.

"Listen, Rakam," she said to me, "they are dust people. They'll never get out of the dust. You're something better. And you will be beautiful. Why do you think you're so black?" I had no idea what she meant. "Some day I'll tell you who your father is," she said, as if she were promising me a gift. I had watched when the Shomekes' stallion, a prized and valuable animal, serviced mares from other estates. I did not know a father could be human.

That evening I boasted to my grandmother: "I'm beautiful because the black stallion is my father!" Dosse struck me across the head so that I fell down and wept. She said, "Never speak of your father."

I knew there was anger between my mother and my grandmother, but it was a long time before I understood why. Even now I am not sure I understand all that lay between them.

We little pups ran around in the compound. We knew nothing outside the walls. All our world was the bondswomen's huts and the bondsmen's longhouses, the kitchens and kitchen gardens, the bare plaza beaten hard by bare feet. To me, the stockade wall seemed a long way off.

When the field and mill hands went out the gate in the early morning I didn't know where they went. They were just gone. All day long the whole compound belonged to us pups, naked in the

summer, mostly naked in the winter too, running around playing
with sticks and stones and mud, keeping away from grandmothers,
until we begged them for something to eat or they put us to work
weeding the gardens for a while.

In the evening or the early night the workers would come back,
trooping in the gate guarded by the Bosses. Some were worn out
and grim, others would be cheerful and talking and calling back and
forth. The great gate was slammed behind the last of them. Smoke
went up from all the cooking stoves. The burning cowdung smelled
sweet. People gathered on the porches of the huts and longhouses.
Bondsmen and bondswomen lingered at the ditch that divided the
gateside from the inside, talking across the ditch. After the meal the
freedmen led prayers to Tual's statue, and we lifted our own prayers
to Kamye, and then people went to their beds, except for those who
lingered to "jump the ditch." Some nights, in the summer, there
would be singing, or a dance was allowed. In the winter one of the
grandfathers—poor old broken men, not strong people like the
grandmothers—would "sing the word." That is what we called reciting the *Arkamye*. Every night, always, some of the people were
teaching and others were learning the sacred verses. On winter
nights one of these old worthless bondsmen kept alive by the
grandmothers' charity would begin to sing the word. Then even the
pups would be still to listen to that story.

The friend of my heart was Walsu. She was bigger than I, and
was my defender when there were fights and quarrels among the
young or when older pups called me "Blackie" and "Bossie." I was
small but had a fierce temper. Together, Walsu and I did not get
bothered much. Then Walsu was sent out the gate. Her mother had
been bred and was now stuffed big, so that she needed help in the
fields to make her quota. Gede must be hand harvested. Every day
as a new section of the bearing stalk comes ripe it has to be picked,
and so gede pickers go through the same field over and over for
twenty or thirty days, and then move on to a later planting. Walsu
went with her mother to help her pick her rows. When her mother

fell ill, Walsu took her place, and with help from other hands she kept up her mother's quota. She was then six years old by owner's count, which gave all assets the same birthday, new year's day at the beginning of spring. She might have truly been seven. Her mother remained ill both before birthing and after, and Walsu took her place in the gede field all that time. She never afterward came back to play, only in the evenings to eat and sleep. I saw her then and we could talk. She was proud of her work. I envied her and longed to go through the gate. I followed her to it and looked through it at the world. Now the walls of the compound seemed very close.

I told my grandmother Dosse that I wanted to go to work in the fields.

"You're too young."

"I'll be seven at the new year."

"Your mother made me promise not to let you go out."

Next time my mother visited the compound, I said, "Grand-mother won't let me go out. I want to go work with Walsu."

"Never," my mother said. "You were born for better than that."

"What for?"

"You'll see."

She smiled at me. I knew she meant the House, where she worked. She had told me often of the wonderful things in the House, things that shone and were colored brightly, things that were thin and delicate, clean things. It was quiet in the House, she said. My mother herself wore a beautiful red scarf, her voice was soft, and her clothing and body were always clean and fresh.

"When will I see?"

I teased her until she said, "All right! I'll ask my lady."

"Ask her what?"

All I knew of my-lady was that she too was delicate and clean, and that my mother belonged to her in some particular way, of which she was proud. I knew my-lady had given my mother the red scarf.

"I'll ask her if you can come begin training at the House."

My mother said "the House" in a way that made me see it as a great sacred place like the place in our prayer: *May I enter in the clear house, in the rooms of peace.*

I was so excited I began to dance and sing, "I'm going to the House, to the House!" My mother slapped me to make me stop and scolded me for being wild. She said, "You are too young! You can't behave! If you get sent away from the House you can never come back."

I promised to be old enough.

"You must do everything right," Yowa told me. "You must do everything I say when I say it. Never question. Never delay. If my lady sees that you're wild, she'll send you back here. And that will be the end of you forever."

I promised to be tame. I promised to obey at once in everything, and not to speak. The more frightening she made it, the more I desired to see the wonderful, shining House.

When my mother left I did not believe she would speak to mylady. I was not used to promises being kept. But after some days she returned, and I heard her speaking to my grandmother. Dosse was angry at first, speaking loudly. I crept under the window of the hut to listen. I heard my grandmother weep. I was frightened and amazed. My grandmother was patient with me, always looked after me, and fed me well. It had never entered my mind that there was anything more to it than that, until I heard her crying. Her crying made me cry, as if I were part of her.

"You could let me keep her one more year," she said. "She's just a baby. I would never let her out the gate." She was pleading, as if she were powerless, not a grandmother. "She is my joy, Yowa!"

"Don't you want her to do well, then?"

"Just a year more. She's too wild for the House."

"She's run wild too long. She'll get sent out to the fields if she stays. A year of that and they won't have her at the House. She'll be dust. Anyhow, there's no use crying about it. I asked my lady, and she's expected. I can't go back without her."

"Yowa, don't let her come to harm," Dosse said very low, as if ashamed to say this to her daughter, and yet with strength in her voice.

"I'm taking her to keep her out of harm," my mother said. Then she called me, and I wiped my tears and came.

It is queer, but I do not remember my first walk through the world outside the compound or my first sight of the House. I suppose I was frightened and kept my eyes down, and everything was so strange to me that I did not understand what I saw. I know it was a number of days before my mother took me to show me to Lady Tazeu. She had to scrub me and train me and make sure I would not disgrace her. I was terrified when at last she took my hand, scolding me in a whisper all the time, and brought me out of the bondswomen's quarters, through halls and doorways of painted wood, into a bright, sunny room with no roof, full of flowers growing in pots.

I had hardly ever seen a flower, only the weeds in the kitchen gardens, and I stared and stared at them. My mother had to jerk my hand to make me look at the woman lying in a chair among the flowers, in clothes soft and brightly colored like the flowers. I could hardly tell them apart. The woman's hair was long and shining, and her skin was shining and black. My mother pushed me, and I did what she had made me practice over and over: I went and knelt down beside the chair and waited, and when the woman put out her long, narrow, soft hand, black above and azure on the palm, I touched my forehead to it. I was supposed to say "I am your slave Rakam, Ma'am," but my voice would not come out.

"What a pretty little thing," she said. "So dark." Her voice changed a little on the last words.

"The Bosses came in . . . that night," Yowa said in a timid, smiling way, looking down as if embarrassed.

"No doubt about that," the woman said. I was able to glance up at her again. She was beautiful. I did not know a person could be so beautiful. I think she saw my wonder. She put out her long, soft hand again and caressed my cheek and neck. "Very, very pretty, Yowa," she said. "You did quite right to bring her here. Has she been bathed?"

She would not have asked that if she had seen me when I first came, filthy and smelling of the cowdung we made our fires with. She knew nothing of the compound at all. She knew nothing beyond the beza, the women's side of the House. She was kept there just as I had been kept in the compound, ignorant of anything outside. She had never smelled cowdung, as I had never seen flowers.

My mother assured her I was clean, and she said, "Then she can come to bed with me tonight. I'd like that. Will you like to come sleep with me, pretty little—" She glanced at my mother, who murmured, "Rakam." Ma'am pursed her lips at the name. "I don't like that," she murmured. "So ugly. Toti. Yes. You can be my new Toti. Bring her this evening, Yowa."

She had had a foxdog called Toti, my mother told me. Her pet had died. I did not know animals ever had names, and so it did not seem odd to me to be given an animal's name, but it did seem strange at first not to be Rakam. I could not think of myself as Toti.

That night my mother bathed me again and oiled my skin with sweet oil and dressed me in a soft gown, softer even than her red scarf. Again she scolded and warned me, but she was excited, too, and pleased with me, as we went to the beza again, through other halls, meeting some other bondswomen on the way, and to the lady's bedroom. It was a wonderful room, hung with mirrors and draperies and paintings. I did not understand what the mirrors were, or the paintings, and was frightened when I saw people in them. Lady Tazeu saw that I was frightened. "Come, little one," she said, making a place for me in her great, wide, soft bed strewn with pillows, "come and cuddle up." I crawled in beside her, and she stroked my hair and skin and held me in her warm, soft arms until I was comfortable and at ease. "There, there, little Toti," she said, and so we slept.

I became the pet of Lady Tazeu Wehoma Shomeke. I slept with

her almost every night. Her husband was seldom home and when he was there did not come to her, preferring bondswomen for his pleasure. Sometimes she had my mother or other, younger bondswomen come into her bed, and she sent me away at those times, until I was older, ten or eleven, when she began to keep me and have me join in with them, teaching me how to be pleasured. She was gentle, but she was the mistress in love, and I was her instrument which she played.

I was also trained in household arts and duties. She taught me to sing with her, as I had a true voice. All those years I was never punished and never made to do hard work. I who had been wild in the compound was perfectly obedient in the Great House. I had been rebellious to my grandmother and impatient of her commands, but whatever my lady ordered me to do I gladly did. She held me fast to her by the only kind of love she had to give me. I thought that she was the Merciful Tual come down upon the earth. That is not a way of speaking, that is the truth. I thought she was a higher being, superior to myself.

Perhaps you will say that I could not or should not have had pleasure in being used without my consent by my mistress, and if I did I should not speak of it, showing even so little good in so great an evil. But I knew nothing of consent or refusal. Those are freedom words.

She had one child, a son, three years older than I. She lived quite alone among us bondswomen. The Wehomas were nobles of the Islands, old-fashioned people whose women did not travel, so she was cut off from her family. The only company she had was when Owner Shomeke brought friends with him from the capital, but those were all men, and she could be with them only at table.

I seldom saw the Owner and only at a distance. I thought he too was a superior being, but a dangerous one.

As for Erod, the Young Owner, we saw him when he came to visit his mother daily or when he went out riding with his tutors. We girls would peep at him and giggle to each other when we were eleven or twelve, because he was a handsome boy, nightblack and slender like his mother. I knew that he was afraid of his father, because I had heard him weep when he was with his mother. She would comfort him with candy and caresses, saying, "He'll be gone again soon, my darling." I too felt sorry for Erod, who was like a shadow, soft and harmless. He was sent off to school for a year at fifteen, but his father brought him back before the year was up. Bondsmen told us the Owner had beaten him cruelly and had forbidden him even to ride off the estate.

Bondswomen whom the Owner used told us how brutal he was, showing us where he had bruised and hurt them. They hated him, but my mother would not speak against him. "Who do you think you are?" she said to a girl who was complaining of his use of her. "A lady to be treated like glass?" And when the girl found herself pregnant, stuffed was the word we used, my mother had her sent back to the compound. I did not understand why. I thought Yowa was hard and jealous. Now I think she was also protecting the girl from our lady's jealousy.

I do not know when I understood that I was the Owner's daughter. Because she had kept that secret from our lady, my mother believed it was a secret from all. But the bondswomen all knew it. I do not know what I heard or overheard, but when I saw Erod, I would study him and think that I looked much more like our father than he did, for by then I knew what a father was. And I wondered that Lady Tazeu did not see it. But she chose to live in ignorance.

During these years I seldom went to the compound. After I had been a halfyear or so at the House, I was eager to go back and see Walsu and my grandmother and show them my fine clothes and clean skin and shining hair; but when I went, the pups I used to play with threw dirt and stones at me and tore my clothes. Walsu was in the fields. I had to hide in my grandmother's hut all day. I never wanted to go back. When my grandmother sent for me, I would go only with my mother and always stayed close by her. The people in the compound, even my grandmother, came to look coarse and foul to me. They were dirty and smelled strongly. They had sores, scars from punishment, lopped fingers, ears, or noses. Their hands and feet were coarse, with deformed nails. I was no longer used to people who looked so. We domestics of the Great House were entirely different from them, I thought. Serving the higher beings, we became like them.

When I was thirteen and fourteen Lady Tazeu still kept me in her bed, making love to me often. But also she had a new pet, the daughter of one of the cooks, a pretty little girl though white as clay. One night she made love to me for a long time in ways that she knew gave me great ecstasy of the body. When I lay exhausted in her arms she whispered "goodbye, goodbye," kissing me all over my face and breasts. I was too spent to wonder at this.

The next morning my lady called in my mother and myself to tell us that she intended to give me to her son for his seventeenth birthday. "I shall miss you terribly, Toti darling," she said, with tears in her eyes. "You have been my joy. But there isn't another girl on the place that I could let Erod have. You are the cleanest, dearest, sweetest of them all. I know you are a virgin," she meant a virgin to men, "and I know my boy will enjoy you. And he'll be kind to her, Yowa," she said earnestly to my mother. My mother bowed and said nothing. There was nothing she could say. And she said nothing to me. It was too late to speak of the secret she had been so proud of.

Lady Tazeu gave me medicine to prevent conception, but my mother, not trusting the medicine, went to my grandmother and brought me contraceptive herbs. I took both faithfully that week.

If a man in the House visited his wife he came to the beza, but if he wanted a bondswoman she was "sent across." So on the night of the Young Owner's birthday I was dressed all in red and led over, for the first time in my life, to the men's side of the House.

My reverence for my lady extended to her son, and I had been taught that owners were superior by nature to us. But he was a boy whom I had known since childhood, and I knew that his blood and mine were half the same. It gave me a strange feeling toward him.

I thought he was shy, afraid of his manhood. Other girls had tried to tempt him and failed. The women had told me what I was to do, how to offer myself and encourage him, and I was ready to do that. I was brought to him in his great bedroom, all of stone carved like lace, with high, thin windows of violet glass. I stood timidly near the door for a while, and he stood near a table covered with papers and screens. He came forward at last, took my hand, and led me to a chair. He made me sit down, and spoke to me standing, which was all improper, and confused my mind.

"Rakam," he said—"that's your name, isn't it?"—I nodded— "Rakam, my mother means only kindness, and you must not think me ungrateful to her, or blind to your beauty. But I will not take a woman who cannot freely offer herself. Intercourse between owner and slave is rape." And he talked on, talking beautifully, as when my lady read aloud from one of her books. I did not understand much, except that I was to come whenever he sent for me and sleep in his bed, but he would never touch me. And I was not to speak of this to anyone. "I am sorry, I am very sorry to ask you to lie," he said, so earnestly that I wondered if it hurt him to lie. That made him seem more like a god than a human being. If it hurt to lie, how could you stay alive?

"I will do just as you say, Lord Erod," I said.

So, most nights, his bondsmen came to bring me across. I would sleep in his great bed, while he worked at the papers on his table. He slept on a couch beneath the windows. Often he wanted to talk to me, sometimes for a long time, telling me his ideas. When he was in school in the capital he had become a member of a group of owners who wished to abolish slavery, called The Community. Getting wind of this, his father had ordered him out of school, sent him home, and forbidden him to leave the estate. So he too was a prisoner. But he corresponded constantly with others in The Community through the net, which he knew how to operate without his father's knowledge, or the government's.

His head was so full of ideas he had to speak them. Often Geu

and Ahas, the young bondsmen who had grown up with him, who
always came to fetch me across, stayed with us while he talked to
all of us about slavery and freedom and many other things. Often I
was sleepy, but I did listen, and heard much I did not know how to
understand or even believe. He told us there was an organization
among assets, called the Hame, that worked to steal slaves from the
plantations. These slaves would be brought to members of The
Community, who would make out false papers of ownership and
treat them well, renting them to decent work in the cities. He told
us about the cities, and I loved to hear all that. He told us about
Yeowe Colony, saying that there was a revolution there among the
slaves.

Of Yeowe I knew nothing. It was a great blue-green star that set
after the sun or rose before it, brighter than the smallest of the
moons. It was a name in an old song they sang in the compound:

> O, O, Ye-o-we,
> Nobody never comes back.

I had no idea what a revolution was. When Erod told me that it
meant that assets on plantations in this place called Yeowe were
fighting their owners, I did not understand how assets could do
that. From the beginning it was ordained that there should be
higher and lower beings, the Lord and the human, the man and the
woman, the owner and the owned. All my world was Shomeke Estate and it stood on that one foundation. Who would want to over-
turn it? Everyone would be crushed in the ruins.

I did not like Erod to call assets slaves, an ugly word that took
away our value. I decided in my mind that here on Werel we were
assets, and in that other place, Yeowe Colony, there were slaves,
worthless bondspeople, intractables. That was why they had been
sent there. It made good sense.

By this you know how ignorant I was. Sometimes Lady Tazeu
had let us watch shows on the holonet with her, but she watched
only dramas, not the reports of events. Of the world beyond the es-

tate I knew nothing but what I learned from Erod, and that I could not understand.

Erod liked us to argue with him. He thought it meant our minds were growing free. Geu was good at it. He would ask questions like, "But if there's no assets who'll do the work?" Then Erod could answer at length. His eyes shone, his voice was eloquent. I loved him very much when he talked to us. He was beautiful and what he said was beautiful. It was like hearing the old men "singing the word," reciting the *Arkamye,* when I was a little pup in the compound.

I gave the contraceptives my lady gave me every month to girls who needed them. Lady Tazeu had aroused my sexuality and accustomed me to being used sexually. I missed her caresses. But I did not know how to approach any of the bondswomen, and they were afraid to approach me, since I belonged to the Young Owner. Being with Erod often, while he talked I yearned to him in my body. I lay in his bed and dreamed that he came and stooped over me and did with me as my lady used to do. But he never touched me.

Geu also was a handsome young man, clean and well-mannered, rather dark-skinned, attractive to me. His eyes were always on me. But he would not approach me, until I told him that Erod did not touch me.

Thus I broke my promise to Erod not to tell anyone; but I did not think myself bound to keep promises, as I did not think myself bound to speak the truth. Honor of that kind was for owners, not for us.

After that, Geu used to tell me when to meet him in the attics of the House. He gave me little pleasure. He would not penetrate me, believing that he must save my virginity for our master. He had me take his penis in my mouth instead. He would turn away in his climax, for the slave's sperm must not defile the master's woman. That is the honor of a slave.

Now you may say in disgust that my story is all of such things, and there is far more to life, even a slave's life, than sex. That is very true. I can say only that it may be in our sexuality that we are most easily enslaved, both men and women. It may be there, even as free men and women, that we find freedom hardest to keep. The politics of the flesh are the roots of power.

I was young, full of health and desire for joy. And even now, even here, when I look back across the years from this world to that, to the compound and the House of Shomeke, I see images like those in a bright dream. I see my grandmother's big, hard hands. I see my mother smiling, the red scarf about her neck. I see my lady's black, silky body among the cushions. I smell the smoke of the cow-dung fires, and the perfumes of the beza. I feel the soft, fine clothing on my young body, and my lady's hands and lips. I hear the old men singing the word, and my voice twining with my lady's voice in a love song, and Erod telling us of freedom. His face is illuminated with his vision. Behind him the windows of stone lace and violet glass keep out the night. I do not say I would go back. I would die before I would go back to Shomeke. I would die before I left this free world, my world, to go back to the place of slavery. But whatever I knew in my youth of beauty, of love, and of hope, was there.

And there it was betrayed. All that is built upon that foundation in the end betrays itself.

I was sixteen years old in the year the world changed.

The first change I heard about was of no interest to me except that my lord was excited about it, and so were Geu and Ahas and some of the other young bondsmen. Even my grandmother wanted to hear about it when I visited her. "That Yeowe, that slave world," she said, "they made freedom? They sent away their owners? They opened the gates? My lord, sweet Lord Kamye, how can that be? Praise his name, praise his marvels!" She rocked back and forth as she squatted in the dust, her arms about her knees. She was an old, shrunken woman now. "Tell me!" she said.

I knew little else to tell her. "All the soldiers came back here," I said. "And those other people, those alemens, they're there in

Yeowe. Maybe they're the new owners. That's all somewhere way out there," I said, flipping my hand at the sky.

"What's alemens?" my grandmother asked, but I did not know. It was all mere words to me.

But when our Owner, Lord Shomeke, came home sick, that I understood. He came on a flyer to our little port. I saw him carried by on a stretcher, the whites showing in his eyes, his black skin mottled grey. He was dying of a sickness that was ravaging the cities. My mother, sitting with Lady Tazeu, saw a politician on the net who said that the alemens had brought the sickness to Werel. He talked so fearsomely that we thought everybody was going to die. When I told Geu about it he snorted. "Aliens, not alemens," he said, "and they've got nothing to do with it. My lord talked with the doctors. It's just a new kind of pusworm."

That dreadful disease was bad enough. We knew that any asset found to be infected with it was slaughtered at once like an animal and the corpse burned on the spot.

They did not slaughter the Owner. The House filled with doctors, and Lady Tazeu spent day and night by her husband's bed. It was a cruel death. It went on and on. Lord Shomeke in his suffering made terrible sounds, screams, howls. One would not believe a man could cry out hour after hour as he did. His flesh ulcerated and fell away, he went mad, but he did not die.

As Lady Tazeu became like a shadow, worn and silent, Erod filled with strength and excitement. Sometimes when we heard his father howling his eyes would shine. He would whisper, "Lady Tual have mercy on him," but he fed on those cries. I knew from Geu and Ahas, who had been brought up with him, how the father had tormented and despised him, and how Erod had vowed to be everything his father was not and to undo all he did.

But it was Lady Tazeu who ended it. One night she sent away the other attendants, as she often did, and sat alone with the dying man. When he began his moaning howl, she took her little sewing-knife and cut his throat. Then she cut the veins in her arms across and across, and lay down by him, and so died. My mother was in the next room all night. She said she wondered a little at the silence, but was so weary that she fell asleep; and in the morning she went in and found them lying in their cold blood.

All I wanted to do was weep for my lady, but everything was in confusion. Everything in the sickroom must be burned, the doctors said, and the bodies must be burned without delay. The House was under quarantine, so only the priests of the House could hold the funeral. No one was to leave the estate for twenty days. But several of the doctors themselves left when Erod, who was now Lord Shomeke, told them what he intended to do. I heard some confused word of it from Ahas, but in my grief I paid little heed.

That evening, all the House assets stood outside the Lady's Chapel during the funeral service to hear the songs and prayers within. The Bosses and cutfrees had brought the people from the compound, and they stood behind us. We saw the procession come out, the white biers carried by, the pryes lighted, and the black smoke go up. Long before the smoke ceased rising, the new Lord Shomeke came to us all where we stood.

Erod stood up on the little rise of ground behind the chapel and spoke in a strong voice such as I had never heard from him. Always in the House it had been whispering in the dark. Now it was broad day and a strong voice. He stood there black and straight in his white mourning clothes. He was not yet twenty years old. He said, "Listen, you people: you have been slaves, you will be free. You have been my property, you will own your own lives now. This morning I sent to the Government the Order of Manumission for every asset on the estate, four hundred and eleven men, women, and children. If you will come to my office in the Counting House in the morning, I will give you your papers. Each of you is named in those papers as a free person. You can never be enslaved again. You are free to do as you please from tomorrow on. There will be money for each one of you to begin your new life with. Not what you deserve, not what you have earned in all your work for us, but what I have to give you. I am leaving Shomeke. I will go to the capital, where I will work for the freedom of every slave on Werel. The Freedom Day that came to Yeowe is coming to us, and soon. Any of you who wish to come with me, come! There's work for us all to do!"

I remember all he said. Those are his words as he spoke them. When one does not read and has not had one's mind filled up by the images on the nets, words spoken strike down deep in the mind.

There was such a silence when he stopped speaking as I had never heard.

One of the doctors began talking, protesting to Erod that he must not break the quarantine.

"The evil has been burned away," Erod said, with a great gesture to the black smoke rising. "This has been an evil place, but no more harm will go forth from Shomeke!"

At that a slow sound began among the compound people standing behind us, and it swelled into a great noise of jubilation mixed with wailing, crying, shouting, singing. "Lord Kamye! Lord Kamye!" the men shouted. An old woman came forward: my grandmother. She strode through us House assets as if we were a field of grain. She stopped a good way from Erod. People fell silent to listen to the grandmother. She said, "Lord Master, are you turning us out of our homes?"

"No," he said. "They are yours. The land is yours to use. The profit of the fields is yours. This is your home, and you are free!"

At that the shouts rose up again so loud I cowered down and covered my ears, but I was crying and shouting too, praising Lord Erod and Lord Kamye in one voice with the rest of them.

We danced and sang there in sight of the burning pyres until the sun went down. At last the grandmothers and the freedmen got the people to go back to the compound, saying they did not have their papers yet. We domestics went straggling back to the House, talking about tomorrow, when we would get our freedom and our money and our land.

All that next day Erod sat in the Counting House and made out the papers for each slave and counted out the same amount of money for each: a hundred kue in cash, and a draft for five hundred kue on the district bank, which could not be drawn for forty days. This was, he explained to each one, to save them from exploitation by the unscrupulous before they knew how best to use their money. He advised them to form a cooperative, to pool their funds, to run the estate democratically. "Money in the bank, Lord!" an old crippled man came out crying, jigging on his twisted legs. "Money in the bank, Lord!"

If they wanted, Erod said over and over, they could save their money and contact the Hame, who would help them buy passage to Yeowe with it.

"O, O, Ye-o-we," somebody began singing, and they changed the words.

> "Everybody's going to go.
> O, O, Ye-o-we,
> Everybody's going to go!"

They sang it all day long. Nothing could change the sadness of it. I want to weep now, remembering that song, that day.

The next morning Erod left. He could not wait to get away from the place of his misery and begin his life in the capital working for freedom. He did not say goodbye to me. He took Geu and Ahas with him. The doctors and their aides and assets had all left the day before. We watched his flyer go up into the air.

We went back to the House. It was like something dead. There were no owners in it, no masters, no one to tell us what to do.

My mother and I went in to pack up our clothing. We had said little to each other, but felt we could not stay there. We heard other women running through the beza, rummaging in Lady Tazeu's rooms, going through her closets, laughing and screaming with excitement, finding jewelry and valuables. We heard men's voices in the hall: Bosses' voices. Without a word my mother and I took what we had in our hands and went out by a back door, slipped through the hedges of the garden, and ran all the way to the compound.

The great gate of the compound stood wide open.

How can I tell you what that was to us, to see that, to see that gate stand open? How can I tell you?

2. Zeskra

Erod knew nothing about how the estate was run, because the Bosses ran it. He was a prisoner too. He had lived in his screens, his dreams, his visions.

The grandmothers and others in the compound had spent all that night trying to make plans, to draw our people together so they could defend themselves. That morning when my mother and I came, there were bondsmen guarding the compound with weapons made of farm tools. The grandmothers and cutfrees had made an election of a headman, a strong, well-liked field hand. In that way they hoped to keep the young men with them.

By the afternoon that hope was broken. The young men ran wild. They went up to the House to loot it. The Bosses shot them from the windows, killing many; the others fled away. The Bosses stayed holed up in the House, drinking the wine of the Shomekes. Owners of other plantations were flying reinforcements to them. We heard the flyers land, one after another. The bondswomen who had stayed in the House were at their mercy now.

As for us in the compound, the gates were closed again. We had moved the great bars from the outside to the inside, so we thought ourselves safe for the night at least. But in the midnight they came with heavy tractors and pushed down the wall, and a hundred men or more, our Bosses and owners from all the plantations of the region, came swarming in. They were armed with guns. We fought them with farm tools and pieces of wood. One or two of them were hurt or killed. They killed as many of us as they wanted to kill and then began to rape us. It went on all night.

A group of men took all the old women and men and held them and shot them between the eyes, the way they kill cattle. My grandmother was one of them. I do not know what happened to my mother. I did not see any bondsmen living when they took me away in the morning. I saw white papers lying in the blood on the ground. Freedom papers.

Several of us girls and young women still alive were herded into a truck and taken to the port-field. There they made us enter a flyer, shoving and using sticks, and we were carried off in the air. I was not then in my right mind. All I know of this is what the others told me later.

We found ourselves in a compound, like our compound in every way. I thought they had brought us back home. They shoved us in by the cutfrees' ladder. It was morning and the hands were out at work, only the grandmothers and pups and old men in the compound. The grandmothers came to us fierce and scowling. I could not understand at first why they were all strangers. I looked for my grandmother.

They were frightened of us, thinking we must be runaways. Plantation slaves had been running away, the last years, trying to get to the cities. They thought we were intractables and would bring trouble with us. But they helped us clean ourselves, and gave us a place near the cutfrees' tower. They were no huts empty, they said. They told us this was Zeskra Estate. They did not want to hear about what had happened at Shomeke. They did not want us to be there. They did not need our trouble.

We slept on the ground without shelter. Some of the bondsmen came across the ditch in the night and raped us because there was nothing to prevent them from it, no one to whom we were of any value. We were too weak and sick to fight them. One of us, a girl named Abye, tried to fight. The men beat her insensible. In the morning she could not talk or walk. She was left there when the Bosses came and took us away. Another girl was left behind too, a big farmhand with white scars on her head like parts in her hair. As we were going I looked at her and saw that it was Walsu, who had been my friend. We had not recognized each other. She sat in the dirt, her head bowed down.

Five of us were taken from the compound to the Great House of Zeskra, to the bondswomen's quarters. There for a while I had a little hope, since I knew how to be a good domestic asset. I did not know then how different Zeskra was from Shomeke. The House of Zeskra was full of people, full of owners and bosses. It was a big family, not a single Lord as at Shomeke but a dozen of them with their retainers and relations and visitors, so there might be thirty or forty men staying on the men's side and as many women in the beza, and a House staff of fifty or more. We were not brought as domestics, but as use-women.

After we were bathed we were left in the use-women's quarters, a big room without any private places. There were ten or more use-women already there. Those of them who liked their work were not glad to see us, thinking of us as rivals; others welcomed us, hoping we might take their places and they might be let join the domestic staff. But none were very unkind, and some were kind, giving us clothes, for we had been naked all this time, and comforting the youngest of us, Mio, a little compound girl of ten or eleven whose white body was mottled all over with brown and blue bruises.

One of them was a tall woman called Sezi-Tual. She looked at me with an ironic face. Something in her made my soul awaken.

"You're not a dusty," she said. "You're as black as old Lord Devil Zeskra himself. You're a Bossbaby, aren't you?"

"No ma'am," I said. "A Lord's child. And the Lord's child. My name is Rakam."

"Your Grandfather hasn't treated you too well lately," she said. "Maybe you should pray to the Merciful Lady Tual."

"I don't look for mercy," I said. From then on Sezi-Tual liked me, and I had her protection, which I needed.

We were sent across to the men's side most nights. When there were dinner parties, after the ladies left the dinner room we were brought in to sit on the owners' knees and drink wine with them. Then they would use us there on the couches or take us to their rooms. The men of Zeskra were not cruel. Some liked to rape, but most preferred to think that we desired them and wanted whatever they wanted. Such men could be satisfied, the one kind if we showed fear or submission, the other kind if we showed yielding and delight. But some of their visitors were another kind of man.

There was no law or rule against damaging or killing a use-woman. Her owner might not like it, but in his pride he could not say so: he was supposed to have so many assets that the loss of one or another did not matter at all. So some men whose pleasure lay in torture came to hospitable estates like Zeskra for their pleasure. Sezi-Tual, a favorite of the Old Lord, could and did protest to him, and such guests were not invited back. But while I was there, Mio, the little girl who had come with us from Shomeke, was murdered by a guest. He tied her down to the bed. He made the knot across her neck so tight that while he used her she strangled to death.

I will say no more of these things. I have told what I must tell. There are truths that are not useful. All knowledge is local, my friend has said. Is it true, where is it true, that that child had to die in that way? Is it true, where is it true, that she did not have to die in that way?

I was often used by Lord Yaseo, a middle-aged man, who liked my dark skin, calling me "My Lady." Also he called me "Rebel," because what had happened at Shomeke they called a rebellion of the slaves. Nights when he did not send for me I served as a common-girl.

After I had been at Zeskra two years Sezi-Tual came to me one morning early. I had come back late from Lord Yaseo's bed. Not many others were there, for there had been a drinking party the night before, and all the common-girls had been sent for. Sezi-Tual woke me. She had strange hair, curly, in a bush. I remember her face above me, that hair curling out all about it. "Rakam," she whispered, "one of my visitor's assets spoke to me last night. He gave me this. He said his name is Suhame."

"Suhame," I repeated. I was sleepy. I looked at what she was holding out to me: some dirty crumpled paper. "I can't read!" I said, yawning, impatient.

But I looked at it and knew it. I knew what it said. It was the freedom paper. It was my freedom paper. I had watched Lord Erod write my name on it. Each time he wrote a name he had spoken it aloud so that we would know what he was writing. I remembered the big flourish of the first letter of both my names: Radosse Rakam. I took the paper in my hand, and my hand was shaking. "Where did you get this?" I whispered.

"Better ask this Suhame," she said. Now I heard what that name meant: "from the Hame." It was a password name. She knew that too. She was watching me, and she bent down suddenly and leaned her forehead against mine, her breath catching in her throat. "If I can I'll help," she whispered.

I met with "Suhame" in one of the pantries. As soon as I saw him I knew him: Ahas, who had been Lord Erod's favorite along with Geu. A slight, silent young man with dusty skin, he had never been much in my mind. He had watchful eyes, and I had thought when Geu and I spoke that he looked at us with ill will. Now he looked at me with a strange face, still watchful, yet blank.

"Why are you here with that Lord Boeba?" I asked. "Aren't you free?"

"I am as free as you are," he said.

I did not understand him, then.

"Didn't Lord Erod protect even you?" I asked.

"Yes. I am a free man." His face began to come alive, losing that dead blankness it had when he first saw me. "Lady Boeba's a member of The Community. I work with the Hame. I've been trying to find people from Shomeke. We heard several of the women were here. Are there others still alive, Rakam?"

His voice was soft, and when he said my name my breath

caught and my throat swelled. I said his name and went to him, holding him. "Ratual, Ramayo, Keo are still here," I said. He held me gently. "Walsu is in the compound," I said, "if she's still alive." I wept. I had not wept since Mio's death. He too was in tears.

We talked, then and later. He explained to me that we were indeed, by law, free, but that law meant nothing on the Estates. The government would not interfere between owners and those they claimed as their assets. If we claimed our rights the Zeskras would probably kill us, since they considered us stolen goods and did not want to be shamed. We must run away or be stolen away, and get to the city, the capital, before we could have any safety at all.

We had to be sure that none of the Zeskra assets would betray us out of jealousy or to gain favor. Sezi-Tual was the only one I trusted entirely.

Ahas arranged our escape with Sezi-Tual's help. I pleaded once with her to join us, but she thought that since she had no papers she would have to live always in hiding, and that would be worse than her life at Zeskra.

"You could go to Yeowe," I said.

She laughed. "All I know about Yeowe is nobody ever came back. Why run from one hell to the next one?"

Ratual chose not to come with us; she was a favorite of one of the young lords and content to remain so. Ramayo, the oldest of us from Shomeke, and Keo, who was now about fifteen, wanted to come. Sezi-Tual went down to the compound and found that Walsu was alive, working as a fieldhand. Arranging her escape was far more difficult than ours. There was no escape from a compound. She could get away only in daylight, in the fields, under the overseer's and the Boss's eyes. It was difficult even to talk to her, for the grandmothers were distrustful. But Sezi-Tual managed it, and Walsu told her she would do whatever she must do "to see her paper again."

Lady Boeba's flyer waited for us at the edge of a great gede field that had just been harvested. It was late summer. Ramayo, Keo, and

I walked away from the House separately at different times of the morning. Nobody watched over us closely, as there was nowhere for us to go. Zeskra lies among other great estates, where a runaway slave would find no friends for hundreds of miles. One by one, taking different ways, we came through the fields and woods, crouching and hiding all the way to the flyer where Ahas waited for us. My heart beat and beat so I could not breathe. There we waited for Walsu.

"There!" said Keo, perched up on the wing of the flyer. She pointed across the wide field of stubble.

Walsu came running from the strip of trees on the far side of the field. She ran heavily, steadily, not as if she were afraid. But all at once she halted. She turned. We did not know why for a moment. Then we saw two men break from the shadow of the trees in pursuit of her.

She did not run from them, leading them toward us. She ran back at them. She leapt at them like a hunting cat. As she made that leap, one of them fired a gun. She bore one man down with her, falling. The other fired again and again. "In," Ahas said, "Now." We scrambled into the flyer and it rose into the air, seemingly all in one instant, the same instant in which Walsu made that great leap, she too rising into the air, into her death, into her freedom.

3. The City

I had folded up my freedom paper into a tiny packet. I carried it in my hand all the time we were in the flyer and while we landed and went in a public car through the city street. When Ahas found what I was clutching, he said I need not worry about it. Our manumission was on record in the Government Office and would be honored, here in the City. We were free people, he said. We were gareots, that is, owners who have no assets. "Just like Lord Erod," he said. That meant nothing to me. There was too much to learn. I kept hold of my freedom paper until I had a place to keep it safe. I have it still.

We walked a little way in the streets and then Ahas led us into one of the huge houses that stood side by side on the pavement. He called it a compound, but we thought it must be an owner's house. There a middle-aged woman welcomed us. She was pale-skinned, but talked and behaved like an owner, so that I did not know what she was. She said she was Ress, a rentswoman and an elderwoman of the house.

Rentspeople were assets rented out by their owners to a company. If they were hired by a big company they lived in the company compounds, but there were many, many rentspeople in the City who worked for small companies or businesses they managed themselves, and they occupied buildings run for profit, called open compounds. In such places the occupants must keep curfew, the doors being locked at night, but that was all; they were self-governed. This was such an open compound. It was supported by The Community. Some of the occupants were rentspeople, but many were like us, gareots who had been slaves. Over a hundred people lived there in forty apartments. It was supervised by several women, whom I would have called grandmothers, but here they were called elderwomen.

On the estates deep in the country, deep in the past, where the life was protected by miles of land and by the custom of centuries and by determined ignorance, any asset was absolutely at the mercy of any owner. From there we had come into this great crowd of two million people where nothing and nobody was protected from chance or change, where we had to learn as fast as we could how to stay alive, but where our life was in our own hands.

I had never seen a street. I could not read a word. I had much to learn.

Ress made that clear at once. She was a City woman, quick-thinking and quick-talking, impatient, aggressive, sensitive. I could not like or understand her for a long time. She made me feel stupid, slow, a clod. Often I was angry at her.

There was anger in me now. I had not felt anger while I lived at Zeskra. I could not. It would have eaten me. Here there was room for it, but I found no use for it. I lived with it in silence. Keo and Ramayo had a big room together, I had a small one next to theirs. I had never had a room to myself. At first I felt lonely in it and as if ashamed, but soon I came to like it. The first thing I did freely, as a free woman, was to shut my door.

Nights, I would shut my door and study. Days, we had work training in the morning, classes in the afternoon: reading and writing, arithmetic, history. My work training was in a small shop which made boxes of paper and thin wood to hold cosmetics, candles, jewelry, and such things. I was trained in all the different steps and crafts of making and ornamenting the boxes, for that is how most work was done in the City, by artisans who knew all their trade. The shop was owned by a member of The Community. The older workers were rentspeople. When my training was finished I too would be paid wages.

Till then Lord Erod supported me as well as Keo and Amayo and some men from Shomeke compound, who lived in a different house. Erod never came to the house. I think he did not want to see any of the people he had so disastrously freed. Ahas and Geu said he had sold most of the land at Shomeke and used the money for The Community and to make his way in politics, as there was now a Radical Party which favored emancipation.

Geu came a few times to see me. He had become a City man, dapper and knowing. I felt when he looked at me he was thinking I had been a use-woman at Zeskra, and I did not like to see him.

Ahas, whom I had never thought about in the old days, I now admired, knowing him brave, resolute, and kind. It was he who had looked for us, found us, rescued us. Owners had paid the money but Ahas had done it. He came often to see us. He was the only link that had not broken between me and my childhood.

And he came as a friend, a companion, never driving me back into my slave body. I was angry now at every man who looked at me as men look at women. I was angry at women who looked at me seeing me sexually. To Lady Tazeu all I had been was my body. At Zeskra that was all I had been. Even to Erod who would not touch me that was all I had been. Flesh to touch or not to touch, as they pleased. To use or not to use, as they chose. I hated the sexual parts of myself, my genitals and breasts and the swell of my hips and belly. Ever since I was a child, I had been dressed in soft clothing made to display all that sexuality of a woman's body. When I began to be paid and could buy or make my own clothing, I dressed in hard, heavy cloth. What I liked of myself was my hands, clever at their work, and my head, not clever at learning, but still learning, no matter how long it took.

What I loved to learn was history. I had grown up without any history. There was nothing at Shomeke or Zeskra but the way things were. Nobody knew anything about any time when things had been different. Nobody knew there was any place where things might be different. We were enslaved by the present time.

Erod had talked of change, indeed, but the owners were going to make the change. We were to be changed, we were to be freed, just as we had been owned. In history I saw that any freedom has been made, not given.

The first book I read by myself was a history of Yeowe, written very simply. It told about the days of the Colony, of the Four Corporations, of the terrible first century when the ships carried slave men to Yeowe and precious ores back. Slave men were so cheap then they worked them to death in a few years in the mines, bringing in new shipments continually. *O, O, Yeowe, nobody never comes back.* Then the Corporations began to send women slaves to work and breed, and over the years the assets spilled out of the compounds and made cities—whole great cities like this one I was living in. But not run by the owners or Bosses. Run by the assets, the way this house was run by us. On Yeowe the assets had belonged to the Corporations. They could rent their freedom by paying the Corporation a part of what they earned, the way sharecropper assets paid their owners in parts of Voe Deo. On Yeowe they called those assets freedpeople. Not free people, but freedpeople. And then, this history I was reading said, they began to think, why aren't we free people? So they made the revolution, the Liberation. It began on a plantation called Nadami, and spread from there. Thirty years they fought for their freedom. And just three years ago they had won the war, they had driven the Corporations, the owners, the Bosses, off their world. They had danced and sung in the streets, freedom, freedom! This book I was reading (slowly, but reading it) had been printed there—there on Yeowe, the Free World. The Aliens had brought it to Werel. To me it was a sacred book.

I asked Ahas what it was like now on Yeowe, and he said they were making their government, writing a perfect Constitution to make all men equal under the Law.

On the net, on the news, they said they were fighting each other on Yeowe, there was no government at all, people were starving, savage tribesmen in the countryside and youth gangs in the cities running amok, law and order broken down. Corruption, ignorance, a doomed attempt, a dying world, they said.

Ahas said that the Government of Voe Deo, which had fought and lost the war against Yeowe, now was afraid of a Liberation on Werel. "Don't believe any news," he counseled me. "Especially don't believe the neareals. Don't ever go into them. They're just as much lies as the rest, but if you feel and see a thing you will believe it. And they know that. They don't need guns if they own our minds." The owners had no reporters, no cameras on Yeowe, he said; they invented their "news," using actors. Only some of the aliens of the Ekumen were allowed on Yeowe, and the Yeowans were debating whether they should send them away, keeping the world they had won for themselves alone.

"But then what about us?" I said, for I had begun dreaming of going there, going to the Free World, when the Hame could charter ships and send people.

"Some of them say assets can come. Others say they can't feed so many, and would be overwhelmed. They're debating it democratically. It will be decided in the first Yeowan Elections, soon." Ahas was dreaming of going there too. We talked of our dream the way lovers talk of their love.

But there were no ships going to Yeowe now. The Hame could not act openly and The Community was forbidden to act for them. The Ekumen had offered transportation on their own ships to anyone who wanted to go, but the government of Voe Deo refused to let them use any space port for that purpose. They could carry only their own people. No Werelian was to leave Werel.

It had been only forty years since Werel had at last allowed the Aliens to land and maintain diplomatic relations. As I went on reading history I began to understand a little of the nature of the dominant people of Werel. The black-skinned race that conquered all the other peoples of the Great Continent, and finally all the world, those who call themselves the owners, have lived in the belief that there is only one way to be. They have believed they are what people should be, do as people should do, and know all the truth that is known. All the other peoples of Werel, even when they resisted them, imitated them, trying to become them, and so became their property. When a people came out of the sky looking differently, doing differently, knowing differently, and would not let themselves be conquered or enslaved, the owner race wanted nothing to do with them. It took them four hundred years to admit that they had equals.

I was in the crowd at a rally of the Radical Party, at which Erod spoke, as beautifully as ever. I noticed a woman beside me in the crowd listening. Her skin was a curious orange-brown, like the rind of a pini, and the whites showed in the corners of her eyes. I thought she was sick—I thought of the pusworm, how Lord Shomeke's skin had changed and his eyes had shown their whites.

I shuddered and drew away. She glanced at me, smiling a little, and returned her attention to the speaker. Her hair curled in a bush or cloud, like Sezi-Tual's. Her clothing was of a delicate cloth, a strange fashion. It came upon me very slowly what she was, that she had come here from a world unimaginably far. And the wonder of it was that for all her strange skin and eyes and hair and mind, she was human, as I am human: I had no doubt of that. I felt it. For a moment it disturbed me deeply. Then it ceased to trouble me and I felt a great curiosity, almost a yearning, a drawing to her. I wished to know her, to know what she knew.

In me the owner's soul was struggling with the free soul. So it will do all my life.

Keo and Ramayo stopped going to school after they learned to read and write and use the calculator, but I kept on. When there were no more classes to take from the school the Hame kept, the teachers helped me find classes in the net. Though the government controlled such courses, there were fine teachers and groups from all over the world, talking about literature and history and the sciences and arts. Always I wanted more history.

Ress, who was a member of the Hame, first took me to the Library of Voe Deo. As it was open only to owners, it was not censored by the government. Freed assets, if they were light-skinned, were kept out by the librarians on one pretext or another. I was dark-skinned, and had learned here in the City to carry myself with an indifferent pride that spared one many insults and offenses. Ress told me to stride in as if I owned the place. I did so, and was given all privileges without question. So I began to read freely, to read any book I wanted in that great library, every book in it if I could. That was my joy, that reading. That was the heart of my freedom.

Beyond my work at the boxmaker's, which was well paid, pleasant, and among pleasant companions, and my learning and reading, there was not much to my life. I did not want more. I was lonely, but I felt that loneliness was no high price to pay for what I wanted.

Ress, whom I had disliked, was a friend to me. I went with her to meetings of the Hame, and also to entertainments that I would have known nothing about without her guidance. "Come on, Bumpkin," she would say. "Got to educate the plantation pup." And she would take me to the makil theater, or to asset dance halls where the music was good. She always wanted to dance. I let her teach me, but was not very happy dancing. One night as we were dancing the "slow-go" her hands began pressing me to her, and looking in her face I saw the mask of sexual desire on it, soft and blank. I broke away. "I don't want to dance," I said.

We walked home. She came up to my room with me, and at my door she tried to hold and kiss me. I was sick with anger. "I don't want that!" I said.

"I'm sorry, Rakam," she said, more gently than I had ever heard her speak. "I know how you must feel. But you've got to get over that, you've got to have your own life. I'm not a man, and I do want you."

I broke in—"A woman used me before a man ever did. Did you ask me if I wanted you? I will never be used again!"

That rage and spite came bursting out of me like poison from an infection. If she had tried to touch me again I would have hurt her. I slammed my door in her face. I went trembling to my desk, sat down, and began to read the book that was open on it.

Next day we were both ashamed and stiff. But Ress had patience under her City quickness and roughness. She did not try to make love to me again, but she got me to trust her and talk to her as I could not talk to anybody else. She listened intently and told me what she thought. She said, "Bumpkin, you have it all wrong. No wonder. How could you have got it right? You think sex is something that gets done to you. It's not. It's something you do. With somebody else. Not to them. You never had any sex. All you ever knew was rape."

"Lord Erod told me all that a long time ago," I said. I was bitter. "I don't care what it's called. I had enough of it. For the rest of my life. And I'm glad to be without it."

Ress made a face. "At twenty-two?" she said. "Maybe for a while. If you're happy, then fine. But think about what I said. Love is a big part of life to just cut out."

"If I have to have sex I can pleasure myself," I said, not caring if I hurt her. "Love has nothing to do with it."

"That's where you're wrong," she said, but I did not listen. I would learn from teachers and books that I chose for myself, but I would not take advice I had not asked for. I refused to be told what to do or what to think. If I was free, I would be free by myself. I was like a baby when it first stands up.

Ahas had been giving me advice too. He said it was foolish to pursue education so far. "There's nothing useful you can do with so much book-learning," he said. "It's self-indulgent. We need leaders and members with practical skills."

"We need teachers!"

"Yes," he said, "but you knew enough to teach a year ago. What's the good of ancient history, facts about alien worlds? We have a revolution to make!"

I did not stop my reading, but I felt guilty. I took a class at the Hame school teaching illiterate assets and freedpeople to read and write, as I myself had been taught only three years before. It was hard work. Reading is hard for a grown person to learn, tired, at night, after work all day. It is much easier to let the net take one's mind over.

I kept arguing with Ahas in my mind, and one day I said to him, "Is there a Library on Yeowe?"

"I don't know."

"You know there isn't. The Corporations didn't leave any libraries there. They didn't have any. They were ignorant people who knew nothing but profit. Knowledge is a good in itself. I keep on learning so that I can bring my knowledge to Yeowe. If I could I'd bring them the whole Library!"

He stared. "What owners thought, what owners did—that's all their books are about. They don't need that on Yeowe."

"Yes they do," I said, certain he was wrong, though again I could not say why.

At the school they soon called on me to teach history, one of the teachers having left. These classes went well. I worked hard preparing them. Presently I was asked to speak to a study group of advanced students, and that too went well. People were interested in the ideas I drew and the comparisons I had learned to make of our world with other worlds. I had been studying the way various peoples bring up their children, who takes the responsibility for them and how that responsibility is understood, since this seemed to me a place where a people frees or enslaves itself.

To one of these talks a man from the Embassy of the Ekumen came. I was frightened when I saw the alien face in my audience. I was worse frightened when I recognized him. He had taught the first course in Ekumenical History that I had taken in the net. I had listened to it devotedly though I never participated in the discussion. What I learned had had a great influence on me. I thought he would find me presumptuous for talking of things he truly knew. I stammered on through my lecture, trying not to see his white-cornered eyes.

He came up to me afterward, introduced himself politely, complimented my talk, and asked if I had read such-and-such a book. He engaged me so deftly and kindly in conversation that I had to like and trust him. And he soon earned my trust. I needed his guidance, for much foolishness has been written and spoken, even by wise people, about the balance of power between men and women, on which depend the lives of children and the value of their education. He knew useful books to read, from which I could go on by myself.

His name was Esdardon Aya. He worked in some high position, I was not sure what, at the Embassy. He had been born on Hain, the Old World, humanity's first home, from which all our ancestors came.

Sometimes I thought how strange it was that I knew about such things, such vast and ancient matters, I who had not known anything outside the compound walls till I was six, who had not known the name of the country I lived in till I was eighteen! That was only five years ago, when I was new to the City. Someone had spoken of "Voe Deo," and I had asked, "Where is that?" They had all stared at me. A woman, a hard-voiced old City rentswoman, had said, "Here, Dusty. Right here's Voe Deo. Your country and mine!"

I told Esdardon Aya that. He did not laugh. "A country, a people," he said. "Those are strange and very difficult ideas."

"My country was slavery," I said, and he nodded.

By now I seldom saw Ahas. I missed his kind friendship, but it had all turned to scolding. "You're puffed up, publishing, talking to audiences all the time," he said, "you're putting yourself before our cause."

I said, "But I talk to people in the Hame, I write about things we need to know—everything I do is for freedom."

"The Community is not pleased with that pamphlet of yours," he said, in a serious counseling way, as if telling me a secret I needed to know. "I've been asked to tell you to submit your writings to the committee before you publish again. That press is run by hotheads. The Hame is causing a good deal of trouble to our candidates."

"Our candidates!" I said in a rage. "No owner is my candidate! Are you still taking orders from the Young Owner?"

That stung him. He said, "If you put yourself first, if you won't cooperate, you bring danger on us all."

"I don't put myself first—politicians and capitalists do that. I put freedom first. Why can't you cooperate with me? It goes two ways, Ahas!"

He left angry, and left me angry.

I think he missed my dependence on him. Perhaps he was jealous, too, of my independence, for he did remain Lord Erod's man. His was a loyal heart. Our disagreement gave us both much bitter pain. I wish I knew what became of him in the troubled times that followed.

There was truth in his accusation. I had found that I had the gift in speaking and writing of moving people's minds and hearts. Nobody told me that such a gift is as dangerous as it is strong. Ahas said I was putting myself first, but I knew I was not doing that. I was wholly in the service of the truth and of liberty. No one told me that the end cannot purify the means, since only the Lord Kamye knows what the end may be. My grandmother could have told me that. The *Arkamye* would have reminded me of it, but I did not often read in it, and in the City there were no old men singing the word, evenings. If there had been I would not have heard them over the sound of my beautiful voice speaking the beautiful truth.

I believe I did no harm, except as we all did, in bringing it to the attention of the rulers of Voe Deo that the Hame was growing bolder and the Radical Party was growing stronger, and that they must move against us.

The first sign was a divisive one. In the open compounds, as well as the men's side and the women's side there were several apartments for couples. This was a radical thing. Any kind of marriage between assets was illegal. They were not allowed to live in pairs. Assets' only legitimate loyalty was to their owner. The child did not belong to the mother, but to the owner. But since gareots were living in the same place as owned assets, these apartments for couples had been tolerated or ignored. Now suddenly the law was invoked, asset couples were arrested, fined if they were wage-earners, separated, and sent to company-run compound houses. Ress and the other elderwomen who ran our house were fined and warned that if "immoral arrangements" were discovered again, they would be held responsible and sent to the labor camps. Two little children of one of the couples were not on the government's list and so were left, abandoned, when their parents were taken off. Keo and Ramayo took them in. They became wards of the women's side, as orphans in the compounds always did.

There were fierce debates about this in meetings of the Hame and The Community. Some said the right of assets to live together and to bring up their children was a cause the Radical Party should support. It was not directly threatening to ownership, and might appeal to the natural instincts of many owners, especially the women, who could not vote but who were valuable allies. Others said that private affections must be overridden by loyalty to the cause of liberty, and that any personal issue must take second place to the great issue of emancipation. Lord Erod spoke thus at a meeting. I rose to answer him. I said that there was no freedom without sexual freedom, and that until women were allowed and men willing to take responsibility for their children, no woman, whether owner or asset, would be free.

"Men must bear the responsibility for the public side of life, the greater world the child will enter; women, for the domestic side of life, the moral and physical upbringing of the child. This is a division enjoined by God and Nature," Erod answered.

"Then will emancipation for a woman mean she's free to enter the beza, be locked in on the women's side?"

"Of course not," he began, but I broke in again, fearing his golden tongue—"Then what is freedom for a woman? Is it different from freedom for a man? Or is a free person free?"

The moderator was angrily thumping his staff, but some other asset women took up my question. "When will the Radical Party speak for us?" they said, and one elderwoman cried, "Where are your women, you owners who want to abolish slavery? Why aren't they here? Don't you let them out of the beza?"

The moderator pounded and finally got order restored. I was half triumphant and half dismayed. I saw Erod and also some of the people from the Hame now looking at me as an open troublemaker. And indeed my words had divided us. But were we not already divided?

A group of us women went home talking through the streets, talking aloud. These were my streets now, with their traffic and lights and dangers and life. I was a City woman, a free woman. That night I was an owner. I owned the City. I owned the future.

The arguments went on. I was asked to speak at many places. As I was leaving one such meeting, the Hainishman Esdardon Aya came to me and said in a casual way, as if discussing my speech, "Rakam, you're in danger of arrest."

I did not understand. He walked along beside me away from the others and went on: "A rumor has come to my attention at the Embassy. . . . The government of Voe Deo is about to change the status of manumitted assets. You're no longer to be considered gareots. You must have an owner-sponsor."

This was bad news, but after thinking it over I said, "I think I can find an owner to sponsor me. Lord Boeba, maybe."

"The owner-sponsor will have to be approved by the government. . . . This will tend to weaken The Community both through the asset and the owner members. It's very clever, in its way," said Esdardon Aya.

"What happens to us if we don't find an approved sponsor?"

"You'll be considered runaways."

That meant death, the labor camps, or auction.

"O Lord Kamye," I said, and took Esdardon Aya's arm, because a curtain of dark had fallen across my eyes.

We had walked some way along the street. When I could see again I saw the street, the high houses of the City, the shining lights I had thought were mine.

"I have some friends," said the Hainishman, walking on with me, "who are planning a trip to the Kingdom of Bambur."

After a while I said, "What would I do there?"

"A ship to Yeowe leaves from there."

"To Yeowe," I said.

"So I hear," he said, as if he were talking about a streetcar line. "In a few years, I expect Voe Deo will begin offering rides to Yeowe. Exporting intractables, troublemakers, members of the Hame. But that will involve recognizing Yeowe as a nation state, which they haven't brought themselves to do yet. They are, however, permitting some semi-legitimate trade arrangements by their client states. . . .

A couple of years ago, the King of Bambur bought one of the old Corporation ships, a genuine old Colony Trader. The king thought he'd like to visit the moons of Werel. But he found the moons boring. So he rented the ship to a consortium of scholars from the University of Bambur and businessmen from his capital. Some manufacturers in Bambur carry on a little trade with Yeowe in it, and some scientists at the university make scientific expeditions in it at the same time. Of course each trip is very expensive, so they carry as many scientists as they can whenever they go."

I heard all this not hearing it, yet understanding it.

"So far," he said, "they've gotten away with it."

He always sounded quiet, a little amused, yet not superior.

"Does The Community know about this ship?" I asked.

"Some members do, I believe. And people in the Hame. But it's very dangerous to know about. If Voe Deo were to find out that a client state was exporting valuable property. . . . In fact, we believe they may have some suspicions. So this is a decision that can't be made lightly. It is both dangerous and irrevocable. Because of that danger, I hesitated to speak of it to you. I hesitated so long that you must make it very quickly. In fact, tonight, Rakam."

I looked from the lights of the City up to the sky they hid. "I'll go," I said. I thought of Walsu.

"Good," he said. At the next corner he changed the direction we had been walking, away from my house, toward the Embassy of the Ekumen.

I never wondered why he did this for me. He was a secret man, a man of secret power, but he always spoke truth, and I think he followed his own heart when he could.

As we entered the Embassy grounds, a great park softly illuminated in the winter night by groundlights, I stopped. "My books," I said. He looked his question. "I wanted to take my books to Yeowe," I said. Now my voice shook with a rush of tears, as if everything I was leaving came down to that one thing. "They need books in Yeowe, I think," I said.

After a moment he said, "I'll have them sent on our next ship. I wish I could put you on that ship," he added in a lower voice. "But of course the Ekumen can't give free rides to runaway slaves. . . ."

I turned and took his hand and laid my forehead against it for a moment, the only time in my life I ever did that of my own free will.

He was startled. "Come, come," he said, and hurried me along.

The Embassy hired Werelian guards, mostly veots, men of the old warrior caste. One of them, a grave, courteous, very silent man, went with me on the flyer to Bambur, the island kingdom east of the Great Continent. He had all the papers I needed. From the flyer port he took me to the Royal Space Observatory, which the king had built for his space ship. There without delay I was taken to the ship, which stood in its great scaffolding ready to depart.

I imagine that they had made comfortable apartments up front for the king when he went to see the moons. The body of the ship, which had belonged to the Agricultural Plantation Corporation, still consisted of great compartments for the produce of the Colony. It would be bringing back grain from Yeowe in four of the cargo bays, that now held farm machinery made in Bambur. The fifth compartment held assets.

The cargo bay had no seats. They had laid felt pads on the floor, and we lay down and were strapped to stanchions, as cargo would have been. There were about fifty "scientists." I was the last to come aboard and be strapped in. The crew were hasty and nervous and spoke only the language of Bambur. I could not understand the instructions we were given. I needed very badly to relieve my bladder, but they had shouted "No time, no time!" So I lay in torment while they closed the great doors of the bay, which made me think of the doors of Shomeke compound. Around me people called out to one another in their language. A baby screamed. I knew that language. Then the great noise began, beneath us. Slowly I felt my body pressed down on the floor, as if a huge soft foot was stepping on me, till my shoulderblades felt as if they were cutting into the mat, and my tongue pressed back into my throat as if to choke me, and with a sharp stab of pain and hot relief my bladder released its urine.

Then we began to be weightless—to float in our bonds. Up was down and down was up, either was both or neither. I heard people all around me calling out again, saying one another's names, saying what must be, "Are you all right? Yes, I'm all right." The baby had never ceased its fierce, piercing yells. I began to feel at my restraints, for I saw the woman next to me sitting up and rubbing her arms and chest where the straps had held her. But a great blurry voice came bellowing over the loudspeaker, giving orders in the language of Bambur and then in Voe Dean: "Do not unfasten the straps! Do not attempt to move about! The ship is under attack! The situation is extremely dangerous!"

So I lay floating in my little mist of urine, listening to the strangers around me talk, understanding nothing. I was utterly miserable, and yet fearless as I had never been. I was carefree. It was like dying. It would be foolish to worry about anything while one died.

The ship moved strangely, shuddering, seeming to turn. Several people were sick. The air filled with the smell and tiny droplets of vomit. I freed my hands enough to draw the scarf I was wearing up over my face as a filter, tucking the ends under my head to hold it.

Inside the scarf I could no longer see the huge vault of the cargo bay stretching above or below me, making me feel I was about to fly or fall into it. It smelled of myself, which was comforting. It was the scarf I often wore when I dressed up to give a talk, fine gauze, pale red with a silver thread woven in at intervals. When I bought it at a City market, paying my own earned money for it, I had thought of my mother's red scarf, given her by Lady Tazeu. I thought she would have liked this one, though it was not as bright. Now I lay and looked into the pale red dimness it made of the vault, starred with the lights at the hatches, and thought of my mother, Yowa. She had probably been killed that morning in the compound. Perhaps she had been carried to another estate as a use-woman, but

Ahas had never found any trace of her. I thought of the way she had of carrying her head a little to the side, deferent yet alert, gracious. Her eyes had been full and bright, "eyes that hold the seven moons," as the song says. I thought then: But I will never see the moons again.

At that I felt so strange that to comfort myself and distract my mind I began to sing under my breath, there alone in my tent of red gauze warm with my own breath. I sang the freedom songs we sang in the Hame, and then I sang the love songs Lady Tazeu had taught me. Finally I sang "O, O, Yeowe," softly at first, then a little louder. I heard a voice somewhere out in that soft red mist world join in with me, a man's voice, then a woman's. Assets from Voe Deo all know that song. We sang it together. A Bambur man's voice picked it up and put words in his own language to it, and others joined in singing it. Then the singing died away. The baby's crying was weak now. The air was very foul.

We learned many hours later, when at last clear air entered the vents and we were told we could release our bonds, that a ship of the Voe Dean Space Defense Fleet had intercepted the freighter's course just above the atmosphere and ordered it to stop. The captain chose to ignore the signal. The warship had fired, and though nothing hit the freighter the blast had damaged the controls. The freighter had gone on, and had seen and heard nothing more of the warship. We were now about eleven days from Yeowe. The warship, or a group of them, might be in wait for us near Yeowe. The reason they gave for ordering the freighter to halt was "suspected contraband merchandise."

That fleet of warships had been built centuries ago to protect Werel from the attacks they expected from the Alien Empire, which is what they then called the Ekumen. They were so frightened by that imagined threat that they put all their energy into the technology of space flight; and the colonization of Yeowe was a result. After four hundred years without any threat of attack, Voe Deo had finally let the Ekumen send envoys and ambassadors. They had used the

Defense Fleet to transport troops and weapons during the War of
Liberation. Now they were using them the way estate owners used
hunting dogs and hunting cats, to hunt down runaway slaves.

I found the two other Voe Deans in the cargo bay, and we
moved our "bedstraps" together so we could talk. Both of them had
been brought to Bambur by the Hame, who had paid their fare. It
had not occurred to me that there was a fare to be paid. I knew who
had paid mine.

"Can't fly a space ship on love," the woman said. She was a
strange person. She really was a scientist. Highly trained in chemistry by the company that rented her, she had persuaded the Hame
to send her to Yeowe because she was sure her skills would be
needed and in demand. She had been making higher wages than
many gareots did, but she expected to do still better on Yeowe. "I'm
going to be rich," she said.

The man, only a boy, a mill hand in a Northern city, had simply
run away and had the luck to meet people who could save him from
death or the labor camps. He was sixteen, ignorant, noisy, rebellious, sweet-natured. He became a general favorite, like a puppy. I
was in demand because I knew the history of Yeowe and through a
man who knew both our languages I could tell the Bamburs something about where they were going—the centuries of Corporation
slavery, Nadami, the War, the Liberation. Some of them were rentspeople from the cities, others were a group of estate slaves bought
at auction by the Hame with false money and under a false name,
and hurried onto this flight. None of them knew where they were
going. It was that trick that had drawn Voe Deo's attention to this
flight.

Yoke, the mill boy, speculated endlessly about how the Yeowans
would welcome us. He had a story, half a joke half a dream, about
the bands playing and the speeches and the big dinner they would
have for us. The dinner grew more and more elaborate as the days
went on. They were long, hungry days, floating in the featureless
great space of the cargo bay, marked only by the alteration every

twelve hours of brighter and dimmer lighting and the issuing of two meals during the "day," food and water in tubes you squeezed into your mouth. I did not think much about what might happen. I was between happenings. If the warships found us we would probably die. If we got to Yeowe it would be a new life. Now we were floating.

4. Yeowe

The ship came down safe at the Port of Yeowe. They unloaded the crates of machinery first, then the other cargo. We came out staggering and holding on to one another, not able to stand up to the great pull of this new world drawing us down to its center, blinded by the light of the sun that we were closer to than we had ever been.

"Over here! Over here!" a man shouted. I was grateful to hear my language, but the Bamburs looked apprehensive.

Over here—in here—strip—wait—All we heard when we were first on the Free World was orders. We had to be decontaminated, which was painful and exhausting. We had to be examined by doctors. Anything we had brought with us had to be decontaminated and examined and listed. That did not take long for me. I had brought the clothes I wore and had worn for two weeks now. I was glad to get decontaminated. Finally we were told to stand in line in one of the big empty cargo sheds. The sign over the doors still read APCY—Agricultural Plantation Corporation of Yeowe. One by one we were processed for entry. The man who processed me was short, white, middle-aged, with spectacles, like any clerk asset in the City, but I looked at him with reverence. He was the first Yeowan I had spoken to. He asked me questions from a form and wrote down my answers. "Can you read?"—"Yes."—"Skills?"—I stammered a moment and said, "Teaching—I can teach reading and history." He never looked up at me.

I was glad to be patient. After all, the Yeowans had not asked us to come. We were admitted only because they knew if they sent us back we would die horribly in a public execution. We were a profitable cargo to Bambur, but to Yeowe we were a problem. But many of us had skills they must need, and I was glad they asked us about them.

When we had all been processed, we were separated into two groups: men and women. Yoke hugged me and went off to the men's side laughing and waving. I stood with the women. We watched all the men led off to the shuttle that went to the Old Capital. Now my patience failed and my hope darkened. I prayed, "Lord Kamye, not here, not here too!" Fear made me angry. When a man came giving us orders again, come on, this way, I went up to him and said "Who are you? Where are we going? We are free women!"

He was a big fellow with a round, white face and bluish eyes. He looked down at me, huffy at first, then smiling. "Yes, Little Sister, you're free," he said. "But we've all got to work, don't we? You ladies are going south. They need people on the rice plantations. You do a little work, make a little money, look around a little, all right? If you don't like it down there, come on back. We can always use more pretty little ladies round here."

I had never heard the Yeowan country accent, a singing, blurry softening, with long, clear vowels. I had never heard asset women called ladies. No one had ever called me Little Sister. He did not mean the word "use" as I took it, surely. He meant well. I was bewildered and said no more. But the chemist, Tualtak, said, "Listen, I'm no field hand, I'm a trained scientist—"

"Oh, you're all scientists," the Yeowan said with his big smile. "Come on now, ladies!" He strode ahead, and we followed. Tualtak kept talking. He smiled and paid no heed.

We were taken to a train car waiting on a siding. The huge, bright sun was setting. All the sky was orange and pink, full of light. Long shadows ran black along the ground. The warm air was dusty and sweet-smelling. While we stood waiting to climb up into the car I stooped and picked up a little reddish stone from the ground. It was round, with a tiny stripe of white clear through it. It was a piece of Yeowe. I held Yeowe in my hand. That little stone, too, I still have.

Our car was shunted along to the main yards and hooked onto a train. When the train started we were served dinner, soup from great kettles wheeled through the car, bowls of sweet, heavy marsh rice, pini fruit—a luxury on Werel, here a commonplace. We ate and ate. I watched the last light die away from the long, rolling hills that the train was passing through. The stars came out. No moons. Never again. But I saw Werel rising in the east. It was a great blue-green star, looking as Yeowe looks from Werel. But you would never see Yeowe rising after sunset. Yeowe followed the sun.

I'm alive and I'm here, I thought. I'm following the sun. I let the rest go, and fell asleep to the swaying of the train.

We were taken off the train on the second day at a town on the great river Yot. Our group of twenty-three were separated there, and ten of us were taken by ox cart to a village, Hagayot. It had been an APCY compound, growing marsh rice to feed the Colony slaves. Now it was a cooperative village, growing marsh rice to feed the Free People. We were enrolled as members of the cooperative. We lived share and share alike with the villagers until pay-out, when we could pay them back what we owed the cooperative.

It was a reasonable way to handle immigrants without money, who did not know the language, or who had no skills. But I did not understand why they had ignored our skills. Why had they sent the men from Bambur plantations, field hands, into the city, not here? Why only women?

I did not understand why, in a village of free people, there was a men's side and a women's side, with a ditch between them.

I did not understand why, as I soon discovered, the men made all the decisions and gave all the orders. But, it being so, I did understand that they were afraid of us Werelian women, who were not used to taking orders from our equals. And I understood that I must take orders and not even look as if I thought of questioning them. The men of Hagayot Village watched us with fierce suspicion and a whip as ready as any Boss's. "Maybe you told men what to do back over there," the foreman told us the first morning in the fields. "Well, that's back over there. That's not here. Here we free people work together. You think you're Bosswomen. There aren't any Bosswomen here."

There were grandmothers on the women's side, but they were not the powers our grandmothers had been. Here, where for the first century there had been no slave women at all, the men had had to make their own life, set up their own powers. When women slaves at last were sent into those little slave-kingdoms of men, there was no power for them at all. They had no voice. Not till they got away to the cities did they ever have a voice on Yeowe.

I learned silence.

But it was not as bad for me and Tualtak as for our eight Bambur companions. We were the first immigrants any of these villagers had ever seen. They knew only one language. They thought the Bambur women were witches because they did not talk "like human beings." They whipped them for talking to each other in their own language.

I will confess that in my first year on the Free World my heart was as low as it had been at Zeskra. I hated standing all day in the shallow water of the rice paddies. Our feet were always sodden and swollen and full of tiny burrowing worms we had to pick out every night. But it was needed work and not too hard for a healthy woman. It was not the work that bore me down.

Hagayot was not a tribal village, not as conservative as some of the old villages I learned about later. Girls here were not ritually raped, and a woman was safe on the women's side. She "jumped the ditch" only with a man she chose. But if a woman went anywhere alone, or even got separated from the other women working in the paddies, she was supposed to be "asking for it," and any man thought it his right to force himself on her.

I made good friends among the village women and the Bamburs. They were no more ignorant than I had been a few years before, and some were wiser than I would ever be. There was no possibility of having a friend among men who thought themselves our owners. I could not see how life here would ever change. My heart was very low, nights, when I lay among the sleeping women and children in our hut and thought, Is this what Walsu died for?

In my second year there, I resolved to do what I could to keep above the misery that threatened me. One of the Bambur women, meek and slow of understanding, whipped and beaten by both women and men for speaking her language, had drowned in one of the great rice paddies. She had laid down there in the warm shallow water not much deeper than her ankles, and had drowned. I feared that yielding, that water of despair. I made up my mind to use my skill, to teach the village women and children to read.

I wrote out some little primers on rice cloth and made a game of it for the little children, first. Some of the older girls and women were curious. Some of them knew that people in the towns and cities could read. They saw it as a mystery, a witchcraft that gave the city people their great power. I did not deny this.

For the women, I first wrote down verses and passages of the *Arkamye*, all I could remember, so that they could have it and not have to wait for one of the men who called themselves "priests" to recite it. They were proud of learning to read these verses. Then I had my friend Seugi tell me a story, her own recollection of meeting a wild hunting cat in the marshes as a child. I wrote it down, entitling it "The Marsh Lion, by Aro Seugi," and read it aloud to the author and a circle of girls and women. They marveled and laughed. Seugi wept, touching the writing that held her voice.

The chief of the village and his headmen and foremen and honorary sons, all the hierarchy and government of the village, were suspicious and not pleased by my teaching, yet did not want to forbid me. The government of Yotebber Region had sent word that they were establishing country schools, where village children were to be sent for half the year. The village men knew that their sons would be advantaged if they could already read and write when they went there.

The Chosen Son, a big, mild, pale man, blind in one eye from a war wound, came to me at last. He wore his coat of office, a tight, long coat such as Werelian owners had worn three hundred years ago. He told me that I should not teach girls to read, only boys.

I told him I would teach all the children who wanted to learn, or none of them.

"Girls do not want to learn this," he said.

"They do. Fourteen girls have asked to be in my class. Eight boys. Do you say girls do not need religious training, Chosen Son?"

This gave him pause. "They should learn the life of the Merciful Lady," he said.

"I will write the Life of Tual for them," I said at once. He walked away, saving his dignity.

I had little pleasure in my victory, such as it was. At least I went on teaching.

Tualtak was always at me to run away, run away to the city downriver. She had grown very thin, for she could not digest the heavy food. She hated the work and the people. "It's all right for you, you were a plantation pup, a dusty, but I never was, my mother was a rentswoman, we lived in fine rooms on Haba Street, I was the brightest trainee they ever had in the laboratory," and on and on, over and over, living in the world she had lost.

Sometimes I listened to her talk about running away. I tried to remember the maps of Yeowe in my lost books. I remembered the great river, the Yot, running from far inland three thousand kilos to the South Sea. But where were we on its vast length, how far from Yotebber City on its delta? Between Hagayot and the city might be a hundred villages like this one. "Have you been raped?" I asked Tualtak.

She took offense. "I'm a rentswoman, not a use-woman," she snapped.

I said, "I was a use-woman for two years. If I was raped again I would kill the man or kill myself. I think two Werelian women walking alone here would be raped. I can't do it, Tualtak."

"It can't all be like this place!" she cried, so desperate that I felt my own throat close up with tears.

"Maybe when they open the schools—there will be people from the cities then—" It was all I had to offer her, or myself, as hope. "Maybe if the harvest's good this year, if we can get our money, we can get on the train. . . ."

That indeed was our best hope. The problem was to get our money from the chief and his cohorts. They kept the cooperative's income in a stone hut that they called the Bank of Hagayot, and only they ever saw the money. Each individual had an account, and they kept tally faithfully, the old Banker Headman scratching your account out in the dirt if you asked for it. But women and children could not withdraw money from their account. All we could get was a kind of scrip, clay pieces marked by the Banker Headman, good to buy things from one another, things people in the village made, clothes, sandals, tools, bead necklaces, rice beer. Our real money was safe, we were told, in the bank. I thought of that old lame bondsman at Shomeke, jigging and singing, "Money in the bank, Lord! Money in the bank!"

Before we ever came, the women had resented this system. Now there were nine more women resenting it.

One night I asked my friend Seugi, whose hair was as white as her skin, "Seugi, do you know what happened at a place called Nadami?"

"Yes," she said. "The women opened the door. All the women rose up and then the men rose up against the Bosses. But they needed weapons. And a woman ran in the night and stole the key from the owner's box and opened the door of the strong place where the Bosses kept their guns and bullets, and she held it open with the strength of her body, so that the slaves could arm themselves. And they killed the Corporations and made that place, Nadami, free."

"Even on Werel they tell that story," I said. "Even there women tell about Nadami, where the women began the Liberation. Men tell it too. Do men here tell it? Do they know it?"

Seugi and the other women nodded.

"If a woman freed the men of Nadami," I said, "maybe the women of Hagayot can free their money."

Seugi laughed. She called out to a group of grandmothers, "Listen to Rakam! Listen to this!"

After plenty of talk for days and weeks, it ended in a delegation of women, thirty of us. We crossed the ditch bridge onto the men's side and ceremoniously asked to see the chief. Our principal bargaining counter was shame. Seugi and other village women did the speaking, for they knew how far they could shame the men without goading them into anger and retaliation. Listening to them, I heard dignity speak to dignity, pride speak to pride. For the first time since I came to Yeowe I felt I was one of these people, that this pride and dignity were mine.

Nothing happens fast in a village. But by the next harvest, the women of Hagayot could draw their own earned share out of the bank in cash.

"Now for the vote," I said to Seugi, for there was no secret ballot in the village. When there was a regional election, even in the worldwide Ratification of the Constitution, the chiefs polled the men and filled out the ballots. They did not even poll the women. They wrote in the votes they wanted cast.

But I did not stay to help bring about that change at Hagayot. Tualtak was really ill, and half crazy with her longing to get out of the marshes, to the city. And I too longed for that. So we took our wages, and Seugi and other women drove us in an ox cart on the causeway across the marshes to the freight station. There we raised the flag that signaled the next train to stop for passengers.

It came along in a few hours, a long train of boxcars loaded with marsh rice, heading for the mills of Yotebber City. We rode in the crew car with the train crew and a few other passengers, village men. I had a big knife in my belt, but none of the men showed us any disrespect. Away from their compounds they were timid and shy. I sat up in my bunk in that car watching the great, wild, plumy marshes whirl by, and the villages on the banks of the wide river, and wished the train would go on forever.

But Tualtak lay in the bunk below me, coughing and fretful. When we got to Yotebber City she was so weak I knew I had to get her to a doctor. A man from the train crew was kind, telling us how to get to the hospital on the public cars. As we rattled through the hot, crowded city streets in the crowded car, I was still happy. I could not help it.

At the hospital they demanded our citizens' registration papers.

I had never heard of such papers. Later I found that ours had been given to the chiefs at Hagayot, who had kept them, as they kept all "their" women's papers. At the time, all I could do was stare and say, "I don't know anything about registration papers."

I heard one of the women at the desk say to the other, "Lord, how dusty can you get?"

I knew what we looked like. I knew we looked dirty and low. I knew I seemed ignorant and stupid. But when I heard that word "dusty" my pride and dignity woke up again. I put my hands into my pack and brought out my freedom paper, that old paper with Erod's writing on it, all crumpled and folded, all dusty.

"This is my Citizen's Registration paper," I said in a loud voice, making those women jump and turn. "My mother's blood and my grandmother's blood is on it. My friend here is sick. She needs a doctor. Now bring us a doctor!"

A thin little woman came forward from the corridor. "Come on this way," she said. One of the deskwomen started to protest. This little woman give her a look.

We followed her to an examination room.

"I'm Dr. Yeron," she said, then corrected herself. "I'm serving as a nurse," she said. "But I am a doctor. And you—you come from the

Old World? from Werel? Sit down there, now, child, take off your shirt. How long have you been there?"

Within a quarter of an hour she had diagnosed Tualtak and got her a bed in a ward for rest and observation, found out our histories, and sent me off with a note to a friend of hers who would help me find a place to live and a job.

"Teaching!" Dr. Yeron said. "A teacher! Oh, woman, you are rain to the dry land!"

Indeed the first school I talked to wanted to hire me at once, to teach anything I wanted. Because I come of a capitalist people, I went to other schools to see if I could make more money at them. But I came back to the first one. I liked the people there.

Before the War of Liberation, the cities of Yeowe, which were cities of Corporation-owned assets who rented their own freedom, had had their own schools and hospitals and many kinds of training programs. There was even a University for assets in the Old Capital. The Corporations, of course, had controlled all the information that came to such institutions, and watched and censored all teaching and writing, keeping everything aimed toward the maximization of their profits. But within that narrow frame the assets had been free to use the information they had as they pleased, and city Yeowans had valued education deeply. During the long war, thirty years, all that system of gathering and teaching knowledge had broken down. A whole generation grew up learning nothing but fighting and hiding, famine and disease. The head of my school said to me, "Our children grew up illiterate, ignorant. Is it any wonder the plantation chiefs just took over where the Corporation Bosses left off? Who was to stop them?"

These men and women believed with a fierce passion that only education would lead to freedom. They were still fighting the War of Liberation.

Yotebber City was a big, poor, sunny, sprawling city with wide streets, low buildings, and huge old shady trees. The traffic was mostly afoot, with cycles tinging and public cars clanging along among the slow crowds. There were miles of shacks and shanties down in the old flood-plain of the river behind the levees, where the soil was rich for gardening. The center of the city was on a low rise, the mills and train yards spreading out from it. Downtown it looked like the City of Voe Deo, only older and poorer and gentler. Instead of big stores for owners, people bought and sold everything from stalls in open markets. The air was soft, here in the south, a warm, soft sea air full of mist and sunlight. I stayed happy. I have by the grace of the Lord a mind that can leave misfortune behind, and I was happy in Yotebber City.

Tualtak recovered her health and found a good job as a chemist in a factory. I saw her seldom, as our friendship had been a matter of necessity, not choice. Whenever I saw her she talked about Haba Street and the laboratory on Werel, and complained about her work and the people here.

Dr. Yeron did not forget me. She wrote a note and told me to come visit her, which I did. Presently, when I was settled, she asked me to come with her to a meeting of an educational society. This, I found, was a group of democrats, mostly teachers, who sought to work against the autocratic power of the tribal and regional Chiefs under the new Constitution, and to counteract what they called the slave mind, the rigid, misogynistic hierarchy that I had encountered in Hagayot. My experience was useful to them, for they were all city people who had met the slave mind only when they found themselves governed by it. The women of the group were the angriest. They had lost the most at Liberation, and now had less to lose. In general the men were gradualists, the women ready for revolution. As a Werelian, ignorant of politics on Yeowe, I listened and did not talk. It was hard for me not to talk. I am a talker, and sometimes I had plenty to say. But I held my tongue and heard them. They were people worth hearing.

Ignorance defends itself savagely, and illiteracy, as I well knew, can be shrewd. Though the Chief, the President of Yotebber Region, elected by a manipulated ballot, might not understand our counter-manipulations of the school curriculum, he did not waste much energy trying to control the schools. He sent his Inspectors to meddle with our classes and censor our books. But what he saw as important was the fact that, just as the Corporations had, he controlled the net. The news, the information programs, the puppets of the neareals, all danced to his strings. Against that, what harm could a lot of teachers do? Parents who had no schooling had children who entered the net to hear and see and feel what the Chief wanted them to know: that freedom is obedience to leaders, that virtue is violence, that manhood is domination. Against the enactment of such truths in daily life and in the heightened sensational experience of the neareals, what good were words?

"Literacy is irrelevant," one of our group said sorrowfully. "The Chiefs have jumped right over our heads into the postliterate information technology."

I brooded over that, hating her fancy words, irrelevant, postliterate, because I was afraid she was right.

To the next meeting of our group, to my surprise, an Alien came: the Sub-Envoy of the Ekumen. He was supposed to be a great feather in our Chief's cap, sent down from the Old Capital apparently to support the Chief's stand against the World Party, which was still strong down here and still clamoring that Yeowe should keep out all foreigners. I had heard vaguely that such a person was here, but I had not expected to meet him at a gathering of subversive school teachers.

He was a short man, red-brown, with white corners to his eyes, but handsome if one could ignore that. He sat in the seat in front of me. He sat perfectly still, as if accustomed to sitting still, and listened without speaking as if accustomed to listening. At the end of the meeting he turned around and his queer eyes looked straight at me.

"Radosse Rakam?" he said.

I nodded, dumb.

"I'm Yehedarhed Havzhiva," he said, "I have some books for you from old music."

I stared. I said, "Books?"

"From old music," he said again. "Esdardon Aya, on Werel."

"My books?" I said.

He smiled. He had a broad, quick smile.

"Oh, where?" I cried.

"They're at my house. We can get them tonight, if you like. I have a car." There was something ironic and light in how he said that, as if he was a man who did not expect to have a car, though he might enjoy it.

Dr. Yeron came over. "So you found her," she said to the Sub-Envoy. He looked at her with such a bright face that I thought, these two are lovers. Though she was much older than he there was nothing unlikely in the thought. Dr. Yeron was a magnetic woman. It was odd to me to think it, though, for my mind was not given to speculating about people's sexual affairs. That was no interest of mine.

He put his hand on her arm as they talked, and I saw with peculiar intensity how gentle his touch was, almost hesitant, yet trustful. That is love, I thought. Yet they parted, I saw, without that look of private understanding that lovers often give each other.

He and I rode in his government electric car, his two silent bodyguards, policewomen, sitting in the front seat. We spoke of Esdardon Aya, whose name, he explained to me, meant Old Music. I told him how Esdardon Aya had saved my life by sending me here. He listened in a way that made it easy to talk to him. I said, "I was sick to leave my books, and I've thought about them, missing them, as if they were my family. But I think maybe I'm a fool to feel that way."

"Why a fool?" he asked. He had a foreign accent, but he had the Yeowan lilt already, and his voice was beautiful, low and warm.

I tried to explain everything at once: "Well, they mean so much to me because I was illiterate when I came to the City, and it was

the books that gave me freedom, gave me the world—the worlds—
But now, here, I see how the net, the holos, the neareals mean so
much more to people, giving them the present time. Maybe it's just
clinging to the past to cling to books. Yeowans have to go toward the
future. And we'll never change people's minds just with words."

He listened intently, as he had done at the meeting, and then
answered slowly, "But words are an essential way of thinking. And
books keep the words true. . . . I didn't read till I was an adult, either."

"You didn't?"

"I knew how, but I didn't. I lived in a village. It's cities that have
to have books," he said, quite decisively, as if he had thought about
this matter. "If they don't, we keep on starting over every generation.
It's a waste. You have to save the words."

When we got to his house, up at the top end of the old part of
town, there were four crates of books in the entrance hall.

"These aren't all mine!" I said.

"Old Music said they were yours," Mr. Yehedarhed said, with
his quick smile and quick glance at me. You can tell where an Alien
is looking much better than you can tell with us. With us, except for
a few people with bluish eyes, you have to be close enough to see
the dark pupil move in the dark eye.

"I haven't got anywhere to put so many," I said, amazed, realizing how that strange man, Old Music, had helped me to freedom
yet again.

"At your school, maybe? The school library?"

It was a good idea, but I thought at once of the Chief's inspectors pawing through them, perhaps confiscating them. When I
spoke of that, the Sub-Envoy said, "What if I present them as a gift
from the Embassy? I think that might embarrass the inspectors."

"Oh," I said, and burst out, "Why are you so kind? You, and
he—Are you Hainish too?"

"Yes," he said, not answering my other question. "I was. I hope
to be Yeowan."

He asked me to sit down and drink a little glass of wine with him before his guard drove me home. He was easy and friendly, but a quiet man. I saw he had been hurt. There were newly healed scars on his face, and his hair was half grown out where he had had a head injury. He asked me what my books were, and I said, "History."

At that he smiled, slowly this time. He said nothing, but he raised his glass to me. I raised mine, imitating him, and we drank.

Next day he had the books delivered to our school. When we opened and shelved them, we realized we had a great treasure. "There's nothing like this at the University," said one of the teachers, who had studied there for a year.

There were histories and anthropologies of Werel and of the worlds of Ekumen, works of philosophy and politics by Werelians and by people of other worlds, there were compendiums of literature, poetry, and stories, encyclopedias, books of science, atlases, dictionaries. In a corner of one of the crates were my own few books, my own treasure, even that first little crude "History of Yeowe, Printed at Yeowe University in the Year One of Liberty." Most of my books I left in the library, but I took that one and a few others home for love, for comfort.

I had found another love and comfort not long since. A child at school had brought me a present, a spotted-cat kitten, just weaned. The boy gave it to me with such loving pride that I could not refuse it. When I tried to pass it on to another teacher they all laughed at me. "You're elected, Rakam!" they said. So unwillingly I took the little being home, afraid of its frailty and delicacy and near to feeling a disgust for it. Women in the beza at Zeskra had had pets, spotted cats and foxdogs, spoiled little animals fed better than we were. I had been called by the name of a pet animal once.

I alarmed the kitten taking it out of its basket, and it bit my thumb to the bone. It was tiny and frail but it had teeth. I began to have some respect for it.

That night I put it to sleep in its basket, but it climbed up on my bed and sat on my face until I let it under the covers. There it slept perfectly still all night. In the morning it woke me by dancing on me, chasing dustmotes in a sunbeam. It made me laugh, waking, which is a pleasant thing. I felt that I had never laughed very much, and wanted to.

The kitten was all black, its spots showing only in certain lights, black on black. I called it Owner. I found it pleasant to come home evenings to be greeted by my little Owner.

Now for the next half year we were planning the great demonstration of women. There were many meetings, at some of which I met the Sub-Envoy again, so that I began to look for him. I liked to watch him listen to our arguments. There were those who argued that the demonstration must not be limited to the wrongs and rights of women, but equality must be for all. Others argued that it should not depend in any way on the support of foreigners, but should be a purely Yeowan movement. Mr. Yehedarhed listened to them, but I got angry. "I'm a foreigner," I said. "Does that make me no use to you? That's owner talk—as if you were better than other people!" And Dr. Yeron said, "I will believe equality is for all when I see it written in the Constitution of Yeowe." For our Constitution, ratified by a world vote during the time I was at Hagayot, spoke of citizens only as men. That is finally what the demonstration became, a demand that the Constitution be amended to include women as citizens, provide for the secret ballot, and guarantee the right to free speech, freedom of the press and of assembly, and free education for all children.

I lay down on the train tracks along with seventy thousand women, that hot day. I sang with them. I heard what that sounds like, so many women singing together, what a big, deep sound it makes.

I had begun to speak in public again when we were gathering women for the great demonstration. It was a gift I had, and we made use of it. Sometimes gang boys or ignorant men would come to heckle and threaten me, shouting, "Bosswoman, Ownerwoman, black cunt, go back where you came from!" Once when they were yelling that, go back, go back, I leaned into the microphone and said, "I can't go back. We used to sing a song on the plantation where I was a slave," and I sang it,

O, O, Ye-o-we
Nobody never comes back.

The singing made them be still for a moment. They heard it, that awful grief, that yearning.

After the great demonstration the unrest never died down, but there were times that the energy flagged, the Movement didn't move, as Dr. Yeron said. During one of those times I went to her and proposed that we set up a printing house and publish books. This had been a dream of mine, growing from that day in Hagayot when Seugi had touched her words and wept.

"Talk goes by," I said, "and all the words and images in the net go by, and anybody can change them, but books are there. They last. They are the body of history, Mr. Yehedarhed says."

"Inspectors," said Dr. Yeron. "Until we get the free press amendment, the Chiefs aren't going to let anybody print anything they didn't dictate themselves."

I did not want to give up the idea. I knew that in Yotebber Region we could not publish anything political, but I argued that we might print stories and poems by women of the region. Others thought it a waste of time. We discussed it back and forth for a long time. Mr. Yehedarhed came back from a trip to the Embassy, up north in the Old Capital. He listened to our discussions, but said nothing, which disappointed me. I had thought that he might support my project.

One day I was walking home from school to my apartment, which was in a big, old, noisy house not far from the levee. I liked the place because my windows opened into the branches of trees, and through the trees I saw the river, four miles wide here, easing along among sand bars and reed beds and willow isles in the dry season, brimming up the levees in the wet season when the rainstorms scudded across it. That day as I came near the house, Mr. Yehedarhed appeared, with two sour-faced policewomen close behind him as usual. He greeted me and asked if we might talk. I was confused and did not know what to do but to invite him up to my room.

His guards waited in the lobby. I had just the one big room on the third floor. I sat on the bed and the Sub-Envoy sat in the chair. Owner went round and round his legs, saying roo? roo?

I had observed often that the Sub-Envoy took pleasure in disappointing the expectations of the Chief and his cohorts, who were all for pomp and fleets of cars and elaborate badges and uniforms. He and his policewomen went all over the city, all over Yotebber, in his government car or on foot. People liked him for it. They knew, as I knew now, that he had been assaulted and beaten and left for dead by a World Party gang his first day here, when he went out afoot alone. The city people liked his courage and the way he talked with everybody, anywhere. They had adopted him. We in the Liberation Movement thought of him as "our Envoy," but he was theirs, and the Chief's too. The Chief may have hated his popularity, but he profited from it.

"You want to start a publishing house," he said, stroking Owner, who fell over with his paws in the air.

"Dr. Yeron says there's no use until we get the Amendments."

"There's one press on Yeowe not directly controlled by the government," Mr. Yehedarhed said, stroking Owner's belly.

"Look out, he'll bite," I said. "Where is that?"

"At the University. I see," Mr. Yehedarhed said, looking at his thumb. I apologized. He asked me if I was certain that Owner was male. I said I had been told so, but never had thought to look. "My impression is that your Owner is a lady," Mr. Yehedarhed said, in such a way that I began to laugh helplessly.

He laughed along with me, sucked the blood off his thumb, and went on. "The University never amounted to much. It was a Corporation ploy—let the assets pretend they're going to college. During the last years of the War it was closed down. Since Liberation Day it's reopened and crawled along with no one taking much notice. The faculty are mostly old. They came back to it after the War. The National Government gives it a subsidy because it sounds well to have a University of Yeowe, but they don't pay it any attention, because it has no prestige. And because many of them are unenlightened men." He said this without scorn, descriptively. "It does have a printing house."

"I know," I said. I reached out for my old book and showed it to him.

He looked through it for a few minutes. His face was curiously tender as he did so. I could not help watching him. It was like watching a woman with a baby, a constant, changing play of attention and response.

"Full of propaganda and errors and hope," he said at last, and his voice too was tender. "Well, I think this could be improved upon. Don't you? All that's needed is an editor. And some authors."

"Inspectors," I warned, imitating Dr. Yeron.

"Academic freedom is an easy issue for the Ekumen to have some influence upon," he said, "because we invite people to attend the Ekumenical Schools on Hain and Ve. We certainly want to invite graduates of the University of Yeowe. But of course, if their education is severely defective because of the lack of books, of information. . . ."

I said, "Mr. Yehedarhed, are you *supposed* to subvert government policies?" The question broke out of me unawares.

He did not laugh. He paused for quite a long time before he answered. "I don't know," he said. "So far the Ambassador has backed me. We may both get reprimanded. Or fired. What I'd like to do . . ." His strange eyes were right on me again. He looked down at the book he still held. "What I'd like is to become a Yeowan citizen," he said. "But my usefulness to Yeowe, and to the Liberation Movement, is my position with the Ekumen. So I'll go on using that, or misusing it, till they tell me to stop."

When he left I had to think about what he had asked me to do.
That was to go to the University as a teacher of history, and once
there to volunteer for the editorship of the press. That all seemed
so preposterous, for a woman of my background and my little learning, that I thought I must be misunderstanding him. When he convinced me that I had understood him, I thought he must have very
badly misunderstood who I was and what I was capable of. After we
had talked about that for a while, he left, evidently feeling that he
was making me uncomfortable, and perhaps feeling uncomfortable
himself, though in fact we laughed a good deal and I did not feel
uncomfortable, only a little as if I were crazy.

I tried to think about what he had asked me to do, to step so far
beyond myself. I found it difficult to think about. It was as if it hung
over me, this huge choice I must make, this future I could not imagine. But what I thought about was him, Yehedarhed Havzhiva. I
kept seeing him sitting there in my old chair, stooping down to
stroke Owner. Sucking blood off his thumb. Laughing. Looking at
me with his white-cornered eyes. I saw his red-brown face and red-
brown hands, the color of pottery. His quiet voice was in my mind.

I picked up the kitten, half grown now, and looked at its hinder
end. There was no sign of any male parts. The little black silky body
squirmed in my hands. I thought of him saying, "Your Owner is a
lady," and I wanted to laugh again, and to cry. I stroked the kitten
and set her down, and she sat sedately beside me, washing her
shoulder. "Oh poor little lady," I said. I don't know who I meant. The
kitten, or Lady Tazeu, or myself.

He had said to take my time thinking about his proposal, all the
time I wanted. But I had not really thought about it at all when, the
next day but one, there he was, on foot, waiting for me as I came
out of the school. "Would you like to walk on the levee?" he said.

I looked around.

"There they are," he said, indicating his cold-eyed bodyguards.
"Everywhere I am, they are, three to five meters away. Walking with
me is dull, but safe. My virtue is guaranteed."

We walked down through the streets to the levee and up onto it in the long early evening light, warm and pink-gold, smelling of river and mud and reeds. The two women with guns walked along just about four meters behind us.

"If you do go to the University," he said after a long silence, "I'll be there constantly."

"I haven't yet—" I stammered.

"If you stay here, I'll be here constantly," he said. "That is, if it's all right with you."

I said nothing. He looked at me without turning his head. I said without intending to, "I like it that I can see where you're looking."

"I like it that I can't see where you're looking," he said, looking directly at me.

We walked on. A heron rose up out of a reed islet and its great wings beat over the water, away. We were walking south, downriver. All the western sky was full of light as the sun went down behind the city in smoke and haze.

"Rakam, I would like to know where you came from, what your life on Werel was," he said very softly.

I drew a long breath. "It's all gone," I said. "Past."

"We are our past. Though not only that. I want to know you. Forgive me. I want very much to know you."

After a while I said, "I want to tell you. But it's so bad. It's so ugly. Here, now, it's beautiful. I don't want to lose it."

"Whatever you tell me I will hold valuable," he said, in his quiet voice that went to my heart. So I told him what I could about Shomeke compound, and then hurried on through the rest of my story. Sometimes he asked a question. Mostly he listened. At some time in my telling he had taken my arm, I scarcely noticing at the time. When he let me go, thinking some movement I made meant I wanted to be released, I missed that light touch. His hand was cool. I could feel it on my forearm after it was gone.

"Mr. Yehedarhed," said a voice behind us: one of the bodyguards. The sun was down, the sky flushed with gold and red. "Better head back?"

"Yes," he said, "thanks." As we turned I took his arm. I felt him catch his breath.

I had not desired a man or a woman—this is the truth—since Shomeke. I had loved people, and I had touched them with love, but never with desire. My gate was locked.

Now it was open. Now I was so weak that at the touch of his hand I could scarcely walk on.

I said, "It's a good thing walking with you is so safe."

I hardly knew what I meant. I was thirty years old but I was like a young girl. I had never been that girl.

He said nothing. We walked along in silence between the river and the city in a glory of failing light.

"Will you come home with me, Rakam?" he said.

Now I said nothing.

"They don't come in with us," he said, very low, in my ear, so that I felt his breath.

"Don't make me laugh!" I said, and began crying. I wept all the way back along the levee. I sobbed and thought the sobs were ceasing and then sobbed again. I cried for all my sorrows, all my shames. I cried because they were with me now and were me and always would be. I cried because the gate was open and I could go through at last, go into the country on the other side, but I was afraid to.

When we got into the car, up near my school, he took me in his arms and simply held me, silent. The two women in the front seat never looked round.

We went into his house, which I had seen once before, an old mansion of some owner of the Corporation days. He thanked the guards and shut the door. "Dinner," he said. "The cook's out. I meant to take you to a restaurant. I forgot." He led me to the kitchen, where we found cold rice and salad and wine. After we ate he looked at me across the kitchen table and looked down again.

His hesitance made me hold still and say nothing. After a long time he said, "Oh, Rakam! will you let me make love to you?"

"I want to make love to you," I said. "I never did. I never made love to anyone."

He got up smiling and took my hand. We went upstairs together, passing what had been the entrance to the men's side of the house. "I live in the beza," he said, "in the harem. I live on the woman's side. I like the view."

We came to his room. There he stood still, looking at me, then looked away. I was so frightened, so bewildered, I thought I could not go to him or touch him. I made myself go to him. I raised my hand and touched his face, the scars by his eye and on his mouth, and put my arms around him. Then I could hold him to me, closer and closer.

Some time in that night as we lay drowsing entangled I said, "Did you sleep with Dr. Yeron?"

I felt Havzhiva laugh, a slow, soft laugh in his belly, which was against my belly. "No," he said. "No one on Yeowe but you. And you, no one on Yeowe but me. We were virgins, Yeowan virgins. . . . Rakam, *araha*. . . ." He rested his head in the hollow of my shoulder and said something else in a foreign language and fell asleep. He slept deeply, silently.

Later that year I came up north to the University, where I was taken on the faculty as a teacher of history. By their standards at that time, I was competent. I have worked there ever since, teaching and as editor of the press.

As he had said he would be, Havzhiva was there constantly, or almost.

The Amendments to the Constitution were voted, by secret ballot, mostly, in the Yeowan Year of Liberty 18. Of the events that led to this, and what has followed, you may read in the new three-volume *History of Yeowe* from the University Press. I have told the story I was asked to tell. I have closed it, as so many stories close, with a joining of two people. What is one man's and one woman's love and desire, against the history of two worlds, the great revolutions of our lifetimes, the hope, the unending cruelty of our species? A little thing. But a key is a little thing, next to the door it opens. If you lose the key, the door may never be unlocked. It is in our bodies that we lose or begin our freedom, in our bodies that we accept or end our slavery. So I wrote this book for my friend, with whom I have lived and will die free.

About the Authors

Nancy Kress

Nancy Kress is the author of seventeen books: three fantasy novels, seven SF novels, two thrillers, three collections of short stories, and two books on writing fiction. She is perhaps best known for the "Sleepless" trilogy that began with *Beggars in Spain*. Her most recent books are *Stinger* (Forge/Tor) and *Probability Moon,* an alien-contact novel based on her Nebula-winning story "The Flowers of Aulit Prison." She has been awarded three Nebulas and one Hugo for her short fiction. "Inertia," her fierce tale of resilience, appeared in the January 1990 issue of *Analog*. In addition to writing fiction, Ms. Kress is the monthly fiction columnist for *Writer's Digest* magazine. She lives in Silver Spring, Maryland, with her husband, SF writer Charles Sheffield.

Connie Willis

"Even the Queen," Connie Willis's hilarious Hugo and Nebula Award-winning story from 1992, gives us a room full of independent and determined women who exemplify the theme of this anthology. They are women who can stand up for themselves no matter what the world dishes out.

Ms. Willis was the first person to win Nebula and Hugo Awards in all four fiction categories. With eight Hugos and six Nebulas, she has been honored with more of these awards than any other author. Ms. Willis received her first two Nebulas in 1983 for the novelette "Fire Watch" and the short story "A Letter from the Clearys." She went on to win a Hugo for "Fire Watch" as well. In 1992 Ms. Willis received the Hugo and the Nebula Best Novel Award for *Doomsday*

Book. To Say Nothing of the Dog, her 1999 novel, also received the Hugo. With the exception of "At the Rialto" (Nebula, 1989), all of Ms. Willis's award-winning short fiction was originally published in *Asimov's Science Fiction* magazine.

Ms. Willis was also the recipient of the John W. Campbell Memorial Award for her haunting novel *Lincoln's Dreams,* and the *Locus* Poll named her the Best Science Fiction/Fantasy Writer of the Nineties. Ms. Willis was the editor of *Nebulas 33,* and her most recent books include *Miracle and Other Stories* and *Passage,* which is just out from Bantam Spectra.

The author has a grown daughter, Cordelia. Ms. Willis lives with her husband, Courtney, in Greeley, Colorado.

Sarah Zettel

Sarah Zettel's dynamic story "Fool's Errand" (*Analog,* May 1993) was the inspiration for *Fool's War* (1997), a *New York Times* notable book of the year and one of the author's five science fiction novels. Ms. Zettel's earliest book, *Reclamation,* won the *Locus* Poll for best first novel. Her most recent SF novel is *Kingdom of Cages.* She is also working on a fantasy trilogy that she swears will really be only three books long. When not writing, she sings, practices tai chi, and dances, but not all at once. The author currently lives in Ann Arbor, Michigan, with her husband, Tim, and their cat, Buffy the Vermin Slayer.

Pat Murphy

Pat Murphy's tale "Rachel in Love" (*Asimov's,* April 1987) may contain the most unusual women in this anthology. It received the Nebula Award for best novelette the same year that her book *The Falling Woman* won the award for best novel. Her fiction has also been honored with the Philip K. Dick Award for best paperback original, the World Fantasy Award, the *Asimov's* Reader's Award, and the Theodore Sturgeon Memorial Award. Her latest novel, *Adven-*

tures in Time and Space with Max Merriwell, is just out from Tor Books. When she is not writing science fiction, Ms. Murphy writes for the Exploratorium, San Francisco's museum of science, art, and human perception. She lives in San Francisco with her husband.

Vonda N. McIntyre

Vonda N. McIntyre won her first Nebula for the powerful tale "Of Mist, and Grass, and Sand" (*Analog,* October 1973). *Dreamsnake,* her 1978 novel that continued this compelling story, received both the Hugo and Nebula Awards. In 1997 she picked up another Nebula for her novel *The Moon and the Sun.* That book has recently been optioned by Jim Henson Pictures. Ms. McIntyre's other books include the novels *The Exile Waiting* and *Superluminal,* the collection *Fireflood and Other Stories,* and the best-selling novel versions of the screenplays for three of the popular *Star Trek* movies: *The Wrath of Khan, The Search for Spock,* and *The Voyage Home.* Ms. McIntyre lives in Seattle, Washington.

S.N. Dyer

S.N. Dyer's hard-hitting "July Ward" (*Asimov's,* December 1991) was a stunning debut for the pseudonym of an author who has had numerous appearances in *Asimov's Science Fiction* magazine. This frightening novelette was a finalist for the 1993 Nebula Award. Like her unforgettable character Watson, Ms. Dyer is a physician. Under various names, she has published over sixty stories and a collaborative novel. The author lives in Chattanooga, Tennessee.

Katherine MacLean

Although her spellbinding "The Kidnapping of Baroness 5" (*Analog,* January 1995) is one of the newer stories in this book, Katherine MacLean was the first author in the anthology to be published. Her earliest tale, "Defense Mechanism," appeared in *Astounding/Analog* in 1949, and that magazine has been the original home to most of her short fiction. In March of 1971, *Analog* published her Nebula Award-winning novella "The Missing Man." Ms. MacLean's works include *Cosmic Checkmate, The Man in the Bird Cage, Missing Man, Dark Wing,* and *The Trouble with You Earth People.* Last year Wildside Press rereleased her 1962 collection, *The Diploids.* She lives in Arundel, Maine.

Octavia E. Butler

Octavia E. Butler received her first Hugo Award for her outstand-ing short story "Speech Sounds" (*Asimov's,* Mid-December 1983). A year later she won both the Hugo and the Nebula for her classic tale "Bloodchild." Additional honors include a 1995 MacArthur Ge-nius Grant, the 1999 Nebula for her novel *Parable of the Talents,* and the Lifetime Achievement Award from PEN West for her body of work. Some of Ms. Butler's best-known novels include *Parable of the Sower, Kindred, Wildseed, Patternmaster, Clay's Ark,* and *Dawn.* The author is currently at work on a new novel, which will be set after the Civil War. Ms. Butler resides outside of Seattle, Washing-ton.

Anne McCaffrey

Anne McCaffrey was the first woman to win a Hugo Award and one of the very first to win a Nebula for her fiction. She is the author of sixty-seven novels and sixty-five short stories. Some of these works are *Dragonflight* (which includes the 1968 Hugo-winning "Weyr Search" and the 1968 Nebula-winning "Dragon Rider"), *To Ride Pe-gasus, Crystal Singer,* and *The Rowan.* The author's favorite book, *The Ship Who Sang,* further develops the remarkable character Helva, whom we met in her moving tale "The Ship Who Mourned" (*Analog,* March 1966). Her most recent novel, *Pegasus in Space,* was published by Del Rey last year. Ms. McCaffrey lives in County Wicklow, Ireland.

Ursula K. Le Guin

Ursula K. Le Guin's intense tale "A Woman's Liberation" (*Asimov's,* July 1995) was the catalyst for this anthology. Rakam, whose wrenching journey leads to her victorious emancipation, epitomizes the strength of character and resolve that can be found in every story in this book. Ms. Le Guin is the distinguished author of seventeen novels, over a hundred short stories, five books of poetry, two collections of essays, eleven books for children, and two volumes of translations. Two of her novels—*The Left Hand of Darkness* and *The Dispossessed*—won both the Hugo and the Nebula Awards, and her short fiction has also received three Hugos and three Nebulas. Other honors for her writings include a National Book Award and the Pushcart Prize. Her latest book, *Tales from Earthsea,* is just out from Harcourt. She lives with her husband, Charles, in Portland, Oregon.

Sheila Williams

Sheila Williams is the executive editor of *Asimov's Science Fiction* and *Analog Science Fiction and Fact.* She has been with the magazines for over nineteen years. Ms. Williams is also the co-founder of the Isaac Asimov Award for Undergraduate Excellence in Science Fiction and Fantasy Writing. In addition, she coordinates the websites for both *Asimov's* (www.asimovs.com) and *Analog* (www.analogsf.com).

Ms. Williams is also the editor or co-editor of over a dozen anthologies, including *Isaac Asimov's Halloween,* which is just out from Ace: *Isaac Asimov's Father's Day* (Ace, June 2001); *Isaac Asimov's Solar System* (Ace, 2000); *Hugo and Nebula Award Winners from Asimov's Science Fiction* (Wings Books, 1995); and *Why I Left*

Harry's All-Night Hamburgers, and Other Stories from IAsfm (Delacorte, 1990). Ms. Williams has also co-edited *Writing Science Fiction and Fantasy* (St. Martin's Press, 1991, 2000) with the other editors of *Asimov's* and *Analog*.

Ms. Williams received her bachelor's degree from Elmira College in Elmira, New York, and her master's from Washington University in St. Louis, Missouri. During her junior year she studied at the London School of Economics. She lives in New York City with her husband, David Bruce, and their eight-year-old daughter, Irene.

Visit us on the world wide web
Analog Science Fiction and Fact: http://www.analogsf.com
Asimov's Science Fiction: http://www.asimovs.com